STAND AND DELIVER!

Jenna turned to go. She couldn't believe she was standing there, half-dressed, in the garden in the middle of the night, casually discussing tobacco with a man who was probably going to kill her betrothed in a duel.

"I shouldn't be here. I'm sorry," she murmured.

"Why did you come out here at this hour?" Kevernwood said, his deep voice turning her around again.

"Flowers have the same effect upon me as your pipe has upon you, my lord," she replied, swallowing her rapid heartbeat. "I couldn't sleep. I wanted to think, and I always do that best whilst communing with nature."

He came closer, hardly limping at all, and as he continued to advance she could no longer control the rush of excitement that pulsed through the core of her sexuality, quickening her heart, setting off alarm bells in her brain....

The Marsh Hawk

Dawn MacTavish

LEISURE BOOKS   NEW YORK CITY

*For all the talented ladies of Coeur de Louisiane,
whose friendship and support has been with me since*
The Marsh Hawk *placed first in their* Romancing the
Tome *contest, when this wonderful journey began.*

A LEISURE BOOK®

July 2007

Published by

Dorchester Publishing Co., Inc.
200 Madison Avenue
New York, NY 10016

ISBN-10: 0-8439-5934-7
ISBN-13: 978-0-8439-5934-5

The name "Leisure Books" and the stylized "L" with design are
trademarks of Dorchester Publishing Co., Inc.

Printed in the United States of America.

Visit us on the web at www.dorchesterpub.com.

The Marsh Hawk

PROLOGUE

Cornwall, England, Spring 1812

It was a perfect night for a robbery on the old Lamorna Road. Jenna waited just inside the copse, praying that her curves were well obscured by the long black cloak, slouch hat, and mask, which hid all but her eyes. The horse beneath her pranced, puffing visible breath from flared nostrils, but she was a skilled horsewoman and soon coaxed him to a reluctant halt. There must be no sound. The highwayman had stopped the coach but a few yards distant. The acrid smell of gunpowder from his pistol shot still lingered on the cool night air. It mingled badly with the metallic taste of fear, like blood—like death—building at the back of her palate.

She swallowed. The coach's passengers had spilled out on the roadway: a man and a woman, well dressed in the silks and frills of the aristocracy. The woman's diamond earbobs sparkled in the half-light, and the gentleman's silver shoe buckles and glittering stickpin gleamed irresistibly. The highwayman wouldn't notice her now, not with the dazzle of their ornaments to distract him. She eased a pistol from beneath her cloak and cocked it.

Cold sweat beaded on her face beneath the black silk mask. It ran in rivulets between her breasts and triggered a chill that riddled her spine until she shuddered. How had it come to this? What was she, the daughter of a baronet, doing on this dark Cornish road in the dead of night, straddling a horse with a pair of loaded pistols at the ready?

There was no time for retrospection, no time for nursing regrets. Moved by a strange mix of terror and exhilaration that was shockingly sexual, she fired a shot in the air, jammed the spent pistol into her belt, and rode from the copse with the other drawn.

"Stand down and deliver, sir!" she cried out in a deliberately disguised voice already muffled behind the mask.

The highwayman wheeled his horse toward her. He was attired almost exactly as she, except that he wore a half-mask that clearly showed her his broad, clean-shaven chin, and a mouth pursed irascibly in a thin, lipless line.

She reined her mount closer. The fleeting rays of a bashful sickle moon peeking through the dense cloud cover cast an eerie halo about him.

"Drop the pistol, sir," she demanded, gesturing with her own, "and the spoils—the jewels, and that reticule there. *Now!*"

He hesitated, thrusting out his jaw. "Who the devil are you?" he demanded.

"Someone you do not want to know, sir. Drop the pistol, and the rest, I say! My patience ebbs low."

The coachman and postilion sat frozen and slack jawed, their arms in the air, too far from the outdated cannon-barreled blunderbuss that had fallen out of reach beneath their feet. Jenna monitored them out of the corner of her eye, as well as the middle-aged couple trembling against each other alongside the wide-flung coach door. Their expressions spoke volumes. The last turn of events any of them expected was one highwayman holding up another. She almost laughed. If they only knew that one of them was a woman.

The highwayman threw his pistol down and dismounted, but he did not relinquish the spoils. Instead, he strolled boldly closer—rather stiffly, she thought—to exhibit them.

"I'm willing to share," he said. His voice was cultured. "What say we join?" He didn't wait for an answer. "There's more than enough here for two."

"Stand where you are," she snapped.

He'd come dangerously close, close enough to agitate her mount, extracting a snort; close enough for her to inhale the jarring aroma of leather, tobacco, and recently drunk wine drifting toward her on the night breeze from his clothing and glistening moist skin. She took the measure of his tall, muscular shape beneath the multicaped greatcoat that didn't quite contain him. Yes, this was the one—the one they called the Marsh Hawk— there was no mistake. His arrogant demeanor damned him.

His eyes were blue fire in the moonlight, blazing toward her through the holes in his mask. They triggered a wave of pulsating heat that surged through her body. She scarcely blinked. Her hatred of his ilk demanded satisfaction and she raised her weapon, motioning him to walk on ahead of her.

"Hold your hands high, where I can see them!" she commanded. "Your business is done here. You're coming with me."

"Afoot?" he blurted. "Where to?"

"You'll see soon enough. *March!*"

He hesitated, his hands still lowered. Was that another pistol concealed beneath his cloak?

Yes! In a blink, he drew it, aimed, and fired, but she was quicker, since her own was already drawn, and her pistol ball knocked him off his feet as it ripped through his shoulder—or was it his chest? It happened so fast, she couldn't be certain.

The bullet from his gun whizzed past her as he fell. Their horses reared, complaining, setting the coach horses in motion, and the coachman quickly grabbed the reins and pulled back hard to hold them. Before Jenna could bring her mount's high-flying forefeet to the ground again, the flabbergasted aristocrats had scrambled back inside the carriage.

"Hyaaah!" the driver bellowed, snapping his whip. And the coach sped off in a cloud of thick, Cornish dust. The highwayman's mount galloped crazily after it.

Jenna stared down at the man writhing at her prancing

mount's feet. For a moment their eyes met—his narrowed in pain, hers wide with a paralyzing mix of horror and triumph. A hot rush of blood surging like liquid flame coursed through her, ignited by the look in those riveting eyes that held her so relentlessly. Then finally, mercifully, they closed and he fell back in the dirt of the road. Was he dead? No, not quite.

Alerted by a rustling sound, Jenna glanced about. They weren't alone. Was someone watching her? She dared not linger. Spurring her mount, she disappeared into the gnarled trees at the edge of the wood.

CHAPTER ONE

Two months later

It was to be a gala three-day event at Moorhaven Manor, the rambling country estate of Lady Jenna Hollingsworth's betrothed, Viscount Rupert Marner. Moorhaven was situated on the eastern fringes of Bodmin Moor, hence its name. Half the Cornish nobility, not to mention a host of peers from London, were to attend the festivities commencing that evening with an elaborate masked ball at which Jenna's engagement to the viscount would be formally announced. A leisurely day of picnicking, riding, archery, and shooting would follow on Saturday, culminating in a formal sit-down dinner. A hunt on Sunday was planned to bring the weekend to a spectacular close, weather permitting, of course. One could never plan such an event with any degree of confidence in Cornwall. Cornish "flaws," as the locals called the unpredictable storms that plagued the coast, were notorious for upsetting the most carefully laid plans.

Jenna would have been much happier at Thistle Hollow, her own family estate near Launceston. That was certainly what should be, according to etiquette, but when Lady Marner approached Jenna's mother with the alternative of Moorhaven, the dowager jumped at the chance. Though the long year of mourning for her husband was over, Lady Hollingsworth welcomed yet another opportunity to prolong the sympathetic attention she'd so enjoyed—milked to the limit as Jenna viewed it—as long as she possibly could.

Truth be told, she would have preferred not to have the celebration at all, or the wedding either, come to that. She had no desire to marry anyone—least of all Rupert of the Vacant Eyes, as she had dubbed him. Not that he wasn't handsome; quite the contrary. But he was also affected and, as rumor had it, promiscuous. Nevertheless, to join their houses with the union was what her father had wanted, what she owed his memory. Besides, independence was impossible now. After what she'd done, she needed protection. Not the insipid protection of the twenty-nine-year-old tedious bore that was her husband-to-be, but of his house. The Marners were respected aristocrats. No one would dare accuse the viscount's wife of anything, and sins did have a way of surfacing after all. Hadn't Lord Fordenbridge's scandalous alliance with wreckers along the coast come out two whole years after the fact? Albeit in self-defense, as it turned out, and not at all what she had intended, she had done *murder*.

Just what she would have done if the highwayman hadn't attempted to draw that pistol, she feared to wonder; she hadn't thought beyond her passion for vengeance at the time. Murder, however, was never a part of the plan. She was determined to do what the law would not: bring a guilty man to justice. Even if she hadn't been recognized, she had been seen. It was like a nightmare, except that she was wide-awake, and the horror was real. Rupert was insurance, nothing more. The marriage was a smart move . . . only that. She'd almost convinced herself.

Carriages of every type had been arriving all afternoon—the high-perch and low-perch phaetons of close neighbors, two-seater broughams, coupes, curricles, cabriolets, with their leather hoods folded back to take advantage of the beaming sun, and chaises in every conceivable color and description. They congested the circular drive. She'd wondered how the carriage house would ever accommodate them all, until Emily, her lady's maid, told her she'd overheard one of the footmen say that the overflow would go to the posting house in the village. How the posting house would ever manage such an influx, she couldn't imagine, as still more vehicles flooded the drive.

"Jenna, come away from there!" Lady Hollingsworth scolded, close in her ear. She lurched at the sound of her mother's voice and spun to face her. The dowager gave a start herself and tottered backward. "You mustn't gawk like a common scullion," she said. "Someone might see you. What can you be thinking?"

"Isn't that why they've all come," Jenna asked tersely. "To size me up?"

"Don't be impertinent. There's never an occasion for it, dear. What ails you? I've never seen you in such a taking as you have been lately."

Jenna couldn't reply to that. She couldn't very well tell her mother she'd killed a man on the old Lamorna Road one dark night on the cusp of spring. It had only been two months, but it seemed like a lifetime ago.

There was no question that her conscience was bothering her. Twenty-two-year old young ladies of quality did not go around committing black murder in the dead of night. And she was regretting her betrothal to Rupert before it had even officially begun. She would never have bent to her mother's will over that if there had been no murder and she were in her right mind. She would never have agreed to the match if her father were still living, even if it was his greatest wish. She could have charmed him out of it if the Marsh Hawk hadn't killed him and robbed her of the chance to try.

"There! You see?" her mother said, jarring her back to the present. "You haven't heard one word I've said."

"I've heard you, Mother," she replied, emptying her lungs on a gusty sigh. She turned back to the window and gestured toward the mullioned panes. "I'm looking for familiar faces. Thus far I've seen none."

"You will, dear," her mother soothed. Peering over her

shoulder, she craned her neck for a closer look below. "There—
the Markhams, and Lady Chester-White, and there . . . the
Warrenfords and their two daughters. You remember? The oldest girl had her come-out last season. What is her name . . .
Rowena . . . Regina?"

"Rosemary, Mother."

"There, beside the garden wall—the Ecclestons' brougham.
See?" Lady Hollingsworth wagged a thick, wrinkled finger, en-
cumbered by an enormous emerald, toward the drive. "Before
the masque is over you'll not only have been reunited with old
friends, you'll have made new ones—important ones for you
and Rupert, dear." She glanced around the room and craned her
neck again, this time in the direction of Jenna's open bedchamber door across the way. "Has Emily unpacked your costume?"

"Not yet," she replied. She had elected to attend the masque
costumed as a swan. The celebrated French modiste, Marie
Flaubert, whose Bond Street salon in London was the talk of
society—generally referred to as the ton—had designed her a
silk gown completely covered in white feathers, with a graceful
cape to match that attached to her arms on silk bands simulat-
ing wings. It featured a lifelike, feathered cowl, complete with
beak that covered her head like a second skin. Thinking of the
costume crammed into her portmanteau with her dinner
gowns, daytime and afternoon frocks, and riding habit, she
could almost hear the modiste's shrill *"mon Dieu"* after carefully stitching each one of those feathers in place by hand.

"I'll fetch the bird-witted gel at once!" Lady Elizabeth
shrilled. She sucked in a hasty breath. "She'll have to steam
those feathers—or whatever one does with feathers to put them
into shape; I have no idea. Meanwhile, go down and eat something, Jenna. You're nearly a married lady. I shouldn't have to
tell you these things. Where is your head, girl?"

An elaborate buffet had been set up in the dining hall downstairs: assorted cold meats and cheeses, and an endless assortment
of hot entrees kept warm in chafing dishes, since the guests
would be straggling in throughout the day. There were delectable desserts as well, an entire table devoted to them, along

with bowls of champagne punch, and ratafia, as well as silver pots of tea for those so inclined, kept hot by liveried footmen decked out in green and gold, who also managed to keep the food in good supply. This would continue throughout the evening, so that the guests could slip in from the masque, held in the Grand Ballroom across the hall, and avail themselves of the fare whenever they wished.

Jenna wasn't particularly hungry. She wasn't opposed to a tray in her room, but she certainly didn't want to pick at food in the dining hall among fawning, gawking strangers. She wanted to preserve anonymity as long as was possible. That meant keeping to herself until the masque. But Lady Elizabeth was just as determined to display her as she was to hide, and with a firm grip on her arm, the dowager steered her into the hall and propelled her toward the landing.

Halfway down the carpeted stairs and still protesting, Jenna froze on the step. A gentleman was watching their descent from the terrazzo floor below. Others were milling around him, but he appeared to be alone, a striking figure of a man, whom she assessed to be in his midthirties, with the most astonishing eyes she had ever gazed into. Long, dark lashes wreathed them, lashes that any woman would have envied; they gave him a dreamy, suggestive look. He was standing beneath a candle sconce, and the flames ignited the deep-set eyes behind those sweeping lashes, making them bluer than they had any right to be. His chestnut hair curled roguishly from a provocative widow's peak. It was pulled back in a queue behind the stand-up collar on the dark gray cutaway coat of superfine that made him appear very tall. The embroidered white waistcoat, black pantaloons, Hessian boots, and meticulously tied neckcloth that completed him were no more than a blur in the shadow of those eyes. Everything else paled before the primal expression in them that almost caused her to lose her footing.

Something stirred inside her, something she wasn't prepared for. Her mother was tugging at her arm, still carping about the importance of good eating habits and the danger of falling down in dead faints for lack of them. Jenna scarcely noticed;

those eyes watching her seemed to have charged the air between them and paralyzed her where she stood.

"Who is that?" she breathed, aware now of the man's broad jawline and sideburns framing straight lips that almost seemed as if they wanted to smile, but didn't.

As she spoke, a man and woman joined him. The woman, young and attractive, wearing blue organdy with a bonnet trimmed to match that complemented her blondness, put herself between the two men, looping one of her arms through each of theirs, and all three turned away. The subject of Jenna's attention walked with a slight limp that in no way diminished his stature.

"Who, dear? Where?" her mother said, her head oscillating ridiculously.

"There," Jenna whispered, nodding. "The one with the long hair." The new short men's hairstyles that had come into fashion and were all the rage in Town had not entirely taken the coast by storm. Some men still wore their hair rather long, as he did, drawn back loosely at the nape of the neck and tied with a silk ribbon, but that was the exception, not the rule, and an oddity among the aristocracy.

"Why, it's Simon Rutherford, Earl of Kevernwood," Lady Hollingsworth said. She narrowed her eyes and honed in on her target with all the aplomb of a ferret. "I didn't know he'd returned."

Jenna looked over in confusion.

"He's been abroad, dear, since the navy invalided him out. He served under Nelson, you know. I heard he was wounded at Copenhagen. See there, he's limping."

"How is it that we've never received him?"

"Lord Kevernwood doesn't spend much time on the coast, dear. He has a town house that he prefers to Kevernwood Hall. I'm surprised to see him here, actually. He usually keeps to himself. There's some sort of scandal connected with that family . . . something to do with Simon's older brother, who died in India. Their father disinherited him, money-wise, long before he was killed out there—cut him off without a cent of al-

lowance. It was something indelicate, dear, very hush, hush."
She pointed. "Look, Simon's valet. See there?"

Jenna followed her mother's finger to a tall, slender, gray-haired man hurrying after the earl and his companions.

"Simon must be staying the weekend," Lady Hollingsworth chattered on. "How odd. He so rarely socializes. I'm sure Lady Marner will have a good deal to say about that. You know how she does go on."

The earl did not look back. The trio seemed to be heading for the dining hall, and Jenna dug in her heels.

"I'm not going down, Mother," she said. "I'm going back to my room and unpack. By the time you locate Emily, my feathers will be beyond repair. She has an eye for one of the footmen. There's something you might want to address, before we have to hear all about that from Lady Marner."

Lady Hollingsworth bristled and spluttered, but Jenna paid no attention. She took advantage of her mother's incredulity to escape and return to her chamber. The earl's liquid sapphire eyes haunted her. Why had that look disarmed her so? And why should she be so distressed that he had witnessed her having a disagreement with her mother? She didn't know, but her embarrassment was unshakable and deep nonetheless.

That odd, unsettling thrill she'd experienced as those eyes impaled her came again, and a rush of heat sped to her cheeks as she unpacked her costume. She was prone to blushing. It had always been an embarrassment; the curse of her coloring. She wondered if she had done so earlier, and her heart leapt at the thought that she might have, and that he might have noticed.

"Thank God it's a masked ball," she thought out loud, slapping at a few bent feathers on her gown.

Moments later, one of the chambermaids appeared with a tray, and Emily followed on her heels wearing flushed cheeks herself. Jenna couldn't tell if the girl's color was result of an encounter with her footman, or an affray with her mother, since the latter seemed to be the order of the day.

Emily disappeared with the costume, and Jenna pulled a Chippendale chair up to the gateleg table, where the maid had set the tray, and lifted the silver cover from a well-rounded plate of rook pie, braised vegetables, and an assortment of bread tidbits and cheeses. She poured herself a cup of tea from the service that accompanied the meal, and nibbled at some of the bread and Stilton. The butterflies in her stomach would not abide rook pie.

Her costume returned no worse for wear, and two footmen arrived with a hipbath, which they set up in the dressing room off her bedchamber. Once the chambermaids had filled it, they left Jenna with Emily, who would assist with her toilette.

The water was heavenly, silkened with oil of lavender, and rosemary. She sponged it all over her body, luxuriating in the fragrant warmth caressing her. She closed her eyes, but when she did, the earl's image popped into her mind, and a hot surge revived the thrill he'd caused earlier and drove it up a notch. There was something excruciatingly exciting, and not a little frightening, about experiencing such a sensation naked in a tub of steamy, perfumed water. That it was the earl's liquid sapphire eyes that triggered it and not Rupert's dull hazel ones was disturbing. So disturbing that she fled the tub.

Emily's cheeks had returned to their normal color by the time she'd dried Jenna's hair and helped her into the costume. Jenna was seated at the vanity trying to decide how to dress her long strawberry-blond mane in order to make it fit beneath the cowl, when her mother, costumed as well, entered from the adjoining suite. Lady Hollingsworth was supposed to be Helen of Troy, but looked more like she had forgotten to put a dress on over her slip, Jenna decided. The dowager was much too short and heavyset to carry the costume well, and the formidable divorce corset underneath that radically divided her ample bosom only made matters worse, propelling the overflow sideways.

"Help us, Mother. We're in a muddle," Jenna said, suppressing a smile. "What shall we do with my hair? It's too thick to put up, and too long to leave down; it will show below the cowl."

First Emily tried to find a solution, and then Lady Hollingsworth tried her hand. The modiste had created the perfect headgear for a baldheaded woman, Jenna thought, before they finally settled on a soft, flat coil at the back of the head held in place snood fashion by a bit of sarcenet.

"Long hair is so out of fashion, Jenna," her mother said, fussing with the results. "You should have cut it long ago." She threw up her hands. "There's nothing for it. When you unmask, dear, just pull the tendrils out around your face. The center part is quite becoming, and the waves are falling naturally at least. It will have to do."

Taking a full-length view in the cheval glass, Jenna had to agree that Madame Flaubert had outdone herself. The swan-head mask fit perfectly. The eyeholes were slanted at just the right angle to follow the natural curve of her silvery gray eyes, and her mouth and chin were visible beneath the beak. Decidedly, she was magnificent.

Soliciting dances beforehand was waived for the evening, since part of the fun was to be attempting to identify one's dance partner—which really didn't promise to be all that difficult in most cases, judging from the gathering. Would Rupert recognize her? Jenna hoped not. She wanted to enjoy herself, or at least to try. Being in costume allowed her to pretend that she wasn't the Lady Jenna Hollingsworth, who had done murder and was about to ruin the rest of her life as result of it; she was a beautiful, graceful swan without a care in the world, and she longed to spread her lovely feathered wings and fly.

That delicious fantasy dissolved, however, the minute she entered the Grand Ballroom. The orchestra was playing a selection from Bach while the guests poured in through the archway, one costume more bizarre than the next. She spotted Rupert almost at once, dressed as a pharaoh, in keeping with the neoclassical movement that had become so popular among the ton. She hadn't remembered until then that John Nash, who had perpetuated Robert Adam's vision in decor, had begun redecorating Moorhaven in the Empire style incorporating concepts brought back by Englishmen who fought Napoleon during the Egyptian campaign. How could she not have noticed? There were evidences of the man's revolutionary touch everywhere. Jenna wasn't sure she approved.

She managed to avoid Rupert for the moment; he had become surrounded by several members of the House of Lords, who had just arrived from London for the event. The betrothal announcement was to be made at midnight. It would be signaled by the arrival of a troop of footmen bearing silver trays laden with champagne glasses already filled for toasting. That, however, was still more than two hours away, and it was going to be difficult to hide dressed in the most conspicuous costume in the hall.

The dancing began with a quadrille. A daring Viennese *valse à deux temps* followed by a gallop and then another quadrille would set the pattern for fourteen dances before a formal break for the announcement. Jenna danced the first quadrille with the Marquess of Roxbury. He was costumed as a magistrate, an older man, overweight and out of breath, who smelled of onions, and couldn't keep his wig on straight. The experience was nauseating, and she was thankful that her stomach was practically empty.

She didn't know her partner for the waltz. He was dressed simply in a voluminous domino and mask, though most of the masks framed by the customary white satin-lined black hoods were spectacular and very inventive. His resembled a hawk. Many of the other masks represented birds as well. There were owls, falcons, ravens—feathered creatures of every species were well accounted for, one more resplendent than the next, and all sporting formidable looking beaks. But birds were not the only species on display. Jenna particularly admired a lion mask worn by Lord Eccleston, whose deep, gravelly voice gave him away. It was designed as a cowl much like hers and covered his head completely. He was her partner for the gallop.

A duke, elaborately dressed as a potentate, was her partner for the second quadrille, during which she observed the ladies' costumes, which ranged from pastoral milkmaids to fairy princesses in every color imaginable. The young, blond woman who had stolen the earl of Kevernwood away that afternoon, was costumed as a toddler in white organdy and lace, complete with ruffled baby bonnet and leading strings. It suited her. Watching her skip effortlessly over the floor with Sir Gerald Markham leading their set sent a disturbing pang of jealousy shooting through Jenna. The girl seemed so happy, so unencumbered by guilt. Not a care in the world.

How dare she, when this is my ball, and I am so miserable? And who was she anyway? Someone who knew Lord Kevernwood well enough to link arms with him, that's who. Yes, that pang was jealousy. Unmistakably. She wouldn't have minded a bit if Miss Blondness had linked arms with her betrothed. Facing that fact was jarring at best.

Rupert was still engaged in conversation with the Londoners. Would she catch a glimpse of the earl? Would he dance, considering his limp? When the quadrille ended, she glanced around the ballroom trying to pick him out among the guests, but there were just too many people at the gathering. What would it be like to glide over that floor in his arms? She fantasized their bodies touching—the warm pressure of his hand at her waist, moving her effortlessly over the polished terrazzo; the illusion was brought on by the orchestra having struck up another waltz, and her eyes were closed as she indulged in it, when a deep, sensuous voice from behind assailed her ears.

"Will you honor me with this dance, my lady?"

At first, she thought that voice was a phantom of her fantasy. But when she turned to be sure, she froze in horror as she faced not her delicious daydream, but her worst nightmare: a highwayman, in black from his tricorn hat to his polished Hessian boots, his blue eyes blazing through the holes in a glistening silk half-mask.

She gasped, swayed, and spiraled unconscious into the man's strong arms.

CHAPTER TWO

When Jenna came to, she was lying on a yellow, satin-striped chaise lounge in an antechamber off the ballroom. Rupert was stooping over her, alongside her mother, who was whimpering and fanning her furiously with Lord Eccleston's donated handkerchief. The earl, who had removed the black half-mask and tricorn hat, stood behind the lounge. The blond girl was at his side, clutching the rigid arm that ended in a clenched fist against his well-turned muscular thigh, her face pressed against his shoulder as they all stared down at her.

Jenna's cowl had been removed, sarcenet and all, and her hair fell over her shoulders resting now on her breast, which began to heave with spastic breaths the minute her eyes focused on the earl in what remained of his highwayman costume. Those astonishing blue eyes glaring down at her had darkened to smalt. They met hers wearing a different look now, one of gravity and bewilderment.

Rupert dosed him with a disdainful glance.

"I told her to eat something," Lady Hollingsworth whined. "She scarcely touched a morsel all day."

"How colossally stupid of you, Jenna," Rupert said. Returning to his full height, he stood arms akimbo. "You've spoiled the masque!"

Clearly nonplussed, Kevernwood stood ramrod rigid, his eyes oscillating between them. There was nothing readable in his handsome face. If there had been something, anything in those lashes-fringed eyes that bespoke compassion, Jenna would have melted under their gaze. Tears blurred his image instead. Though he'd unmasked, her terror was still with her, and she reacted more like a frightened sparrow than the poised and graceful swan that she appeared.

"Kevernwood," a gruff voice said from the doorway. It belonged to Lord Eccleston, absurdly carrying his lion's head under his arm. Tall and broad shouldered, in his sixties, he was one of the Hollingsworths' closest neighbors, and one of Jenna's father's oldest friends on the coast.

The earl's broad jaw shot upward in his direction in reply, and when Lord Eccleston motioned him closer, he disengaged himself from the clutches of Miss Blondness and strode toward him.

The young man who had accompanied them that afternoon took the earl's place at the girl's side, looking confused. Jenna assumed that he must have been in the dining hall when she fainted, and had no idea what had occurred.

Her mother was chattering in her ear like a magpie. Jenna scarcely heard. Her head was still reeling. It pounded unmercifully. Her cheeks were on fire, and she couldn't meet Rupert's eyes. It was all she could do to persuade herself not to jump to her feet and slap his petulant face.

She glanced toward the doorway where several other men had joined Kevernwood and Lord Eccleston. All at once the earl's head snapped toward her, and his eyes—those liquid sapphire eyes that had so mesmerized her—wavered briefly.

His limp was more pronounced when his steps were brisk, as they were then, returning to her. She wasn't afraid of him now that she realized he was neither a ghost nor a real highwayman. The flood of mixed emotions that coursed through her body then was so complex, however, that she nearly fainted a second time. Not the least of these was an overwhelming desire to be in his arms again; she barely remembered their touch. How cruel was providence. She had fantasized being in those arms, and when it happened she wasn't even conscious to experience it.

"My lady, please forgive me," the earl murmured. "You must believe me, had I known, I would never—"

"Well, you should have known, shouldn't you?" Rupert snapped, interrupting. "Get out of that rig, Kevernwood. What could you have been thinking?"

"How could his lordship have possibly known, Rupert?" Lord Eccleston defended, coming closer. "He's only just come home."

Jenna nodded her awkward acceptance to the earl and attempted to rise.

"No, don't!" Miss Blondness erupted. "My lady, stay. You look frightful. Doesn't she, Crispin?" She was addressing the young man at her side, the man who possessed the other arm she'd linked that afternoon.

Jenna stared at them bewildered. Drat and blast! Who *was* this woman?

"Forgive me, my lady," the earl said, as though he'd read her mind. "May I present Lady Evelyn St. John, and her brother, Crispin St. John; they are my houseguests at Kevernwood Hall."

Jenna managed the correct amenities.

All at once, Lady Carolyn Marner, tall and regal, and totally in character in her Valkyrie costume, parted the growing crowd gathering at the antechamber door, her dull-witted husband, just as totally out of character as her Viking counterpart, trailing at her heels.

"Are you unwell, Jenna, my pet?" she intoned. "The marquess tells me that you swooned in the ballroom."

"Kevernwood here frightened her in that getup," Rupert put in.

"I'm sure he didn't mean to, Rupert, dear," she purred. Then close in his ear, though they all heard, she added, "How could his lordship possibly have known that her father was killed by a highwayman?"

"Can we get on with this, or not?" Rupert snapped, throwing up his hands in a gesture of impatience. "The rest of us may as well unmask and have the announcement. We all look ridiculous."

"No, please," Jenna interrupted. Anger, jealousy, and embarrassment raised her to her feet. She dared not meet the earl's eyes then. She would have come undone. A strange heat radiated between them that she would not probe to identify in front of that gathering. It was taking unmerciful liberties with the most private regions of her anatomy. "Don't let me spoil the ball," she faltered. Her lower lip had begun to tremble, but she would not give any one of them the satisfaction of her tears. "Go on with your merrymaking," she murmured. "No one is at fault. Please, everyone, I beg you excuse me."

She scarcely reached the landing before the tears came—a flood of them. She could barely see the steps. Her knees were still shaking from shock and anger and humiliation.

"How could you do this, Jenna?" her mother's voice rang in her ears. "Rupert is livid!"

"Rupert can go to—to *Jericho!*" she cried.

It was more than she could bear, and she covered her ears with her hands to shut out her mother's strangled gasp, and fled to her suite before the dowager's stutter became words.

Emily was waiting to help Jenna undress. Madame Flaubert's elegant feathered gown fell disrespected in a heap at her feet on the floral carpet. She gave it a vicious kick, scattering loose feathers into the air. How dare Rupert humiliate her in front of all those people? How dared Miss Blondness—St. John—Lady Whatever-Her-Name-Was, tell her she looked frightful? The woman was staying at Kevernwood Hall—under the same roof with those sensuous liquid sapphire eyes.

The maid had scarcely helped her into her nightgown, when a knock at the door of her sitting room brought an end to Jenna's assault on the feathers.

"If that is Mother, I have already retired, Emily," she warned the girl. Then, closing her bedchamber door, she climbed into the four-poster just in case her mother wouldn't take the maid at her word.

Seconds later, a light rapping at the door put her on guard.

"It's me, my lady," Emily called from the other side.

"Come," Jenna said, relieved.

The maid entered with a folded and sealed missive, and offered it.

Jenna didn't bother to examine the seal. How dare Rupert think that he could smooth the situation over with a few empty words scribbled on a piece of parchment? She crumpled it into a ball and threw it across the room.

"Leave me!" she sobbed, burying her hot, tear-stained face in the eiderdown pillow.

Downstairs, the ball was still going on. The announcement must have been made by now, and the rest of the guests had no doubt unmasked. It was official: she was Viscount Rupert Marner's betrothed. She could almost hear the violins playing another of those scandalous Viennese waltzes, just as they had done when Kevernwood asked her to dance. He was probably gliding over the floor with Miss Blondness close in his arms at that very moment, just as she'd imagined him holding her earlier, their bodies almost touching, his warm hand firmly resting on the small of her back—leading her—moving them to the music as one. Her heart sank. If only he hadn't worn that deuced costume.

Fresh tears seeped through her closed eyes—a stream of them, hot and salty. When had she become such a watering pot? She pounded her pillow relentlessly, indulging in the luxury of those tears, and it was some time before she cried herself to sleep.

Jenna did not go down to breakfast at ten with the rest. A tray was brought to her room, but she didn't touch it. The dowager didn't make an appearance, which meant that she was still angry. Jenna was almost grateful. She loved her mother dearly, but there were times when she didn't particularly like her. This was one of them. Was her mother's eagerness to join the two houses and share the benefits that such alliances afforded the ton more important than her daughter's happiness? Was it easier to add to her daughter's humiliation than to defend her, for fear of losing favor among the almighty Marners? Evidently. Her father would never have stood for it.

She got out of bed and glanced at her reflection in the vanity mirror. Her eyes were hopelessly red and swollen from crying. She dabbed at them with a splash of cold water from the pitcher, but there was no help for it. She looked like a chipmunk, just as she always did after a bout of tears, which was why she indulged in them so seldom.

Turning back to the bed, she stepped on the missive she'd discarded the night before and snatched it up from the carpet. Smoothing it out, she examined the seal. It wasn't Rupert's at all—not the Old English letter *M*, for Marner, but a gracefully scrolled *R*.

Her hands shook as she broke the seal and unfolded the parchment. She couldn't hold it still as she read:

> *My Lady Jenna,*
> *I am much distressed over what occurred in the ballroom tonight. If you will allow me, I should like to make a proper apology to you in person. I will be in the library after breakfast.*
>
> > *Your humble servant,*
> > *Kevernwood.*

Assignations of this type were quite acceptable between visiting guests, when two people wanted to speak privately. The library was the usual choice, quite above reproach. The earl had tendered a most decorous invitation. Why, then, did it seem like an invitation to a tryst . . . or was that wishful thinking?

It was well past the breakfast hour. Emily was nowhere to be found, and she hurried to dress her hair in a high chignon with the customary tendrils that always seemed to style themselves in damp weather, and wriggled into her pink lawn dress, perfectly acceptable for daytime wear, though irresistibly fetching.

The earl was just leaving the library when she arrived, and his face was unreadable as he stepped back over the threshold and ushered her inside. She accepted his bow, made a demure apology for her tardiness without explaining why, and waited for him to make the first move.

He was well attired in a tan cutaway jacket and trousers with a cream-colored waistcoat, appropriate for casual day wear, his demeanor controlled to a fault. No doubt a byproduct of naval discipline.

"My lady, I cannot tell you how sorry I am that I frightened you last evening," he said. "I needed to say that to you personally."

"You didn't frighten me, my lord, your costume did. You evidently now know why, and it is I who am sorry for your embarrassment."

"I don't embarrass easily, my lady," he said, flashing a lopsided smile that dissolved her heart. "Though there are those who take pleasure in trying to achieve it. I am quite thick-skinned, I promise you."

Hot blood rushed to her temples, and the fingers of a blush crawled up her cheeks. Looking into those eyes at close range was like drowning in a sapphire sea.

"Forgive me, but you have been crying," he said. "Is there anything I can do?"

"No, my lord," she murmured. Her face was on fire now. How could she have forgotten to put talc on her blotches? They must be flaming. She lowered her eyes, glad of the opportunity to rescue herself from drowning, and picked up a book for something to do with her hands. "I was distraught over having spoiled the masque," she said. "Lady Marner put so much effort into it. I was quite beside myself over that, I'm afraid."

"Nothing was spoiled except, of course, for you," he said. He smiled and it touched her soul. "Please don't reproach yourself. The masque was most enjoyable."

Jenna thought for a moment before curiosity overcame good sense.

"Why did you choose that costume, my lord?" she asked. "Surely you know that highway robbery is a scourge upon the coast these days, just as it is everywhere else?"

He gave it thought, his brows knit in a mischievous attitude that caught her off guard. He looked more like a schoolboy who had just committed the perfect prank than a dignified war hero.

"As a protest against the aristocracy, my lady," he said. "I was making a political statement, showing my disapproval."

Jenna put the book she'd been perusing to avoid eye contact back on the drop-leaf table and stared at Kevernwood unabashedly. "But, my lord, you *are* the aristocracy," she reminded him.

He laughed outright. His teeth were perfect and white, and provocative dimples punctuated his laugh lines.

"An accident of birth, my lady, I assure you," he said. "Underneath it all, I have a quite provincial soul. That costume was, I will admit, a low blow, and it backfired on me, as indeed it should have. Unfortunately, you were caught in the crossfire, and for that I am exceedingly sorry. I would not have had that happen for the world, I vow."

"Think no more about it. Your apology is gratefully accepted, my lord," she assured him, with as much dignity as she could muster in such close proximity.

"When is the wedding to be?" he probed. "I ask because I doubt I will be invited after this, and I would like to tender my felicitations in an appropriate manner when the time comes."

She clouded, hesitating. She'd forgotten all about Rupert. There was an odd, unreadable expression in the earl's face again, just as there had been when she'd first set eyes on him, and when she'd come to in the anteroom after fainting. He was studying her, and that enigmatic look was more disarming at close range than anything she'd encountered in his presence yet.

"We plan a winter wedding, my lord," she said, her voice steady for all that she was a shambles. "The actual date has not been set. I must go to Paris first. My trousseau is incomplete."

Silence replied to that. He was still observing her.

"B-before the new year, though," she added during the awkward gap his hesitation rent in the conversation.

He strolled dangerously close—so close the body heat between them was palpable. The intoxicating aroma of leather and tobacco infused the air. The marriage of scents was dizzying, and provocative. How he towered over her. They were almost touching, and she had to bend her head back to meet his eyes, which studied the curve of her slender throat and décolleté. Drat and blast! Why hadn't she worn her Brussels lace chemisette?

All at once he took her hand and lifted it to his lips, which were warm, riddling her with prickling swells of unexpected sensation, like shock waves, coursing to regions of her shuddering body that were heretofore virgin territory. His moist breath on her skin set swarms of butterflies loose in her stomach and threatened her balance.

"I hate to be the one to make an end to this delightful meeting," he said, lifting his mouth at last. "However, considering the situation, I do not think it wise that we linger here longer. I've cost you enough distress this visit, my lady. Any more would be unforgivable. Permit me to leave before you. I think it would be best."

"Of course, my lord," she murmured, crestfallen that the interview had come to an end so soon. Dazed, she swayed as he gave up her hand. "Will you be staying on, then?" She wished she hadn't said it the moment the words were out. Ninnyhammer! Why wouldn't he stay on? What a jingle-brained thing to say.

"Oh, yes, my lady," he said. He flashed her a positively diabolical grin, and his left eyebrow lifted in punctuation. "I wouldn't miss it for the world." He bowed then, and moved toward the door, but turned back when he reached it. "About the wedding, my lady," he said, taking hold of the knob. "In the spirit of friendship, I ask you to consider a thought from one older and more . . . experienced than yourself."

"My lord?"

"Think carefully, my lady," he said softly, crossing the threshold. "You do not love him."

The heat that rose in her cheeks narrowed her eyes, but the door closed behind him. Her heart was pounding visibly, moving the pink lawn bodice of her frock with every breath. How dare he issue directives! Albeit true, who was he to make such an assumption—and on so brief an acquaintance? Her blood was boiling. No, this was definitely no tryst. Why did the man's eyes say one thing and his lips another? Was he making mock of her?

Tears welled in her eyes again, but the library door opened suddenly and she blinked them back as Lady Evelyn waltzed into the room in a cloud of butter-colored muslin that matched her hair. She was alone, and the last person Jenna wanted to see in that moment. She was trapped. She couldn't run: that would be impolite. She plucked a book from the shelf and pretended to read again.

"Good morning, Lady Jenna," the girl chirped. "Feeling better, I hope?"

"Much," Jenna replied succinctly.

"We missed you at breakfast."

"I had a tray in my room."

"Ahhh! Well, you look much improved. That was dreadful last night. You gave us quite a fright. Simon was awfully upset. I saw him leaving the library just now. I'm sure he's told you it was all terribly innocent."

"Have you known Lord Kevernwood long?" Jenna queried, unable to help herself.

"Have I known Simon long," the girl parroted. "Simply forever. We see a great deal of Simon in town. We're often his guests there as well. When you visit London, you will have to come with us to Almack's. Have you ever been?"

"No, I'm afraid not." There had been no social whirl of fetes and balls, teas and jaunts to such establishments as Almack's for Jenna. She wouldn't elaborate. She wasn't about to confide in this maddening little social butterfly that her father's declining health had delayed the plans for her come-out until she was well past twenty. And she certainly wouldn't confide that his untimely death at the hands of a heartless thatchgallows, and her mother's subsequent spiral into pseudomelancholia had made an end to the prospect of a season in Town for her altogether. She would not bear the girl's pity—especially since it wasn't necessary. Jenna was perfectly happy without all the stirabout and pother of a social event in London. It wasn't as though she was husband hunting, after all. There was hardly a need for entering the marriage mart, since Rupert Marner had always been a foregone conclusion. "I don't go often to Town," she said to the girl's incredulous gasp. "I'm quite content here on the coast."

"Well, you must come . . . you and the viscount, of course. The orchestra is simply divine there. That's where I learned the quadrille. Lady Jersey herself taught me! Can you imagine it? She's one of the patronesses there, and a very dear old friend of Simon's. And the ambience! Well, there's simply nothing like Almack's anywhere. You'll see. Everyone who's anyone goes. It's very exclusive, one must be approved, but I'm sure you'll have no difficulty. Simon can manage simply *anything*."

Jenna took the girl's measure. She was beautiful, young, and vital. No wonder the earl had a *tendre* for her.

"We may have to do without Simon," Lady Evelyn babbled on. "He's become quite stodgy since Copenhagen. But that's to be expected, what with his leg and all. He's so unconventional, is Simon. Crispin and I have been trying to get him to cut his hair for ages. That dreadful tail of his is so outdated. Why, it's positively passé. No one wears long hair anymore—not even we ladies. But Simon will be Simon. He is quite the revolutionary, you know. He utterly defies convention. But that's part of his charm, isn't it? I positively *adore* him."

The tears Jenna had blinked back were threatening again, and she returned the tome she'd been staring at to the shelf with no idea of its topic. Lady Evelyn was eyeing her coiffure now, with not a little interest. Was this gushing girl about to comment on the unconventional length of her hair as well?

"Excuse me," Jenna murmured, and fled without giving her the chance.

CHAPTER THREE

The weather held for picnicking and the men's shoot that afternoon. Jenna did not see the earl again, and Rupert was conspicuous in his absence as well. He was evidently still angry. She was relieved that they were both missing and had no desire to see either of them. She even attempted to beg off the picnic, wanting no more encounters with Lady Evelyn either, but her mother wouldn't hear of it.

"You cannot spoil the rest of the weekend, Jenna," her mother intoned. "I simply will not allow it. What's gotten into you? Rupert is awaiting your apology, dear. I've given him my word that—"

"You've *what*? Mother, how dare you? You heard the way Rupert spoke to me last night in front of everyone. I shan't forget that you took his part. How could you? You heard, and you actually think that *I* should apologize to *him*?"

"He expects it, dear. This is your engagement, Jenna. You are twenty-two years old. If you ruin this you shall have to put on your caps! It's too late for a Season now. Do you *want* to be a spinster? Why, Lady Marner was saying just this morning—"

"Oh, bother Lady Marner! We should have had this farce at

Thistle Hollow—or not at all. It sickens me to see you bow and scrape to Lady Carolyn Marner and that . . . that Sassenach of a husband of hers. There goes Rupert ten years hence—living like a piece of lint in the Prince Regent's pocket, and earning about as much respect! I want to go home. At least on my own ground I'd have the advantage."

"Well, you can't. The Marners have been kind enough to host this weekend out of sympathy for me . . . for *us*, because of your father, dear."

"Father has been gone for over a year, Mother. Don't you dare bring him into this. He isn't here to take sides. But you know full well whose side he would be on if he was. There is no reason why you couldn't have hosted this travesty at Thistle Hollow."

"Well, it's too late now, dear. We are here, and you are going to see it through. You will dress and go to the picnic. At your earliest opportunity, you will apologize to Rupert. And when we go down to dinner tonight, you will smile. You will not hold me up for ridicule and gossip, Jenna. I simply will not have it!"

Jenna wore her white muslin afternoon dress to the picnic. It was held at precisely the noon hour on the well-manicured east lawn of the estate, a picturesque expanse of rolling green that sloped down to an orchard. Only a few of the older gentlemen attended. The rest were occupied with the shoot.

Jenna avoided Lady Evelyn St. John, and opted instead for the company of the Warrenfords' two daughters. The Warrenfords spent a good deal of time in London, in and out of Season, and she attempted to extract whatever tidbits she could about the St. Johns from them. The yield was scant. All she was able to discover was that they were twins, distant relatives of the duke of York, that both their parents were dead, and that Simon Rutherford, the ton's most eligible bachelor, was rarely seen in public without them. *Stuck like glue* was the term Rosemary Warrenford had used. It was like rubbing salt in an open wound.

Her interview with Rupert did not go quite so smoothly. He appeared at the picnic late in the afternoon, exchanged amenities with the Warrenford girls, took Jenna's arm and steered her toward the orchard.

The earl put in an appearance at about the same time. His limp was more pronounced now than it had been earlier, yet his movements were elegant in spite of it. He strolled straight to Lady Evelyn's side, offered his hand, and helped her up from the picnic cloth she occupied with several young people whom Jenna did not recognize. She deliberately navigated her course with Rupert to pass directly in front of them. Then, snuggling closer to her betrothed, she flashed him her most disarming smile, ignoring the earl altogether as they sailed past. That would teach his lordship to keep his advice to himself.

Rupert studied her with a skeptical eye through his quizzing glass. He was tall and slender, with close-cropped hair the color of wheat swept toward his face in the latest à la Brutus style. Whether the occasion was casual or formal, she could not fault him. His toilette was always up-to-the minute, and correct.

"You're feeling better I see," he said.

"Much better, thank you. And what of you? Are you in a more agreeable temper after your shoot?"

"I heard you had a rendezvous with Kevernwood this morning," he replied, his avoidance of the question obvious.

"I'd hardly call it a 'rendezvous,' Rupert. He apologized for last night and I accepted him. It was all quite proper."

"Mmm," Rupert said, tucking the quizzing glass back into his waistcoat pocket.

"Who told you?"

"You should have," he flashed. "I shouldn't have to hear such on-dits from my servants."

"We aren't married yet, Rupert. I do not have to account to you for every second of my time. At least he had the good manners to apologize."

"I want you to stay away from him, Jenna," he said. They had reached the orchard, and he turned her toward him. "I mean this. The man's a Jackanapes. Just look at the cut of him. He knows long hair went out ages ago, and yet he will insist upon wearing that ridiculous queue. He does it for attention."

"Oh, I don't know, I rather think it's quite attractive."

Rupert's jaw dropped and an incredulous grunt escaped his throat. "That whole business last night was a put-down," he said. "One simply does not cut his hosts in that way."

"He didn't know about Father, Rupert."

"But he knew that costume was in bad taste. He wore it apurpose."

"I've accepted his apology."

"Yes, yes, so you've said. Now let that be the end of it. Leave him to the St. Johns. Let them ruin their reputation aligning with him."

"You act as if I dragged them here. You invited them, Rupert."

"Not actually. Mother invited *him*. He took it upon himself to bring the St. Johns, those hangers-on he's entertaining. Colossal cheek, by God!"

"Did he ask permission to bring them?"

"What does that matter?"

"Did he, or didn't he?"

"Yes, he did, but he shouldn't have; we aren't acquainted."

"Well, we are now, aren't we?" She couldn't believe that she was actually defending the St. Johns—defending the earl's right to include them, of all things. She wished she'd never set eyes on any of them.

"I beat him in the shoot, you know."

"*You?* Rupert, you are terrible with a pistol."

"Exactly!"

"He must have let you win."

"He did not! He's a lousy shot I say, for all his bragging about holding a record at Manton's Gallery. It's a good thing Nelson got him and not Wellington. It's sure as check, the blighter'd need to make use of a ship's cannon to hit anything."

"Rupert, this pettiness is beneath you."

"All right." His impeccable posture collapsed and he breathed a nasal sigh. "Let's not quarrel," he said in an undertone.

"Is that supposed to be an apology?"

He gave a start and blurted, "You were expecting one?"

"Don't answer a question with a question, Rupert. You do that a lot, you know, and it's such bad form. And, yes, I was expecting an apology. You behaved like a boor last night and embarrassed me in front of everyone."

"I've been expecting an apology from *you*!" was his incredulous reply.

"For what? For passing out at the sight of someone looking the part of my father's murderer?"

"No, for swooning for lack of nourishment when this house is packed to the rafters with enough to feed Wellington's army!"

"You've been listening to Mother."

"She's concerned about you, Jenna."

"She's concerned that I might break the engagement and ruin her social standing."

Rupert stared.

Why was there nothing in those empty hazel eyes? Why didn't they quicken her heart and turn her knees to water?

"Is that what you're of a mind to do?" he asked, gravel voiced. "I love you, Jenna."

"Then I would suggest that you rethink who needs to apologize to whom before this weekend is over. What I have 'a mind to do' depends upon it."

The rest of the afternoon was uneventful. Jenna returned to her suite to rest and change for dinner, which was to be held at eight. Lady Hollingsworth insisted she wear her embroidered dinner gown of sage green patterned silk, citing that it tinted her silver-gray eyes the color of seawater. Jenna would have preferred her burgundy voile, with the rosebud trim, but she allowed the green to avoid an argument. It was to be her first dinner *à la russe* since she had come out of mourning, and it was a treat to wear any color at a formal affair after a dismal year of paramatta, black bombazine, and crepe.

She was seated between Crispin St. John and Rupert. Kevernwood sat diagonally across the table from her, flanked by

Lady Evelyn and Rosemary Warrenford. Jenna tried not to look in the earl's direction, but his eyes, like magnets, drew her own.

Liveried footmen served the courses from food laid out on the sideboard. Menus were posted at every third place on porcelain menu plates. There would be multiple courses, beginning with Soup à la Reine, followed by turbot, salmon, and trout, all appropriately sauced. There would then be game hens, roast saddle of mutton, ham, braised beef, and spring chicken. Fruit compote, apple charlotte, and Neapolitans would be served for dessert along with the usual assortment of sweet dessert wines.

To Jenna, it all tasted like sawdust.

The table was spread with elegant damask linens, fine crystal, and flowers: pink and lavender sweet peas overflowing round silver bowls. She studied her distorted reflection in the bowl between herself and the earl. To her dismay, her face was deeply flushed, and she'd hardly touched any wine.

Lady Evelyn chattered incessantly. Nobody seemed to mind. It was plain that the gentlemen all found her quite charming in her rose-colored silk gown and coronet of matching silk ribbon rosebuds. Lady Hollingsworth had chosen a pale green plume for Jenna's hair ornament, insisting that it was exquisite against her strawberry blond hair, but she felt like a circus horse straight out of Astley's Amphitheatre in it. Why had she settled for the green? Why hadn't she dug in her heels and held out for the burgundy?

The dinner went well until after the third course. The footmen had removed everything on the table, including the tablecloth, and the butler began setting out the ratafia and sweet wines, while the under-butler and maids busied themselves laying down the dessert plates and silver at each diner's place. It was when the footmen began to serve the desserts that the conversation became dangerously political.

The earl and Sir Gerald Markham were discussing the economy. Much was being made of the economic decline amongst the upper and lower classes since the war with the Colonies.

"Since the postage rates went up again, my tenants can't afford it," Sir Gerald said. "They come begging to me, when their letters arrive, to pay the post. And arrive they do. The lower classes breed like rabbits. They have relations scattered all over the Empire. I myself do not receive such a quantity of mail. And as if that isn't enough, they steal from me. How do you deal with your cottagers, Kevernwood? You're an absentee landlord for the most part. How do you keep your tenants from poaching and robbing you blind? I've had to set out mantraps and spring guns, and hire overseers myself."

"My tenants do not steal because they do not have to," the earl replied succinctly, almost smiling.

"There's wisdom in that somewhere I suppose," Rupert chided.

"There is," the earl agreed. He did smile then, but it was a cold smile that chilled Jenna to the bone. "Cottagers become unruly when they are forced to live in the squalor and cramped quarters of unsympathetic landlords. If one is sensitive to one's tenants' needs and gives them no cause to harbor ill will, they would have no inclination to steal. Consequently there would be no necessity for going to the expense of hiring overseers to maim or kill poachers with traps."

"You don't share a like mind with your father, m'boy," Sir Gerald observed. "Now, there was a true nobleman. He kept his cottagers in line. No cosseting in that camp, by God!"

"We live in different times, sir," the earl said, expanding his posture until the chair creaked beneath him. "They call for different tactics and more liberal minds. Had such existed in my father's day, we would not be in the state we are at present."

"You actually believe that drivel, then, do you?" said Rupert.

"My tenants will testify that I have proven the point."

"Come now, Kevernwood," Rupert taunted through a guttural chuckle. "The lower classes hate the aristocracy."

"With good cause," the earl replied. "We condone pouring good money after bad in the Colonies—at their expense, mind you—and then lose the war." He made a hand gesture. "Look around you. Who has suffered? Certainly not we, the almighty aristocracy; we thrive. Good, loyal men, a vast number conscripted, mind, who fought for this country—men whose wounds have seen them cashiered out—are come home to properties that we have meanwhile confiscated for unpaid taxes in their absence, and they are begging in the streets of London, sir, while we languish on their lands in style."

"If you ask me, the forgers are at fault for the state of the economy," the Marquess of Roxbury interjected dryly. "Forged notes have been flooding the market since 'ninety-seven. Whatever became of all those suggestions for a solution that the people were supposed to have submitted years back? It seems to me that if the lower classes are so concerned with the economy, they should take an active part in improving it. But there it is, they haven't the intelligence. That's why it's left to the aristocracy."

"It's easy enough to lay the blame anywhere but where it belongs"—the earl said, setting his fork down, "—upon ourselves."

"Just what do you propose we do about it, Kevernwood?" Rupert said with raised voice. "Open our coffers and make them all as rich as Croesus? That sort of rubbish smacks of colonialism. It belongs amongst the savages in America, not in civilized England."

At the far end of the table, Lady Marner cleared her voice, rousing her husband, who had begun to nod off.

"Hear, hear!" he hooted, bolting upright in his chair.

"Do be still, Archibald," his wife said in an aside, dosing him with a baleful glance then centering her attention on the diners. "Can we not save this sort of conversation until the ladies have retired? It is hardly proper table discourse, Rupert, dear."

"No. I want him to answer," Rupert insisted, raising his hand in a gesture to stay her.

"The colonists do have ground to stand on," the earl replied. "After all, they did win the war."

"Take care, Kevernwood, you go too far," Rupert warned.

"Unless the aristocracy take an interest in the dilemma of the lower classes, we could see revolution," the earl opined. "You can only push the hungry so far. Look to France for her example. Have we learned nothing from her mistake? Our king wanders in and out of madness. His heir, whom we have just made Regent, God help us, is a gambler, a philanderer, and a notorious elbow bender. Imagine that? The man can't even manage a marriage. How fit is he to rule the British Empire?"

"You speak treason, sir!" Rupert shouted, vaulting out of his chair.

"I speak truth."

"Rupert!" Lady Marner shrilled. "His lordship is our guest."

"He is *your* guest, Mother, not mine."

"Her ladyship was right earlier," the earl said, rising from the table. "This is hardly the forum for such a discussion. We gentlemen shall take it up amongst ourselves at another time."

"We shall take it up on the dueling ground," Rupert decreed, tossing down his serviette. "You leave me no choice but to call you out, sir. You have cut this house too many times these past two days for me to stand for treason spoken under its roof to boot! Since it is customary to postpone arrangements for such things until daytime hours, I would appreciate it if you would remain in residence until my second visits you in the morning."

"Your servant, sir," said the earl, offering a crisp bow.

Jenna's eyes oscillated between Kevernwood and Rupert. Her cheeks were on fire. She wanted to run from the dining hall, but her legs betrayed her. She couldn't move. Around her the gathering had become a milling mass of confusion. The women's cries and murmurings reached an ugly crescendo of sound that made her head swim. The men were rising from the table, their rumbling monotone impossible to translate. Across the way, Lady Evelyn had risen. She had thrown herself into the earl's arms and begun to cry. Her brother skirted the table and went to her side. Kevernwood's eyes met Jenna's. She couldn't read their message, but that molten, blue-steel gaze held her relentlessly, pierced her to the core before moving on to impale Rupert. She was numb. It was a numbness Rupert's cold fingers couldn't penetrate as they clamped around her arm. She was paralyzed, caught between the crossed swords of the two men's glaring eyes, as Rupert spirited her away.

CHAPTER FOUR

Jenna scarcely had time to exchange her dinner gown for the frilly ecru negligee that Emily had laid out for her, when an assault on her sitting room door sent a shiver along her spine. She was alone. Emily was closeted with her mother, who had nearly collapsed in the dining hall, a circumstance that Jenna attributed more to the divorce corset she'd poured herself into than any genuine malaise over the duel.

The knock came again—rapid, urgent, almost desperate—and she threw the door open to Lady Evelyn St. John.

For a moment, they stared at one another across the threshold.

"Please, my lady . . . ?" the girl murmured. Her eyes were red and swollen, and she was trembling.

"It's late, Lady Evelyn," Jenna said, stepping aside to let her enter, "and we have all had an unpleasant evening. I was just about to retire."

"How can you sleep? They're going to kill each other! Don't you care, my lady?"

"What can I possibly do?"

"You can reason with the viscount. There is no necessity for this."

"It's far too late for that."

"You really *don't* care, do you?" Lady Evelyn accused, discovery lifting her voice. "How will you feel when one of them lies dead, knowing that you might have prevented it?"

"You credit me with much too much. Why don't you speak to his lordship?"

"It was your betrothed who challenged Simon, my lady. Simon tried to avoid this—you heard him down there. Now he cannot back down from the challenge. He is a gentleman. He will die in that duel first, albeit against the law. I cannot let that happen. The viscount must withdraw."

"You don't know Rupert, Lady Evelyn. He would never."

"Then we are lost. Someone will die. I shan't be able to bear it if Simon . . ."

Jenna couldn't bring herself to inquire about the obvious. She wanted no details. Why did her heart feel as though this woebegone creature before her had just pierced it through with a dagger? She stared at the girl. So this was what love was like. This was what she should be feeling for Rupert. But it was not Rupert that she was thinking of. She wasn't ready to delve deeper into the recesses of her wounded heart to uncover more of that, however—not then. It was enough of a shock realizing what love *wasn't*.

Jenna had never felt so alone as she did in that moment, an unwilling spectator looking into the breaking heart this desperate girl had laid bare before her.

"I'm sorry, Lady Evelyn," she murmured. "I don't know what sort of relationship you presume that I have with Rupert, but I assure you, he is his own man. Right or wrong, lawful or not, nothing I could possibly say would alter anything."

Lady Evelyn nodded her lowered head in defeat.

Jenna stared toward the girl's collapsed posture. She almost pitied her. Did the earl know she'd come? No. Kevernwood impressed her as being his own man, as well—certainly not the type to let a woman fight his battles for him. Poor girl. Jenna did pity her. This duel wasn't about the fragile state of the British economy, or the tenant farmers, or the poor king's madness. It was Rupert's jealousy that threw down the gauntlet.

"Go and get some rest," she said, turning the girl toward the door. "There's nothing to be done now but pray that they have the good sense not to go through with this insanity."

Jenna sank down on the edge of the four-poster. It was long past midnight and she was too overset to sleep. She went to the window and looked down toward the garden wall. A tall, sculptured hedgerow all but prevented her from seeing the cluster of French lilac trees burgeoning just beyond the arbor. She opened the window, closed her eyes, and breathed deeply, inhaling the exquisite perfume living in the still night air. These lilacs were a more delicate variety than the ones in her own gardens at This-tle Hollow, deep amethyst in color, and a thousand times more fragrant, if that could be.

She heaved a ragged sigh and closed the window. She needed to think. It wasn't that she wanted to. The thoughts were ham-mering at her brain, and if she were to let them in it couldn't be in that house.

Foraging through her clothing, which Emily had hung neatly in the wardrobe, she unearthed the long cashmere pelerine she had brought along to ward off the evening chills, slipped it on over her negligee, and went below to the garden.

But it wasn't the delicious fragrance of French lilacs that filled her nostrils when she entered through the arbor. It was the provocative aroma of tobacco, an exotic blend she'd never smelled before, and yet there was something vaguely familiar about it. She wasn't alone among the lilacs, and her heart nearly stopped as he stepped from the shadows of a tall tree close by.

Kevernwood.

Her quick intake of breath caught in her throat as he emerged still dressed as he'd been at dinner, minus the black cutaway jacket. He'd also removed his neckcloth, and his ruffled shirt was open at the throat exposing a patch of dark hair curl-ing beneath.

"F-forgive me, my lord," she stammered. "I couldn't sleep. I didn't know . . . I didn't mean. . . ." It was no use. The traitor-ous emotions rippling through her body had tied her tongue.

"I wanted a smoke," he said, strolling closer. "I didn't think it wise to have it in the house, considering. God knows but that your betrothed might deem it a hanging offense and, alas, I have but one life to give for king and country this season."

"And I've spoiled it for you," she regretted, ignoring the sarcastic last.

He began tapping the ashes from the bowl of a small clay pipe against the trunk of the tree beside him.

"No, don't!" she cried. "Please. I will leave. There are other gardens, my lord."

"No—no, do not trouble. I've finished, really."

He had taken away her excuse to escape, and she stood studying him for an awkward moment trying to invent another.

"My father used to smoke a pipe," she said meanwhile. "I loved the aroma of his tobacco. I have never smelled anything quite like yours before, though, and yet . . . there is something vaguely familiar about it. Is it a custom mixture?"

The earl nodded. "I have it blended by a tobacconist in London," he said, tucking the pipe into his pocket. "He flavors it with licorice, whiskey, rum, and a little latakia from the Mediterranean. Most women object to it as being too overpowering, but I find it a very satisfying smoke."

Jenna turned to go. She couldn't believe she was standing there, half-dressed, in the garden in the middle of the night, casually discussing tobacco with a man who was probably going to kill her betrothed in a duel.

"I shouldn't be here. I'm sorry," she murmured.

"Why did you come out here at this hour?" he said, his deep voice turning her around again.

"Flowers have the same effect upon me as your pipe has upon you, my lord," she replied, swallowing her rapid heartbeat. "I couldn't sleep. I wanted to think, and I always do that best whilst communing with nature."

He came closer, hardly limping at all. For a moment she toyed with the idea of telling him about Lady Evelyn. She'd almost decided against it, but when he continued to advance she could no longer control the rush of excitement that pulsed through the core of her sexuality, quickening her heart, setting off alarm bells in her brain.

"Lady Evelyn paid me a visit in my rooms earlier," she blurted. "She is afraid for you."

His smile disappeared and he stopped in his tracks. The moon shone down on them and there was something in his eyes that she couldn't identify, though it sent cold chills the length of her spine. He was very close, searching her face in the moonlight.

"She shouldn't have done that," he said.

"She wanted me to use my influence with Rupert . . . to persuade him to withdraw the challenge."

Consistently, his blank expression told her nothing.

"She was dreadfully overset," Jenna went on. "I'm afraid I couldn't offer her much hope in that regard. Rupert is quite fixed in his ways."

For a long moment their eyes met trembling in the moon-light before he prowled closer. The evening dampness had framed her face in tendrils, and he reached to brush a stray one from her cheek.

"I told you, you do not love him," he murmured, seizing her in strong arms that pulled her close.

Before she could catch her breath, his mouth closed over hers. He tasted of the tobacco and traces of sweet wine. He deepened the kiss and swallowed her moan as his warm, skilled tongue glided between her parted teeth and entered her slowly—totally.

It was wrong, but she didn't resist. She was being compromised, alone, past midnight, half-dressed in the arms of another, while her unsuspecting betrothed slept in the manor but a few yards away. If someone were to see, her reputation would be ruined. But the earl had stirred her passion awake and she was beguiled, as foxed by his closeness as a lord in his cups.

His massive hand roamed beneath the pelerine and took possession of her waist. Slowly the hand inched upward. Deftly, his tongue teased, pulling back, then plunged deeper, and a husky groan resonated from his throat to hers as her trembling tongue responded.

Her heart leapt. An involuntary pulse throbbed wildly at her very core, spreading a delicious, achy warmth through her most private regions as he crushed her closer still, molding her body to his, grown turgid with arousal.

All at once she remembered where she was and what was happening to her. What was he thinking—that because she wasn't begging him to spare Rupert in the duel she didn't care? Or was it that he thought to take her favors as payment for Rupert's safety? These thoughts, coming in rampant flashes, were stabbing at the sexual stream that flowed between them, mortally wounding the magical sensations his touch had ignited.

His hand found its way to her face and slid down the length of her arched throat. He spread the cape wide and murmured her name against her lips as his fingers slipped lower. But it was when the roughened skin of his palm explored her décolleté that she sobered. What happened inside her when he touched her there was so terrifying that she wrenched free and slapped his face, with all the strength she could muster.

Unprepared, he staggered backward.

"How dare you!" she demanded, her breast heaving with passion and indignation beneath the pelerine she pulled tight around her. "I've just told you that a woman who worships you came begging me to plead with my betrothed to cancel the duel. Is this how you would betray that heart?"

Breathing hard, he stared. His handsome face showed her no emotion.

"Rupert warned me that you were a Jackanapes," she said to his silence. "I'm sorry now that I didn't believe him. You are no gentleman, my lord."

"So I was wrong," the earl said, his voice like gravel. "You do love him after all?" He raked his hair back. His moist brow, pleated by a frown, glistened in the moonlight. "Well, you can put your mind at ease, my lady," he said. "Your precious Rupert will not be seriously harmed in the duel, nor arrested for instigating it. You didn't have to try and buy his safety with your charms."

"W–with my—"

"You didn't have to degrade yourself. I've already instructed my second that we shall use swords, not pistols."

"*Swords*?" That possibility hadn't occurred to her. "What kind of swords?"

"Fencing swords, the *épée de terrain*. Sword fights are outlawed in England, my lady. If one kills someone with a sword these days, he can no longer excuse himself as having acted in self-defense, hence duels fought with the sword are not fought to the death . . . unless, of course, one of the duelists is an out and out bounder. Once one of us is blooded or disarmed, the duel will end."

"But . . . I don't understand. Why did you choose the sword over the pistol?"

"Because your betrothed is hopelessly inept with the pistol, my lady." A husky laugh lived in his throat. "I would surely kill him with one."

"He says much the same of you, my lord," she snapped haughtily.

"We shall never know now whom you should believe, shall we?" His eyes darkened and he smiled, but there was neither humor nor warmth in it. "The thing I find amusing is that you nearly compromised your honor for naught. But your virtue is still reasonably untarnished, and since, contrary to your belief, I *am* a gentleman, your secret is quite safe with me. Sleep well, my lady." He offered a crisp bow and brushed by her, stirring the air.

The aroma of his exotic tobacco teased her nostrils as he passed. It overpowered the lilacs. Where had she smelled it before? Was it in the library when he'd made his apology? Her brain was too addled to recall. The pressure of his kiss still numbed her mouth. The touch of his hands on her skin still lingered. Her breast still tingled from his roughened fingers. How could he have thought she would have sacrificed her chastity? But he had, and what's more she had nearly let him take it. She shuddered. He had stolen the warmth from the garden. A cold wind rose stirring the lilacs, it riddled her damp, flushed skin with gooseflesh. Pulling her pelerine close about her, she crept back unseen to her rooms.

Phelps, his valet, was waiting when Kevernwood stomped into his dressing room wilted from dampness, rubbing Jenna's smarting raised handprint on his left cheek. The valet's right eyebrow lifted. It was enough to earn him a scathing look.

"Don't start," the earl warned.

The valet's eyebrow inched a little higher before it lowered. "I haven't said a word, my lord," he intoned.

"But you will," Simon said. He yanked his shirt out of his pantaloons, flopped in the wing chair beside the dead hearth, and raised his legs. "Just help me out of these first, if you don't mind. The deuced dampness has got me soaked clear through."

The valet took hold of the Hessians the earl aimed toward him, clicking his tongue as he yanked them off, first one and then the other. The lawns had been freshly scythed for the weekend, and the boots were covered with grass spears.

"I'll have to use the new boot polish—the one with the champagne base," the man observed. "The old will never address this fine state you've put them in."

The earl grunted, struggling out of the rest of his clothes, and stood while the valet helped him into his burgundy brocade dressing gown. He cinched the sash ruthlessly and flopped back down in the chair again.

"I take it that the viscount has not cried off?" Phelps said, setting the earl's clothes aside. He poured a brandy and handed it over.

"Hm?" the earl grunted, taking the snifter. The duel was the farthest thing from his mind just then. His lips still tingled from Jenna's kiss, and stubborn waves of pulsating warmth still grieved his loins. How could he have been so mistaken about the girl? How had he misread her furtive glances? He shifted uncomfortably in the chair. The pressure of her slender body was still with him, molded to his with precious little in between—nothing but that ridiculously thin pelerine and gauzy nightdress. He would have bet his blunt that she was not in love with Rupert Marner. The man was a coxcomb. He couldn't even be termed a Corinthian; he hadn't the measure of a sportsman—reckless or otherwise. Were the Hollingsworths in Dun territory that they had to contract such a union? He hadn't heard of it. And that was his business, after all, keeping tabs on who among the aristocracy were plump in the pockets or parvenu, and who were putting on tick. That could only mean that Jenna was in love with Marner, as if he needed to wonder. Hadn't she just proven that? Hadn't she just nearly sacrificed her honor to ensure his safety? Yes, his pride was wounded, but it was more than that. His heart had taken a direct hit the moment he clapped eyes on her on that staircase. She was the most exquisite creature he had ever seen.

The valet cleared his voice, bringing him back to earth. "The viscount, my lord," he prompted. "Perchance, has he had the good sense to withdraw?"

"Of course not."

"And, I don't suppose that you—"

"What? And have it bruited about at court that the Earl of Kevernwood is a coward? You know better than to even ask."

"I warned you not to accept the Marners' invitation, my lord. Why ever did you, when you know that they hold you up to ridicule?"

Phelps had been with him since he was a boy, and Simon considered the valet more the father he wished he'd had than the loyal servant he was, hence the liberties the man sometimes took were often overlooked. Their relationship was such that, the earl's body language often sufficed for the spoken word, like now, when his telltale clenched fists bespoke a warning—which, much to his chagrin, however, also like now, rarely served to keep the servant in his place.

"For two reasons," Kevernwood replied. "Firstly, I thought it prudent to put Evy and Crispin forward in society. Evy is about to have her come-out, as you well know, and Crispin is embarking upon a naval career. Such weekends are important to them, Phelps. And just because I am ostracized by jealous fops such as Marner does not credit them being shunned as well. I've put too much effort into ensuring just the opposite."

The valet waited a diplomatic interval, and when no further discourse followed said, "And . . . the other reason?"

"You know perfectly well the other reason," the earl snapped, scowling. "Look around you, Phelps. You're no nodcock. All these chickens to be plucked, how could I resist?"

"But that costume, my lord! What could you have been thinking? I told you—"

"Do let me have my bit of fun," Simon interrupted.

"The lady did not appreciate your wit, my lord," the valet responded, wagging his head in disapproval.

"That was unfortunate," the earl agreed. His face fell, and he breathed a tremulous sigh.

"I take it that is her . . . er . . . signature on your face there, my lord?"

"Deuced female misrepresented herself," Kevernwood growled, rubbing his cheek.

"That's odd. I took her for quite well to pass."

"Yes, well, you are hardly an expert on the wiles of women, old boy."

The valet never smiled, yet somehow Simon always knew when his humor was appreciated.

"She is betrothed, my lord," Phelps pressed on. "What made you think your advances would be welcome?"

"I didn't 'think,' I hoped."

"Ahhh, so it isn't just the usual dalliance, this. You've formed a *tendre* for the lady."

"Nothing of the sort," Simon barked. Damn it all! How was it that the man could always see into his heart and soul? Was he so transparent? It was most exasperating.

"I have seen you every which way with women over the years, my lord," said Phelps, "but I have never seen you lose your heart before. It is quite disconcerting to witness—and dangerous, I might point out, considering your . . . enterprise, if you take my meaning?"

"I have not lost my heart, I've lost my head—temporarily. My brother made the fatal mistake you accuse me of, if you remember? I shan't be tarred by the same brush."

Phelps cast him an articulate look down his slightly crooked nose that told him he did not believe a word.

"If you must know, since I can see I shall have no peace 'til I tell you, she was ready to compromise her reputation to ensure that popinjay's safety in the duel."

"That's another thing," Phelps said. "You aren't in any condition to fight a duel. And with the épée, no less! Have you gone addle witted? Think of the exertion. You're scarcely recovered from the shoulder wound. Pistols would have been the better choice."

"That would have taken unfair advantage. Besides, he's hardly worth hanging over."

"So, you're giving him the field?"

"Just stubble it! I know what I'm about."

"I hope you do, my lord. I certainly hope you do."

The earl shifted in the chair again. Jenna was still with him—he could taste her. He was steeped in her scent: the intoxicating fragrance of lavender married with rosemary.

"I want a bath," he announced, surging to his feet.

"A *bath*, my lord?" Phelps blurted. "Where am I to get hot water at this hour?"

"I'll have it cold."

"*Cold*? Will that be good for your leg, my lord?"

"My leg is not the part of my anatomy that concerns me at the moment, Phelps. Dash it all, man, just fill the damned tub!"

CHAPTER FIVE

The duel was to take place on a secluded tract of heath on Bodmin Moor not far from the fabled Stowe's Hill, a longtime favorite dueling ground among the upper classes on the coast. It was a level stretch among the patchwork hills carpeted with bracken, gorse, and wild, fragrant heather, and hemmed in on the north by a stand of dwarf pines, crippled by the scathing Cornish wind that never ceased to blow. Since the hunt was scheduled for Sunday, the duel was set for the following morning at dawn. Crispin St. John had volunteered to act as the earl's second, and Sir Gerald Markham would serve Rupert. Lord Eccleston was to referee.

Kevernwood had not changed his plans, which was something that had worried Jenna. He had the right to choose the weapons and the field. It was, indeed, to be the épée, and the ground was chosen for its convenience to Moorhaven Manor, and for its distance from Kevernwood Hall, which stood on an august bluff overlooking the sea on the outskirts of Newquay. It was there that he had sent Lady Evelyn, along with her personal maid, far afield of the dueling ground. Jenna interpreted that as his need to eliminate all distractions and spare his lady distress should he be injured. For, while the épée was by far the safest choice, it was by no means incapable of doing serious—even permanent—damage.

The earl did not stay on at Moorhaven. As soon as the arrangements were finalized, he departed along with Phelps and Crispin St. John for the Heatherwood Arms, a public house of rather dubious reputation near the dueling ground, whose name by far outclassed its image, to spend the night there until the duel the following morning.

Jenna was relieved that the earl had left the manor. Her anger and embarrassment over what had occurred in the garden was overwhelming. But more alarming were the rogue waves of excruciating ecstasy his embrace had ignited that kept recurring whenever his image stole across her mind.

She was also glad of Lady Evelyn's absence. She couldn't have faced her after what had happened between herself and Kevernwood, and worse still, she couldn't endure the thought of the girl in those strong arms being touched and aroused, being made to feel what she had felt. Imagining it was unbearable. Unfortunately, Lady Evelyn's absence did little to erase those images, either.

The hunt was staged on schedule. By ten in the morning, the circular drive was swarming with mounted guests wearing traditional habits. Dogs ran helter-skelter over the courtyard, their discordant barks out of sync. Liveried footmen wearing royal blue and gold moved among them bearing silver trays of silver goblets filled with wine. The gaiety of the occasion in no way suggested that a duel loomed on the horizon.

Jenna was among the best when it came to horseback riding, but her heart wasn't in it that day. She wanted to spur her mount and ride like the wind until she'd put as much distance between herself and the circumstances as she possibly could. But Rupert was watching her with too close an eye for that to be anything but a fantasy.

"You look rather pale this morning, my dear," he said, maneuvering his spirited bay alongside her mild-mannered Thoroughbred sorrel. "Are you unwell, Jenna? Because, if you are you'd best stay behind this morning. Enough of this weekend has been spoiled, I should think, without your coming down again in the middle of the hunt."

"I am quite all right, Rupert. You needn't worry that I'll spoil your hunt."

"Mmm. What did you do to your lip there?"

She had tried to disguise a slightly bruised swelling that the passion in Kevernwood's kisses had left behind. Evidently her attempt had failed.

"You know perfectly well that I sometimes chew my lip when I'm overset," she lied.

"Self-mutilation. How utterly childish."

"And what is dueling, Rupert?"

"There's nothing to worry over you know, love," he crooned. "I'm quite skilled with the épée, actually, albeit out-dated for dueling these days. I can't think why the fool chose it. I'm much better with swords than pistols—not that I'm any man's piker with decent firearms, mind," he hastened to add. "I told you how I beat him in the shoot."

Jenna rolled her eyes. "You told me," she said on a gusty sigh.

"Would you have rather had the blighter blow my head off?" he blurted, through an incredulous grunt.

Jenna looked daggers at him.

"I think you actually would, I'll be bound!"

"Don't talk nonsense, Rupert."

"You know, Jenna, you need to take stock. You're becoming more and more like your mother every day. I shouldn't want to marry a harpy."

Woefully, there was some truth in that. She'd begun to realize it herself, but only where he was involved. She wasn't prepared to admit it, however, least of all to him.

"Well, I shouldn't like to marry an insensitive brute who humiliates his bride-to-be in company, either," she retaliated. "And while we're on the topic of mothers, considering your take on chivalry under *your* mother's tutelage, you'd have been better off if beasts in the wild had taken you to task!"

Another incredulous grunt answered her.

"What? Are you going to challenge *me* to a duel now, too, Rupert?"

The grooms had come out with the fox, and the subject needed changing before the chaos began, but she was still flushed with rage, and anger spoke.

"I don't suppose you've given any thought to apologies?"

Rupert stared, slack jawed.

"You've got till midnight."

Before he could form his sputtering into an answer, the fox was freed, and Viscount Archibald Marner's cry of, *"Tally-ho!"* began the hunt.

Jenna proved her riding skills by keeping up with Rupert, who was an exceptional horseman when he wanted to be. Her preoccupation with that was all that mattered then—anything to keep her mind from straying toward Simon Rutherford. She wondered if Lady Evelyn was an accomplished equestrian; wished that she could flaunt her skills before the girl, and Kevernwood, too, come to that.

The hunt went on for some time before the fox found its way back to its underground hole and dove down into it. Jenna and Rupert were at the forefront, their horses milling about while the dogs—small, sleek hounds—began to dig furiously at the opening until they'd widened it enough for the sleekest among them to burrow down into the fox's den.

The air, filled with the strident sounds of whinnies, snorts, and barking, was heavily scented with the pungent, musky odor of lathered horseflesh mingled with mulch, and rich, black earth sodden with damp. They had come to the part that Jenna had always found gruesome. The fox had cubs, and the dogs began dragging their mangled little bodies out first, one at a time, and setting them down at the hunters' feet on proud display. That done, they went back in after the mother fox as the hunters cheered and clapped and egged them on. Jenna heard the guttural snarling of the dogs tearing at the cornered fox; she watched them fighting for possession as they dragged it out of the hole bloodied and still twitching, but not dead, and spat it out with the others. Then came the guns, and the mad volleys as the hunters blasted the poor thing to bits where it lay.

She looked away. She'd forgotten how this ritual sickened her. All at once it wasn't a fox at all lying there; it was a man all dressed in black writhing in the dirt on the old Lamorna Road, and she had fired the gun that killed him. The murderous scene brought it all back.

Tears welled in her eyes and, moaning, she wheeled around and drove her horse hard at a gallop through the incredulous hunters grouped there—through the milling, yelping hounds, their mouths foaming with spittle, their coats streaked with saliva and blood—and rode straight back to Moorhaven Manor.

Dawn broke dreary and damp over Bodmin Moor, with a fine, misty drizzle leaking from leaden clouds. Well hidden among the dwarf pines and hedgerows at the edge of the clearing, Jenna dismounted and picked a spot that offered her a good vantage from which she could watch the duel without being seen. She arrived just before Rupert's brougham pulled into the clearing, and her heart leapt when she realized how close behind her he had been. The earl's barouche parted the low lying fog shortly thereafter from the opposite direction, and the men climbed out of their respective carriages and met in the center of the field.

The heath was steeped in an eerie mist that swirled about them in the quiet. The rain had not yet chased it from the hollows. Lord Eccleston offered a selection of swords. Kevernwood chose first, and then handed his pick to Crispin. While Rupert was deciding, Phelps called the earl aside uncomfortably close to where Jenna hid among the shrubs.

"My lord, this is sheer madness," the valet said. "I beg you, do not continue."

"We've been all 'round this, Phelps. I must, you know that."

"Think of the exertion, and your leg—your balance, not to mention the rest. It's too soon I tell you. Who gives a Tinker's curse what these gudgeons think? I beg you, reconsider this."

"It isn't a duel to the death, Phelps, for God's sake. I'm going to try and disarm the blighter if I can. I don't want him harmed. His betrothed would hardly appreciate it."

"Please, my lord . . ."

The earl cast the valet a look that told him he'd wasted his breath, gripped his arm briefly, and turned back to the clearing.

It wasn't until that moment, as she watched him limp out on the field, that Jenna admitted to herself that this wasn't just a physical attraction; she was falling in love with him. What had he sacrificed to spare her betrothed? Her heart was pounding in her ears; the blood pulsing as it coursed through the artery in her neck. Not even the cold splinters of rain that had already begun to penetrate her riding habit could cool the fever in her skin.

Crispin St. John took the earl's coat while Sir Gerald Markham took Rupert's. Lord Eccleston stood between them, and when he spoke, the solemnity in his voice made her hot blood suddenly run cold.

"Gentlemen, the entire body shall be your valid target," Lord Eccleston said. "Any wound sufficient to cause the hand to shake, or otherwise give reasonable evidence against continuance, will end the duel. When I give the command, you will stand *en guard*. You will engage until one of you is blooded, disabled, or disarmed, or in the event that you, Marner, should be wounded, or blood be drawn and shall at that time ask Kevernwood's pardon—"

"Yes, yes, Eccleston, get on with it," Rupert interrupted. "I assure you that shan't happen."

Jenna swallowed dry. It never occurred to her until Lord Eccleston spoke the rules that one of them could be seriously harmed, and gooseflesh that was totally unrelated to the elements inched along the length of her spine.

"A disarm shall be considered the same as a disable, at which point the duel will end," Eccleston continued. "He who still possesses his blade will be declared the winner. Are these conditions clear?"

Both men nodded.

"Then, seconds, arm your contenders!" Eccleston barked.

Once Crispin and Sir Gerald had given Rupert and the earl their chosen blades, and they had saluted each other by kissing the crossguards of their épées, Eccleston called: *"En guard!"*

The duel was begun.

Rupert lunged at once. Jenna watched his back leg stiffen and his front leg move him forward with flawless grace. The earl met him with a thrust, threatening with the tip of his sword, and they closed in until their blade guards clashed together, making a clang that echoed in the stillness. She shuddered. The cold, metallic rasp of metal against metal ran her through as though their swords had skewered her where she stood.

"Disengage!" Eccleston thundered. And then, "Recover!" and finally, *"En guard!"* The two men obeyed each shouted command.

The earl advanced, and Rupert deflected his blade with a beat. Kevernwood staged a counterattack, and Rupert lunged, circling the point of the earl's blade in a counterparry; but the earl counterattacked with a riposte.

Rupert attempted to lure Kevernwood with an invitation, and the earl made a quick thrust, which was blocked by Rupert's parry. Then they moved so fast that Jenna couldn't tell who had the advantage. She did, however, finally realize the disadvantage that Kevernwood's leg injury imposed upon him. He was tiring, losing ground. His strides had become ragged, and his heavy breathing was audible at her distance. Only then did she fully understand the valet's warning and concern. Kevernwood was in pain, but he would not yield, and Rupert, thrusting like a man possessed, would give him no quarter. It seemed to go on forever.

All at once Rupert made a running attack, but the earl countered the flèche brilliantly by closing in. When their blade guards came together this time, Jenna could have sworn she saw sparks fly from the steel, and her heart skipped a beat watching Kevernwood struggling with his stance. She could scarcely see the men's feet for the mist that encircled their Hessians like ropes. But that was short-lived. Suddenly the heavens opened.

The rain the black-edged clouds had promised sluiced down over them. And the mist drifted off in Jenna's direction as if it had the intelligence to choose shelter among the trees.

Again Lord Eccleston's deep voice thundered the commands: "Disengage! Recover! *En guard!*"

And the duelists began again.

The earl advanced, taking short, deliberate steps, but a sharp tap from Rupert's blade deflected his thrust. The earl counterparried again, circling the point of Rupert's blade. Rupert staged a feint, but Kevernwood's glide countered the false attack, and another furious engagement of thrust and parry ensued in rapid succession.

Both men were breathing hard and crying out with their thrusts now. Their ruffled shirts were plastered to their bodies. The ground beneath them had become slippery. The rain was undermining their balance, and even Rupert staggered, trying to keep his footing. Jenna gasped aloud as she saw the earl nearly go down in the morass their bloodlust had made of the field. Watching their every move, she had bitten into her lower lip. It was numb. Her heart was racing, rising in her throat with every deadly thrust and parry.

All at once, the earl made a wild lunge. Jenna couldn't imagine what it took for him to straighten his leg like that. Rupert hadn't expected it, either. That was his mistake. He parried, but the earl staged a quick counterattack that caught Rupert off guard, and disarmed him with a well-aimed beat—a sharp, well-executed tap of his épée that sent Rupert's sword flying from his hand.

"Forfeit!" Eccleston cried out. "End of contest! Kevernwood has won!"

Both men's shirts were streaked with blood. They had moved so fast that Jenna had no idea when the wounds occurred.

The earl handed his sword to Crispin and turned to Phelps, who now had custody of his coat. Lord Eccleston and Sir Gerald made a mad dash for Rupert's brougham as a fresh tear in the cloud fabric overhead unleashed heavy sheets of horizontal rain over the scene, driven by a blustery wind that had risen out of nowhere.

No one but Jenna was watching Rupert, standing, fists clenched in the teeming rain, his breast heaving with rage and his eyes narrowed to slits upon Kevernwood. All at once, he dove for the épée at his feet and made a running attack at the earl from behind.

"Simon! Look out! Behind you!" she shouted, bolting from the thorn hedge.

Startled, the earl froze for the space of a blink, then ordered himself and looked to his valet.

"Phelps!" he commanded.

The valet arrested Jenna as she ran out onto the field, and her breath caught as the earl spun around toward another skirmish. Crispin had stepped in Rupert's path and engaged him.

Battling wildly, Rupert executed a parry, then a thrust in rapid succession. Crispin met the thrust with a quick parry himself, but he was clearly no match for Rupert, and Jenna screamed as Kevernwood put himself between them and shoved Crispin out of the way, taking a wound in his side that brought him to his knees momentarily.

Rupert hesitated just long enough in the confusion for the earl to snatch his épée from Crispin, and execute a thrust and beat that closed them in, blade guards locked, as he staggered upright.

Lord Eccleston's hoarse voice was thundering commands to deaf ears. Still tethered by the valet, Jenna screamed at the top of her voice. Why would no one hear her?

A quick left-hand maneuver by the earl disengaged the swords and, in the blink of an eye, he executed a coup that sent Rupert's sword flying a second time.

Kevernwood plucked up the fallen épée from the heath, raised his knee, and broke the blade in two over it. A collective gasp issued from the onlookers trailing off on the wind as he tossed the broken weapon down at Rupert's feet, since it was against the code of ethics of the duel for the challenged party to break the challenger's sword, no matter the circumstances.

"You haven't heard the last of this, Kevernwood," Rupert snarled, his eyes still wild with battle madness. "Our swords will cross again, sir."

"Then mine will be the only one you'll ever have to fear," the earl sallied. "No self-respecting gentleman in the realm will engage with a backstabber. You lost more than the duel today, Marner. You lost your reputation. I shall see to that."

Jenna, who had finally broken free of the valet's restraining hands, rushed into the earl's arms. "You're hurt! You're bleeding!" she cried, seeing the bloodstains on his torn shirt. The wound was low, just above the right side of his waist.

"So I was right after all?" he murmured, searching her eyes deeply. "You gave yourself away just now . . . you called me 'Simon' back there. I am in your debt, my lady."

They had nearly reached the earl's chaise when Crispin caught up to them.

"Uncle Simon, is it bad?" he cried.

"*Uncle* Simon . . . ?" Jenna breathed.

The earl dosed Crispin with a reproving glance.

"I . . . I'm sorry. I forgot myself," the youth regretted. "You're bleeding badly, sir." Only then did Jenna realize how young the boy was.

" 'Tisn't serious," Kevernwood assured him. "There's a doctor in the village." He turned to Jenna. "Did you come by carriage?"

"No, I rode. My mount is tethered by the trees there," she said, pointing.

"Is that horse yours, or Marner's?"

"It's Rupert's."

"Turn that gelding loose," he said to Phelps, nodding toward the snorting animal straining at the tether. "I am no horse thief."

"B-but . . ." she sputtered.

"You shan't need it," he said. "You aren't going back. You're coming with me."

CHAPTER SIX

Simon dragged himself up the cobblestone walk that led to Holy Trinity Vicarage and addressed the arched door with his fist—three raps, a pause, then another—and rested his forehead on the thick, iron-hinged wood, waiting. He hadn't been all that truthful with Jenna about his wound. The laudanum the doctor had given him had worn off, and the pain in his side was no longer bearably dulled. He gritted his teeth and soothed it with his hand. There was fresh blood on his shirt that had seeped through the bandages during the jostling coach ride from Bodmin Moor; his fingers came away wet with it. The doctor had warned him he ought to go to hospital for a proper mend, but, of course, that was out of the question. He would not leave Jenna vulnerable to Rupert's threats.

He rapped at the door again in the same rhythm, louder this time. It was well into the wee hours, and the vicar was undoubtedly asleep, but he wouldn't mind the intrusion. How often had they played this scene out over the years? He couldn't count the times. Slumped there, inhaling the seasoned oak as the cool, damp wood soothed his brow, he savored the peaceful silence. It came at a price. There would be a lecture, sure as check. That was inevitable.

He was just about to knock a third time, when the door came open in the hand of Vicar Robert Nast, Simon's closest friend since their school days, standing barefoot, mouth agape in his nightshirt, with a worn green dressing gown thrown hastily over it, the fringed sash trailing on the parquetry. His wheat-colored hair was disheveled, and his eyes were still glazed with sleep when recognition sparked in them.

"Simon?" he breathed, all but dropping the candlestick in his hand. "Good God, you're bleeding!" He hauled him over the threshold and poked his head out, looking left and right. "Where's your horse? Are any in pursuit?" He slammed the door and bolted it. "I told you this would happen one day!"

"I came by coach," Simon explained. "I sent it back to the Hall, and no one is following."

"Well, that's a switch," said the vicar ruefully, taking him in from head to toe. "Here, let me help you to the study. You could use a stiff brandy by the look of you. What's *happened*?"

"I've met . . . a woman," Simon told him.

The vicar jerked to a stop and stared, slack jawed. "And *this* is the result?" he blurted, taking his measure again.

"Not directly," Simon growled, "but yes, this is the result."

"Well, I hope you've sent her packing," the vicar said, leading him through the door of a small, sparsely furnished room with book-lined walls.

"I'm going to marry her," Simon announced flatly. The familiar aroma of leather laced with lemon polish greeted him the minute he crossed the threshold. He breathed in deeply. It put him at ease.

"The devil you say?" the vicar erupted, meanwhile setting his candlestick on the gateleg table nearby. "Are you foxed? No . . . you aren't, are you? You're serious! This I've got to hear, but not before we get you cleaned up. Sit." He poured a brandy and handed it over. "Drink this," he charged, "and stay put. I'll be back directly."

Simon tossed back the brandy before the vicar had quit the

room, and poured himself another, which he sipped with more aplomb. He sank into the chair, leaned his head against the cool leather, and leaked a soft moan. He was exhausted. The snifter dangled precariously from his fingers, and he made a conscious effort to hold on to it as he felt himself slipping away. He had almost lost the battle, when the vicar padded back into the room carrying a basin of water and a bottle of antiseptic, with a wad of bandage linen and a clean shirt tucked under his arm. Between them, they re-dressed the wound, while Simon told him how he'd met Jenna, and recounted the particulars of the duel.

"You were unarmed when he did this?" the vicar queried. "By the look of it, the bounder tried to kill you, and damn near succeeded." Setting the basin aside, he sank down on the lounge opposite as Simon gingerly tugged on the shirt.

"Damned fool, Crispin, jumped in and engaged the blighter when he came at my back. That boy was no match for Marner, Rob; he'd have gutted him. I shoved him out of the way, and Marner got me before I could wrestle the épée out of Crispin's hand."

"Well, he got you good. The stitches are holding —just barely, but you need to get off your feet for that to mend properly. What the deuce are you doing here? You ought to be home abed."

"I can't go home," Simon returned. "Jenna is there unchaperoned. I can't compromise her like that."

"You've got her at the Hall?" the vicar cried. "Have you lost your mind? We'll have scandal all over again here!"

"I'm going back to Town with the twins in the morning, after I've asked Jenna to be my wife," Simon explained. "I don't want her to know how serious the wound is. I told her it was only a scratch."

"Outstanding!"

"I mean it, Rob. There is no need to overset her. It'll mend at the town house with no one the wiser. I'll be there at least a fortnight arranging for Crispin's commission, and getting things underway for Evy's come-out." He frowned. "I don't know the first thing about managing that. I'm hoping Jenna will lend a hand with it if she accepts me, or perhaps Lady Jersey if she doesn't; she's always bent over backward to accommodate the twins. The woman's been a godsend. But no! I don't want to even give rise to that possibility with conscious thought. Jenna *has* to accept me."

"This is madness! Absolute madness! How long have you known this gel—less than a sennight, and you're contemplating marriage? *You?*"

"I love her, Rob."

"But . . . *marriage*. Simon, is that wise? Think! Think what you're about. It's bad enough that Phelps and I know. What if it all comes out? You know it's bound to, sooner or later. It's only a matter of time, and what happens to her then?"

"You don't imagine I'm going to tell her, do you?" Simon retorted. "Give me some credit, for God's sake."

"You cannot start a marriage like that!" the vicar said with raised voice. "Besides, a sennight ago the gel was betrothed to Marner—"

"She wasn't in love with him," Simon flashed. "I knew that the minute I met her."

"Let me finish!" the vicar barked. "How well could you possibly know each other on such short acquaintance? Whirlwind romances almost always end in failure. I ought to know. I've married enough lovesick buffleheads in my time. Their sour stares haunt me in that pulpit next door." He gestured roughly. "I will not suffer yours among them."

"You needn't worry about that."

"No, I expect not. How long has it been since you darkened that door? Hah! I can't even recall when you last came to a Sunday service."

"Stubble it!"

The vicar's posture collapsed. "Simon, don't you think I want to see you happily married? Don't you know I pray for that? But . . . as things are . . . with so much at stake, it just isn't practical. You need to take stock. If that's what you really want, it's time to lay this . . . alter ego of yours to rest. Then, once you've gotten to know her—"

"I *love* her," Simon intoned. "And I can't give the other over. Not yet. But soon."

The vicar threw his hands in the air. "Fine! Have it your way. Just remember what 'love' did to your brother. It drove him straight to his grave. He'd still be here—alive and well—if he'd controlled his . . . urges, and waited it out until your father died. You want to follow in his footsteps? Be my guest. Just don't expect me to have a hand in it. Don't even think to ask."

"You haven't even met her."

"That's right, I haven't. You want me to, I take it? That's what this is about, is it?"

"Of course I want you to, but with an open mind."

"This is ludicrous!"

"No, it's *necessary*," Simon corrected him. "I need your help, Rob. I need you to keep an eye on things . . . on her, while I'm gone. I needn't tell you that Marner isn't exactly ecstatic about the outcome of his gala engagement weekend. He made some pretty cryptic threats against the both of us on that dueling ground. I'm hardly concerned for myself, but I am for Jenna, since I can't be here to physically protect her—not until we wed. I'm leaving Phelps behind to look after things, and none of the servants will admit Marner, should he be fool enough to attempt to lay siege to Kevernwood Hall. I'll see to that, but I'd rest a good deal easier if I knew that you were keeping watch as well."

"And do what, exactly—sacrifice my anonymity in your madness defending a fair maiden in the castle?"

"If needs must."

"I believe you have attics to let. You won't be happy till they hoist us both up the Tyburn Tree, will you?" He breathed a nasal sigh, and threw up his hands again in a gesture of defeat. "All right—all right, you win. I will keep an eye out, but don't you dare come grousing to me when this brew you're stirring boils over and scalds you. You were warned."

"I knew you wouldn't let me down."

A strangled laugh replied to that, and Simon flashed a lop-sided smile at the sound. He'd heard that reproving guttural chuckle more times than he could tally over the years, but, be that as it may, the outcome was always the same. Robert Nast never refused him. The maddening thing was, he was probably right, as always, but that didn't matter. All that remained was to persuade Lady Jenna Hollingsworth to be his bride.

"I'm free for the most part day after tomorrow," the vicar grumbled. "I'll go 'round then. It would be good of you to let her know I shall be paying a call."

"Splendid!" Simon rejoiced, offering a crisp nod. "Of course I'll prepare her."

"For the inquisition, eh?" the vicar blurted, dourly.

"Just don't fall in love with her yourself."

"You must really have caught one of Cupid's darts. You've always trusted me with your wenches before."

"This is no 'wench,' Rob. She's a lady. Not just titled, but literally. God knows I've known enough of the other sort to make a fair distinction."

"Yes, well, I shall have to take your word for that, shan't I? Not being acquainted with her, what other choice have I?" He shook his head. "I don't know . . . the whole damned thing just seems a bit rash to me—even for you. I'd like nothing better than to see you married well . . . and happy—God knows you've earned it—and she may be the one; I just wish you weren't rushing into this with such a crashing disregard for common sense."

"Meet her first, before you judge her—or me, come to that. Be fair. You do have a tendency to be a tad judgmental you know."

"It comes with the calling."

"Hmmm, don't go all vickerish on me now. That tack has never worked in the past, and it shan't on this occasion, either, I assure you. What I need more than this deuced lecture at the moment is some sleep, if I am to be about the business of proposing marriage in the morning. What say we call a truce? After I've pressed my suit, I'll stop by on my way to Town and tell you the outcome. If all goes well, she is to be my wife, Rob. Don't be formal. Her name is Jenna. Make her feel welcome."

"Her name is 'Lady' Jenna till she dictates otherwise," the vicar amended. "That must come from her. And when have you ever known me to be unwelcoming to any of your friends—lady *or* ladybird—I'd like to know?"

"Sorry, old boy. That's never mattered before." He flashed a sheepish grin. "Since you're obviously set upon playing your role, will you pray for me at least?"

"That I will do. You can bet your blunt upon it!"

CHAPTER SEVEN

Jenna woke in a hand-carved mahogany sleigh bed late the following morning. For a moment she was disoriented in her new surroundings: a spacious suite of third-floor rooms overlooking the sea at Kevernwood Hall. It was the sound of the sea that woke her. The flaw was at the full height of its fury, flinging diaphanous clouds of spindrift over the brow of the cliff below. Little by little the events of the past twenty-four hours trickled back across her memory and her heart leapt. It wasn't a dream. Rupert had disgraced himself on the dueling ground and they had left him standing in the teeming rain on Bodmin Moor, shouting ugly threats after them as Simon's carriage sped away.

They had arrived at Kevernwood Hall very late. The earl needed stitches, and his doctoring in Bodmin village took longer than anticipated. While that was taking place, Phelps saw that she and Crispin were well fed at the Heatherwood Arms, since they wouldn't be stopping again until they reached Newquay in an effort to outrun the storm that was headed west toward the rocky coast.

During the earl's absence, Jenna had plenty of opportunity to question Crispin, but she decided against it. She remembered

Simon's disapproving look when Crispin called him "uncle." The explanation for that needed to come from the earl himself, not secondhand. She would not invade his privacy. She kept the conversation as casual as was possible under the circumstances, but that by no means kept her from wondering. She used the time instead to observe the young man, who was as handsome as his sister was beautiful, fair and blue-eyed, with a likable manner that showed good breeding. She was dying to solve the mystery surrounding them both, but that would have to wait.

By the time the earl returned from the surgeon, Phelps had loaded his luggage on the chaise, as well as Crispin's, and the small leather valise that housed the valet's own toilette. Jenna had nothing but the clothes on her back. Exhausted, more mentally and emotionally than physically, she let the swaying of the coach rock her to sleep in the earl's arms for the last lap of the journey. They arrived at Kevernwood Hall at two in the morning, and though she was bursting with questions, the earl insisted that they postpone discussing their circumstances until they'd both had a good night's rest. Now, morning had come, and she was almost sorry. What on earth would she say to the man whom she had literally let abduct her?

She swung her feet over the side of the bed. They'd scarcely touched the carpet when a light rap came at the door, and her head snapped toward the sound. She was wearing a cream-colored flannel nightgown that smelled fresh, of pine tar soap, which was donated by the housekeeper, Mrs. Rees, who had been unceremoniously roused from a sound sleep upon their arrival the night before. Middle-aged and good-natured, the woman had taken Jenna's bedraggled riding habit down to the servants' wing to dry beside the fire and press with the flatiron. The knock came again, and Jenna clutched the quilt over her nightgown.

"C-come," she called guardedly, fearing that it might be the earl himself.

To her great relief, it was the housekeeper who entered, bearing a tray. A chambermaid followed on her heels carrying Jenna's riding habit, which the girl carefully draped over a wing chair at the edge of the Aubusson carpet in the center of the room. She then went straight to the hearth, where she began to coax the dwindling fire to life again with fresh logs and the bellows.

Mrs. Rees set the tray down on the drop-leaf table across the way and folded her hands across her crisp, white apron, like a quaint mechanical doll.

"The master wants the fires kept going in your rooms, my lady," she said. "It's cold here on the water clear into June sometimes, what with the storms and all."

"How is the master this morning?" Jenna queried.

"He's just come home, my lady."

"Just come home, did you say?" Jenna frowned, perplexed. Where on earth had he gone at two in the morning?

"Just a bit ago," the housekeeper replied with a nod. "He's waiting for you down in the conservatory, my lady."

Jenna got up and reached for her riding habit.

"Oh, no—no, not till you've eaten, my lady," Mrs. Rees said, raising a quick hand in protest. "The master was most particular about that. You're to take your time, my lady."

The maid, a plain little mouse of a girl, whom Jenna had heard the housekeeper address as Molly, straightened up from her chore at the hearth and helped Mrs. Rees carry the drop-leaf table closer. They left her then, after giving her directions to the conservatory, and she began to eat the delicious fare consisting of coddled eggs, grilled sausages, and warm cheese scones oozing freshly churned sweet butter. In spite of the housekeeper's directive, she ate quickly, and flushed it all down with the wonderful Darjeeling tea that accompanied the meal. It was a wonderful breakfast, and she regretted that she was far too anxious about her situation to enjoy it.

The halls were cold and damp out of the fire's reach, and Jenna began to appreciate the reasoning behind having them lit into June. Thistle Hollow, her own estate east of Launceston, was far enough inland to be spared much of the battery of wind and water that plagued the Cornish seacoast, and it wasn't nearly as dank.

The conservatory was on the first floor facing the drive, far from the threat of flogging by storms driven landward by the sea. Towering walls of leaded glass jutted into the courtyard. Inside, a veritable jungle of plant life, both domestic and exotic, thrived in a near-perfect atmosphere. Situated on the southeast corner of the house, the breathtaking room got sun most of the day, when the coast was lucky enough to see it.

When she entered, the earl was standing beside the east wall watching heavy sheets of rain slide down the panes. Though her step was light, it turned him around, and he reached her in three strides. Taking her in his arms, he gazed deep into her eyes, with his own eyes dilated and penetrating in the half-light called by the storm.

"Did you sleep well?" he said.

"Yes, my lord," she murmured.

"I liked it better when you called me Simon."

"That's going to take some getting used to," she said. "I misspoke. It's hardly proper." Hot blood rushed to her cheeks. Was she blushing again, in spite of her resolve?

He smiled and pulled her closer. "Nothing else about this business is proper. Why should we stand upon ceremony over names? Besides, it is what I wish . . . when we are alone, if that better suits your sensibilities."

"Take care! Your wound!" she cried, as her hand grazed the bandage beneath his cambric shirt.

"I told you, it's nothing to worry over—just a scratch." He hesitated a moment before asking, "Why did you come to the dueling ground?"

"I couldn't bear it, yet I had to see—to be there. I was so afraid . . ."

His liquid sapphire eyes looked into her soul.

"The land we fought on is rich in legend, you know," he told her. "The tale goes that, back in the mists of time, the saints and giants fought on Bodmin Moor. The saints were claiming too many wells and erecting too many crosses to suit the giants, who elected Uther to represent them in a duel of sorts—a rock throwing contest. It was St. Tue, who fought

Uther for possession of the place. The rocks they threw took form in the shape of a standing stone, and all went well for the saints until the last toss. The final rock was too heavy for St. Tue, and, as legend has it, an angel came and carried that stone up to crown the Cheesewring menhir, where it sits defying gravity to this very day."

"How perfectly lovely," Jenna murmured. "I thought I knew all the legends, but I've never heard that one."

"While we're on the subject of saints, there is a Cornish saint named 'Kevern,' you know. He is the namesake of my title, but I am not he, by any means—or anything like him. I am no saint, Jenna, I promise you, and I have never believed in legends, or angels, either until now. Until a heavenly creature saved my life in that place yesterday. Thank you, my angel."

"When I saw Rupert running at your back . . ."

"I would have challenged the blighter myself if he hadn't saved me the trouble, after the way he humiliated you in company at the masque," he said, his strong hands soothing her. "But I would have chosen a more appropriate place to call him out. A title does not a gentleman make. Whatever possessed you to accept his suit, Jenna—a man like that?"

She clouded. Part of her desperately wanted to confess to him then and there, to tell him that she had done murder on the old Lamorna Road two months ago, and that she feared her sin would come back to haunt her and wanted shelter from it among the Marners. There needed to be honesty between them, and she needed to lift the burden weighing upon her conscience. She hadn't been able to confess it to Rupert. She hadn't trusted him enough. But this was the man she loved.

"My father wished it," she said instead. "And, after he died, Mother pressed for it."

It was a half-truth.

"I've loved you from the first moment I saw you on that staircase," he revealed. "I don't pretend to be able to explain it, but there it is. I can't begin to tell you what it did to me thinking that your response to me in that garden was because of your love for Marner . . . because you thought to buy his safety with those kisses."

"And I thought that you were offering *me* that proposition."

He held her away and stared with wounded eyes that told her such a thing had never occurred to him. She couldn't bear to look into them.

"It seems that we have been blundering along at cross purposes," he said, "but not anymore." He produced a gold ring encrusted with rubies and diamonds from his waistcoat pocket and slipped it on her finger. "Will you marry me, Jenna?"

She stared into those earth-shattering sapphire eyes and melted. They were like whirlpools, sucking her down into unfathomable depths. It was madness. She'd only known of the man's existence for five days. She knew nothing about him except what she needed to know—that, bizarre though it was, he loved her and she loved him.

"Yes, Simon," she murmured, and surrendered her lips to his kiss.

It was a soft, gentle embrace, not the volatile explosion that had rocked her in the garden, but it aroused her more totally. And she moaned at the firestorm of rapturous excitement pulsing through her from nothing but the slightest touch of those warm, sensuous lips that were capable of much, much more.

She wanted more.

After a moment, he held her away and searched her face.

"You're sure?" he murmured.

"I'm sure."

"My God," he said, holding her close, clearly loath to let her go.

But there was something she needed to know, something that had played havoc with her curious nature since the dueling ground. Still . . . if he had wanted her to know, he would have explained, wouldn't he? It took her a moment to summon the courage.

"Simon," she began at last. "Crispin called you 'Uncle' yesterday. Are you . . . ?"

A frown stole his smile and wrinkled his broad brow. Taking

her arm, he led her to a white wicker love seat beside the south wall, and sat with her there.

"Jenna, I must ask you to forget you heard that," he said. "You couldn't possibly imagine the lengths I've gone to in order to preserve anonymity . . . for both their sakes. Even in this house. Phelps is the only one under this roof who knows. He's been with me since I was a boy, and he is privy to all of my personal affairs. I'd trust him with my life, and have done so on more occasions than I care to tally."

"Of course, I shan't betray your trust. You don't even have to tell me, I only—"

"No—no, I want to tell you," he interrupted, laying a gentle finger over her lips. "There must be no . . . secrets between us."

A pang of conscience stabbed her at that, and her eyes clouded, recalling the dark secret she had elected to keep from him. But the moment passed, defeated by curiosity.

"I had a brother, thirteen years older than myself," he was saying. "I wasn't quite fifteen when he met and fell in love with a distant cousin of the Duke of York. They committed an indiscretion, and the girl became pregnant. Father wouldn't sanction their union, and he disinherited my brother in all but title and lands. He would have stripped those from him as well if the law allowed, but since he couldn't, he cut him off without a halfpenny when he married her without his approval. Edgar—that was his name—stole enough blunt from Father's vault to buy himself a commission in the army, eloped with the girl to Gretna Green, then took his bride with him to India. Though it wasn't encouraged, there were provisions at the post for the wives of officers, with the proper connections, of course, and Edgar was well liked.

"There was a dreadful scandal here on the home front, as you can well imagine. Cutting one's eldest son and heir off without a feather to fly with hardly goes unnoticed by the ton. The girl's family reacted in much the same way that Father did, which is probably one of the reasons I so resent the aristocracy—the self-serving social hypocrisy that drives them to put more store in things material than in humanity. It's what killed my father, that. He died a bitter old man."

"How awful for you," Jenna said.

"I loved my brother," he went on. "I never saw him alive again. He was killed by bandits in the hills near Delhi—the Thuggee, a secret society of religious fanatics who performed ritualistic murder in the name of some heathen Hindu god. British officers were highly prized targets. Edgar was carrying out a routine dispatch exchange between posts and just . . . disappeared. Eight months later, they found his remains buried under a pile of rubble. The twins were just three years old. Their mother died shortly after of cholera."

"Oh, Simon, I'm so sorry."

"The army contacted Father, of course, but he refused to acknowledge the children. Neither would their mother's family. I was still at school. There was nothing I could do on my own without losing my inheritance, and I couldn't risk that if I were to help them once Father passed.

"Making short of it, I appealed to the Church, and the twins were brought home and fostered by a good family until Evy was old enough to be housed at a convent school in Yorkshire, and Crispin at an Anglican boy's boarding school in Manchester. I couldn't go against Father's decision and acknowledge them as family without making them illegitimate. I couldn't do that to my brother's memory, or to them. But they know. At least I have the satisfaction of that, and Phelps knows, because it was he who helped me achieve it."

The rain was drumming on the glass walls as if begging admittance, and Jenna shuddered. Pulling her closer, he soothed her absently.

"When Father died," he continued, "though they were entitled to nobility, I had to reinvent it for them because of the way Father cut Edgar off. I literally blackmailed the Duke of York into allowing the truth—well, a stretched version of it, anyway—to circulate that they were, in fact, quite legitimate distant relatives, hence their titles. Since the duke's branch of the family is so convoluted, no one questioned it.

"You see, I knew that York's mistress, Mary Anne Clarke, was selling commissions and promotions. I threatened to put that knowledge into the right hands and he agreed to acknowledge the twins as distant relations." He popped a cryptic chuckle. "The whole coil came out anyway, and the poor blighter was forced to resign his military commission two years ago. For all I know, he thinks I'm at the root of that. I'm not, I assure you. It was his own carelessness that damned him. But I do permit myself to wallow in the irony of it from time to time.

"It all turned out well in the end. York's just been reinstated, and I brought Evy and Crispin out of hiding with their new identities. They're finally secured, but all of that will be for naught if the truth should surface now."

"You never need fear that I shall make it known," Jenna said. All at once she clouded. "I feel awful about Evelyn. I'm afraid I was quite jealous of her, Simon, and not very pleasant. I'm dreadfully sorry about that."

"Don't be sorry, my love," he said. He ground out a guttural chuckle. "But for your jealousy, I never would have suspected that you might return my feelings."

Jenna stared. She was incredulous.

"You were quite obvious," he told her. "Charmingly so."

"She's in love with you, you know."

"She has a adolescent crush on me, which I have never encouraged, yes," he said. "She's only eighteen, Jenna, and I am her benefactor; it's only natural."

She gasped. "I took her for much older!"

"They're just children yet. At least I see them that way." He smiled that heart-melting smile, all the more precious for its rarity. "Once Evy is presented to society, she'll find a proper suitor, and I'm buying Crispin a naval commission. All that should have been in the works long ago, and would have been but for Copenhagen."

"You were injured," she responded.

He nodded. "Along with a hundred and sixty-three other men on our vessel alone, Jenna. Nearly seven hundred men were wounded in that battle, and over two hundred and fifty died. My piddling wounds seem quite insignificant compared to that. Despite it all, we won."

"Were many ships lost?"

"Not a one, though many were badly damaged. Ours was one of the worst hit. I served on the *Monarch*, under Commander Mosse. A friend of mine from my school days, Nathaniel Ridgeway, the Earl of Stenshire, was aboard as well. We were a scandalous pair. We'd shipped together many times and always watched each other's backs, but that day was like no other. There was no time for antics. We were caught between the sand banks in the King's Channel when we engaged the Danish fleet. We both took a hit. He fared better than I did, and went on to take more hits in other battles. I wasn't so fortunate. But we weren't the only ones who fell that day. We lost fifty-six men. It was quite an event. I'll tell you about it sometime."

"And that is the kind of future you want to buy for Crispin?" She couldn't imagine it.

"That, my love, is the only justification I can allow for my ties to the aristocracy," he said, clouding, "the only investment a decent man can make that will benefit the country, not just line the pockets of high-in-the-instep, toadying 'pinks of the ton,' like Marner. It is a noble profession, and in it a poor man can be just as noble as a rich one. That is the lesson I hope to teach Crispin."

Jenna's take on that issue was strictly maternal; his was fraternal. They were polar opposites. That conflict was old as eons. They would never agree, and she was wise enough not to pursue it. Instead, she nodded. Something else was still troubling her, something closer to the moment.

"Simon, I would like to apologize to Evelyn. I need to see her."

"That will have to wait," he said. "There'll be plenty of time later for mending fences . . . all the time in the world." He took her hands in his. "Jenna, I know you were planning an elaborate society wedding with Marner, but do you really need to have all that folderol to be happy?"

She stared. His meaning was unclear, and she didn't know how to answer.

"I don't want to wait," he explained, "not while you complete your trousseau, not until all the social brouhaha is played out. I don't want to alarm you, but I didn't like some of the menacing remarks Marner made when we left him on Bodmin Moor. He's no gentleman; he's proven that. I want you to remain right here at Kevernwood Hall until we can be married. I want you under my protection."

"I don't need a fancy wedding, Simon. I was using my trousseau as an excuse to delay my marriage to Rupert."

"I'll buy you the most elegant trousseau on the continent—"

"I don't want to wait, either, Simon," she said, laying a finger over his lips to silence him as he had done to her earlier.

"What about your mother?"

Jenna gave a start, and gasped. She'd totally forgotten about her mother.

"Shall I send Phelps to Moorhaven to fetch her?"

"No!" she cried, shaking her head. "God, no!"

"We can't just leave her there, Jenna," he scolded, suppressing a smile.

"No, but we don't have to bring her here, either. Mother can take care of herself, Simon; she's well able. I'm not being unkind. It's just how she's made. She thrives upon drama. She's a survivor, quite capable of dealing with the situation, I assure you."

"I have no doubt, but I would like to get off on the right foot with her, if it's all the same to you, and there is a rather stiff code of etiquette regarding prospective in-laws, you know. *I* may be rather unconventional, but I'm sure, judging from what I've observed of the lady, that your mother is not."

"You aren't marrying Mother."

"God be praised for that! But still, I rather think she'd make a better ally than she would an adversary. That aside, technically, you know I should have spoken with her beforehand, and but for these bizarre circumstances—"

"Oh, no!" she cut in. "Don't worry about Mother. Let me deal with that. I'll compose a missive and have it posted to Thistle Hollow." She laughed. "I'll have her send some of my things on as well." She fingered the skirt of her riding habit. "This is all I've got. My portmanteau is still at Moorhaven."

"Leave it," he said. "There's a dressmaker in the village.

Evy's used her and she's quite good. I'll have her come 'round and see to your needs at once."

"I hardly think that would be proper," she protested.

Simon let loose a hearty guffaw. "Nothing about any of this is 'proper' in the academic sense," he said, "and yet, impossible though it seems, never in my life has anything ever seemed more proper."

He got to his feet and pulled her up alongside him. The air around them smelled of the extraordinary plant life that made its home there. She picked out top notes of acanthus, eucalyptus, and, oddly, rue, along with several different species of mint, all thriving in huge porcelain pots resting on the slate floor amongst similar containers overflowing with forget-me-nots. Mingled with the exotic aroma of Simon's tobacco, the result was practically hallucinogenic.

His gaze was drawing her in again—in behind those incredible dark lashes—into the very essence of him. He was so incredibly handsome, and yet there was a hint of sadness in those eyes that cast a mysterious aura about him. There was something he hadn't told her, something he hadn't exorcised. It fed the desperation in his embrace. Wild, feral lights flashed in those eyes. They were dilated with desire as he buried his hand in her hair and arched her head back, bending slowly, excruciatingly slowly, until their lips met.

He deepened the kiss, and she tasted the lingering presence of latakia sweetened with wine in his mouth. It heightened her senses. He had probably drunk the wine for courage to propose—wine, because it wouldn't cloud his mind like brandy, but would blunt the edges of his apprehension that she might refuse his suit. She adored him.

The tongue that had parted her lips and glided between her teeth probed gently, exploring, curling around her own, conjoining with it in a strange, voluptuous dance she was powerless to resist. The more it coaxed, the more hers followed, plunging passionately inside the satiny depths of his warm mouth, and their moans combined as he encircled her waist and pulled her against his lean, corded body.

He was aroused. The bruising power of him leaned against her. It was a delicious pain that called her closer not even understanding why, or what the harnessed power in that magnificent body was capable of unleashing.

The jacket of her riding habit was open, exposing the low-cut underbodice gathered with ruching, and he spread it wider. His lips glided to her throat; the roughness of stubble just beginning on his chin excited her, the contrast of textures sending shock waves of fiery warmth to the same mysterious recesses that he had ignited when he'd first held her.

Perspiration beaded on his brow. The exotic scent of tobacco and wine grew stronger, seeping from his pores, spread by the heat radiating from his skin beneath the cambric shirt. Her heart was racing, beating wildly against his. Her blood had caught fire also, kindled by the skilled tongue sliding now along the curve of her arched throat. Her whole body seemed about to burst into flame. Was he reminded, as she was, of the touch of his roughened fingers against the soft exposed flesh overflowing her décolleté, when he'd held her in the moonlit garden perfumed with lilacs at Moorhaven?

Yes!

His hand slipped lower. She held her breath. This was forbidden. So were the feelings his touch aroused. She had never even let Rupert—or anyone else for that matter—kiss her the way Simon did, much less touch her intimately. But somehow with Simon it seemed perfectly natural, and right.

His fingers deftly undid the ties and spread the ruching on her underbodice. Her breath caught as his hand plunged inside and came to rest above her heart . . . then lower still. For a moment, she thought he would kiss her there. She scarcely breathed in anticipation of that silken tongue and rough stubble against the tender skin of her breast. She could almost feel the tug of those sensuous lips encircling the nipple that had hardened under his touch, and a new wave of ecstasy riveted her. If he were to do so, she was certain she would surrender—or faint—or die. But he didn't.

All at once, those renegade fingers, so gentle for their size, closed her jacket with painstaking control, though his hands were shaking. Then, crushing her close in his arms again, he buried his moist face in the cloud of her hair that his passion had set awry.

"I have to go," he murmured, his voice husky with longing.

"*Go?* Go where?"

"To London, Jenna. I cannot stay here with you in this house . . . not now . . . not like this. I shan't compromise you in that way."

"But, Simon—"

"Shhhh," he murmured. His warm mouth closed her lips. When he lifted away, she looked into his hungering eyes, darkly glazed and half-shuttered. "If I stay, I won't be able to stop myself, Jenna," he said. "And I won't do that to you. I want it to be perfect between us, my love. I want us to remember it always."

"I don't want you to leave me," she murmured, blinking back tears.

"I shouldn't even be here now," he said, "but we needed to have this conversation. I love you, Jenna. I will do nothing ever to cause you harm."

Their lips met again, but briefly, and though he held her away, the ghost of his arousal still lingered.

"I'll go 'round to the church in the village on my way and see to the arrangements," he said. "The vicar there is a close friend of mine. We were at school together before he entered the University and took Orders. He knows about the twins as well. It was he who gave me the idea to contact the Church for help years back. You'll like him. His name is Robert Nast, and he will call upon you. I spent the night at his vicarage after I brought you here. I couldn't stay under the same roof with you without a chaperone, Jenna—not after the way I literally abducted you from that dueling field before witnesses."

So *that's* where he'd gone. She loved him more than ever, if that could be possible.

"How long will you be away?" she wondered, unable to disguise her disappointment.

"You won't see me again until our wedding day, my love," he said. "I will not have vicious gossip damning us the way it damned my brother." He loosed one of his signature guttural chuckles. "Believe me," he murmured, "it shan't be long."

CHAPTER EIGHT

The storm spent itself on the coast through the night, and the following dawn broke steeped in a breathless mist that clung with stubborn persistence to the estate for most of the day. Jenna woke at first light lonely for Simon. But for the exquisite ruby and diamond ring on her finger, she would have sworn the events of the past few days had been a dream.

She passed most of the morning familiarizing herself with the house and the servants. There were a number of footmen, stewards, kitchen maids, scullery maids, chambermaids, and laundresses. There was a butler and underbutler, a cook, a groundskeeper and his wife, a gamekeeper, and several grooms. Entirely too many for her to hope to remember all their names on short acquaintance, and she decided to concentrate on the ones with whom she would have the most contact. These included several of the primary footmen, Lawrence, Charl, and Peter; the housekeeper, Mrs. Rees; Horton, the butler; her chambermaids, Anna and Molly; and, of course, Phelps, who to her surprise had not gone on to London with Simon. She wondered about that, but there were just so many other things to think about then that she didn't dwell long upon it.

Before he left, Simon asked her if she wanted him to send for Emily, but she declined. Since she shared Emily with her mother—not out of necessity, but rather because her mother had her first and couldn't bear to part with her—Jenna didn't want to uproot the girl. Besides, she could only imagine how her mother must be coping with the situation. Taking Emily from her now would be disastrous. Simon offered to hire a personal maid for her, but she declined that offer as well and chose instead the mousy little Molly, who was delighted over the elevated new station that would take her eventually to London, and all of the excitement of Town life. It was a good choice. Everyone was pleased, and with that decided, Jenna set out to explore Kevernwood Hall.

Mrs. Rees explained that the mansion itself was almost three centuries old, except for the conservatory, which Simon's father, the second Earl of Kevernwood, had added before Simon was born. The house, nearly half-covered with ivy, was hewn of stone, seeming to rise from the very granite that formed the base of the cliff it crouched upon. It was an enormous rambling structure, four stories high, rising from a well-landscaped lawn with its back to the sea. To her amazement, it even had battlements.

There were a number of outbuildings on the estate, including the stables, carriage house, groundskeeper's cottage, gamekeeper's cottage, and a strange-looking round stone tower almost hidden in the orchard. Constructed of the same stone as the Hall, it looked like a miniature medieval keep.

Inside the manor proper, the corridors were narrow and damp, the rooms enormous and full of stone presence. The hearths were very spacious; the mantels on nearly all of them held in place by elaborately carved marble statuary. Over the years much of the house had been renovated, but the effect was jarring. Modern trappings such as the Chippendale, and Duncan Phyfe furniture, Persian rugs, and odd pieces upholstered in chintz and brocade that dominated seemed out of place, and had been chosen for comfort rather than any pretense at aesthetics. Few women had had a hand in the decorating, Jenna decided. It was definitely a man's house. The crossed swords, standing halberds, trophies, and formidable-looking Rutherford ancestors glowering from gilt-edged frames only reinforced her theory. It was cold and depressing and damp, to say nothing of dreary, and she was beginning to understand why Simon spent so little time on the coast.

The fourth floor was closed off. Mrs. Rees explained that unless there was to be a hunt and a large number of guests were expected, none of the chambers there were ever used. They browsed through all of the third-floor guest chambers, and the second-floor suites. On the main floor, they toured the breakfast room, ballroom, salon, sitting rooms, library, parlor, trophy room, and drawing room. All seemed converted from something decidedly Elizabethan. Jenna came to the conclusion that she liked the conservatory best, but that, she admitted, was probably because she'd nearly given herself to Simon there.

They ended the tour in the dining hall, where the housekeeper informed her that all meals would be served, and Jenna marveled at the size of it. The dining hall at Thistle Hollow would have fit inside it twice. It boasted a high vaulted ceiling embellished with frescoes in a woodland theme and fitted with Austrian crystal chandeliers, three of them suspended above the endless banquet table in the center of the room. A fine linen cloth had been draped across the end where her place had been set for nuncheon.

The walls were painted a deep shade of rose with gilded plasterwork, and matching medallions holding sconces. On the east wall, the raised arms of tall marble wood nymphs supported the mantel over the hearth. Opposite, a built-in mahogany sideboard, nearly as long as the table it matched, was laid with salvers of cold meats and cheeses, and silver chafing dishes housing a variety of entrees, one more delectable-looking than the next. It was all very beautiful, but Jenna insisted that, in the future, unless the earl was in residence, she would just as soon take her meals in the breakfast room—or in her dressing room upstairs, for that matter. Eating alone in that vast, empty hall would only make her more lonesome for Simon.

Once she'd eaten, she set out to explore the grounds. The mist still clung stubbornly to the hollows and floated over the courtyard that sloped down to the orchards in the south, half burying the odd-looking derelict tower. The sun hadn't yet made an appearance, and by the look of the jaundiced sky threatening overhead, she wondered if it would for some time.

Drenched and stirred by the wind, the garden foliage perfumed the air with exquisite scents. Though hidden from view by the fog milling inside artistically carved openings in the tall hedgerows that formed the garden wall, Jenna picked out the fragrances of rose, peony, honeysuckle, and lilac, to name but a few. She didn't need to see them to know that they were there. The heady perfume stirred her senses awake, reminding her of another garden, and a pulsating tremor moved inside her that almost made her lose her footing.

The outbuildings were situated in a wide, sweeping semicircle around the courtyard and gardens, accessed by a narrow, well-kept lane, and she started out in a westerly direction, past a stand of stunted elms that stretched between the house and the stables. The day was warm for April despite the dampness, and she was grateful for that since she didn't have her cloak. She did have her riding habit, however, and owing to that, she decided to make use of it and do her exploring on horseback.

The stables were situated just beyond the trees. The carriage house stood alongside, with paddocks and a well in back. Emile Barstow, the chief groom, a bow-legged, gray-haired man past sixty, with hunched posture and a thick mustache, was only too happy to present her with a Thoroughbred sorrel mare named Treacle for the occasion. He was impressed at once with Jenna's seat and knowledge of horses, and his sparkling blue eyes, filled with admiration, promised friendship and loyalty. Jenna eagerly looked forward to both. All of the servants at Kevernwood Hall had treated her royally, but this man was special. He reminded her of her father.

She passed the gamekeeper's cottage next. A smokehouse stood beside it. It looked deserted, as did the groundskeeper's cottage farther on, set back beside a wall of rhododendron.

Picket fencing separated vegetable and herb gardens. The combined scents of hawthorn, gentian, comfrey, bramble, briar rose, and the sweetness of wild rhubarb rode the breeze. The rabbits smelled them, too, and she laughed aloud watching them take unmerciful advantage of everyone's absence. She hadn't laughed in a long time—not since the night she killed the Marsh Hawk.

She was relieved that no one was at home. Though she did want to meet everyone, she wasn't really up to socializing. Not then. She wanted a closer look at the peculiar-looking round tower in the orchard. The mist was denser there, wandering aimlessly among the rows of budding apple trees that were just beginning to promise blossoms. It groped her body to the waist while she dismounted and tethered Treacle in a clump of bracken. The roughly hewn surface of the structure was half-covered with woodbine creepers, as was the land around it for some distance in all directions. A little path had been cleared in the groundcover leading from the narrow drive she'd been following, suggesting that the keep was frequented on a somewhat regular basis. Curious as to what it could be used for, she tried the arched wooden door, but it was locked, and she ambled around toward the back in search of another entrance. There wasn't one, but there was a small window on the side almost at eye level, fitted with tinted glass panes set into diamond-shaped fretwork. There were two others like it higher up as well, one in front and one in back.

She stood on tiptoe and began pulling the vines away from the lowest pane. It was black as pitch within, and she wiped away the dusty, salty crust that had collected over time on the tinted glass, cupped her hands around her eyes, and tried to see inside. Intent on that, when a man's hand clamped around her arm, she spun around and gasped.

It was Phelps.

"You frightened me!" she breathed, clutching her breast as if to keep her heart inside her body. "Where did you come from, Phelps?"

"You'd best come away, my lady," he said. "We don't use the tower."

"It's locked," she said, paying no heed to his directive. "Is there a key?"

"I do not have the key, my lady, only his lordship. The tower is very old, you see. There is structural damage, my lady; it isn't safe. You'd best come away now."

"It looks sound enough to me," she said, appraising the building through a frown.

"The damage is on the inside, my lady, though some of the outer is falling now as well. His lordship has been meaning to repair it, but he is here so seldom . . ."

"I've never seen anything like it. What was it used for?"

Phelps hesitated and finally said, "Storage, my lady. Tobias Heath, the groundskeeper here, used to keep his tools inside until it became . . . unsafe. He keeps them in the root cellar now. Please come away, my lady. His lordship would never forgive me if you came to harm out here. Why, just last week some slates fell from the roof, so they tell me. It really isn't safe, my lady."

"Did you follow me here, Phelps?"

"Well, actually . . . no, my lady," the valet said, turning as white as the mist. "That is . . . I was paying a call on Tobias when I saw you ride this way."

"He isn't at home."

"I realize that now, my lady; it's market day. I should have remembered, but we—"

"Yes, yes, I know—you come to the coast so seldom," she interrupted, finishing the sentence he was struggling with. Now she realized why Simon had left the valet behind. The stressed look on his face confirmed it. "Did his lordship leave you here to look after me, Phelps?" she said with her most fetching smile.

"Well, actually . . . yes, as a matter of fact, he did, my lady."

She nodded, agreeing with her conclusion. At least the man was honest.

"I would still like to see inside," she persisted. "You're sure there isn't a key?"

"I'm sure, my lady. Please come away now. There's a fresh flaw on the make. It often happens in the spring—the prevailing wind's to blame. One storm often spawns another along this coast. Sometimes it goes on for weeks."

"Perish the thought."

His nervous smile disturbed her. The tower looked too sound to warrant his distress, and that only piqued her curiosity further. It was neither the time nor the place to challenge him over it, however, and she followed him back to their horses.

As he hung back at the edge of the path once she'd loosened Treacle's tether, she called "Aren't you coming, Phelps?"

"I'll wait for Tobias, my lady. He should be returning soon."

So she mounted then, and rode back toward the stables, eerily aware of the valet's eyes on her the whole distance. There was such a thing as carrying protection too far. She would definitely speak to Simon about it. Phelps was right about the storm, though. She was all too familiar with Cornish flaws, though she had never experienced one so close to the sea. She tasted the salt on the air and on her lips now that she was alerted to it. She shuddered, imagining the sort of weather that had driven sea salt far enough inland to coat the leaded windows in the tower. Those thoughts dissolved the minute she reached the stables, however. Her heart plunged in her breast at the sight of a chaise in the drive being led by a different groom toward the tack room. It bore the Hollingsworth device.

Jenna hurried back to the house. She was met at the door by Horton, the butler, a tall man with a long, straight nose, inscrutable gray eyes, and a shiny bald head fringed sparsely with silver hair.

"Your mother has arrived, my lady," he warbled. "I put her in the parlor."

"Thank you, Horton." She glanced at the three portmanteaux on the floor and said, pointing, "That one may remain. Please have the footmen return the others to the chaise, and tell the grooms not to unhitch the horses. My mother will not be staying."

"Yes, my lady. Will that be all, my lady?"

"Did she arrive alone?"

"No, my lady, her personal maid was with her. I took the liberty of having tea served to the girl in the servants' hall, and a tray has been brought to the parlor as well. Was that all right, my lady?"

"Of course, Horton, thank you."

Jenna dismissed the butler, squared her posture, marched down the corridor through the broad medieval arch that led to the main floor renovations, and entered the parlor. It was a spacious, unwelcoming room somewhat outdated in decor, with the musty, telltale odor of disuse. She commended the butler mentally on his choice.

The dowager spun around from the terrace doors, sloshing tea from her cup into the saucer in her hand when she entered. Taking one look at the indignant scowl on her mother's face— sour enough to clabber cream—Jenna braced herself. She knew that posture all too well.

"Jenna Hollingsworth, how *could* you!" the dowager spluttered, slapping her teacup and saucer down on the serving tray with little regard for their frailty.

"Sit down, Mother."

"I will *not* sit down. Jenna, explain yourself at once!"

"Mother, *sit!*"

Lady Hollingsworth bristled, passed an incredulous grunt, and dropped like a stone into a wing chair upholstered in faded blue velvet resting beside the vacant hearth. A cloud of dust rose around her upon contact. Aggression having failed miserably, she whipped out a handkerchief, and Jenna's eyebrow lifted. It was edged with the familiar black of mourning. So that's how it was to be, was it?

"Put it away, Mother," she said. "That tactic is quite shopworn, and beneath you. You know as well as I do that if Father knew what sort of man Rupert Marner really was, he never would have approved our betrothal, much less pressed for it."

"Jenna, what have you *done?*" her mother shrilled. Her breath caught in a gasp. "Has the scoundrel . . . ruined you? Have you let him—"

"No, Mother, I have not let him 'ruin' me," she replied, laughing in spite of herself.

"Rupert is livid, dear. You've broken the poor man's heart."

"Rupert has no heart, Mother. He's a coward, you know. After Simon won the duel, your precious Rupert came at his back and wounded him—at his *back*, Mother! He would have killed Simon if I hadn't been there. There were witnesses: Sir Gerald, Lord Eccleston—and you know how upright *he* is—Phelps, Simon's valet, and Crispin St. John, Simon's . . . houseguest. Don't pretend that one among them hasn't told the tale. Rupert's behavior was unconscionable. How dare you defend him?"

"And what of your behavior, Jenna? You run off with a man—unchaperoned—in front of half the aristocracy, and take up residence with him in this godforsaken wilderness out here on the coast? Who do you think is going to pay for damaged goods? Regardless of what went on between the bedsheets, you've put paid to your reputation, my girl, it is *ruined*!"

"I have not taken up residence with Simon, Mother. He isn't even here. He's gone to London with his guests. Not that I need to tender you an explanation, because I do not. I'm of age; twenty-two—ready to put on biggins and embrace spinsterhood, as you yourself continually remind me. But since you must know, Simon brought me here and left me at once. Everything is quite proper. I am here because Rupert made some very ugly threats before we left the dueling ground, and in this house I am under Simon's protection. I wouldn't be at Thistle Hollow, and you know it. You'd let Rupert in without batting an eye. Simon isn't going to do that, and neither will his staff. They are taking very good care of me until we can be married."

"*Married?*" the dowager shrieked. "Jenna, you can't, so soon after your betrothal to Rupert. What ever are you thinking? What will people say? Ha! You *know* what they'll say, that you *had* to marry the man, just like his brother had to marry that girl years ago."

"Simon has proposed, and we *are* going to be married, Mother. There is nothing you can do to prevent it." She held out her hand, and Lady Holingsworth examined the exquisite ruby and diamond ring on her finger. Her expression softened at once, and Jenna pulled her hand away. "Oh, *Mother!*" she scorned.

"Well, I suppose we could make the best of things," the dowager chirped, wriggling in the chair. "He is titled, and more prestigiously than Rupert, I daresay. And he is a war hero, after all. I shall see to the arrangements, of course. I must have you to Paris at once to complete your trousseau. Yes! And we'll have the wedding in London, since his lordship prefers it to the coast."

"So it's 'his lordship' now, is it? What happened to 'that scoundrel' who has ruined my reputation? Really, Mother."

"That will save me the bother of refurbishing Thistle Hollow—and the expense," the dowager babbled on. "And, of course, I shall tack 'Rutherford' onto 'Hollingsworth.' Hyphenated names are so in fashion today, and 'Rutherford' is so much more impressive than 'Marner'! As soon as I unpack—"

"No, Mother," Jenna interrupted. "You will unpack at Thistle Hollow. I've already had your portmanteaux put back on the chaise. As soon as you and Emily have finished your refreshments, you will leave. This is my home now, and I will have things my way in it. Neither Simon nor I wish a showy society wedding. We want it to be simple and private. I do not mean to be rude, but you had no business coming here without an invitation. I can see by your expression that you mean to oppose me. I wouldn't if I were you. I would hate to have you put out bodily, but I will if you persist."

"*Well!*"

"And one more thing . . . if you ever dare presume to 'tack' Rutherford onto *anything,* I will take legal action against you."

"Why, you ungrateful girl," the dowager wailed, bursting into crocodile tears. "I nearly *died* giving birth to you—two days in labor—and this is my reward? How can you be so cruel to your mother? If your poor father were alive—"

That tweaked a nerve.

"If Father were still alive," Jenna said with raised voice, "I wouldn't have had to . . ."

"You wouldn't have had to what?" her mother snapped.

"Never mind. Please finish your tea and leave before I say something we'll both regret. And in the future, please remember that when I want you to visit, I shall send you an invitation." Then, wheeling around, she sailed through the drawing room door intoning, "Good bye, Mother," without a backward glance.

CHAPTER NINE

The dressmaker arrived the following morning, and Jenna was closeted with her for the better part of the day. Her name was Olive Reynolds, and Simon had given her carte blanche in creating Jenna an entire new wardrobe, including her wedding gown.

Miss Reynolds arrived with two assistants bearing bolts and swatches of silk, cashmere, moiré, and lawn. There were trimmings of tulle, and of Mechlin, Matise, Brussels, and Honiton laces, and sheaves of patterns to pore over. Everything from bonnets to ball gowns was represented. Simon had been very thorough; he had even ordered several new dresses and appropriate accessories for Molly that were more in keeping with her elevated status as lady's maid.

The dressmaker was a plain-looking woman in her fifties, with sharp features and a tongue to match, who, at the outset, made it plain that house calls were not her usual practice, but that since it was for the Earl of Kevernwood, she would make an exception. Jenna realized at once that the woman was fishing for an explanation as to why she couldn't have come to her salon like the rest of the populace, but since Simon hadn't given her one, she was not about to do so, either. That aside, the woman possessed impeccable taste and fingers that were almost as skilled as Madame Flaubert's. Jenna was more than pleased.

There was no real wardrobe emergency now that she had her portmanteau, of course, but Simon had given explicit instructions that there were to be dozens of frocks made, morning and afternoon dresses, party, ball, and presentation gowns, lingerie and outer wear, including two pelisses to wear over her new finery once the weather turned colder—one of fur, and one of fine Merino wool trimmed in chinchilla—as well as spencers and cloaks in various colors and weights. He had also left word with the cobbler at the local bootery, who would see to her footwear.

It was all very improper, of course, for him to do such a thing, and she couldn't help but giggle imagining what her mother would have to say about it were she to find out. There was no question that she would be positively scandalized. But Jenna knew Simon's mind in the matter, and what's more, his heart. It was as though he was trying to erase every shred of her existence before him, and she adored him for it, especially because it went against his principles to indulge in the materialistic fripperies of aristocratic pretentiousness. It wasn't hypocrisy on his part, either; it was love, and it melted her heart. As Lady Evelyn had once so aptly put it, Simon Rutherford was, indeed, a revolutionary. Had society done that to him, or was he born that way? Jenna didn't know, and it really didn't matter. She was happier than she had ever been in all her life, happier than any woman had any right to be, except for the one matter nagging at her conscience, the dark cloud spoiling her horizon, threatening that happiness . . . the burdensome secret she needed so desperately to confess.

Jenna was amazed at how quickly that need was to be tested. The dressmaker had scarcely departed, when Horton announced that the vicar, Robert Nast, had invited himself to nuncheon and was awaiting her in the breakfast room. Her head was still a jumble of silk and lawn and Honiton lace, when she got that news. She quickly changed into a demurely correct afternoon frock of dove gray organdy, which was trimmed in the palest of pale pink silk ribbon roses, thanking God that her mother had brought her portmanteau.

The breakfast room had been chosen because it was the only room on the first floor of the house that offered a view of both the courtyard and the garden, from the terrace doors on the south, and from the wide bay window built into the southwest corner, respectively, and because it was the vicar's favorite. It was Jenna's favorite as well. When she'd breakfasted there earlier, the fog had just lifted, exposing the tall hedgerow that formed that segment of the garden wall, where great arches were cut out making visible different vignettes of the garden beyond. They were planted in such a way that the groupings were framed like fine works of art. Even without the sun, the effect was breathtaking, like looking at miniature landscapes inside sugar eggs. She particularly loved the one that displayed delphinium and foxglove, with snowdrops and lilies of the valley at their feet. Their tall, colorful stalks seemed to be resting on clouds. Everything bloomed early in Cornwall. To Jenna it had always seemed a land enchanted, but never had it seemed so magical as it did then, viewing the Kevernwood gardens from that panoramic spectacle of sparkling glass.

It was beside the bay window that a drop-leaf table had been opened up and spread with a creamy lace-edged linen cloth. The footmen had just finished at the sideboard, setting out potted blue cheese, fresh bread wedges, and chutney made of apples, rhubarb, and melon. There was also a flavorsome salad of fresh garden greens, nasturtium, onion, leek, and fennel, dressed with garlic oil and vinegar, and warm vegetable pasties. The footmen carried a tea service to the table and were just setting out the chairs when the quick patter and slide of Jenna's feet on the polished floor announced her arrival.

As she skittered to a halt on the threshold, her breath caught in surprise. The vicar wasn't what she'd expected at all. Her mental image of him was of someone rather plain, older, and dreadfully stuffy. Before her stood a man in his early thirties, tall and strongly built, with hair like summer wheat, and piercing eyes the color of amber. In jarring contrast, he wore somber black, with the crisp white neckcloth of an Anglican clergy-man. But he was no cliché. She was standing face-to-face with yet another enigmatic revolutionary.

Her surprise was such that she scarcely remembered extending the hand that he lightly kissed and returned to her. She didn't even realize she was standing in front of the sideboard, until he put a plate in that same hand and nodded for her to make her selection before him. He obviously read her expression, because the first words he spoke came on the tail of a laugh.

"It's quite all right, my lady," he said, "you're not exactly what I expected, either."

"I beg your pardon," she gushed. "Please, do forgive me, Vicar Nast, I didn't mean to stare, but you have the right of it; you aren't at all what I expected."

"Which was . . ."

"Someone . . . older . . . more, well, sour-looking, actually."

"Someone infected with ecclesiastical malaise, eh?" he said, tongue in cheek. "Does serving God make men sour, do you think? It's supposed to go the other way 'round."

"It seems to have done to most of the clergy I've seen," Jenna said frankly.

"There is joy in God. At least there ought to be." He smiled, and it was like sunshine breaking through the bleak gray afternoon. "Perhaps I'll start a trend. I sometimes think that is why I've become what I've become; to make a difference. Is that awfully idealistic of me?"

"It's admirable, I think."

"You are most kind, my lady, but then, I was told to expect that."

"Simon mentioned that you would be stopping by."

"At the outset, let me say that I do not usually invite myself to nuncheon," he said, clouding briefly as he spooned a dollop of chutney onto his plate. "Simon asked me to pay a visit and introduce myself, and such things always seem to go much more smoothly over food, I've discovered. It gives the participants something to do with their hands . . . and their eyes. Rest assured, I shan't make a habit of this."

"You are most welcome any time, Vicar Nast. Is there a Mrs. Nast?"

"No, my lady, not yet." He chuckled, and quickly added, "So far, I'm afraid no one will have me."

Jenna laughed, and they made their selections and took their seats at the table. He had put her at ease. She liked him at once, but she couldn't imagine the circumstances that had thrown him together with Simon.

"You were at school with Simon, so he tells me," she probed, taking his teacup to fill it.

"Quite so," he said. He took the cup and saucer from her and set it beside his plate. "Simon and I started out in the same social predicament; we're both second sons, he of an earl, I of a baronet. The most useless creatures on the planet, I'll be bound, second sons; nobody seems to know what to do with them. At any rate, I didn't share Simon's zeal for the military life—I'll come back to that—and I didn't have the patience or the inclination to pursue a future in politics or law—"

"And so you took Orders?"

"Yes," he said, nodding. "Getting back to my conscientious objection, I plumbed the depths of that and found it had roots that were decidedly clerical; hence the seminary. And here I am, the vicar of Holy Trinity out by the quay!"

"Is your tea all right, Vicar Nast?" she inquired, after tasting her own.

"Oh, quite. Simon's cook is a master blender." He looked off in the distance around a sip and declared, "China, gunpowder, and common green—her traditional 'house tea' as she calls it. She has a blend for every occasion, has Cook: 'company tea,' 'breakfast,' 'afternoon,' and 'dinner tea.' Small wonder she keeps the tea cabinet locked, and the key on her chatelaine. This is indeed worth stealing."

"At home we have to take care whom we send to market," she told him. "They need their wits about them. The poor folk dry their used tea leaves and sell them back to the tea vendors, who doctor the leaves and then foist them off upon unsuspecting patrons—sometimes at first quality prices. Can you imagine?"

"That sort of thing goes on all over. One can't help but feel for the poor unfortunates who are driven to such lengths in order to survive these days. Meanwhile, the rich in this country run mad with extravagance."

Evidently he shared Simon's philosophy on the human condition, and she began to wonder who had influenced whom.

"You and Simon think alike in that regard," she said.

"What is your take on it, my lady?"

"Truthfully, I'd never given much thought to economics until I met Simon. But I have to say that I quite agree with him. Some of what goes on is . . . criminal." She cocked her head and studied the vicar as he raised a forkful of salad to his lips. "Tell me, Vicar Nast, do you address Simon as 'your lordship'?" she wondered.

"No," he said, laughing huskily. "I've never called him anything but Simon, come to think of it."

"Then, let us please not be so formal. I am to be his wife, after all. It would please me if you would call me Jenna."

"I should like that," he responded. "Simon wished it, but the invitation for such a familiarity had to come from you. Simon calls me Rob."

"No," she said thoughtfully. "That is special between you and Simon, from your childhood. I shall call you Robert—with permission, of course."

"Fair enough," he agreed. "Since I hope that means we shall be friends, I have a confession to make. Two, actually."

"Confession?" The word stuck in her throat and she choked on a bit of the bread she was nibbling.

"Are you all right, my dear?"

"It's just a crumb," she lied, taking a swallow of tea.

"First off," he began, "I'm sure you are aware that Simon asked me to keep an eye on you here in his absence. He's made me privy to what occurred at Moorhaven, and on Bodmin Moor. Secondly . . . I don't quite know how to put this . . ."

"I've always found it best to speak my mind," Jenna said at his hesitation.

"Very well, then, at the risk of having repetition damn me, Simon and I have been close friends practically all of our lives. Simply put, he is not a happy man, and I want him to be. He's spent his whole life thus far living for others. I want him to have a happy life of his own. You are much younger than Simon, and—"

"I am twenty-two," she interrupted. Would no one let her forget that she was practically putting on her caps?

"Eleven years between a man and woman is . . . significant, and I was concerned over the rashness of it all. Simon isn't like that. It's almost seemed as if he were . . . driven. I know he's had several close calls of late, and that can put one in touch with one's mortality, I daresay, but it seemed to me almost as if . . . how shall I put this . . . as if he wasn't acting with a level head, and that is *not* usual for Simon."

Jenna stiffened, bolting upright in the chair. Another word and he would have gone beyond the pale. Was he friend or foe, this enigmatic clergyman?

"Please don't misunderstand me," he went on before she could reply. "Simon and I are as close as brothers. I was concerned that he might be . . . following the call of some mad, midlife desperation."

"You use the past tense. Does that mean you aren't concerned any longer?"

"Of course, my dear. I would hardly be confessing the thing if I were still inclined toward the same opinion, would I? The truth is, I failed to credit what love can do to a man's sanity. You see, I'd seen Simon with women, of course, but I'd never seen him in love before. I couldn't recognize him. Now that I've met you—though I daresay there is no logical reason why it should—it all somehow makes perfect sense."

Jenna brightened. She stared deeply into the piercing eyes of the man across the table and longed to tell him everything. From somewhere in the garden she could hear a peacock crying; she had since she'd come to Kevernwood Hall, but she had yet to see one. It was a desolate, mournful sound, like that of a melancholy child, and it stole the sparkle from her mood suddenly.

"Is something wrong, my dear?" the vicar said, frowning.

Jenna hesitated. Yes, something was very wrong, and she longed to unburden herself as he had done. But there were questions that needed to be addressed first.

"When someone confesses to the Anglican clergy, are vicars bound to secrecy as the Catholic clergy are?" she queried.

"You aren't churched, then, I gather," he said, answering his own question.

Realizing her blunder too late, she lowered her eyes, as hot blood rushed to her cheeks. If she were churched, she wouldn't have had to ask that question. What a birdwit she was. Now he would likely take her for a heathen.

"I've had a rather sporadic religious education, Robert," she recovered steadily, though she was anything but. "When Father was alive . . . things were different." Her voice trailed off altogether, and she studied her reflection in the rich, amber-colored liquid swimming in her teacup.

"Simon tells me that you are just recently out of mourning," Nast said, soft of voice.

"Yes, that's true."

"I'm dreadfully sorry for your loss. Does it bother you to talk about it?"

Jenna shook her head. Maybe if he understood what drove her out on the old Lamorna Road that night, he might not judge her too harshly.

"My father was returning from Truro by chaise, when a highwayman overtook the coach and made him stand down," she began, reaching for his empty cup to refill it. "Father had a bad heart," she continued, passing it back to him. "It had been failing for years. He . . . resisted, and the man beat him with his pistol, robbed him and . . . left him lying bloodied in the road."

"When was all this?"

"A year ago February," she said, around a tremor.

"You needn't go on, my dear. This is upsetting you."

"No," she insisted. "I haven't spoken of it since, and I need to now, if you will allow me?"

Though the vicar nodded, he seemed uncomfortable. His amber eyes had grown dark and troubled.

"Very well, as long as it shan't distress you," he conceded.

"Lionel, our driver, put Father in the chaise and brought him home. We sent for the doctor at once, but later that night, Father suffered a seizure and died in his sleep."

"Did he regain consciousness . . . give a description of the bounder?"

Jenna shook her head no. She wanted to tell him about what she'd done—needed to tell him, to tell *someone* and receive absolution before she dared tell Simon. It was on the tip of her tongue, but she couldn't bring herself to speak it. It was too terrible, and their acquaintance was too new. Tears welled in her eyes. She blinked them back.

"Lionel got a good look at the man," she went on. "He said he was the one they call the Marsh Hawk. The guards from the Watch, of course, would do nothing. I needn't tell you what a sham the law is hereabouts, civilian volunteers paid off by thatchgallows to look the other way while they prey upon innocent travelers. It's shameful! At least in Town there are constables and Bow Street Runners and magistrates to keep the peace, but here—"

"He was certain?" the vicar interposed. "The Marsh Hawk, to my knowledge, has never harmed anyone. His reputation is that of a gentleman bandit. He preys on the rich, yes, but to rob, not to kill. At least I've never heard of it. He's quite the local legend hereabouts."

"Lionel described a man who looked like Simon did in that costume at Moorhaven, except for the hair," she told him. "His hair was short, not long like Simon's. He wore no queue."

"Dressing like that was sheer stupidity. I told him so."

"It wasn't Simon's fault, Robert. It was a costume ball. He had no way of knowing about Father."

"You *have* . . . told all this to Simon since, though . . . that your father was a victim of the Marsh Hawk?" he said haltingly.

"No . . . not exactly; at Moorhaven Manor, Lord Eccleston told him that Father was killed as result of a highway robbery, but he didn't go into detail in front of the gathering out of respect for my privacy. Everything's happened so quickly since, I haven't had the chance to discuss it with Simon."

"You really ought, you know. You need to . . . let it go, and confession is good for the soul, so they say. That reminds me! We've strayed from the path. You asked me about that very thing earlier. Why? Was there something you wanted to . . . confess?"

Jenna stared at him over the rim of her teacup. Inside she was screaming, *Yes—God, yes!* But the words just wouldn't come.

"No . . . I was just . . . curious," she murmured instead.

"I see, well, the answer to your question is yes, we are bound by the same canon. Confessions are private and sacred. If you should ever need to . . . talk to someone, I hope you won't hesitate to call upon me. I sincerely mean that, Jenna."

"Thank you, but I think you're right. What I need to say, I need to say to Simon. Please keep my confidence—about the Marsh Hawk, that is. I should like to tell him myself."

"Of course, my dear," he replied. "In regard to the wedding, Simon wants to waive the banns in favor of a special license. He will do what he will do, but since his business in London is going to take at least another fortnight anyway—three weeks more than likely, I'm going to post banns regardless. 'Tisn't necessary, what with the license, and we shan't have the customary four-week publishing, but it will please me nonetheless, making this announcement, considering the unfortunate past, and I will indulge myself."

"Another *three weeks*?" She was crestfallen.

"He's buying a naval commission for Crispin, and arranging for Evelyn's come-out after your wedding," he explained. "Brace yourself. You're going to get drawn into that. Simon has no one else to turn to in that cause."

"I'd be . . . delighted," she replied, trying to muster enthusiasm.

"Good! Simon will be relieved." He set his serviette aside then and tilted his head in a manner that told her there was no use trying to hide from those all-seeing amber eyes. "You do love him very much, don't you?" he observed.

"Yes, Robert, I do."

"Then talk to him, Jenna. And if you ever feel the need to talk to me about anything, please don't hesitate, my dear."

CHAPTER TEN

Vicar Nast paid several more visits during the three long, dreary weeks that followed. Jenna was grateful for his company, and his cheerful good humor helped her bear her loneliness for Simon. She sent for the vicar herself on one occasion, when Simon's solicitor, Olin Wickham, arrived at the end of her first week at Kevernwood Hall to go over the marriage settlement.

The legalistic jargon concerning such matters as the equity system, Chancery Court, separate estates, and jointure quite boggled her mind. She was wise enough to know when she was out of her depth and sent one of the footmen to bring the vicar, who cheerfully presided over the stuffy little man's visit.

While the vicar reviewed the staggering sum the agreement entailed without batting an eye, Jenna was nearly prostrate from shock learning that she now owned a keep in Scotland, as well as a sizable tract of farmland not far from her family's estate, which were entirely her own to do with as she pleased without restrictions. There were also generous clothing and pin money allowances to be paid to her monthly, and a staggering sum provided by way of a jointure to be settled upon her in the event of Simon's death. She closed her ears to that and fled to the garden while Robert Nast concluded with the solicitor. She simply would not hear of Simon dying. No amount of money could compensate her for that. What shocked her most was that Simon had filed the settlement agreement with both the Chancery and Equity Courts before he had any inkling of the amount the Hollingsworth dowry would bring into the marriage, since the bride's dowry was usually the barometer that governed what the groom's investment would be.

A fortnight later, Olive Reynolds brought her bridal gown for the final fitting. Jenna had insisted that it be simple, since it was to be a quiet wedding, and it was—elegantly so, of ivory silk embellished with Honiton lace, with a veil of the same delicate fabric, and slippers custom-made by the cobbler of the same ivory silk that the dressmaker had used for the gown. She was to wear a dainty wreath of moss rosebuds and wildflowers from the Kevernwood gardens in her hair, and carry a matching bouquet.

It would be some months before Miss Reynolds would be able to complete her wardrobe. However, the dressmaker was able to supply her with enough of a selection to add to her own that would suffice for the wedding trip, which was to be a month-long stay at Lion Court, her new holding on the verge of Roxburghshire in Scotland, an older, more venerable, though smaller structure than controversial Floors castle across the Tweed River.

A missive arrived that morning from Simon, and as soon as the dressmaker's coach rolled away down the drive, Jenna took it into the garden to read in private. Having managed to elude Phelps, whose hawklike surveillance was driving her mad, she stole to the gazebo at the east end of the garden. The sun had finally chased the flaws, and the air was warm with the promise of kinder days. A gentle wind rippled the parchment in her hands as she read, mildly distracted by the two peacocks that had joined her and begun to circle the structure, strutting and preening and raking the rolling green lawn with their great sweeping tails. She was proud of herself for having won them over. When they followed her to the stable on her way to exercise Treacle earlier in the week, even Barstow remarked that the elusive, unsociable birds had never warmed to anyone else on the place since Simon bought them.

He was coming home. Two more days and they would be wed. She could scarcely believe it. Those words were all she really saw, or wanted to see. She gave only passing notice to the rest of the letter, and hardly any at all to the paragraph explaining that Evelyn and Crispin would be coming home with him for the wedding. *Simon was coming home!*

She folded the parchment, slipped her hand through the side slit in her frock that gave access to the flat little embroidered pocket she wore on a silk cord about her waist, and tucked the missive inside. The sun was warm, laying slanted rays of brilliance at her feet in a checkered pattern through the whitewashed latticework. Its heat married the many garden fragrances around her into one exotic perfume, and she wished she'd brought a book from the library to read there and would have done but for her haste to avoid Phelps. She had just about decided to go back inside and choose one, when the birds suddenly fled in a rush of displaced feathers and irate screeching. As she stepped out of the gazebo to see what had frightened them, a man's strong hands seized her. To her horror, it was Rupert. She screamed, but his hand clamped over her mouth cut it short.

"What? You didn't imagine I'd just leave you here—give you up without a fight, did you, Jenna?" he said, tethering her close. She bit down hard, and he pulled his hand away, examining the teeth marks on his fingers. "Bitch!" he spat, lowering the flat of his wounded hand across her face. "You are my betrothed!"

"I *was* your betrothed, Rupert. No longer. You showed me a man I could never marry on Bodmin Moor. I'm only sorry I didn't see him sooner. You came at Simon's back, and then ran his side through before he could arm himself. I *saw* you! How dare you come here? I am Simon's betrothed now, and you had best leave at once!"

"Or what? He'll come to your rescue and save your honor? Don't be ridiculous. For one thing, he isn't even here. For another, you have no honor to save, m'dear. It was lost the minute you set foot into that man's house unchaperoned."

She struggled fiercely, awarding his shins a healthy drubbing with the pointed toe of her slipper, and clawed at his arms; but his grip was strong as he dragged her toward the orchard.

"Where are you taking me? Let me go!" she cried.

"You don't think for a moment that I'm fool enough to come by way of the drive in broad daylight, do you? I've a carriage waiting in the orchard. I've been watching the place for days."

"Let me go, Rupert! I'm not going anywhere with you. I'll scream!" It was an empty threat. His grip was so tight she could scarcely breathe.

"I'm not going to let the bounder have you, Jenna. You've shared his bed, haven't you?" He shook her. *"Haven't you?"* He repeated. "I'm the only titled suitor you'll ever find now who's going to settle for used merchandise. You should be grateful. No one else will have you after this."

She dug her heels into the damp sod, ruining the perfect lawn with deep ugly trenches in a desperate attempt to slow his progress.

"Simon and I are going to be married," she gritted. "Let me go!"

"Hah!" he erupted. "Everyone knows he's diddling that ripe little packet of flesh he's carting all over Town. Don't you see, my dear, he may well marry you, but the lovely Lady Evelyn goes with the arrangement, part and parcel."

It was unfounded, of course, but Jenna hadn't quite exorcised the demon, jealousy, where Evelyn and Simon were concerned. Though she knew there was nothing threatening of a physical nature between them, she couldn't help being a little jealous that they were together in London, enjoying the Season—the fetes, the opera, Drury Lane Theatre, Almack's—all that the ton afforded, while she was alone and miserable without him at Kevernwood Hall. That manifested itself in a fresh assault upon Rupert's shins, which earned her another slap. This time his fingers left marks.

His hand on her mouth prevented her scream now. Every step was taking her farther away from the house, and help. The strong hand clamped around her arm bent it behind her back. He was propelling her toward the sound of horses whinnying unseen among the budding apple trees. She made a valiant struggle, and he needed both his hands to restrain her. With her mouth free, her screams grew louder and more desperate. All at once he spun her toward him and his cruel lips reduced the sound to a whimper. They siphoned off her breath, and she was close to passing out from lack of air as his hand on her breast tore at the thin, lace chemisette that rose high at the throat of her peach-colored lawn frock, filling her with a panic she had never experienced. It came with the realization that he had the strength to overpower her.

"Stop that!" he snapped through his teeth, shaking her. "I'm doing you a favor, damn you, Jenna. Our union will save your reputation. You'll still be received—still be welcomed by the ton. I can do that for you. Can he? The man is ostracized from polite society. He's a revolutionary. I can lay the ton—the whole world—at your feet."

"I'd rather die!" she shrilled. "And you are the one who is ostracized, Rupert. The ton does not favor backstabbing cowards. It is you who have fallen from grace."

His eyes dilated with rage, Rupert drove her down into the woodbine at the edge of the path and fell upon her there, anchoring her hands to the ground at her sides.

"You'd lie down for him—and have done, I'll be bound. You belong to *me*, and I mean to have you."

She screamed at the top of her voice, but his savage mouth cut it short again. It was no use. Pinned beneath him, she couldn't break free.

All at once a thunderous shot rang out close by, and Rupert's head snapped toward the sound. As he scrambled to his feet, Jenna rolled out from under him, scrabbled up, and ran straight into the arms of Vicar Nast, who had come running from the direction of the tower with a smoking pistol in his hand. Meanwhile, Emile Barstow, armed with an obsolete flintlock rifle, sprinted over the courtyard with the agility of a man half his age and three stone lighter, as Phelps converged upon them coming from the manor. They reached her in seconds, but after another warning shot from the vicar's weapon, Rupert fled to his waiting carriage and escaped.

The vicar made brief eye contact with Phelps and glanced in the direction of the tower, which loomed darkly in the shade of the orchard, meanwhile gesturing with the pistol, still trailing smoke. Watching the exchange, Jenna caught a hitch in the valet's expression, but the groom distracted her before she could analyze it.

"Are you all right, my lady?" he asked.

She glanced down, assessing the damage. Her dress was grass stained, the puffed left sleeve had been torn, and the high-waisted skirt of her frock had become separated from the bodice where Rupert had stepped on it. Her hair had come down. It hung awry about her shoulders. Her cheek stung where he'd struck her, her tooth had pierced her lip, and she dabbed at the blood with her handkerchief.

"Yes, thank you, Barstow," she said. "But for the obvious, I'm just winded."

"Good God, man, put that thing down before you do yourself a mischief," the vicar said to the groom, glancing at his rifle. "Is that the best you've got back there at the stable? The thing's positively antiquated!"

The groom scowled. "She may be old, but she still shoots straight enough, does Effie here—straight enough to pepper the pants of the likes of that jackanapes what just run off."

"Well, I shan't argue the point, but, all due respect to 'Effie,' I shall speak to his lordship about updating the arsenal at Kevernwood Hall at my earliest opportunity; you can count upon it."

"As you please," Barstow said, patting the stock of his gun with affection. "But I'll just stick to good old Effie all the same, thank you kindly, Mister Nast."

The vicar handed his pistol to Phelps. Jenna couldn't bear to look at it, yet she couldn't look away. It reminded her of that night on the old Lamorna Road. It was a large piece, a twelve-inch holster pistol. She admired the sleek walnut handle and smooth brown patina of the metalwork. She picked out the English Tower proof markings, and, on the center plate, the royal cipher. It wasn't a gentleman's handgun. It was a British Military Sea Service pistol; quite similar to the army type the thatchgallows had stolen from her father during the robbery. The very one she wished she'd had at her disposal for her mission that terrible night two months ago, and all the other nights that went before, when she'd gone searching for the Marsh Hawk. In its absence, she had chosen instead smaller, lighter flintlocks from her father's collection, overcoat-size models that weren't as formidable looking, but fit her hand more comfortably. She shuddered, reliving the instant she squeezed the trigger, and the vicar reacted, pulling her close in the custody of strong arms.

"You're trembling," he said. "Let's get you back to the house and clean you up, then you can tell me what the devil went on out here."

"Shall I send Peter to fetch the constable, Mister Nast?" the groom said.

"No!" Jenna cried. "Please, Robert, I don't want Simon to know!"

The vicar's eyebrow lifted and he soothed her against his shoulder, meanwhile shaking his head in a silent *no* to the groom. "We're going to have to talk about that, Jenna," he said, steering her back toward the house.

An hour later, Jenna and the vicar were having lemonade in the gazebo, the groom had gone back to the stable, and Phelps had disappeared. She hadn't seen him since they left the orchard.

She had changed into an ivory-colored afternoon frock, with a Brussels lace scarf demurely obscuring the décolleté. The welts on her face had been painted with a paste Mrs. Rees had made of marshmallow root from the Heaths' herb garden, to reduce the redness and swelling.

She took a sip from her glass and sighed, glancing around the gazebo. They sat at a small wicker table, with chairs to match, that had been brought and spread with a cloth edged in Battenburg lace. A bowl of flowers from the garden squatted in the center of it, alongside a salver holding a crystal pitcher filled with the tangy refreshment.

"I was so enjoying this place before it . . . happened," she lamented.

"That's why I had the lemonade served here," the vicar confessed, "to erase some of the unpleasantness. Simon wouldn't want you to feel uncomfortable anywhere on his land."

She cocked her head and studied him. The man was a mystery.

"You are very kind," she observed, with heartfelt appreciation.

"Are you certain that you're all right?" he pressed, "That's a nasty cut on your lip there."

She nodded. Her abrasions would mend. She was worried about Simon's reaction to them.

"Robert . . . I really don't want Simon to know what happened here today. I mean this," she said.

The vicar set his glass aside and leaned back in his wicker chair. It creaked from disuse with his shifted weight. Those articulate eyes of his told her she had wasted her breath.

"Jenna, he has to know," he murmured. "What's more, I've got to tell him before Phelps or Barstow or one of the other servants does. If I don't, and it comes out, which such things always seem to do, he's going to wonder why *you* didn't tell him. You don't want to start your marriage like that. Besides, look at yourself! If Mrs. Rees's famous cure-all should fail, I won't have to tell him."

Her posture collapsed and she looked away. A bee had settled on the flowers in the center of the table, and she concentrated on its methodical course as it flitted from one bloom to another.

"He's going to think he has to challenge Rupert, and we'll have it all over again." She groaned. "I couldn't bear another duel."

"You mustn't sell Simon short. Rupert is no match for him. The bounder needs a comeuppance. He nearly raped you!"

"No, I was never in danger of that—not really," she refuted. "Rupert views me as a possession. He takes loss badly. In his warped, egotistical mind he believes that Simon has stolen something that belongs to him. He was merely trying to take it back."

"Hah!" he erupted. "You defend him well enough."

"There is no defense for his behavior. I simply mean that I understand the way his mind works. That is why I left him."

"And you don't think the man's dangerous?"

"I don't think he'll try it again."

A guttural laugh rumbled in the vicar's throat. There was no humor in it.

"Well, I doubt Simon is going to want to take that chance, and I shan't advise it. You aren't going to convince me that you could have handled the situation if I hadn't happened along."

He was probably right, but she wasn't about to tell him so. It didn't matter if he was. She would be more diligent next time.

"Where did you come from?" she said, deftly changing the subject. "And, what were you doing with that pistol?"

"There's a narrow road, more path than road actually, beyond the orchard that winds down 'round the quay. I often come that way. The distance is shorter," he explained. "I saw the coach half-hidden among the trees. The driver was dozing. I was just about to wake him and ask him why he was loitering in Simon's orchard, when I heard you screaming. Lucky I came on when I did."

"And the pistol? That was no pocket pistol, Robert; it was a military weapon, a Sea Service pistol, if I'm not mistaken. What ever would a vicar be doing with one of those?"

His eyebrow lifted, and he dosed her with his piercing amber stare. It was a look she'd almost come to fear. He seemed to see into the thoughts she was so desperately trying to hide.

"Astute of you!" he blurted. "You know your guns. I'd like to hear the whys and wherefores of that, I'll be bound!"

"My father kept a rather extensive arms collection—guns, swords, truncheons, tipstaves; I believe he was a frustrated Bow Street Runner. That's what makes the way he died so horrible. At any rate, he owned a pistol very similar to yours, except that it was army issue; he'd used it himself in the Colonies. But what were you, a vicar, doing with such a weapon?"

"It isn't mine. It's Simon's, the very one he used at Copenhagen. When he retired from duty, he lent it to me. There was a rash of church robberies at the time, you see. The vicar of a church on the outskirts of Wadebridge was badly pistol-whipped in his own vestry. I'm often on the road, traveling alone, and what with the threat of highwaymen in these parts, Simon thought I'd best have protection. I keep it in the cabriolet usually. I'm glad I had it with me today. I'd never really shoot anyone, of course, but it makes a god-awful noise. It scared Marner well enough, didn't it? A pity that decent folk have to resort to such tactics these days."

"Were you . . . aiming?"

"Of course not. I might have hit *you*. I only fired a warning into the air. I'm a terrible shot, my dear."

"I don't like guns," she said frankly, cracking the paste that had dried on her cheek as she spoke, "and I don't like war. I'm glad Simon is out of it. I cannot believe that he's buying a commission for Crispin. The boy's so terribly young."

"All men answer the call to arms, Jenna," he replied. "It's in the blood—in the gender."

"But not you."

"No, not me. But I understand the drive. You need to understand it, too. Oh, I don't mean that you have to agree, of course, but if you love Simon, you need to understand his need to follow the call, and his frustration that he can no longer do so."

"He's living vicariously through Crispin, is that what you're saying?"

The vicar sighed, weighing his answer. "To a degree, I suppose," he said. "Part of him wants to do right by his brother—to do what Edgar would have done for the boy. It's a point of honor. Another part of him wants to secure the boy's future . . . in case something should happen to him, God forbid. And then there's the part that frustration feeds."

"I'll never understand it," she lamented.

"Jenna, Simon fought under Nelson during the Battle of the

Nile. Nelson was rear admiral then. Simon idolized the man. He was in the thick of it, a lieutenant, and he watched Nelson rise. He was on the *Foudroyant* when she captured the *Genereaux*, but it was another, more experienced lieutenant, Lord Cochran, who, as prizemaster, took her into Port Mahon. Afterward, Cochran was given command of the *Speedy*, a fourteen-gun brig."

"And Simon felt slighted?"

"No—no, he wanted the chance to win his own command, and then came Copenhagen. He would have done it, too, but for his wounds."

"How dreadful he must have felt. How disappointed."

"Don't ever let on that I told you, but he considered his life over when he couldn't be in the thick of things. A good friend of his, a lieutenant like himself, Nathaniel Ridgeway, Earl of Stenshire, was also injured at Copenhagen, but not as badly. He went on to fight in other battles, while Simon could not. After that, Simon gave up, spiraled into a deep depression . . . until you, actually. I'm going to tell you something else to keep under your hat. I didn't want to see him come to harm, of course, but I was almost glad when he got blasted at Copenhagen. As you said, he's well out of the madness now, thank God. He would have eventually been killed. The man's got a death wish, I'll be bound. He saved the lives of three conscripted midshipmen when the *Monarch* took the hit that crippled her—pushed them out of the way of a falling mast and took the brunt of it himself. That shove finished his career, but there are three very grateful midshipmen who shan't ever forget it. He was duly decorated, of course. Small consolation, considering."

"He did mention his friend, Stenshire, but other than that I knew nothing of this," Jenna regretted.

"That is one of the drawbacks of marrying in haste," Nast replied. "You don't really know each other."

"Thank you for telling me," she said, avoiding a response to what had all the earmarks of an imminent lecture. "I saw the sadness in him, loved him all the more for it, wanted to sooth it all away—but I couldn't name it."

"It got worse after Spain declared war on us," the vicar continued. "Nelson was blockading Toulon. Simon wanted to be with him, and he couldn't. And then . . . Trafalgar. Simon was devastated when Nelson fell. Now there's talk of more trouble in the Colonies. There will always be something—something he cannot be part of."

Jenna clouded, and said in a small voice, "Robert, I don't want you to think that there is a . . . physical reason for our marrying in haste."

"I don't."

"We had that discussion about confession. You hardly know me, and I just don't want you to presume—"

"I don't have to know you. I know Simon."

She hesitated. "While we're on the subject, there *is* something I would like to . . . confess. I know it's foolish, and I know I've no reason to be, but I'm ashamed to say that I've been . . . jealous of Evelyn."

The vicar looked pained suddenly. His color faded, taking his buoyant good nature with it, and she wished she hadn't spoken.

"You know the situation there," he said. "You know that's impossible."

"I know, but . . . Rupert inferred that . . . well, he as much as said that they are lovers, and that everyone in Town knows it."

"You know where that's coming from."

"Of course I do, but she is infatuated with Simon, Robert, and that frightens me."

"Marner doesn't know that Evy is Simon's niece, Jenna— nobody does. He sees them together, and with the sort of mind the man possesses, he reads what he wants to into it, because of his own improprieties and jealousy. The man's a maw-worm, my dear."

"I realize that. What I'm concerned about is Evelyn's feelings for Simon. I want to be her friend, and I can't with this between us. I hate to impose, but . . . could you possibly . . . have a word with her about it? She would resent it coming from me, and that would only make matters worse."

He made a strangled sound, and winced as though he were in pain.

Her hand flew to her mouth. Could he have feelings for the girl? Of course! What a birdwit she was not to have seen it. She saw it now. Her thoughts reeled back on their conversation. His demeanor had changed the minute the subject of Evelyn came up.

"Oh, my God!" she breathed. "Oh, Robert, I . . . o-oh, Robert . . ."

"Now you know why I've never married," he said. "But this is supposed to be your confession, not mine."

"How could I have been so insensitive—so blind?" she moaned. "Rupert was right. He told me I needed to take stock. Robert, I beg you forgive me. I'm not usually like this. I know it's no excuse, but I haven't been myself since Father died."

"Here now, none of that!" he responded, bolting upright in the chair.

"Does Simon know?"

"I've never told him."

"But, this is dreadful. I'm so sorry, Robert."

"Keep it to yourself, eh? I wouldn't want her to—"

"How can you even ask?" she interrupted.

"As you've said, I hardly know you."

"Well, you must trust me nonetheless to expose your heart to me in this way. I shan't betray it." There was a moment of awkward silence, and then she said, "Thank you for what you did before. You're right. I've never seen Rupert as he was today. He was like a madman. I don't know what would have happened if you hadn't . . ."

"You do see now why I must tell Simon?"

"More so now than ever," she murmured, nodding her lowered head.

"Excuse me? I don't follow."

"I received a letter from Simon today. I was reading it here in the gazebo before Rupert accosted me. I had just put it in my pocket. It's gone, Robert, pocket and all. I missed it out by the orchard. It could have been torn away when I was struggling with Rupert and still be out there somewhere, of course, but suppose he has it? It told all of our plans . . . where we're going to be . . . everything."

"I'll give the orchard a good going-over before I leave."

"How will you ever tell him?"

"He'll be coming to me at the vicarage before he comes to you. The plan is to drop Evy here at the Hall, then he and Crispin will drive out to Holy Trinity and spend the night at the vicarage. He isn't going to compromise you in any way, Jenna. I'll tell him then."

"He's going to be furious. Please, God, don't let there be another duel!"

"Don't worry, Jenna, there won't be. You just leave it to me."

CHAPTER ELEVEN

"What is it?" Simon demanded the minute the vicar's study door clicked shut. "Come, come, man. I know something is amiss. I knew it the minute I entered the vicarage. You're a lousy actor, Rob. That face would damn you in the gambling hells. Well? Out with it!"

Robert Nast had never been able to hide his feelings from Simon. He'd done his best to affect a casual air, but Simon's silent exchanges during dinner were pregnant with unspoken questions. When Simon literally dismissed Crispin after the meal, and the vicar found himself being steered toward the study without ceremony, he conceded defeat.

"Settle down, Simon," he said. "There was an incident at the Hall, but it was handled—"

"Why didn't you send for me?" Simon demanded.

"It would have done no good. You were already en route."

"What 'incident'? Don't make me choke it out of you, Rob. Something's happened to Jenna hasn't it? I asked you to do one simple thing—keep an eye on her—"

"And I did. We *all* did."

"Then—"

"Marner tried to abduct her from the Hall in broad day-light," the vicar interrupted with raised voice. "Suffice it to say that we spoiled his plan—Phelps, Barstow, and myself. Now then, if you want the tale told in detail, pour yourself a brandy, light that damnable pipe of yours, and sit! I refuse to talk to a moving target."

There was no mistaking the cold light in Simon's eyes, and the vicar chose his words with care. He left nothing out, though he deftly skimmed over the details of Jenna's assault. When he'd finished, Simon surged to his feet and began to pace.

"She wasn't harmed?" he urged.

There was no use to lie; he would see for himself in the morning. "Not . . . seriously," the vicar hedged. But Simon's rigid stance, his narrow-eyed stare, and jutting chin clearly de-manded more. "She was mauled a bit, yes," he went on. "She fought him like a tigress before we intervened, and—"

"'*Mauled*'?" Simon gritted out.

The vicar gave a deep nod. "Mauled—roughed up—jostled about," he elaborated. "The blighter thought you two were sharing the same bed, which, in his warped mind, put paid to gentility, and gave him license to expect the same. You only have yourself to blame for that, you know, Simon, whisking her out here so impetuously. That's what *everyone* is likely think. You may have meant well, but you've done the girl a great disservice. And haring off to London hasn't helped anything, either. The ton will believe what they want to believe; the juicier they can make the on-dits—true or false—the better."

"You're *defending* that maw-worm?" Simon bellowed, in-credulous.

"Shhh! You'll have Crispin down here! No, I'm not defend-ing Marner. I'm simply trying to tell you that you might expect more of the same, considering your bizarre abduction of that girl. Whatever possessed you to throw propriety to the winds and make such a foolhardy blunder? What could you possibly have been thinking?"

"I was 'thinking' that I couldn't leave her at Moorhaven with Marner—not after what happened on the dueling ground. My judgment on that was sound enough, by God! Your 'incident' proves the point. As to the whys and wherefores of my actions, I shan't waste my breath explaining them. You wouldn't understand if I did. You've never been in love with a woman."

The vicar stifled a groan. Should he tell his friend of his feelings for Evelyn—prove Simon wrong here and now? No. Nothing would be served in it, though he was tempted. Nevertheless, he needed to do something to shock the man back to his senses.

"You don't approve of her," Simon accused. "I'd hoped . . . once you got to know her . . ."

"It's not Jenna that I don't approve of, Simon; she's delightful. It's this mad rush to the altar that I can't conscience."

"If you're insinuating—"

"No, no, it's nothing like that. Were she enceinte, it would make sense! Let me ask you this—did you know that she is more knowledgeable about firearms than the both of us put together?"

Simon's blank look replied.

"I thought not!" the vicar responded. "Did you know what an outstanding horsewoman she is—that she rides for sport, and is skilled in the art of dressage? Hah! Even Barstow knows that! We've been 'round all this before. You hardly know each other. *That's* what I'm insinuating."

"We know all we need to know," Simon defended. "That we love each other and want to spend the rest of our lives together. I never thought this would happen to me, Rob. Now that it has, I want to grab fast and hold on to it for dear life. I never expected this reaction from you. I would have thought, all things considered, that you'd be happy for me."

"I *am* happy for you, Simon . . . I want to be happy for you, but you aren't thinking clearly. What about the Marsh Hawk? Is he going to fade into oblivion at last, praise God? You can't think to lead this insane double life right under your bride's nose. Jenna is no birdwit, you know; she'll find you out in a trice! Then what? I shouldn't have to remind you that she has a rather poor opinion of highwaymen." It was as far as he was prepared to go, as far as he *could* go without betraying her trust. This was dangerous ground, and if he had any sense, he'd set aside his promise to let Jenna tell Simon about her father herself, and have done. But he'd given his word as a vicar. The least he could do was give her the chance to do as she wished.

"The Marsh Hawk has not yet completed his mission," Simon replied. "I needn't remind you that I've funded two hospitals out of pocket, Rob. The aristocracy is going to help pay for the third, and for the lands they've stolen from the conscriptees while they were fighting for this country on foreign soil—with the Marsh Hawk's management, of course. Once that's accomplished, the Marsh Hawk will retire."

"And if the Marsh Hawk should slip up and get himself caught, while blind passion undermines his common sense and clouds his heretofore levelheaded thinking, what happens to Jenna then? You need to talk to her, Simon. You need to tell her. If she loves you as you say, it will make no difference. If not, you need to know it now, before—"

"I can't do that. I can't risk losing her. If all goes as planned, I'll be out before winter sets in, and she need never know. There's no need for you to be involved any longer, if that's what's bothering you. Phelps and I can manage on our own from here. I've put you in jeopardy much too long."

Robert Nast's involvement in the Marsh Hawk's escapades was hardly in keeping with his vocation, or something he was proud of. However, Simon's safety was now—and always had been—paramount. He couldn't remember how he'd gotten embroiled in the Marsh Hawk madness. He and Simon had always been there for each other for as long as he could recall. It wasn't as though he had to don a mask and ride alongside Simon on forays. The service Robert provided was simply a safe haven on occasion, and an irreproachable alibi if needs must. It didn't hurt that, contrary to what he'd told Jenna, he was an expert marksman and had proven himself at Manton's Gallery in London on numerous occasions in his impetuous youth. That latent talent had come in handy many times since it all began, the latest of these, only two days ago in Simon's orchard at Kevernwood Hall.

"That's not what's bothering me, and you know it," he snapped. "I gave you my word at the onset of this insanity that I would help you, and I will continue to do so—especially now, when your addled wits are likely to get you killed, or hanged at Tyburn. But if I am facing being hoisted up the gibbet alongside you after you slip up and earn us both a rope, I need to understand. Talk to me, Simon! Why now? After all these years, why such a mad dash down the aisle, as though your breeches were afire? Why can't you wait until the Marsh Hawk has retired to marry?"

"My obligation to Evy and Crispin is soon fulfilled. Evy's come-out will surely yield her a respectable match, and that can't happen too soon— she's entirely too attached to me; it isn't healthy. Crispin is about to embark upon a naval career that will assure him a prestigious future, I've just seen to that personally. I have lived for this moment, and now that I've found my soul mate, I can't think why I should postpone my life a minute longer. Besides, I . . . we can't go on as we are. She can't stay on at the Hall unchaperoned, else she be compromised, and I don't trust that mother of hers to keep Marner at bay if she returns to Thistle Hollow. The woman is salivating over any such match."

"I agree with most of what you've just said, but how can there be anything but a physical attraction between you on such short acquaintance? That isn't enough to base a marriage upon. The physical element fades all too quickly. Then what? A marriage needs to be built on an emotional and spiritual attraction as well if it's to work. My point, which you continue to avoid, is that you haven't known her long enough for all that."

"I will admit that at first the attraction was purely physical. From the first moment I saw her, I knew I had to have her. But Jenna felt the same thing at the same time. I'm not going to presume to understand or explain it, Rob; it's just the way things are."

"But you've been attracted to women in such a manner before. Don't tell me you haven't. Why, just last year—"

"*Ladybirds*, Rob, not ladies. I shan't deny that I've been attracted to women that I knew could give me pleasure—women skilled at pleasing a man without the courtship rituals that ladies demand. Considering my 'agenda,' as you like to call it, it seemed the most practical solution for me at the time. I never met a lady of quality who was anything but an insipid milk-and-water miss. You should come to Town for a Season, Rob. Whoever called it 'coming out' named it well. They swarm out of the gate like lemmings after the eligible males. Why do men marry such creatures? To get a respectable heir, that's why. Meanwhile, they take mistresses for someone to engage in stimulating conversation—someone to relax with, who promises lively bed sport. How have these marvels escaped you? Until Jenna, I never met a woman that I could respect for her intelligence as well as her virtue. Even Evy is all fluff and chatter—charming, certainly, but hardly the sort to keep a man from straying for long."

"Evy's young yet, Simon. How can you presume to level such harsh judgments against her?" Robert scolded. He couldn't help himself. He couldn't resist coming to the girl's defense, even if Simon was right. Hot blood surged to his temples. Would Simon guess? No. He was clearly too wrapped up in his own dilemma.

"Growing up without a mother hasn't helped," Simon went on. "I'm hoping Jenna will be able to offer some guidance there." He popped a guttural chuckle. "And there's another thing," he said. "That Jenna has turned out as she has with such a harridan for a mother is in itself a miracle, and a credit to her, I daresay. It's honed her intellect and sharpened her wits. She's vibrant—alive, and passionate, Rob—no milk-and-water miss, she. I know all I need to know. I mean to have her now—right now. Anyone who presumes to stand in the way of that can go straight to the Devil."

The vicar said no more by way of argument, though Simon raved on for some time before they retired; there wasn't any use appealing to his rational side. He had no rational side—not when he dug in his heels as he did now. He'd seen Simon in such a taking many times before, but never over a woman. That had him worried, since there was no valid precedent to hold up as example. And so, Robert did what he could—what he always did when faced with the impossible. He listened, and he prayed.

CHAPTER TWELVE

The wedding took place at Holy Trinity Church on Sunday morning as scheduled. A reluctant Evelyn, dressed in pink tarlatan, served as Jenna's bridesmaid, and Crispin acted as bridegroom's man for Simon.

Wearing a dark blue frock coat, a white waistcoat, and buff-colored trousers with a simply tied neckcloth and white gloves, Simon stood, fists clenched, ramrod rigid as Robert Nast performed the ceremony. His eyes never left Jenna's face. Her lip was still slightly swollen, and traces of Rupert's fingers remained on her cheek despite her skillful doctoring with talc. She didn't need to wonder if the vicar had told him about her encounter with Rupert. The look in those fiery blue eyes was so strange and complex a meld of love, desire, and rage, it physically pained her to meet it.

There was only one guest on her side: her mother. Jenna had relented and invited her, largely because she knew her mother could help with Evelyn's come-out. The arrangements for that needed to be addressed at once if they planned to have it before the Season ended, and Jenna knew that the wedding trip would have to be cut short in order to see to it otherwise. Though she didn't want to admit it, Lady Elizabeth Hollingsworth was the answer. She certainly had the necessary skills and connections, with an added bonus: she had the credentials to arrange for Evelyn's presentation at court. And who but her mother would be better qualified to preside over the social whirl of fetes and balls that would follow? She would be in her element.

After much soul-searching and several lengthy conversations with the vicar over the matter, Jenna had finally conceded that her mother was essential to the situation. The invitation was sent, with a warning: If anything even close to what happened at their last meeting were to occur, she would find herself packed off to Thistle Hollow straightaway. Jenna's mother, appropriately humble, arrived in time for the wedding.

The dowager was not, however, made privy to Evelyn's relationship to Simon. As far as she knew, the St. Johns were distant relations of the Duke of York, and close friends of the Rutherford family. Simon had opened an account in Crispin's name so that it would appear as though he were providing for his sister. Their extended stay as his guests, both at Kevernwood Hall and at the town house, instead of their own home in Dorset, was explained away as stemming from Simon's sponsorship of Crispin's naval commission, and his commitment to see to Evelyn's come-out—promises he'd made to the parents before their deaths. It was half-truth, but Lady Hollingsworth didn't question. It was obvious to all that she was only too happy to accept the situation as a social substitute for the grand society wedding Jenna had denied her. Evelyn received the formidable dowager's sponsorship with the kind good manners of a well-bred young lady, though she did so without heart.

Another not elated with the arrangement, aside from Evelyn, was the vicar, but Jenna surmised that was because he feared that once Evelyn had her come-out, some dashing young aristocrat would snap her up in a heartbeat. The key word in that thought was *young*. Not that Robert Nast wasn't youthful, because he was—and handsome besides. It was just that Evelyn simply didn't see him that way, and he knew it. She didn't see him at all.

Jenna's heart went out to Robert, and to Evelyn. And during their correspondence, she convinced Simon to hold the girl's come-out ball at Kevernwood Hall instead of the town house as was originally planned, in hopes that bringing the celebration to the coast would somehow work a miracle for Robert Nast. All of the fine tuning for the affair would have to be done in London, of course, where her mother would have easy access to the Bond Street shops, and to the engravers for the all-important cards and invitations, and other such necessary details. Not the least of which would be seeing to it, meanwhile, that Evelyn was well displayed in the right circles. Time, however, was of the essence. In order to accomplish all this, when all the other eligible young ladies in Town were already bombarding the establishments and depleting their supply, the dowager and the St. Johns would have to leave right after the festivities, much to Jenna's profound relief.

Lady Hollingsworth didn't seem to notice Evelyn's chagrin. The wedding had her full and fierce attention then. She went along with Jenna's simple ceremony, but she dug her heels in at the prospect that there not be a reception, protesting that a wedding breakfast was positively de rigueur. Jenna finally gave in and let her arrange it through a local confectioner for the sweets, since the decision was reached far too late for Simon's cook to prepare a respectable wedding cake. The cook was, however, able to provide cold viands consisting of chicken, ham, tongue, fish, and game pie, all laid out in the dining hall around the confectioner's elegant wedding cake, richly decorated with sugar flowers, and crowned with real orange flowers gathered from the Kevernwood orangery in the orchard.

Fine champagne, imported from the House of Ruinart in France, had been brought up from the wine cellar, and all of Simon's crofters and servants were invited to enjoy the fare as well and toast his ravishing new bride. All, that is, except Phelps, who was mysteriously absent from the festivities.

Simon endured with grace and a cheerful manner, but the strain in his demeanor was evident. He hadn't mentioned what Jenna knew he'd suppressed for the occasion, which went on late into the afternoon. The dowager and the St. Johns had planned to set out for London the following morning, but as the day wore on, the sun reneged on its promise and a fine sheeting rain began to dampen the coast, forcing them to leave ahead of schedule. It forced Simon and Jenna to change their plans as well. They decided to wait until morning to leave for Scotland, since the storm, which had all the earmarks of a ripping northeaster, would make traveling to Roxburghshire treacherous at best in the dark.

Jenna was relieved at that. Her first time with Simon was going to be difficult enough on familiar ground. It would have been a little unsettling in a strange place, not to mention a strange land. With so much going on, it wasn't until then that she realized what was about to happen. The dowager had barely touched the subject of marital relations during their mother-daughter discussion on the eve of her engagement to Rupert. All she had volunteered was that Jenna would be expected to share her husband's bed and submit. Submit to what exactly wasn't entirely clear. Jenna had seen animals mating, of course, but no . . . *surely not*

It was long after dark when the vicar and the last of Simon's tenants finally took their leave, and Jenna made her way to her dressing room adjoining the bridal chamber on the north, where Molly was waiting to ready her for bed. Simon repaired to his own dressing room, adjoining the bedchamber on the south, there to manage his own toilette with the help of the footman Charl, since Phelps was still conspicuously absent.

Jenna looked at her reflection in the cheval glass in her dressing room, evaluating the very fine batiste nightgown, so airy it was nearly transparent, from every angle. It was trimmed with delicate white-on-white ribbon embroidery work and satin piping, with a drawstring closure at the neck. She had just left the hipbath that Molly had prepared. The steamy water perfumed with rosemary and lavender was meant to relax her. It had heightened her senses instead, and though it did impart a somewhat languid feeling, aided by the champagne she'd drunk more of than was prudent, it also set her pulse racing with anticipation.

She sat at the vanity, while Molly brushed her long hair loose over her shoulders from a center part. It tumbled like waves of spun gold about her face. Jenna was glad she'd resisted her mother's directive to cut it short after the current fashion. What all the fuss was about, she couldn't imagine. Long hair could be made to look short, she reasoned, but short hair could not be made long. Simon was certainly no slave to fashion, either. He hadn't run to the barber for the sake of style. He made his own. That was one of the things she so admired about him.

"You look so fine, my lady," said the maid, her words riding a giggle. Her large round eyes shone like two chestnuts in the candle glow. "And he's so handsome, the master," she added boldly.

"If only I weren't so . . . flushed," Jenna said to the girl's reflection in the glass. "It makes the bruises look much worse than they really are. Oh, I wish . . ."

"You aren't frightened are you, my lady?" the maid asked. "It's the wine to be sure that's making me so cheeky, but you oughtn't worry. It only hurts the first time, so they tell me. After that it can be quite pleasant—so they say, begging your pardon, my lady."

Jenna was about to say *what hurts?* when a light rap on the dressing room door made her lurch, and she rose from the vanity bench, taking one last look in the mirror.

"That will be all, Molly," she murmured. "I shan't need you again tonight."

Another giggle was forthcoming, and the maid curtsied and crept out in a manner that reinforced her evaluation of the girl as mouselike.

Squaring her posture, Jenna opened the dressing room door to find Simon on the threshold wearing his gray satin dressing gown. He didn't speak, but took her hand and led her into the master bedchamber.

The chambermaids had turned down the coverlet on the mahogany four-poster bed. A fresh bottle of the French champagne sat in a silver bucket surrounded by shaved ice on a Chippendale table at the edge of the carpet. Two glasses waited beside it. But Simon led Jenna instead to the candle stand, and tilted her face toward the light, tracing the shape of the bruises on her cheek lightly with his fingers.

"I'm all right, Simon," she murmured.

His mouth had formed a hard, lipless line, and his jaw muscles had begun to tick. The candle flames danced in his eyes, which were smoldering blue coals boring into her in a manner that set chills loose along her spine. It was a look she had never seen in those eyes, and yet . . .

"I should have been here," he said through a dangerous tremor.

"Please, Simon, it's over," she murmured, raising a finger to his lips. "Please don't spoil this."

There came a shift in his deportment then, and he searched her face in the candle glow with a softer look come into his eyes that threatened to undermine her balance. When he cupped her face in his hand and delivered a gentle, reverent kiss, she melted against him. He didn't deepen it this time. Instead, after a moment he withdrew his lips and led her to the table, where he poured them each a glass of champagne.

"I want you to drink this—all of it—Jenna," he murmured. Then, to her look of surprise, he said, "It's all right, my love. It will relax you."

She was still a bit light headed from what she'd drunk earlier, and wondered at the wisdom of further consumption. It hardly seemed wise.

She hedged. "I've already had some, it was quite delicious."

"I know. I want you to have a little more."

Jenna sipped the wine. The bouquet filled her nostrils, and the sweet effervescence teased her tongue and tickled her nose. It tasted wonderful, and when she'd finished he refilled the glass and put it in her hand again.

"One more . . . for me."

Jenna giggled. "Are you trying to get me foxed?" she said.

"Something like that," he replied with a lopsided smile. "It's all right. Just drink it, Jenna."

"Simon," she said, clouding, "I'm not sure . . . I mean, I don't quite know how . . ."

"I know," he whispered, slipping his arm around her. "Do you trust me?"

She nodded that she did.

"Good. I'm going to show you how. Sometimes it hurts a bit the first time. That's why I've asked you to drink the wine. It will help. There will be pleasure, too, I promise. I love you, Jenna. I do not ever want to hurt you, and I apologize beforehand for what has to be."

More talk of pain. She wouldn't show her ignorance. She drank the second glass dry, a little too quickly, and set it aside. At first it didn't seem to have any effect. It wasn't until he took her in his arms again and began kissing her—deep, soulful kisses that set her pulse racing and pumped the alcohol into her blood—that she began to feel pleasantly dizzy.

After a moment, he took her arm and led her toward the four-poster, extinguishing the candles one by one with the palm of his hand until the room was in semidarkness, the only light issuing from the mellow glow of the fire burning low in the grate to chase the dampness. When they reached the bed, he untied the sash that closed his dressing gown and let it gap open, taking care, she noticed, to spare her the sight of his deeply scarred right knee. Turning her toward him, he untied the satin ribbon that gathered her nightgown at the neck. Sliding it down over her shoulders, he let it puddle at her feet and feasted upon every inch of her body, his hooded eyes becoming smoldering black sapphires, dilated with anticipation. They followed the curve of her arched throat to her breasts and narrow waist, and slid along the curve of her hips and over her belly and thighs.

"Good God, you are exquisite," he said, his voice husky with longing as his fingers lightly followed the same route his eyes had taken. When they reached her breasts, Jenna held her breath as fire surged through her loins. He drew her closer, and she melted in his arms.

His satin dressing gown, so cold pressing against her, couldn't cool the fever rising in her blood. His runaway heart was beating against her naked skin through the fabric. It was racing, pounding, echoing in a wild, hypnotic rhythm that resonated throughout her quivering body. He was erect, his greatness touching her. When he guided her hand there, she uttered a strangled gasp as his sex responded to her touch.

All at once he struggled out of the dressing gown, lifted her in his arms, and laid her on the bed. Her head was reeling. The champagne had taken effect. It blurred her vision as he gathered her close and held her there murmuring her name. Emboldened by the wine, and intoxicated by his maleness, she threw her arms around him, pressing him closer, and slid her fingers along the length of his spine. When they reached his taut buttocks, his body convulsed and shuddered against her. He groaned, folding her closer, his chest hair like silk against her breasts.

Who was this paradox she had married—this man, so strong and virile, yet capable of such incredible tenderness as this he showed her now? It made him seem almost childlike, vulnerable in her arms. Her heart ached with love for him.

He kissed her again, holding back at first as he had before, then more deeply, urgently. The effect was dizzying. He tasted of wine and traces of latakia as his skilled tongue opened her mouth and entered her, savoring each slow, silken advance. Waves of intense sensation began to pulse through her belly and thighs at the touch of his hand on her breast. When his lips traveled there, usurping his fingers, she called out his name.

She had imagined this since he held her in the garden at Moorhaven—wished for it, longed for it. Now her delicious fantasy had become real, and nothing in her wildest imaginings could compare to the touch of these warm lips, sucking, tugging—surrounding her aching nipple, grown tall and hard against his tongue.

Jenna arched her throbbing body against him. It seemed to have a will of its own. Her heart leapt at the abandon with which her flesh reached out for his in the heat of raw passion. Involuntary sighs trembling from the very depths of her became husky with desire. The vibration was more than she could bear, and when her lips parted to release the sound, his warm mouth closed over them and swallowed it. Conjoined, their moans gained volume, thrumming wildly in her blood—pulsing through her body as she moved to the strange erotic rhythm coursing through her.

Jenna's heart began to race as his gentle fingers left her arched throat and traveled to her breast. It nearly stopped when they moved over her belly and along the inside of her thighs. She held her breath as he opened her legs, and her body tensed. What must he think of her wanton behavior?

"It's all right," he murmured. "Relax, Jenna."

She did as he bade her, and he probed further into the soft, moist hair curling between the thighs she'd opened to him—slow, rhythmic strokes that tantalized her deep inside with waves of warm, achy heat. She spread her legs wider, writhing against his fingers, leaning into the pressure of his strokes. That pressure grew more intense, the rhythm more rapid. Her breath quickened as his fingers inched deeper—then deeper still! His lips moved over her breast, closed over the tight, hard peak, his flicking tongue teasing it taller. He began to suck, and when his teeth nipped lightly, she uttered a hoarse, throaty groan. The sound was so foreign she almost didn't recognize her own voice.

There was pain then, but oh what glorious pain, as those skilled fingers glided inside her, wet with the first dew of her awakening. Was this what all the pother was about, this excruciating ecstasy that riddled her body so rapturously with pleasure she had never imagined?

But no!

All at once he pulled back and gazed down at her, his broad chest heaving, his hooded eyes glazed with arousal, glistening with the reflection of the dying embers in the grate.

"Hold me, Jenna," he panted.

As she reached to pull him close, he withdrew his fingers and filled her instead with his engorged sex. Jenna cried out as he entered her, but he stifled the cry with his warm lips, meanwhile guiding her legs around him.

Jenna shuddered with pleasure and pain as he plunged deeper, igniting her loins with drenching fire. And she matched his thrusts with a rocking rhythm that halted him momentarily, their moist bodies trembling, their runaway hearts hammering in unison. But the moment was short-lived. He gathered her closer, and they clung to each other in a frenzy of mindless oblivion.

Her hands, seeming to act on their own again, flitted over his moist skin—caressing, reverencing, exploring forbidden regions of his well-muscled body in shameless abandon. What shocking fervor had he awakened in her? What primitive force was this over which she had no control in this man's arms? Whatever it was, this was the consummation of what she'd felt from the very first moment she'd set eyes on him at Moorhaven Manor. It was *right*. This wasn't just a mating of their bodies; it was a mating of their souls.

When she took his face in her hands, he threw back his head and gritted out, "Now, my Jenna . . . please . . . I beg you . . . now . . ."

Jenna murmured his name and he groaned, taking her deeper and deeper until his sex froze inside her. Then, pumping wildly, it convulsed in a spasm of pulsating contractions that filled her with the warm rush of his seed.

Simon let his breath out on a long, low moan. His thrusts eased to mild undulations. He dropped his moist brow on her shoulder, his breath coming short, and folded her close in his arms.

Jenna wasn't dizzy anymore. Her vision had almost become normal again, though her whole body throbbed like a pulse beat. It was a long moment before his warm mouth found her lips, and he shifted his weight, though he didn't withdraw.

"Are you all right?" he murmured.

His warm breath puffed in her ear, and she nodded against his lips.

"Was there much pain?"

"A little," she said. It would serve nothing to lie. "But then . . . oh, Simon!" she whispered in reflection. How tenderly he had managed it.

He gathered her close again, then gently withdrew himself and relaxed, heaving a ragged sigh.

Jenna soothed him with caressing hands, but when her fingers slid upward across his shoulder, he stiffened against her. Her hand was resting on something rough and puckered—still tender, judging from his reaction to her touch—and she pulled back, examining what she'd discovered.

The room was almost in total darkness. Only the faintest embers still glowed in the hearth, but in what light they spared, she picked out the ragged shape of a scar just below his collarbone. The wound was recent, and deep.

"Simon, what is this?" she breathed.

"Nothing to trouble over," he said. Lifting her hand from the scar, he raised it to his lips and kissed first her palm, and then her fingers, fondling them gently.

A surge of hot blood rushed through her veins. It crippled her. Her mind reeled backward in time. The aroma of latakia and wine seemed stronger suddenly, drifting from his moist skin, invoking a memory older than Moorhaven, as she stared up into eyes gazing back like blue-black fire. But she saw them instead, not dilated as they were now, with passion, but in *pain*, blazing through the holes in a black silk half mask. Her throat closed over a gasp.

"When did it . . . happen?" she murmured.

"Months ago. Before we met," he said almost tersely.

"H-how?"

Simon kissed her again. He took hold of the counterpane and wrapped it around her, pulling her close in his arms. "It's nothing, Jenna, nothing at all. Cover up. You're trembling."

"Simon—"

"Shhhh," he whispered, nuzzling her throat. "It's been a long, difficult day. Go to sleep, my love."

But Jenna couldn't sleep. She lay wide-eyed in Simon's strong arms while he slept peacefully beside her well into the wee hours of that long, stormy night. Outside, banshee winds howled about the pilasters. It was a mournful, melancholy sound that reminded her of the peacocks' cries, and rain tapped against the windowpanes like the anxious fingers of some lost soul begging admittance. Was guilt causing her imagination to run wild, or was this development worse than her worst nightmare? Though Jenna didn't want to address that question, it gave her no peace.

Why had Simon been so evasive about the wound? He had almost become angry when she persisted about it before he drifted off to sleep. Her thoughts kept returning to that awful night on the old Lamorna Road. The highwayman had seemed to walk stiffly. Was he disguising a limp the way she'd so often seen Simon do? She'd smelled exotic tobacco and wine on the man when he approached her that night. Was that why Simon's latakia blend sparked recognition the very first time she'd inhaled its distinctive aroma? She recalled the eyes of the man—the blue fire burning toward her through the holes in his half-mask. Was that why she'd fainted at the ball: not because Simon represented her nightmare, but rather because she'd literally seen a ghost that her conscious mind wouldn't let her accept? What was it he'd said when she asked him why he'd worn that costume—that it was a protest against the aristocracy, that he was making a statement, showing his disapproval. He'd made his convictions plain. Had he put them into practice? Was that costume a blatant reality, a daring insult, a slap in the face to a houseful of examples of the very decadence he so abhorred? How did he dare take such a gamble that they wouldn't see him for who he really was? Maybe it wasn't such a gamble. He evidently knew they wouldn't make the connection, or he wouldn't have taken such a risk. But then, he seemed to thrive upon risk. At best the man was a paradox. No wonder he distanced himself from the ton, kept such a low profile. He was hiding this, protecting his alter ego. Could it be?

All at once her own words came back to haunt her: *Long hair could be made to look short, but short hair could not be made long!* Was he simply a revolutionary as Evelyn had observed, or was his unconventional hairstyle a clever ploy to throw suspicion off himself should the need arise? She wracked her brain trying to remember if his queue had been visible on the night of the ball, or tucked up inside that antiquated tricorn hat—another signature of the Marsh Hawk—but she couldn't. She'd passed out before taking notice.

Her heart was pounding, keeping time with the runaway brain that repeatedly harkened back to the same terrible thought: *Dear God, could that highwayman have lived? Could Simon be the Marsh Hawk? Have I fallen in love with and married the man responsible for my father's death?* Whatever the cost, she had to know. Somehow, she had to discover the truth. With that decided, she succumbed to physical and emotional exhaustion and let the peaceful sound of Simon's deep breathing lull her into a deep, dreamless sleep.

CHAPTER THIRTEEN

Phelps's encrypted knock at the dressing room door called Simon from his marriage bed. While the wedding guests had been sampling the delectable viands and drinking French champagne at the wedding breakfast, his valet was closeted at the Heatherwood Arms, plying one of Rupert Marner's tigers with enough of the inn's black ale to loosen the man's tongue in regard to Rupert's travel plans. The volatile brew, known to have doubled as a furniture stripper on occasion, had done its job. As Simon feared, the viscount was, indeed, privy to their itinerary, and was about to set out for Roxburghshire. At that news, dressed in his highwayman garb, with Phelps in tow, the earl rode into the oncoming storm at breakneck speed and reached the stretch of wooded road just west of Widdon Down in time to intercept Rupert's brougham.

Well hidden among the trees that formed a natural canopy over the narrow thoroughfare in that sector, and sheltered somewhat from the persistent rain, Simon donned his half mask and loaded his pistols.

"My lord, it's madness, this," Phelps pleaded. "Are you certain you want to take such a risk?"

"The bounder's got to answer for Jenna, Phelps," Simon stated, speaking in a dark mutter. He tucked his tied-back hair underneath his old-fashioned tricorn hat, and adjusted the mask around it, anchoring it in place. "Nothing else could have gotten me out of that bed just now, old boy. I had planned on waking with my wife in my arms. What he's done, not to mention what he's planning, demands satisfaction. You know that."

"What satisfaction, my lord, when he won't even know that it was you who have leveled it—and why?"

"*My* satisfaction," Simon returned, thumping his chest with a balled-up fist, "in that I've put paid to the score."

The valet wagged his head in an all too familiar manner, and Simon heaved a gusty sigh that flared his nostrils and answered the gesture. "What? Would you rather have another duel?" he said.

"At least there would be honor in it, my lord. You've never stooped to what you're planning. The Marsh Hawk has never—"

"I don't intend to kill him, Phelps. Stubble the melodrama."

"What do you plan to do, then?"

"I plan to prevent him from spoiling my wedding trip. I plan, Phelps, to meddle with *his* travel plans. Just how much of a meddle depends upon him. Now, ride back 'round the bend and crow when you see the blackguard's coach. I don't want to meddle with anyone else this trip. Oh, and, Phelps," he added, as the valet turned, "no matter what occurs, you are not to interfere."

The valet offered a cursory nod and did as bidden, making no sound as he walked his horse through the underbrush and disappeared into the eerie green pallor of the wood.

Simon nodded in approval. Phelps would perform well, for this was his usual procedure. The one thing all of his victims remembered of an encounter with the Marsh Hawk was the cry of a real hawk before he appeared; hence his title. But it was never the Marsh Hawk himself who uttered the cry. It was Phelps, and the cry of the hawk was the valet's signal for Simon to continue according to plan.

Simon didn't have long to wait. The stubborn rain had just begun to drip from the corners of his hat, making hollow splats on the broad, caped shoulders of his greatcoat, when he heard the valet's piercing cue. And he drew his pistol and rode out onto the highway, firing a shot in the air that stopped the listing black brougham that rounded the curve.

"Stand and deliver!" he shouted, his voice booming like thunder, amplified by the storm. Then, to the driver he charged, "You there, coachman, throw down your weapons and hold your hands high where I can see them."

A flintlock rifle came crashing to earth, landing in a puddle, and Simon's narrowed eyes—reduced to slits behind the half mask—glared through the rain-spattered coach window.

"You in there, step down!" he commanded.

The coach team shied and pranced in place, set in motion by the nervous right leader, nearest to Simon. With a careful eye upon the animal, Simon walked his own prancing mount closer as a slow hand pushed the coach door open and Rupert Marner stepped out on the sodden road, wearing a dour look of indignation.

"Well, well," Simon taunted, knocking Rupert's beaver off his head with the point of his pistol, "a born-to-the-purple toady, I'll be bound."

"H-how dare you stop this carriage? D-do you know who I am, you want-wit?" cried Rupert in falsetto, reaching too late to retrieve his hat, which had rolled upside down into the puddle between them, and joined the coachman's gun.

Simon ground out a guttural chuckle, meanwhile crushing the hat beneath his mount's prancing forefeet. He laughed outright as Rupert danced quickly away to spare his pantaloons a splattering with mud.

"Oh, aye, that I do—a fat chicken to be plucked," he replied, disguising his cultured voice. He slid out of the saddle, looped his mount's reins around a clump of bracken at the side of the road, and strolled closer. "Turn out your pockets, gov'nor," he charged, "and hand over your purse, that quizzing glass, stickpin—and the gold watch you're trying to conceal there, too."

"I'll see you swing at Tyburn for this," Rupert snapped, tossing the lot after the hat into the puddle.

"You will, eh?" Simon drawled. He took down a coiled length of rope from his saddle, advanced—pistol in one hand, rope in the other—and said through a dangerous tremor, "Off with the driving coat."

Rupert hesitated, but Simon pressed his pistol barrel against the man's corseted stomach.

"It would be a pity to spoil this with a bullet hole, such a fine wool coat; a real pity," he said, his thumb caressing the hammer.

Rupert stripped off the coat and tossed it down roughly.

"Now the tails, and the waistcoat—be quick about it!"

Rupert complied, his furious eyes raking Simon from head to toe, and hurled the blue superfine coat and embroidered ivory satin waistcoat at his feet.

"Now the shirt, and the rest—corset, boots, pantaloons. Everything, right down to the drawers—if you're wearing any, that is."

"You bastard!" Rupert snarled, removing his neckcloth and shirt with rough hands. "I've given you my jewels and purse—"

"Not nearly enough," Simon interrupted. "Get those boots off!"

Again Rupert hesitated, mumbling complaints under his breath, clearly unhappy about consigning his Hessians to the pile. He removed the right one, but when he tugged off the left boot he straightened up, swinging it.

Simon sidestepped the attack aimed to disarm him, and the boot missed its mark, dislodging his tricorn hat instead and sending it flying, exposing the tied-back hair he'd tucked underneath it. The heavy barrel of his pistol lowered hard across the viscount's face made an end to the incident. Howling, Rupert clutched his face. Simon, spewing a string of profanity he hadn't indulged in since his seafaring days, snatched up his hat and put it back on, hoping that Rupert hadn't noticed the queue he'd again tucked away.

He hauled Rupert to his feet and yanked him close to his face. "Now the rest," he commanded. "Unless you want help?"

Rupert obeyed until, barefoot and stripped to his drawers, he stood shivering in the rain.

Nudging him with the pistol, Simon shoved him up against
an oak tree at the edge of the road, and tied him to it.

"You there, unhitch those horses!" he shouted to the terrified coachman.

Hopelessly trembling, the little man climbed down and fumbled with the harnesses, Simon looking on, until the four
matched stallions were freed of the tangled leather tack. Then,
firing a shot in the air, Simon slapped the rump of the skittish
right leader, and the team galloped off in a shower of mud and
water churned up from the road by their high-flying hooves,
trampling Rupert's clothes in the morass underfoot.

Whimpering in spasms, the coachman backpedaled, slip-
sliding in the ooze as Simon stalked closer.

"Throw down those bags, and give me the horsewhip!" he
demanded of the coachman, gravel voiced.

The man scrambled back up to the driver's seat, reached behind, and tossed Rupert's two small travel bags and the whip to
the ground. Simon secured the bags to his mount's saddle, and
plucked up the horsewhip in a white-knuckled fist.

"Now get your arse down here," he trumpeted. "Into the
coach. *Move!*"

The panic-struck coachman climbed down, plunged into the
carriage, and shut the door after, whimpering like a woman.
Had he soiled himself? Sure as check. Simon laughed, but only
briefly, viewing the little man's eyes—round as an owl's—
gaping through the coach window, watching him crack the
whip and lower it full force to Rupert's back. Again and again
it struck its mark, until the scourging finally buckled Rupert's
knees. The viscount moaned, and it wasn't long before his posture collapsed altogether, his dead weight driving him down
along the tree trunk until he slumped there like a rag doll,
scarcely conscious. Satisfied, Simon tossed the bloodied whip to
the ground and gathered up every last piece of clothing from
the muddy road.

"You stay put," he warned the coachman, "unless you want a
dose of the same."

A terrified eruption of indistinguishable babbling answered

him. Simon paid it no mind. Tying Rupert's belongings into a neat bundle, he hefted that up alongside the travel bags he'd secured on his horse's saddle earlier, then mounted and rode off without a backward glance.

It wasn't until Rupert's shrill voice knifed through the quiet that the terrified coachman finally poked his gray head out of the carriage window.

"Get down out of there and get me out of this, Wilby, you lack-witted dolt!" his employer bellowed.

The coachman climbed out of the carriage and began loosening the rope binding Rupert to the oak tree. "The brigand's done a proper job," he said, sucking in his breath as he steadied him. "This needs attention. He's striped you badly, sir."

"A fine help you were!" Rupert snapped through a grimace.

"*Me*, sir? What on earth could I have done?"

"Never mind. He'll pay for it, mark my words."

"Was it the Marsh Hawk, sir?"

"It was. Fetch my clothes, you nodcock. And see if you can find that blasted team. We'll have to go back. I cannot continue to Scotland like this."

"Oh, they're long gone, sir. You'll not catch those beasts tonight in this storm."

Rupert loosed a spate of profanity that backed the coachman up a pace.

"My clothes, man! Fetch my clothes! I shall catch my death here," he bellowed.

"I . . . I can't, sir. He's taken them."

"The Hessians, too?"

The coachman nodded.

Another deluge of curses followed.

"Give me yours, then. Be quick, man!" Rupert demanded.

"*Mine*, sir?"

"Do you see anybody else about?"

"But, sir . . ."

"Come, come, the coat and breeches at least. I can hardly go about as I am."

The coachman peeled off his coat and soiled breeches, and handed them over reluctantly.

"Oh, yes, the whoreson will pay for this," Rupert vowed, wincing as he slid the coat over his raw back.

"There's many a nobleman on this coast who would like to see the Marsh Hawk pay, sir," said the coachman solicitously.

"Ahhh, but I have the advantage," Rupert returned.

"Sir?"

"I know who the blighter is! And in my own time, I'll hoist him with his own petard. He'll pay royally for this night's work, you have my oath upon that."

CHAPTER FOURTEEN

It was nearly noon when Jenna stirred and stretched awake in the mahogany four-poster, and her heart turned over in her breast when she realized she'd overslept. Her eyes flashed toward the indentation Simon's body had left in the feather bed beside her. There on the pillow lay a perfect moss rose, and a folded parchment. Jenna bolted upright and read:

> *Forgive me, my love, for not being here when you woke. Our wedding trip must wait. There is an urgent matter concerning one of my cottagers that I must resolve before we go. We will leave when I return on Wednesday. Until then, my Jenna, my heart is with you.*
>
> *Simon*

She was almost relieved. She couldn't have faced him then. She needed to order her thoughts first. They were still over-shadowed by suspicion; sleep hadn't changed anything in that regard.

She dressed in a morning frock of white sprigged muslin and went downstairs. Nuncheon had been laid out for her in the breakfast room. There were platters of aged Stilton and mature cheddar, loaves of Cook's cobbled, soda, and herb breads, along with salvers of spiced chicken, smoked salmon, and baked ham. But Jenna availed herself of tea only. She was too overset to think of food.

Looking on in utter dismay, the housekeeper delivered a spate of apologies for not having a breakfast tray brought to her room earlier, explaining that the earl had left word that she not be disturbed. Her wrinkled brow knit in a worried frown, she vowed to leave the nuncheon fare awhile, in case Jenna should have a change of heart.

It was the frazzled housekeeper who told her that Phelps had returned as mysteriously as he'd disappeared in the wee hours, only to turn right around and leave again with Simon shortly after. Jenna wondered why Simon had taken the valet this time on such a short mission, when he had left him behind for over three weeks while he went off to London with the St. Johns—especially since her pocket and its contents had never been re-covered. There was no explanation for that but that Rupert had taken it, which meant he knew their plans, and his interference was very probable. But those thoughts bothered her only mar-ginally. She was glad of the valet's absence. His incessant hover-ing had begun to make her extremely uncomfortable. She needed time to think, and to form some sort of plan. In order to do this she needed to be alone, with no interference. She was having enough trouble dealing with the distraction of Simon's passionate embrace in the mahogany four-poster, which col-ored her cheeks and sent waves of relived pleasure surging through her body each time it ghosted across her memory. This was all so new to her.

She decided to begin her search for the truth in Simon's dressing room off the bridal chamber, which was, in fact, the master bedchamber. The rooms several doors away that would, as was the custom, ultimately be hers when she returned from their honeymoon.

The chambermaids had already been and gone by the time she reached the suite. Though it was scarcely two in the after-

noon, the room was in semidarkness. The rain had ceased, but
the storm still generated bilious clouds that imprisoned the sun.

Holding a lighted branch of candles high, she poked her
head into the dressing room. The flickering light revealed a
large compartment with a definitive masculine presence, from
the Turkish carpet in the center of the floor, similar to the one
in the bedchamber next door, to the large mahogany armoire
casting tall shadows in the corner. A mullioned window separated a matching chiffonier and dressing table, where the usual
grooming implements were neatly assembled. Across the way, a
horseshoe desk squatted by the hearth, and a small drum table
beside the door held smoking tools, and a brandy decanter and
glasses. A separate alcove on the east housed a tub, and boot
chair, and beyond, Phelps's quarters.

Jenna took a deep breath. More than proving her suspicions,
she desperately wanted to refute them. For a moment, as she
stood scanning the room in the candlelight, she almost decided
to turn and leave and close the door upon the entire mystery.
Sadly, she knew that no matter what she discovered, it wouldn't
change her love for Simon—only her ability to live with him.
If he had done what she feared, she would have to leave him.
But the point of no return had passed; she'd crossed the threshold, and so she carried the candle branch to the wardrobe and
threw open the thick, carved doors.

Everything seemed in order. Simon's clothes were neatly
hung inside. She ran her hand along the collection of frock
coats, swallowtail coats, morning, dress, and riding coats, over-
coats, and waistcoats. She fingered the assortment of trousers,
cord breeches, pantaloons, pants—both loose and tight fitting—
and shirts of cambric, linen, and Egyptian cotton for every season and occasion. Disturbing the clothes stirred the exotic scent
of Simon's latakia blend laced with whiskey and rum that lingered about them. A draft lifted the aroma toward her nostrils,
and she quickly closed the wardrobe doors. That provocative
scent infiltrated her resolve and ignited her senses.

The chiffonier was the next target to suffer her scrutiny. One
by one she opened the drawers, evaluating the neat piles of

breeches, silk stockings, handkerchiefs and neckcloths. Aside from a velvet-lined gun case that held a brace of small flintlock pistols, nothing seemed out of the ordinary there, either.

She moved on to the horseshoe desk. The drawers and cubbyholes held the usual things—parchment, ink, quills, sealing wax, and the familiar scrollwork *R* seal. There were correspondences from the Naval Office, personal account books, and records. But one small drawer above the writing surface was locked. She searched the other drawers for the key but found nothing. Examining the locked drawer, she discovered that it had no keyhole. All at once she remembered a desk in her father's study with such a drawer that was accessed by pressing a button underneath the writing surface that activated a release spring. Bending, she groped beneath the desktop, running her hand along the smooth wood, and her fingers came to rest upon the mechanism that snapped the drawer open. She gave a start even though she expected it.

Holding the candles closer, she peered into the drawer, but all that lay inside was a large brass key on a faded red silk cord. The cord was crimped and open at the top as though it had been untied, suggesting that more than one key belonged on it, but though she searched the other drawers again, she found no other.

Jenna closed the drawer and glanced around the room again. She had overlooked nothing, and a flood of relief brought her posture down. It was accompanied by not a little guilt over her trespass, and she stole back to the bedchamber through the adjoining door and closed it behind her with a gentle hand, as though reverencing a sacrosanct cloister.

Nothing unusual was found during a similar search in that room, either, and she was just about to sink down on the bed and put her fears to sleep until the supper hour, when Molly came to tell her that Robert Nast had come to call.

"So much for not making a habit of it," Jenna murmured in an undervoice, though she regretted the uncharitable thought the moment it left her lips. Aside from Phelps, the vicar was closest to Simon, after all. Perhaps he could shed some light upon the situation. Engrossed in that possibility, she'd sailed halfway down the stairs before she thought to wonder how he knew she would still be there.

The lamps and candles had been lit in the breakfast room. As bleak as the day was, that was still the cheeriest spot in the house, with the flowers peeking through the garden wall brightening an eerie green darkness that had settled like a pall over the coast.

Watching the vicar fill his plate, Jenna was glad that Mrs. Rees had left the food there after all. He was obviously hungry, and it certainly wouldn't do to let the poor man eat alone. She cut a slab of Cook's round cobbled bread, speared a sliver of smoked salmon, and took her place opposite him at the table, where she poured them each a cup of tea from the fresh pot one of the footmen delivered.

"You picked a dreadful day to call," she said, taking in the festering sky bearing down upon the landscape through the window. "The storm isn't over, evidently."

"Simon wanted me to keep . . . eh, to come 'round," he said, stumbling over the words through a sip from his teacup.

He was about to say "keep an eye on her"—she knew it. Nothing had changed. Simon had taken Phelps, but the vicar had replaced him. She was still under guard. She was almost angry, but she didn't address it.

"You must have seen him earlier today, then," she probed instead, "or you would have thought we'd gone on to Scotland."

"Last night, actually, or rather early this morning. He had to pass by the vicarage on his way to the Pillsworths'. It was late, but I was still up, and he was most distressed about having to leave you like that. He asked me to stop by and cheer you up."

"The Pillsworths'," she puzzled. "His cottagers?"

"One of the families, yes. You met them at the wedding breakfast."

"I met so many," she defended. "I fear I shall never remember them all. Do they live far? I would have thought he'd be back by now."

"Not very. He tells me you two will be leaving for Scotland on Wednesday."

She nodded. The conversation seemed stilted, strained, not at all the easy flow she had enjoyed between them on his previous visits. Was it her imagination, or was he a jot more paradoxical than usual?

"Robert," she murmured, "when we spoke of my father last week, you said that the Marsh Hawk doesn't usually . . . that he doesn't brutalize his victims. How do you know that for certain?"

"I myself do not know anything 'for certain,'" he replied, shifting uneasily in his chair. He shrugged. "It's simply common knowledge, Jenna. The Marsh Hawk's exploits are legendary in these parts."

"But if he holds people up at gunpoint and steals—"

"Oh, he steals, but only from the very rich. And what he steals does not line his coffers; it finds its way to the needy—the poor disenfranchised who haven't a feather to fly with."

"You sound as if you condone such a thing."

"Of course I don't condone it," he hastened to say. "I'm only trying to explain the man in simple terms. Brutality doesn't appear to be in his nature. He seems more disposed toward spreading the wealth amongst those folk who are down at the heels, in dire need."

"Suppose he was opposed by one of his victims. Suppose they . . . resisted, as my father did. What then?"

"I cannot presume to get inside the man's head, Jenna," the vicar said on an audible breath. "I only know that, to my knowledge, he has never harmed anyone." He cleared his throat. "Yet."

"Is that why the land guards turn a blind eye, do you think?"

"I don't know that they do."

"Oh, yes! No attempt was ever made to apprehend the man responsible for my father's death. *None*. Either the man is paying them off, or they're afraid. If he is what you say, a gentleman bandit, some sort of . . . Robin Hood, what have they to fear?"

"Jenna, you have serious issues . . . because of your father," he said haltingly, "but I sense that there is more to it than what appears on the surface. You haven't mentioned any of this to Simon yet, as I asked you to, have you?"

"No," she said. "I haven't had the opportunity. There hasn't been time."

"Something is deeply troubling you. I've known that since our first conversation. You need to confide in Simon. But if not that, I wish you would confide in me. You can, you know; I told you that. Whatever you say will remain between us two. Whatever you tell me in the guise of confessor is protected under canon law. You have my word."

She pushed her teacup aside and shook her head no. Tears threatened, but she blinked them back, meanwhile toying with a piece of bread on her plate to avoid eye contact. How right he was about such conversations best indulged in over food.

"My father and I were very close, Robert," she said. "I am lost without him. Someone took him from me on a dark lonely road in south Cornwall. He was traveling at night in order to return from Truro in time for my birthday celebration. Do you remember when I told you that my father had a pistol similar to the one you frightened Rupert with that day out by the tower?"

The vicar nodded. He had lost his color, and his amber eyes were riveted to her.

"My father was carrying the pistol I spoke of the night he was set upon. When the highwayman tried to rob him, he drew it and the bounder took it from him, beat him with it, and then stole it, along with everything Father had on him, and left him for dead. He died in the wee hours on my birthday."

"Are you certain it was the Marsh Hawk?"

"Our driver seemed certain it was."

"Did the highwayman identify himself as such?"

"No, but—"

"Jenna, have you any idea how many highwaymen roam this coast? You cannot accuse a man without proof. Why, Simon himself was set upon just two months ago, and shot by a high-wayman who was definitely not the Marsh Hawk."

"W-where . . . did it happen?" she murmured. Paralyzed, she stared. The cold fingers of a chill crept over her scalp, and pin-points of white light starred her vision.

"Out on the old Lamorna Road."

"How can you be so certain that it wasn't the Marsh Hawk who shot him, Robert? Did Simon . . . did he recognize the . . . man?"

"Simon said not. He was younger, with a slight build—a newcomer evidently, and quite inept, though his blunder served him well enough for a novice. Simon would have bled to death if it weren't for Phelps, who came on just after. They were trav-eling together, but Phelps was delayed. His horse had thrown a shoe. Had he been at Simon's side, that highwayman would be dead today. Phelps is an excellent shot. He was Simon's batman while he served under Nelson, you know, and more than once he took it upon himself to step beyond his orderly duties, or Si-mon wouldn't be here today."

Jenna's hands were trembling, and she returned the morsel of bread she'd unconsciously been shredding to her plate as crumbs. So it was Phelps she'd heard rustling the brush that night. That being so, the valet was well aware of the situation; he was *part* of it. Her mind reeled back to the morning of the duel and the valet's concern. When he'd warned that it was too soon, it wasn't Simon's leg injury that worried him at all. It was the wound *she* had inflicted. Still, she had to be certain.

"Robert, I noticed that . . . Simon has a fairly recent wound in his shoulder, is that . . ."

The vicar nodded.

"I asked him about it. He wouldn't tell me."

"Because of your father. He didn't want to remind you. He worships you, Jenna."

A dry sob died in her throat as she rose from the table, pray-ing her legs wouldn't fail her.

"Forgive me, Robert. I . . . Forgive me," she murmured, and

fled the breakfast room with the words half-uttered before he
had a chance to glimpse her tears.

Jenna refused the dinner tray Mrs. Rees sent up to the master
bedchamber, and she sent Molly away when the maid came to
undress her. Her heart was breaking and her brain was numb.
Her worst fears were realized. There wasn't even any comfort
in the knowledge that she hadn't committed murder after all.
She threw herself across the counterpane on the mahogany
four-poster and sobbed herself to sleep.

Her dreams were dark and troubled, of highwaymen garbed
in black with smoking pistols drawn. Dreams of the night she'd
left the man she loved to die in the dirt of the road just as he
had left her father to die. Dreams of liquid sapphire eyes—blue
fire—searing her through the holes in a black silk half-mask,
and of those same eyes hooded with desire devouring her,
quickening her pulse, igniting her passion.

She awoke in the wee hours still dressed in her sprigged
muslin afternoon frock. It was wrinkled, the ribbonwork
crimped and spoiled. It was doubtful that even a flatiron could
save the delicate flowers and leaves that embellished the neck-
line and framed the décolleté. It didn't matter. Nothing mattered anymore.

The storm had passed over, and a bright wafer moon cast
slanted beams of silver light through the windowpanes. Dust
motes danced along the shafts. They traveled back and forth as
if they had a purpose. Would the night never end? It was the
longest she had ever endured, and the loneliest.

Her eyes were nearly swollen shut, and the quilt beneath her
face was damp and cold. That was what had awakened her: the
cold, wet cloth against the fever in her cheek. Her hair had
come down. The ivory combs that had held it in a neat high
coil were lost somewhere in the rumpled bedclothes. She didn't
bother searching for them.

After a time, the light dimmed in the room. Though it shone
still, the moon was no longer visible through the window
frame, and she lay in the bleak semidarkness before dawn. It was

no use. There would be no more sleep, and she struggled to her feet and went to the window. Below, the courtyard and the garden wall were visible, and beyond, the tall, dark skeleton of the tower in the orchard loomed eerily. She started to turn away and then turned back again. Had her eyes deceived her? No. There was a light in the tower.

Hypnotized, she strained in the darkness through smarting eyes toward the glow issuing from the lowest window, and then in a blink it was gone. She was just about to dismiss it as a will-o'-the-wisp, a figment of her imagination, when, in the fractured light of the waning moon, she caught sight of a figure emerging from the tower.

It was Simon. Even at this distance, she recognized his ragged gait in the moonlight.

Her heart leapt for fear that a confrontation was imminent. One look at her face and he would know that she had been crying, just as he knew that morning in the library. Her blotches would give her away. She couldn't let that happen now—not until she had decided what to do. But Simon did not cross the courtyard toward the house. Instead, he mounted the horse tethered in the groundcover that she hadn't even noticed until then, and rode off in the opposite direction. She followed him with her swollen eyes until he had disappeared amongst the trees in the orchard.

She began to pace. Her mind was racing. The course she traveled took her back to the window. All at once she gave a start and ran to her dressing room, where she opened her armoire and snatched out her new indigo cloak of Merino wool that the dressmaker had delivered along with the frocks for her wedding trip. The mornings were still cold and damp so close to the sea. Tossing it over her shoulders in transit, she burst into Simon's dressing room and triggered the spring that opened the secret drawer in the horseshoe desk. Her hands were shaking as she lit the candle on the desktop and stared down at the key inside the drawer. Could it be a spare key to the tower? A split second was all it took for her to blow out the candle and pluck out the key. Then, making no sound, she stole to the scullery, lit a lantern, and ran out into the gathering predawn mist.

The hems of her cloak and frock were drenched with the morning dew before she ever reached the courtyard. Their cold, wet heaviness clung to her ankles. Crossing the drive, she waded through the woodbine creepers to the narrow footpath that led to the tower. Her heart was pounding in her ears, and she swallowed the metallic taste of fear that threatened to close her throat and stop her breathing.

Slipping the key from the pocket in the lining of her cloak, she turned it in the lock, and the tower door creaked open on rusty hinges. She stepped inside on hesitant feet and glanced around. It was one room, with a spiral staircase hewn in the round walls that led to two upper levels steeped in darkness.

She raised the lantern. There seemed to be no visible signs of the structural damage Phelps had warned of, no cracks in the thick stone walls that were frosted with mildew, veined with cobwebs, and running with damp. The room was sparsely furnished, only a chifforobe, a large teakwood chest lurking in the shadows of the stone stairwell, and a horsehair lounge. The chest was locked, but the chifforobe was not. Her hand trembled as she opened it and held the lantern closer. It wasn't needed. From behind, the pearly glimmer of first light had begun to filter through the leaded panes illuminating its contents—the tricorn hat she remembered all too well, the silk half-mask, black cloak, coat, and trousers. It was all there, heavy with wetness. There were other like costumes as well, and in the first drawer, a mahogany case containing a brace of target pistols, long and sleek and deadly.

She set the lantern down, lifted one of the guns from the burgundy baize lining, and fingered the octagonal swamped barrel. She ran her hand over the walnut stock and checkered grip, and traced the floral engravings on the frizzen and cock. It was French, marked *Peniet Of Paris*. The other was identical. Both were well seasoned and had been fired recently.

Solemnly, she replaced the pistol in the case alongside the powder flask, mallet, and loading rod, and closed the lid. She opened the second drawer and stared down at a small flintlock pocket pistol, and something else wrapped in a piece of green baize. Unwrapping it, she unearthed a Sea Service pistol identical to that which Robert Nast had used in coming to her rescue. Could it be the same one? Her mind raced back to the odd exchange between the vicar and Phelps that day, and her breath caught in her throat. She wiped her moist palms on her cloak and shut the drawers.

The sun had cleared the horizon, flooding the coast with light. Streaming through the window at her back it broke over her shoulders, but it gave her no comfort, and spared her no warmth. It promised to be a beautiful day, but she resented the morning for shining upon her discovery, and her despair.

Jenna glanced around again, then blew the unnecessary lantern out, and left it. Closing the door, she turned the key in the lock, and trudged back across the courtyard, but she did not return to Kevernwood Hall. She went to the stable instead.

CHAPTER FIFTEEN

Jenna reached Holy Trinity Church, rising from a field of burgeoning bluebells on a little slope within sight of the quay, just as the sun spilled over the moor striking the rose window in the tall, square bell tower. It was the vicar himself who answered her frantic pounding on the vicarage door. Throwing it open, he stared, sliding his amber gaze over the bedraggled sight she was on his doorstep. She looked down in dismay at what he was staring at: She was covered with dust and grime from the tower. Her soiled frock and cloak were plastered wet to her legs and ankles. Her hair was falling loose from a center part over her shoulders, and her dirty hands and arms were pockmarked with rain spots. She could only imagine the condition of her face, between the rain and the dirt and the tracks of her tears.

She all but collapsed in his arms.

"Jenna!" he said through a gasp. "What's happened to you?"

"Robert, please . . . I know it's early, but . . . you said that if I ever—oh, Robert!"

"Let's get you inside," he replied to her stuttering; meanwhile he led her to the study, where he settled her in a leather wing chair beside the vacant hearth. "Mrs. Baines, my house-keeper, hasn't arrived yet this morning. Let me light a fire and fetch a pot of coffee . . . or tea. You need something hot. You're soaked through."

"No!" she cried, halting him as he bent over the wood box. "No, Robert. Let me do this while I still possess the courage . . . please. There *is* something I must confess. I should have long ago."

"Have you been . . . harmed?" he said. Turning back, he took her measure again.

Jenna shook her head that she hadn't been.

"All right, then, catch your breath, my dear," he soothed, offering his handkerchief.

"I've done something . . . unforgivable," she murmured, wiping her eyes.

"There is nothing unforgivable, Jenna, so long as there is true contrition. You look more than contrite to me, and to God, I have no doubt, whose assessment is the only opinion you need concern yourself with, after all."

Other than conducting her wedding ceremony, Jenna had never heard the vicar's official voice before. Thus far their conversations had all been light and cordial. This now was Vicar Robert Nast speaking, and she was not a little impressed.

"I don't know where to begin," she moaned.

"Take your time, Jenna. Nothing could be so grave as that face supposes."

"Oh, but it is, Robert . . . it *is*!"

"You know I'll help in any way that I can," he said, sinking down on the lounge across the way.

"There is no help for this. I don't know what to do! Simon will despise me if he learns of it."

"You have been . . . unfaithful?" he said, his voice charged with disbelief.

"No, no, never, Robert. Worse!" she blurted. "When Father was killed, I went to the land guards to seek justice, but they only laughed at me. Mother should have done so, but she and Father . . . well, they were never really close, you see. They had the sort of relationship I would have had if I'd married Rupert—a social disaster, like so many marriages among the ton."

The vicar hung on her every word, his eyes so intense, Jenna dared not meet them directly.

"The guards looked on me as an hysterical female, nothing more," she continued. "It made no difference that Lionel, our driver, provided them with a description. They were patronizing and insensitive, and I . . . I took retribution upon myself."

"*You*, but . . . how? Forgive me, I don't follow."

"Father had no sons to avenge him. It was up to me . . . at least that's how I saw it. If the law would not do anything, then I would. The plan was to apprehend the man myself and have him before the authorities to answer for Father's death and let right be done. Father would have been pleased. I told you he was a frustrated Bow Street Runner. It goes back to his days during the war with the Colonies, when he served as provost marshal. Robert, it never occurred to me that the plan was irrational . . . or that I might actually have to . . . use the pistol I carried."

"Go on," the vicar said in a voice she didn't recognize.

"I would slip out at night dressed as a highwayman and follow the post chaise routes. I didn't fear the law. They had turned blind eyes away from the situation."

"But, why dressed as a highwayman? I don't understand."

"I couldn't very well go out like this," she said, slapping at her skirt. "I would have put myself at risk—a woman, alone at night on the highway in the company of gallows dancers? Dressed as a highwayman, I hoped, at the very least, to disarm— to give the brigand enough pause for thought to allow me to get close enough to affect a capture. I knew I'd find the man sooner or later. The old Lamorna Road was the most dangerous, and the most notorious. I haunted the spots where robberies had occurred in the past, and one night . . . I came upon the highwayman—the one they call the Marsh Hawk—holding up a carriage. I . . . I interrupted him. Lamorna Jail was not far off, and it was my intent to see him there on foot at gunpoint, and let the guards deal with him. They could no longer deny me. I had caught him red-handed, after all."

The vicar swallowed. He had lost all color, and he didn't seem to be breathing.

"The man threw down his gun but not the spoils, and approached me offering to share," she went on. "He . . . had another pistol concealed beneath his greatcoat. When he drew it on me and fired, I fired back. I . . . I had no choice. I'm an excellent shot, Robert; Father taught me. He had no son to share his weapons collection with, and I did so want to please him. Then I heard someone coming and I fled. I . . . left him there! Robert, it was Simon, and I . . . left him there to die."

"So that is why you've never mentioned the Marsh Hawk to Simon?"

"No, not at first. It wasn't until I saw the wound in his shoulder that I began to wonder. And then yesterday, when you told me that a highwayman had—"

"Simon did not cause your father's death, Jenna," he interrupted.

"How can you possibly know that?" she flashed, her eyes filled with scorn and brimming with tears.

"Because I know Simon. You do not, or you wouldn't doubt. I told you once that two people ought to get to know one another before they—"

"You are aware of this!" she cried, her gasp cutting him short. "You know that Simon is the Marsh Hawk," she realized, vaulting to her feet. "You've known it all along!"

"I know he did not cause your father's death," he conceded. Getting up from the lounge, he approached her.

"The day when Rupert accosted me, you didn't have that pistol in the cabriolet at all. You took it from the tower, didn't you?" She gasped again, avoiding his outstretched hand. "You must have a key, too! You do, don't you? I just saw that pistol there in the chifforobe with three others, and Simon's . . . costumes. That business about your not being skilled with a gun was all a lie. You know exactly how to handle a pistol, don't you, Robert? My God, you're part of this!"

"You need to talk to Simon, Jenna. I've been telling you that since our first meeting."

"It's too late for that," a cold voice interrupted from the doorway.

They both spun toward the sound.

It was Simon.

"Simon, please . . . I asked you to let me handle this," the vicar pleaded, shaking his head in an emphatic no.

Simon stayed him with a raised hand and a look that turned Jenna's blood cold. His eyes then came around toward her, and the expression in them exuded more hurt than anger cooling their blue fire, which had darkened despite the shaft of bright sunlight flooding the study. Had he been there all the while? He must have been. Of course! This must have been where he'd ridden off to when she watched him leave the tower.

She looked away, unable to bear that terrible wounded look. Was the man awaiting an apology? She would not tender one. Though every fiber in her ached to run to him, to feel those strong arms folding her close, igniting her passion, she would not—could not—yield to the man who had robbed and bludgeoned her father, and left him for dead. Moaning her despair, she shoved the vicar aside with rough hands, fled past Simon into the corridor, and ran from the vicarage leaving the doors flung wide behind her.

Simon wheeled around and started after her, but the vicar reached him in two strides and clamped a firm hand around his rock-hard arm.

"No, let her go," he said, "Simon, how could you? You know confession is sacrosanct. I told you to leave it to me."

"Leave it to you, eh?" Simon thundered, ripping his arm free. "What in hell's been going on between you two behind my back?"

"I'm going to pretend I didn't hear that," the vicar said.

Simon stared. Pent-up anger and hurt and the bitter taste of betrayal roiled in him, launching a white-knuckled fist that hesitated just short of connecting with the vicar's rigid jaw.

"Go ahead, plant me a facer if it will make you feel better," the vicar said. Unflinching, he squared his posture in obvious anticipation.

Simon raked his hair back from a moist brow and balled his hand into a fist again, this time at his side.

"Talk!" he seethed. "And you had better make it good."

"What?" the vicar said. He popped a strangled grunt. "You heard all that just now. I was just as taken aback as you were."

"But you knew there was . . . something."

"Yes, I did," he said, giving a deep nod. "I knew she suspected the Marsh Hawk of her father's murder, and I knew she was mistaken. I tried to convince her of that without overstepping my bounds with either one of you, and I told her repeatedly to speak with you about what was troubling her. I can see now why she didn't. Simon, she thinks you murdered her father!"

"You know that's absurd."

"*I* do, yes, but I don't matter. You've got to make *her* see it, or your marriage is over before it's begun."

Simon clouded. All at once the pure ecstasy of Jenna's soft, naked body, molded to the contours of his own, visited him. The heady scent of rosemary and lavender threaded through his memory—her scent; it overpowered him. He relived the eager abandon with which she let him approach her innocence, with which she let him take it. In spite of himself, his loins tightened.

"You should have let me go after her," he snapped.

"No, Simon, not like this. Not till you've calmed down. You're a headstrong, bungling fool in a passion, and enough harm's been done as it is."

"You haven't let me finish," Simon returned. "You should have let me go after her while I was still of a mind to do so; it's too late for that now."

"Simon, you've got to."

Simon shook his head.

"But . . . why? You two have got to talk this out. She knows who you are. Are you mad? You never even made an effort to defend yourself—not one word!"

"I shouldn't *have* to. Not to her," he flashed. "She should know better. Do I come off as the sort to bludgeon old men to death—military men, at that? You know why the Marsh Hawk rides, and you know who he targets."

"But she doesn't! That's why you've got to set her straight—and quickly. You should have made a clean breast of it long before now. Do you want to swing at Tyburn? Hah! I'll likely swing right alongside you, for complicity, just as I've said all along. If you don't give a tinker's curse for your own neck, you might have a care about mine. She knows I'm involved now as well."

"If you're so worried over your neck, then *you* talk to her," Simon ground out through a deep, throaty chuckle. "I'm off to London."

"To lick your wounds?" the vicar snapped.

"Don't preach to me, Rob, I'm at the end of my tether. I warn you!"

"You never should have gotten into this Marsh Hawk madness. I warned that you would rue the day you took to highway robbery, no matter how noble the cause."

"Yes, well, don't worry. I absolve you of your complicity."

"That isn't funny, Simon."

"Maybe not, but you have to admit it's in keeping with the 'sacrosanct' flavor of the morning."

"Simon, put yourself in Jenna's place."

A mad laugh replied.

"Be reasonable here. It wasn't personal. She didn't know it was you she gunned down on that road."

"I'm not leaving because of that. I can almost forgive that she bloody near killed me. She was trying to avenge her father, and she evidently didn't set out to do murder." He breathed a ragged sigh. "You know, I almost envy her resolve . . . and that she had a father worth avenging. No, I can't fault her for that."

"*What*, then, for God's sake?"

"This here today wounds me far more deeply than that bullet ever did, Rob. She should have come to *me* with that confession, not you. That's what's stuck in my craw. That's what's ripping a hole in my heart, and that is what I don't believe I can ever forgive."

CHAPTER SIXTEEN

Jenna had no idea where she was going, only that she must leave Kevernwood Hall posthaste, and she packed as though her very life depended upon it. She would not take any of the lovely things Simon had given her, only her own frocks and garments; those which her mother had delivered in the portmanteau she had left behind at Moorhaven Manor while fleeing with Simon after the duel.

She stared down at her mud-soaked, sprigged muslin frock. It was one of the lovely creations that Simon had commissioned the dressmaker, Olive Reynolds, to make for her. It took only seconds to wriggle out of it. She rummaged through the pile of rumpled clothing she had heaped on the bed and snaked out her riding habit. For a moment she crushed it close to her breast. She remembered Simon's strong arms holding her in that habit in the conservatory when he proposed to her, remembered the gentle strength in his hands caressing her through the thin Merino wool, arousing her, leading her to the brink of ecstasy. But it was only a brief reverie. Reliving those steamy memories stirred something awake inside that caused the habit to jump from her hands and join the sprigged muslin at her feet as though it had caught fire and burned her.

She never wanted to see it again.

Choosing instead a dove gray traveling costume that held no memories and invoked no passions, she struggled into it and continued packing.

Her heart was numb. The awful look in Simon's eyes haunted her—the hurt and the anger in his blue-fire stare. That look had run her through. She would take it to her grave. He hadn't even tried to defend himself. He hadn't even made an attempt to deny his guilt. His silence damned him. It had broken her heart, and her grief was so overwhelming that she couldn't even rejoice in the fact that she hadn't done murder after all on that dark night which seemed a lifetime ago.

She had never felt so alone. In the space of a few short hours, she had lost both her husband and her confidant. All at once the dimity frock she'd been folding slipped from her hands. She sank down on the edge of the bed beside the overflowing portmanteau and stared through the tall mullioned panes toward the light streaming in through the window. It was golden and warm pressed up against the glass. How dare it shine upon her sorrows? The rampant thoughts banging around in her brain were so hopelessly bizarre a jumble that she groaned aloud under the weight of them—not the least of which were: Where would she go? What was she to do? Though she loved Simon more than life itself, how could she ever live with him now? More poignantly, how could she ever live *without* him?

When the knock came, she vaulted off the bed as though she'd been launched from a catapult, and stood trembling head to toe, her eyes riveted to the barred door of her chamber.

"Are you in there, my lady? 'Tis Molly. Horton says you've had the coupe brought 'round. He says you're leavin'! It's that upset, he is! Will you be taking me with you, my lady, and should I pack?" The knock came again. "Are you all right, my lady? Why is the door locked? You're scaring me now. Horton says you were that overset, and Barstow won't hear of any of the other grooms taking you. He's sitting out there in that coupe himself, yes ma'am, he is!"

Jenna crammed the rest of her things into the portmanteau, slammed it shut, and shrugged on the spencer that matched her costume. Molly knocked again, more urgently, and Jenna snatched up the portmanteau, unbolted the tall, gilded door, and swept past the nonplussed maid teetering on the threshold.

"My lady! Am I not to go with you?" the girl shrilled.

"No, Molly, you shall not," Jenna said with conviction, starting toward the staircase. "I've no right to take you from Kevernwood Hall. Your place is here."

"But, my lady, surely you aren't going for good?"

"I'm sorry," said Jenna over her shoulder as she struggled down the stairs with the portmanteau.

"But you can't just run off all on your own, my lady. 'Tisn't proper—'tisn't safe!" the maid pleaded. Having relieved her of the portmanteau, the girl struggled along with it close on her heels. "Where will you go? Who'll care for you?"

"I assure you I'm well able to take care of myself. I'm going . . . home," Jenna decided, choking back tears. Thistle Hollow was the last place she wanted to go, but she had no other options.

"You *are* home!" said a booming voice that stopped her in her tracks halfway down the staircase.

It belonged to Robert Nast, who stood, arms akimbo, blocking the landing at the bottom of the stairs.

Jenna hesitated only briefly before she continued to descend.

"Don't try to stop me, Robert," she warned. "Please stand aside."

"We have unfinished business, Jenna," he returned. Taking her arm in one hand, meanwhile relieving Molly of the portmanteau with the other, he dismissed the maid with a nod and said to Jenna, "After I've had my say, you can go with my blessing . . . if you're still so inclined. But hear me out, you will—now come."

With no more said, he steered her along the corridor to the

conservatory despite her protests, and planted her squarely on the selfsame wicker love seat where Simon had proposed to her. How cruel was the man? Did he not know what she was suffering? Why didn't he just let her go? He knew it was hopeless. He knew Simon was the Marsh Hawk. He'd known it all along.

"Robert, please," she murmured, blinking back tears. She would be red with blotches in a minute if he didn't let her go. "I trusted you and you deceived me—betrayed me," she cried. "We have nothing to say to one another."

"I haven't betrayed you, Jenna," the vicar said wearily, sinking down beside her on the love seat. "I've bungled badly trying my best to serve you both separately. That was wrong of me—terribly wrong. I've hurt you both instead, and I shall never forgive myself for that."

"None of that matters any longer, Robert. It's over."

"Only if you let it be."

She stared into the vicar's soulful amber eyes. They seemed so sincere. No matter how he saw it, he *had* betrayed her. She could give no other name to it. He knew. All the while he pretended to be her friend, he *knew*. He knew exactly what she was suffering, what she was wrestling with, and he had let her go right on suffering. He'd *married* them knowing. She was the complete want-wit for allowing those traitorous soulful eyes to flummox her so thoroughly.

"I told you from our first meeting that the Marsh Hawk did not murder those he robbed, Jenna," he said, as though he read her thoughts. "Nor did he ever manhandle or abuse them. I told you that his mission was a benevolent one. I call that not deception."

"What . . . 'benevolence' could possibly come from highway robbery, pray?"

"I told you how passionately Simon championed those with pockets to let, especially those among them that have been cashiered-out by the military. Simon took the issue to the proper authorities, but nothing to speak of was done. Whether it be the poor king's madness, or the Prince Regent's indifference—in that his attention seems to be centered . . .

elsewhere, to put it delicately—and since the aristocracy will not take a step but that the Regent lead them, Simon took matters into his own hands. What he steals from the aristocracy benefits those down-at-the-heels souls that have been disenfranchised and forgotten. These include the unfortunate conscriptees—men taken by force from public houses, gambling hells, and, yes, brothels—who have meanwhile had their lands seized for nonpayment of taxes while they were in His Majesty's service on other shores.

"Many of the wives of such men have been transported, Jenna, and their children incarcerated in workhouses, for their having sunk to stealing and prostitution to feed their families. Many of the mustered-out men who served this country well—many maimed and wearing the medals they've earned—are begging in the streets of London and other cities in this land as we speak. Some of those men fought alongside Simon at Copenhagen. Many fought beside Nelson at Trafalgar, and God alone knows how many fought beside Wellington—*still* fight beside him and soon will join their number. These are Simon's cause."

"And you condone his methods?"

"No, I do not. I never have, but Simon is my friend, Jenna, and I will stand beside him in whatever madness he employs, because I know his heart, and I know that he would do the same for me. And, yes, I will protect that bond however I have to. I know what he's sprung from—what he's risen above, if you will. He has lived his life thus far for others. What he has done for Evelyn and Crispin doesn't even scratch the surface of the man. Did you know that he has funded two veterans' hospitals—sold plantations in the Indies, and holdings in the Highland to do it, and invested half of his fortune besides in these unfortunates and their families? No. And you never will from Simon's lips. You have no inkling of the measure of the man you've married."

"Still . . ." Jenna responded, shaking her head.

"Jenna, Simon had a dreadful childhood. His father was a mean-spirited, unfeeling tyrant, as stingy with his affections as he was with his wealth, who hung all his hopes on Simon's elder brother, Edgar—his heir. When Edgar disappointed him, he didn't turn to Simon, whom he'd kicked aside; he turned in on himself and died a miserable, embittered old man. I conducted his funeral ceremony. Simon was the only soul in attendance."

"And you've come here now to plead his case, is that it?" Jenna said icily. "He *has* no case, Robert. Simon is the Marsh Hawk. He didn't even try to deny it!"

"Yes, he is the one they call the Marsh Hawk," the vicar returned, "but the Marsh Hawk is not responsible for your father's death, Jenna. And, no, I haven't come to plead his case. Speaking with you is entirely my idea. Simon doesn't know. I've come with a message for Phelps, actually."

"Then you'd best deliver it. I have to go. I want to leave before Simon returns."

"Simon isn't returning," the vicar said, getting to his feet. "He's on his way to London. I have come to instruct Phelps to join him en route."

Jenna's face fell. Something wrenched her stomach as though a fist had clenched around it, and her lower lip began to tremble. Why should she care? She was running from him, after all, wasn't she? Why did this news seize her heart in such an icy grip?

"Jenna, you and Simon love each other," the vicar said, interrupting her thoughts. "You need to talk this through. Running away is never the answer."

"Tell that to Simon!" she retorted. "He has a head start on me, so it seems."

"I just did."

"Well then, there it is!" Jenna snapped, throwing up her hands.

"He isn't angry that you shot him, you know. He's hurt that you could actually believe him capable of murder, and that you didn't trust his love for you enough to make your confession to him instead of to me."

Jenna rose from the love seat as steadily as her trembling

knees would allow. "I have to go," she said. "The coupe is in the drive, and I don't want to keep Barstow waiting."

"Where will you go?"

"Home . . . to Thistle Hollow. I shall hire a coach in Newquay, and Barstow will return with the coupe straightaway."

"You're taking Molly, of course."

"Molly is part of Simon's household," she said, her voice frosty. "I want nothing of his, Robert."

"But . . . it isn't safe, a woman alone . . . unchaperoned! There are dangers . . . there are . . . there are—"

"Highwaymen?" Jenna said. She flashed a cold smile. "Nothing I could possibly suffer at their hands could compare to that which I have suffered at the hands of my 'friends.' Now, if you will excuse me? I don't want to keep Barstow waiting."

"Jenna, are you going to . . . Will you expose him?"

She had been expecting that question, but it didn't make it any easier to hear, especially from Robert. That she held his words in contempt was evident; she made no effort to hide it. For a long moment, she stared at him through angry tears.

"Will you?" he urged during her silence.

"Good bye, Robert," she murmured with disdain, and fled.

CHAPTER SEVENTEEN

It was dark in the taproom at the Heatherwood Arms, where Simon waited out of patience in a shadowy corner, nursing a flagon of bitter black ale. Was he nursing his wounds as well, as the vicar had accused? Possibly, though he wouldn't admit to it then, not even to himself, as he absently drew on his clay pipe. It tasted flat—as bitter as the ale. Not even his custom-blended tobacco satisfied. He wondered if it ever would again.

The barmaid across the way was vying for his attention—a furtive glance, a well-displayed bosom strategically arranged to catch the lamplight. There was a time when he might have accepted the invitation in those doelike brown eyes trained so seductively upon him, but that was all a very long time ago, before he'd fallen in love with a mysterious beauty with hair like spun gold in the setting sun and eyes that shone like mercury.

All at once Jenna's image passed before him and he recalled those quicksilver eyes dilated with desire, glazed with a passion that he alone had awakened. Oh, how she had loved him. With what unfettered abandon had she reverenced—yes, that was the word—*reverenced* him. No lover had ever reverenced him before. And he knew with a sinking heart that he would never again know so complete a surrender of rapturous innocence. What heaven it had been to be drenched in the dew of her first awakening. No woman would ever again receive him with so pure and complete a submission to the very essence of love.

A soft moan escaped him, and he drowned it in a rough swallow of the Heatherwood Arms' infamous black ale. He grimaced as it burned all the way down to the empty, growling pit of his clenched belly, mercifully cooling the fire that those bittersweet memories had kindled in his loins. The notorious brew wasn't potent enough, however, to extinguish that fire altogether. Something primeval still stirred in the very core of him, reliving that ecstasy, and he shifted uneasily in the chair that creaked with his sleek, muscular weight.

He took another swallow—just to be sure that heat was doused—and grimaced again. No, not quite. And if this poisonous stuff couldn't do it, he was doomed. Would nothing quench the damnable fire? In that wretched, turgid moment, if he were a betting man, he would have wagered heavily against it.

Phelps was nearly upon him before he saw the straight backed valet threading his way through the crowd. He tapped the dead ash from his pipe against a salver on the table, and tucked the pipe away inside his waistcoat pocket as he got to his feet, scudding the chair out behind him.

"Well, it's about time!" he complained. "What kept you, man? It will be dark in an hour, and we've a long ride ahead. Who's driving the coach?"

"I haven't got the coach, my lord," said Phelps. "There is a graver press."

"What 'press'? What's happened now?" he queried, with a hitch in his stride as he led the valet toward the taproom door.

"The countess has taken it upon herself to run off to Thistle Hollow, my lord."

"And?"

"*Alone,*" Phelps pronounced, his eyebrow inching up in its inimitable manner.

"Bloody hell!" Simon spat through clenched teeth, steering the valet outside into the warm, late afternoon haze. "How has she gone, Phelps?"

"Barstow drove her into Newquay in the coupe. Mister Nast said she planned to hire a coach there to take her on to Launceston."

"Alone and unchaperoned—with night coming on? And he couldn't stop her, go after her?"

"Evidently not, my lord. A burial has detained him, that's why he sent me to bring you. He was most distressed, my lord. He said for me to tell you that no matter what your feelings for my lady, neither of you needs her meeting with foul play upon your conscience. Begging your pardon, but what did he mean by that, my lord?"

"Never mind!" Simon snapped. "Go round back, fetch my horse and follow me. I'm taking yours. We've got to make some time by nightfall."

"Oh, no, my lady, I'll not hear of it!" Barstow barked, hat in hand. Decked out in full coachman's regalia from red woolen scarf and caped coat, to cord knee breeches and painted top boots, he was facing Jenna beside the carriage house at the coaching station in Newquay. His outburst had turned more than one head as he argued with her. "I know my place right enough," he said to her indignant sputtering, "but I also know my duty, and you'll not be going on to Launceston in the dead of dark all on your own. Why, the master'd kill me if I let you! He'd skin the hide clean offa me if I ever let you go off alone with night coming on. You was raised here in Cornwall, my lady, you know night comes quick on the coast. You see that sky up there? It'll be black as coal tar pitch in an hour."

Jenna stamped her foot in defiance. She didn't want Simon's coupe or his groom or *anything* that belonged to him. That was all supposed to end right there at the Newquay Coaching Station. She needed no reminders of her broken heart.

"You don't seem to understand," she said, aiming for restraint in her fractured tone. "I'm not coming back, Barstow. I'm going home for good."

"That's between you and the master," he said with a shrug. "This here is between you and me, and I'll not have you spoil my sleep for worrying over what's become of you. I'm taking you on to Launceston, and that's the end of it. I've got old Effie up top; she's loaded and at the ready, and I'll use her if needs must to get you where you're going safely. It's a pretty rough stretch between here and Launceston, my lady. If I'd known this was what you was planning, I never would have stopped. I'd have drove right through!"

"Barstow, please," Jenna pleaded. "I know you mean well, and I bless you for that, but I really want to go on alone."

"You've got enemies, my lady, I seen it myself, and you can't deny it," the groom argued. He folded his arms and thrust his bearded chin out stubbornly. "You can hire yourself a carriage if that's your pleasure; I can't stop you, but you'll be wasting your blunt, since I'm going to follow right along after you. So you might as well get right back into this coupe here."

As frustrated as she was, Jenna almost smiled. Barstow had an endearing quality about him, she had recognized and bonded with it at their first meeting. His incontrovertible demeanor told her that he meant every word. Considering his point, she had to admit that his presence was a comfort, and so was his trusted flintlock, Effie. The light was fading fast. Soon it would be full dark. She dared wait no longer to set out for the south, and she took a ragged breath that brought her posture down.

"Very well, Barstow, you win," she conceded.

"Give me your valuables," he said, holding out his leathered palm; it looked as though it belonged on a man twice his age.

"Excuse me?" she murmured.

"Them earbobs there, and your rings, my lady," said the groom. "I'll not lie to you, the roads hereabouts are crawling with thatchgallows. Unless you want to be donating those doodads to the first brigand that stops us, you'd best let me hide them away up top."

She glanced down at her hands. She had meant to leave her jewelry behind with everything else Simon had given her, but she'd left in such a hurry she'd forgotten all about it. She took off her earbobs, and the beautiful ruby and diamond ring Simon had slipped on her finger when he proposed, and handed them over without batting an eye. But when she came to her wedding ring, she hesitated, clouding, before she yanked it from her finger and thrust it toward him also.

"Better give me what's in that reticule, too," Barstow prompted, gesturing. She held the purse out toward him, but he fended it off with a raised hand. "No, my lady, leave a pound or so, and whatever coins you've got in it, and give me the rest to hold for you. If we are stopped and the gallows dancers find your purse empty, they're bound to be suspicious, and it could get ugly. It's best to let them have a little if it comes down to it, rather than suffer a search of your person for the lot they think you've put by, if you take my meaning, my lady."

Jenna gulped and handed him the notes. Was that the sort of thing Simon would stoop to on his forays? She shuddered to wonder, but the picture it painted in her mind caused jealousy to arise right along with disdain.

"There's a space under the seat—a false bottom so to speak," Barstow explained. "The master had one built inta all his coaches. Your notes and gewgaws will be safe enough up top under my arse. Begging your pardon, my lady."

Jenna didn't reply. The blood drained away from her face suddenly. He was right, of course. It all seemed like a nightmare, and she prayed that she would wake beside her husband in the spacious mahogany four-poster. She prayed there would be no wound in his shoulder, no highwayman costume in the tower, and no pistols—still warm, smelling of gunpowder—in the drawer of the chifforobe there. But the nightmare was real, and she climbed into the coupe and leaned back against the padded leather squabs in defeat, while the groom snapped the whip and set the horses in motion.

It wasn't long before darkness fell and Barstow lit the carriage lamps. Clouds hid the moon, bringing to Jenna's mind another night, dark and still—perfect for highway robbery. Cold chills played along her spine upon making that comparison. She couldn't help dwelling upon Barstow's precautions. Was she being unduly overset and he overly cautious? She wanted to believe it, but she still wished she had the sort of security one of the weapons from her father's collection would have provided.

Nothing was visible through the isinglass windows of the coupe. Tall oaks and ancestral chestnut trees formed a natural arbor over the road for long stretches, barring what stingy spurts of moonlight the clouds begrudged now and then. There wasn't even the flicker of lantern glow from the coaches of fellow travelers to comfort her; the road ahead and behind was deserted.

Now and again she heard Barstow's scratchy voice asking after her comfort as the milestones zipped by unnoticed in the dark. In spite of herself, she was glad that she'd given in and let the faithful groom convey her after all. She felt safe with him in the driver's seat, and it wasn't long before the rhythmic clopping of the horses' hooves and the swaying of the coupe as it sped over the highway began to nudge her toward sleep. Finally, she gave in to it.

Soon, however, another sound bled into that sleep, touching off strange dreams of cracking whips and mad commands to horses that seemed suddenly to fly, their hooves scarcely touching the ground. All at once it seemed as if she were cast adrift in a rocking boat instead of the compact two-seater coupe, listing this way and that as it careened around the treacherous hairpin curves of her dream. Then came the gunshots at close range, and Jenna tumbled out of her nightmare and into heart-stopping reality as she pitched forward off the seat and landed in a heap on the floor of the carriage as it pulled to a creaking, shuddering halt in the darkness.

"Stand and deliver, I say!" a strange voice boomed gruffly, close beside the shuddering coach window.

The acrid stench of gunpowder rose in her nostrils. Barstow's voice was barking something that she couldn't make out over the frantic snorts and nervous shrieks of the horses prancing and pawing the ground. Before she could collect herself and regain her seat, the coach door was yanked open by a black-gloved hand, and she was lifted to the ground.

"Let go of me!" she shrilled, struggling against the man's vise-like grip. She cried out in earnest as he jerked her to a standstill.

"Make no resistance, my lady!" Barstow warned her from the driver's seat. "Do as the bounder says!"

"Wise words," said the highwayman to Barstow. "I told you to get down from there! Step lively, old man."

"Do you want to get trampled?" Barstow shouted, struggling with the reins as the horses reared. "These horses will bolt if I do!"

"Toss down your weapons, then!"

"I've got no weapons. Hurry it up and get on with it. I can't hold these beasts, I'm telling you."

All at once the pistol fired again, and Barstow's low-crowned coachman's hat went flying as the bullet ripped a gaping hole in its wide brim.

"The next will put your lights out," the highwayman snarled, his voice raised over Jenna's scream. "Now, like I said, throw down your weapons."

Jenna's heart sank as Effie came crashing to earth at the highwayman's feet.

"That's all I've got," Barstow shouted. "Come and see if you don't believe me."

"Keep those hands high, then," the man charged, meanwhile shoving Jenna's bonnet back from her face with the tip of his pistol barrel. He raked her with familiar eyes.

She gasped, watching the highwayman slip his pistol into his greatcoat pocket and withdraw another gun—one more familiar to her. Even in the darkness, with no light but the coach lamp to illuminate it, she recognized it at once. She'd seen it often enough in her father's gun case in the trophy room at Thistle Hollow. It was the army service pistol that had bludgeoned him to death. There was no question. She recognized the notches and initials her father had carved in the stock.

She took the man's measure then, and her breath caught

again. It could have been Simon standing there. The tricorn hat and dark clothes were nearly identical to those she'd discovered in the round tower in the orchard at Kevernwood Hall. Was the man emulating Simon—riding on his coattail, as it were? Was he sullying the Marsh Hawk's benevolent reputation to safeguard himself from making his own? Whatever the situation, it was easy to see how Lionel had mistaken this brigand for the true Marsh Hawk. The likeness was substantial.

The man's dark eyes held her relentlessly. He smelled unwashed, and of strong whiskey; his breath was fetid with it. He groped for her reticule and ripped it from her arm. Examining the contents, he did not remove the notes and coins inside, but rather crammed the little purse into his pocket and examined her hands for jewels.

"I have nothing else," she snapped in defiance.

"Nothing, eh?" the man scoffed. "Off with the spencer. I'll see for myself, me lady.' "

She fumbled with the buttons on her jacket. Impatient, the highwayman helped her out of it with rough, pinching hands, removed her bonnet, and spun her around. Pearl combs held her neat chignon in place. He ripped them out, and her hair tumbled over her shoulders.

"Nothing, eh? What's these, then, me lady?"

"Take them!" Jenna shrilled.

"I've *got* them, little ladybird. What else have ye got, eh?"

"N-nothing else. *No!* Let me go!"

"Here! Let her be!" Barstow erupted. "Have my watch, 'tis gold."

The groom tossed it down, and the highwayman caught it in flight.

"Thank ye!" he blurted, tossing it in his hand before he jammed it into his pocket fob, alongside Jenna's reticule.

If she hadn't been so paralyzed with fear, she would have recognized the earth trembling beneath her thin leather slippers as the vibration of horses' hoofbeats. Instead, she took it for her own helpless trembling, until another pistol shot rang out, ripping through the darkness.

Muttering a string of curses, the highwayman let her go, snatched his horse's reins draped over the branch of a sapling by the roadside, swung himself into the saddle, and galloped off into the night.

Jenna scarcely blinked before Simon leapt off his lathered mount and reached her side in two long-legged strides. She could have sworn he didn't even limp. Phelps was nothing more than a blur streaking past them in pursuit of the highwayman, his own pistol blazing.

"Are you all right, my lady?" Barstow queried, attracting Simon's attention. "I did my best to outrun the bounder. When I seen he'd stopped another coach up around the bend, I spun this buggy clean around—almost upset her tryin' to put some distance between us. But he was too quick for me."

It wasn't until then that Jenna realized they were facing in the opposite direction, toward Kevernwood Hall. Choked with emotions, not the least of which were raw fright, relief, and gross embarrassment, she read the look in Simon's blue-fire eyes, and looked away. They were searing her at close range, and all she could manage was a nod.

Though he stood so close that his warm breath puffed on her face, Simon hadn't touched her. One glance toward the white-knuckled fists clenched at his sides made her glad of it. When he spoke, it was not to her, but to Barstow, though it took a moment for him to switch his glower toward the driver's seat during the delivery.

"You and I have issues"—he launched toward the groom, whose brow had become pleated in a frown—"and you can bet your blunt we'll have them out when we get back to Kevernwood Hall."

The last place Jenna wanted to go was Kevernwood Hall, and a protest caught in her throat. If he noticed, he showed no evidence. Taking her elbow, he steered her unceremoniously toward the coach without a word.

She was just climbing in when Phelps rode back alongside. Simon jutted a granite jaw in the valet's direction, posing a silent question, and the look ran Jenna through. She'd seen it before, in the anteroom at Moorhaven Manor, when she'd come around after she'd fainted; Simon had addressed Lord Eccleston with that look. It had thrilled her then. The memory brought tears to her eyes now. She refused to let him see them.

"I lost him in the wood, my lord," Phelps said, with a regretful wag of his head. "His mount was not so worn to a raveling as this beast of yours underneath me."

Simon snatched the reins of the horse he'd arrived astride, and thrust them toward the valet, directing him with a nod, and followed Jenna into the coupe. Taking his seat opposite her, he struck the roof of the coach a vicious blow with his pistol barrel, signaling Barstow to move on. Then, leaning back against the squabs, he folded his arms across his broad chest, his eyes smoldering toward hers.

Jenna averted her gaze, unable to bear that riveting look.

"Are you . . . hurt?" he queried after a painfully long hesitation, in a tone that utterly contradicted the feral look in those sizzling eyes. "He didn't . . . harm you?"

"No," she murmured emptily, shaking her lowered head. "He was . . . the one."

CHAPTER EIGHTEEN

"Am I to be kept prisoner here, my lord?" his wife asked coolly as Simon ushered her inside the master bedchamber at Kevernwood Hall.

He did not cross the threshold. He hadn't spoken another word to her the whole distance to the estate. Halfway there, Robert Nast joined them on horseback, at which point Simon left the coupe and rode behind it alongside Phelps and the vicar the rest of the distance. He needed time to order his thoughts, which were all tangled up with his urges.

"You cannot think to keep me here against my will," she said to his silence.

"I prefer to call it 'protective custody,'" he returned succinctly. "It's clear that you aren't able to manage on your own."

"How dare you!" she shrilled.

"Oh, I dare, my lady? I *have* to dare. I cannot afford the luxury of trust here now. Too much is at stake."

"You think I mean to expose you," she breathed.

"Suffice it to say, my lady, that until I've taken steps to protect myself, I cannot afford to take the chance that you might."

"You do not know me very well, my lord."

"And you, my lady, do not know me at all!"

Blue eyes dueled with silver. What had ever made him think he could lead a normal life—marry, and live a peaceful existence? Yes, he needed time. Those beautiful eyes—even in anger—dissolved his heart.

"Good night, my lady," he said, the words clipped and unequivocal.

Closing the door to shut that quicksilver stare out of his view, he turned the key in the lock. Ignoring the frantic pounding of Jenna's fists and shrill protests from the other side, he stalked off down the corridor toward the staircase, where Phelps met him at the landing.

"I've locked the dressing room doors as you requested, my lord," he said loftily, after his fashion. "Are you sure this is wise?"

"Wise?" Simon blurted, incredulous. "Good God, man, it's imperative—at least until I've thought this coil through."

"As you say, my lord."

"You don't approve," Simon observed, noting the valet's telltale raised eyebrow.

"It's not for me to approve or disapprove, my lord," Phelps returned. He ground out a guttural, humorless laugh. "I just don't think it's practical." He inclined his head toward the master bedchamber door. "She'll bring the house down with that god-awful caterwauling."

"Let her," Simon replied, cracking a grim smile. He clapped the valet on the shoulder and continued down the stairs. "She'll keep," he said. "Right now, Rob is awaiting me in the library, and then I have a few choice words for Barstow."

"Will you want me to draw your bath, my lord?"

"Bath?" said Simon, wheeling around on the step. "There won't be time for that, old boy. Meet me at the stable. We're going to try and find that whoreson."

Jenna's hands were red and smarting when she finally gave up her assault on the master bedchamber door. She sank down on the bed, her posture hunched in defeat, flexing her fingers and soothing the knuckles she'd scraped against the ancient wood. It had only been an hour since Simon left. It seemed like an eternity. She had only ceased her attack on the door during that time long enough to discover that, while the dressing room doors which led to the master bedchamber on either side remained open, both of the doors giving egress to the corridor outside were locked.

No one had come to her rescue, not even the mouselike Molly, whom she had been certain would liberate her. Did Simon mean to imprison her here indefinitely? Angry tears burned her eyes at the thought. She batted them back with moist lashes, and pounded the counterpane with clenched fists. The man had turned her into a veritable watering pot. She had shed more tears in the few short weeks since she'd met her paradox of a husband than she had in her entire life beforehand.

She pounded the bed again and vaulted off it. She hadn't lit the lamps, but a weak shaft of moonlight breaking through the clouds laid itself at her feet, and she followed it to its source and strained the darkness below for some sign of activity on the grounds. All at once her scalp began to tingle, and cold chills riveted her spine.

There was a light in the tower.

Scarcely breathing, she waited, her smarting eyes fixed upon the ghostly glow in the orchard until it disappeared and two figures emerged, their identity shrouded in the swarthy darkness, their images detectable only through their motion, as they mounted and rode off into the blackness. One of them was Simon. She recognized his ragged stride. But where could he be going in the wee hours, and who was with him?

She stood beside the window for some time pondering that before exhaustion dragged her eyelids down and tampered with her balance. Haloed in an eerie puddle of fractured moon glow, the bed looked inviting. Dared she accept? She shuffled toward it wearily, and crawled beneath the coverlet, shoes and all. No. She would not disrobe. She would be ready to make her escape the minute a hand turned the key in that lock across the way—

no matter who that hand belonged to. That was the plan. Having decided upon it, she closed her swollen eyes, and slept.

For all her resolve, her plan was foiled when she awoke to bright sunlight streaming through the mullioned panes, and to Simon standing over her with a breakfast tray in his hands. She bolted upright and threw back the counterpane. Before she could rise, however, Simon tethered her with the tray, planting it squarely over her lap, and stood back, arms akimbo, an eyebrow raised, taking the measure of her wrinkled gray serge traveling costume and morocco leather slippers.

"Did you imagine that I would take advantage of you, my lady?" he said, frosty voiced. "You really don't know me, do you? No matter. I expect much of that is my fault. So says Rob, at least."

She set the tray aside with not a little force, and swung her feet to the floor.

"I am dressed, my lord, because I mean to leave. You cannot entomb me here."

"Jenna," Simon entreated, his tone turned solemn. "May we have a truce? We need to talk."

"We have nothing to discuss, my lord. You made it perfectly clear at Holy Trinity that you don't care to hear anything I have to say. I think it best that we leave it at that."

"But I have something to say to you. May I sit?" he inquired, sweeping his arm toward the hearth-side chair.

Jenna didn't answer. Seeing her chance, she bolted toward the door and tugged frantically at the knob, but it was locked, and she spun around to face Simon exhibiting the key.

He strolled toward her, his limp scarcely noticeable, and she backed away until the door made an end to her retreat. He was so close that his body heat warmed her, and the aroma of latakia drifting from his moist skin dizzied her like a drug. Tears welled up in her throat and puddled in her eyes. She choked them back. His image swam before her, and her heart began to hammer visibly, moving the dove gray bodice of her traveling dress. Something wrenched her heart and turned her knees to jelly. For a moment, she thought he was about to kiss her. If he had taken her in those strong, muscular arms, she would have yielded to his kiss—a single kiss. But no, those sapphire eyes holding her so relentlessly were not dilated black with passion; they were glazed over with anger and pain, and the look in them turned hers away.

"May we have a truce?" he repeated.

"My lord?"

"Jenna, please. I am not your lord; I'm your husband. I'm not asking you to honor your vows if that's what's bothering you; quite the contrary. I was on my way to Town when you decided to put yourself in harm's way. I'd be there, well out of your way, but for that, and now, *because* of that, I cannot go."

"I've no idea what you're talking about," Jenna snapped.

"It's obvious that we've made . . . a mistake," he said, tight-lipped, his voice hollow and strained. "Rob was right. We married too quickly, without really getting to know each other. I shan't pretend it will come about overnight—these things are frowned upon, and it could take years—but I have friends in the Court of Arches, and I'm well acquainted with the Archbishop of Canterbury. If you want to be released from your vows, I'm sure something can be arranged, and I shan't stand in your way. We can work out the particulars once the process is begun. I was a fool to think that I . . . Well, never mind. The point is, I will take steps to release you from our . . . marriage, but first I need your cooperation in a truce because of something totally unrelated to us."

"And just what might that be?" Jenna said in defiance. Rebellion was her only weapon against the scandalous reaction his closeness had ignited inside her.

"Evy's come-out," said Simon.

"E—Ev . . ."

"There's no need to take a pet," he replied to her incredulous stuttering. "It was you who insisted upon holding the deuced ball here at Kevernwood Hall, if you remember. I wanted to hold it at the town house. Well, it's been arranged for Saturday next. The invitations have been sent. They cannot be unsent,

and I wouldn't do that even if I could at this juncture. I owe
Evy as fine a come-out ball as I can provide. I will not have that
darkened by our . . . difficulties. It would have been better held
in Town. The ambience is much more suitable there, the ballroom is more than adequate, and it's far more convenient than
this mausoleum is for the guests. I can't for the life of me understand why you insisted upon having it here."

"Because of Robert," she blurted. Her hand flew to her
mouth, and she chewed her lip the moment the words were
out. She hadn't meant to deliberately betray the vicar. Thinking
on it in that moment, however, she couldn't see why she owed
him allegiance after he'd betrayed her so cruelly. Anger, bitter-
ness, and disappointment roiled in her, reliving that betrayal, but
it was defiance that spoke.

"He's in love with her," she said.

"Evy?" Simon erupted. His posture clenched, and he took a
ragged step back.

"She doesn't know he's alive, of course; she's so busy pining
over you, and he's sworn me to secrecy. But I no longer feel
obliged to honor that oath—not after the way he's betrayed me."

"Rob hasn't betrayed you, Jenna."

"Oh? What would you call it, then? He let me pour out my
heart, let me bare my soul, and all the while he knew you were
the Marsh Hawk. He'd been protecting you—abetting you!"

"Shhhhh!" Simon hissed. "No one else here knows that except Phelps."

"Phelps! Hah! I should have guessed. I suppose Evy knows as
well?"

"Evy is the last one I would want to get wind of it."

"Why doesn't that surprise me? All right, just what do you
expect of me in this . . . truce of yours?"

"Just that you pretend things are well between us until after
the ball. I won't have our difficulties marring Evy's emergence
into Society. I've labored too long and hard to achieve it for
her. When it's done, you may go anywhere you wish with my
blessing. I am not your jailor. Will you do this one thing for
me, Jenna?"

She gave it thought. He didn't deserve a quick answer. *Evy—always Evy! Why must it always be Evy?* She savored his discomfort before she spoke.

"Very well, my lord," she said at last, "for *Evy*." There was no mistaking the jealousy in her tone; she'd made no attempt to hide it. She was beyond caring what he thought. Evy, indeed!

"Thank you," he pronounced, his delivery crisp and curt.

"Now will you let me out of this room?" she snapped.

"After Molly's cleaned you up," Simon returned. "You cannot go about here looking like that."

"Wait," Jenna said, as he moved past her toward the door. "Just to set one thing straight . . . I know now that it wasn't you, who . . . that you didn't—"

"Now that you've seen the real Tyburn tripper, eh—now that you've got your proof?" he snapped bitterly. He smiled, but it was cold—riddling her with gooseflesh. "You should have known without it, Jenna." Unlocking the door, he set it ajar and turned back. "I'll send Molly up directly." He jerked his head toward the tray on the bed. "You'd best eat that," he said. "It's awhile yet till dinner."

"I shan't be coming down to dinner, my lord," she informed him.

" 'Simon,' " he corrected. "It's a truce, remember? And you *will* come down to dinner tonight, washed and coifed and made presentable; you're going to have to."

"And why, pray, is that?"

"Because your mother and Evy have just come to work a miracle and set this place to rights for a ball in a sennight, and they will be expecting you to dine with them. I think I'll have Rob join us. I want to have a look at him in Evy's company for myself and see if there's anything to this business you say. I'll make your excuses until then." He ran a gentle finger along her cheek. His touch ran her through like a javelin. "You need time to doctor these blotches," he observed. "And, Jenna . . . no matter what you think, you have naught to fear from me. Nor have you ever."

CHAPTER NINETEEN

They were to gather in the drawing room before dinner, and Jenna went down early. The last thing she wanted to do was make a grand entrance in a room filled with people with whom she had issues—not an ally amongst them.

Her heart sank at the sight of Simon and the vicar engaged in strained conversation beside the open French doors. The heady aroma of moss rose and night-blooming botanicals wove a mystical spell drifting in on the evening breeze, recalling another garden, and the ghost of lilacs.

The vicar's amber eyes were troubled and sad as he greeted her, while Simon's liquid sapphire gaze appraised her frock. She'd chosen a cream-colored muslin evening dress, with an overskirt picked out with delicate violets. A wide green grosgrain sash positioned under the low décolleté was tied in a bow at the back trailing streamers. Molly had styled her hair in a high chignon framed in tendrils all around, and threaded it through with narrower matching green grosgrain ribbons. Simon nodded, evidently in approval, and went back to his conversation with the vicar.

Jenna had never felt so alone in her life, or so awkwardly out of place. When her mother and Evelyn swept in through the doorway, matters went from bad to worse. The dowager entered rambling on to no one in particular about nothing of consequence in a voice so shrill that Jenna winced. Meanwhile, Evelyn, wrapped in a diaphanous cloud of sprigged muslin, ran to Simon and threw her arms around his neck, peppering his cheek with kisses and gushing over how terribly she had missed him. It wasn't even a sennight since the silly chit left Kevernwood Hall. Jenna was caught between nauseated and incensed, watching the girl cling to Simon so relentlessly. Though Simon soothed her with a touch that could be deemed naught but fraternal, Jenna's heart ached recalling the ecstasy of those strong arms holding her, those skillful hands soothing her, and in that moment she would have given anything to trade places with Lady Evelyn St. John.

The dowager was still babbling when Simon offered his arm to escort her to the dining hall. Not to be abandoned, Evelyn, breaking every protocol, seized Simon's free arm, snuggling her head beneath his shoulder as he showed the pair of them over the threshold. This he did gingerly, owing to his awkward gait and the dowager's circumference, which challenged the door frame. The girl's posture sent shock waves of déjà vu through Jenna that rocked her visibly. It was the very stance—clinging and possessive—that she had opened her eyes to in the anteroom at Moorhaven Manor. Would the traitorous memories never cease? Rooted to the spot, she gave a violent lurch at the touch of Robert Nast's gentle hand at her elbow guiding her to follow.

Simon took his place at the head of the table, with Jenna on his right and the dowager on his left. Nast was seated across the table, next to her mother, and Evelyn sat beside her, directly opposite the vicar. Jenna did not question the odd seating arrangement. It was plain that Simon wanted to keep the gathering close, and Evelyn and the vicar where he could observe them. It was also plain that they had no idea they were being scrutinized, or why.

Being separated from Simon had clearly vexed Evelyn, who pouted and fidgeted, restless to a fault, tossing her golden curls and leaking petulant sighs that Simon didn't seem to notice. He was occupied trying to juggle dancing attendance to Jenna's mother and observing Robert Nast. Jenna surmised from the girl's demeanor that she had in the past enjoyed close proximity to Simon at table. She refused to acknowledge the display.

"Isn't that so, Jenna, dear?" her mother warbled.

"I beg your pardon?" Jenna said. She had no idea what her mother had been saying.

"Are you sure you're feeling well, dear?" the dowager queried, bristling. "You haven't heard one word I've said thus far this evening."

"I'm fine, Mother," Jenna said tersely. "What were you saying?"

"I was saying, dear, that your engagement weekend at Moorhaven Manor came off without a hitch on shorter notice than this, and everything in sixes and sevens if you recall."

"Yes," said Jenna, "it did." She rolled her eyes. Why in the name of divine providence would she have to bring that up?

The dowager rambled on while one of the liveried footmen began serving the soup course. Jenna stared into her plate. The soup smelled good, but it looked inedible, an anemic broth devoid of vegetables that wasn't dense enough to hide the blue swirls of the china pattern on the bottom of the bowl.

Spoons clicked out of sync against china, and she shuddered, listening to her mother's loving little moans as she literally inhaled the savorless liquid. More than once Jenna caught Simon looking in her direction; no doubt, she thought, to reassure himself that she meant to keep the bargain. She caught his furtive glances toward Evelyn and the vicar as well, since she was in a perfect position to monitor them herself without making her observance obvious. There really was no need to monitor Evelyn, however. Her eyes were glued to Simon.

Drat and blast. What did it matter?

It was a mercy when one of the footmen removed the soup plates, and another served the oysters au gratin. No one was eating except the dowager, who continued what Jenna appraised as a vulgar love affair with the cuisine. Still sulking, Evelyn was chasing her oysters around her plate with a vengeful fork, while the vicar looked on, forlorn. Simon, scrutinizing them with knit brows, didn't look Jenna's way at all for a time, until her mother's high-pitched voice fractured the awkward silence.

"I have the most deliciously wicked on-dit to share," she said. Then, leaning her protruding bosom over her oysters as though she were about to disclose a state secret, she almost whispered, "I'm not altogether certain that this is the proper forum for it, but I fear I shall burst if I have to keep it inside another moment longer."

"Then, by all means, Mother, enough gibble-gabble. Out with it!"

"Well, dear," the dowager began, wriggling in her chair, "it concerns Rupert Marner."

"Nothing you could possibly have to say involving Rupert Marner could be of the remotest interest to me, Mother," Jenna said.

"Oh, I wouldn't be too sure," the dowager replied. "He's had his comeuppance!"

Jenna watched the vicar freeze over his plate, his amber eyes leaving Lady Evelyn's face for the first time since she swept into the drawing room. They flashed now toward the head of the table and fastened upon Simon, who seemed almost to smile, taking up his fork at last. Jenna gave her plate her full attention.

"Rupert was on his way to the Highlands, so it seems, and he hadn't gotten far when his carriage was held up at gunpoint," the dowager continued.

"That's nice, Mother."

"Jenna! It was the Marsh Hawk, dear—the very bounder who killed your poor father."

Jenna's head came up slowly, a speared oyster suspended on her fork, and she stared at her mother, who had begun wriggling in her chair again across the table.

"The thatchgallows made him strip down—inexpressibles and all—took his valuables, pistol-whipped him, lashed him to a tree in naught but his drawers, and horsewhipped him senseless. Then the scapegrace turned poor Rupert's horses loose, took all his clothes, even his Hessians, and left him there practically naked! Rupert had to walk all the way back to the coaching station at Tavistock in his groom's coat and breeches, where he collapsed and had to be taken back to the Manor by post chaise. I had it from Lady Jersey herself. It's all over Town."

Nobody spoke.

Jenna lowered her fork, oyster and all. She glanced at the vicar, but he didn't meet her eyes. Simon did, however, dosing her with one of his maddening blank expressions, his long-lashed gaze meeting her wide-eyed stare head on.

"When was this, Mother?" Jenna said, not taking her eyes from Simon's.

"Why, it happened on your wedding night, dear, well . . . in the wee hours following, that is."

So that's where Simon had gone—not to the Pillsworths' at all. Her posture clenched. A quick look in the vicar's direction proved her theory. His neck had turned beet red around his clerical collar, and he didn't know where to direct his eyes. A tremor in Simon's hard gaze betrayed him as well, though neither Jenna's mother nor Evelyn seemed to notice.

The dowager surrendered her cold oysters au gratin in anticipation of the larded pheasant being distributed along with a delectable array of entremets and removes.

Jenna was certain her face had turned crimson. The heat in her cheeks had narrowed her eyes. Her heartbeat echoed in her throat. She imagined Rupert lashed to a tree, imagined Simon's fury wielding the horsewhip that buckled his knees. She knew full well the rage that had driven his heavy hand, and why. She'd seen it herself, held in check all through the wedding and afterward, before another passion took its place, at least for a little while. Rupert had paid for his trespass on Rutherford soil, and his assault upon her person. That's what Simon must have just returned from when she'd made her discovery in the tower. That's what he was evidently reporting to the vicar when she pounded so frantically upon the vicarage door and made the confession that had cost her the only man she had ever loved, or ever would love.

The pheasant on her plate swam in her tears; she would not let them fall. Simon was watching her, and she would not give him the satisfaction. She hated him for making her such a watering pot. She hated her heart for loving him—hated her body for betraying her even now, for she longed to fling her arms around his neck and pepper his face with kisses just as Evelyn had done earlier.

Instead, she was utterly alone at the table with the vicar who had betrayed her, the husband who had abandoned her, and the woman who, albeit differently, had captured Simon's heart in a way that she never could. Not to mention her mother, who, for all of her yearlong spiral into mourning, seemed more moved by the advent of Rupert Marner's encounter with the Marsh Hawk than she had been with Jenna's father's death.

Anger dried Jenna's tears, but she would not show it. She took her anger out instead upon the succulent larded pheasant on her plate. It tasted like straw, as did the venison, and braised potatoes in parsley sauce that followed. Not even the dessert wines, vol-au-vent of pears, Charlotte Russe, or raspberry tart could sweeten that moment.

When time came for the ladies to repair to the parlor for coffee, leaving Simon and the vicar to their brandy and tobacco, the dowager begged off, complaining of gastric distress, which didn't surprise Jenna one bit after having watched her inhale everything edible in sight. That, however, presented Jenna with the awkward situation of being alone in Evelyn's company. It only took one furtive glance in the girl's direction to discern that Evelyn wasn't looking forward to the circumstance any more than she was.

Neither really wanted coffee, and it remained on the tray growing cold. Finally, it was Jenna's sigh that broke the strained silence hanging like a pall over the dreary antiquated room.

"You don't like me very much, do you, Evelyn?" she said.

"It isn't a matter of 'liking,'" the girl said frankly. "I just don't believe you are right for Simon, that's all."

"Well, well! And, what sort of woman would you approve of for your uncle, then?"

"Someone who would appreciate him," the girl flashed, looking daggers.

"Evelyn, you would not approve of *any* woman your uncle chose," Jenna accused. "No, wait!" she cried to the girl's back as she sprang toward the door. "We're going to have this conversation whether you like it or not; it's long overdue . . . and necessary."

"There's really no point, Jenna. You shan't change my opinion."

"Perhaps not; that remains to be seen, but you will hear me out. Please come back and sit down. No matter what you think, I am not your enemy. It saddens me that you obviously think so."

Evelyn hesitated a moment, and then, tossing her golden curls, she floated back to the Chippendale chair at the edge of the carpet she'd fled, and resumed her seat with flourish.

"Thank you," said Jenna. "I wish to know why you do not think me suitable for your uncle."

"Simon is *Simon*. I do not think of him as my uncle."

"That is the problem, I think. He *is* your uncle, you know, whether you think of him that way or not. There can never be anything between you, Evelyn. Certainly you know that."

"I'm sure I have no idea what you mean," the girl said, bristling.

"You are a bright young woman—no jingle-brain with attics to let. I think you know exactly what I mean. You are quite blatantly infatuated with your uncle, and I threaten those feelings. You don't dislike me personally; you don't know me well enough. That is something I hope to change. You resent me, however, just as you would anyone who encroached upon your space where your uncle is concerned. That is understandable, considering your situation in that he is your benefactor and you've formed a natural attachment. But . . . is it fair, now that you are . . . enlightened in the matter?"

"*Fair*? What has fair to do with anything? Is it 'fair' for you to continually refer to Simon as my uncle, when you know I dislike it?"

"That is what he *is*, Evelyn," Jenna pointed out. "I'm trying to make you see that you need to acknowledge it." She hesitated, then said on an audible breath, "I was jealous of you, you know . . . in the beginning, because you occupy a place in your uncle's heart that I can never touch, a part of him that I can never reach. Never enter. I told him that I wanted to apologize to you for that."

"Y-you've discussed all this with Simon?" Evelyn shrilled, surging to her feet again.

"Of course," said Jenna. "I discuss everything with your uncle. He is my husband, Evelyn."

"Y-you told him what is in my heart . . . that . . . that I—"

"Oh, no, I didn't have to," Jenna interrupted. "He already knew that. Your uncle is most intuitive. He loves you very much. You are his brother's child, and important to him. Nothing will ever change that. You occupy a special place in his heart, as I've said, as does Crispin. What is needed here is that you recognize and stay in that place, for the good of your own heart, as well as your uncle's. Because, while you pine over what cannot be, you miss an opportunity that already exists on another front, and that will sadden your uncle dreadfully, considering the nature of it."

"You make no sense. What opportunity? What . . . other front?"

"I was hoping that by now you would have seen it for yourself," Jenna said, hesitating. "But since you haven't . . ."

"Yes?" Evelyn prompted, tapping her foot on the carpet.

"I will have to break a confidence to tell you," Jenna went on. "Not that it matters anymore. But if I can see some good come from all this before I . . . Well, never mind. The truth is, there is someone right under your very nose, you silly goose, whose heart is bursting with love for you, and you don't even know he's alive!"

"And, who might that be, pray—Phelps, I suppose?" Evelyn snapped. "Or the good Vicar Nast, perhaps?"

Jenna didn't answer. Meeting Evelyn's blue-eyed rage with a steady gaze that spoke for her, she folded her arms, inclined her head, and waited.

Clearly shaken, Evelyn sank like a stone into the Chippendale chair, her moist eyes flashing as though she were viewing past events on the wall, on the floor, in the very air in front of her.

"W-who told you such a thing?" she breathed.

"He did," Jenna returned. "Have you never noticed the way he looks at you? Just now in the dining hall, he scarcely took his eyes from you, Evelyn."

"I saw no such thing."

"No, you wouldn't have, would you, pouting so over not being able to sit beside your uncle. It was painfully obvious to everyone else."

"I don't believe this—believe you! Why, he's *old*! He's positively—"

"He is no older than your uncle, and he worships you. Don't take my word for it; see for yourself. It shouldn't be too difficult. The poor man wears his heart on his sleeve, and his pain in his eyes."

"*Oh!*" Evelyn sobbed. And before Jenna could reply, she'd fled the room.

It took two brandies and one pipe full of his special blend to loosen Simon's tongue in the matter that needed addressing, and even at that, he wasn't sure speaking out was wise, since the vicar had only downed one glass—not even. There was nothing else for it, however. Jenna was right. How had he never seen it? More to the point, why had Rob never broached the subject with him? He was almost angry. It was, of course, the perfect answer all the way round. All that remained was to make the bufflehead see it.

Another brandy first. He poured it, flushed some down, and leaned back in the carver's chair, openly studying his unsuspecting companion.

"What?" said the vicar to his scrutiny. It was that obvious.

"Why have you never told me?" Simon asked, laying his clay pipe aside. The ash had grown cold in the bowl and it tasted foul.

"Told you what?" the vicar replied around a nervous laugh.

"Christ, don't fence with me, Rob. Don't insult my intelligence. You're in love with her! You're in love with Evy. How could I not have seen it until now? Am I all that self-centered, then?"

The vicar lost his posture and looked away. "Jenna's told you," he murmured.

"I saw for myself tonight."

"She doesn't know I'm alive, Simon."

"Whose fault is that, I wonder?"

"That isn't fair. I'd rather take it to my grave than be held up to ridicule for it."

"Why did you confide in Jenna and not me?"

"For the same reasons Jenna confided in me and not you."

"And they are?"

"Simon . . ."

"Please. I want to know. Am I so difficult to talk to? Did you think I wouldn't approve? Did you think I would laugh at you? What?"

"I don't believe I could have stood it if you had."

"You don't know me—either of you."

"Simon, I am a man of the cloth. People are *supposed* to confide in me, and I had nothing to lose in confiding to Jenna. Besides, I didn't confide in her—not really. She found me out, and I asked her to keep my confidence."

"I'm glad she didn't. I might not have noticed otherwise; I'm too caught up in my own coil these days."

"What are you going to do about that, Simon?"

"Don't shift the subject!"

"You can't let her go. You love her!"

"I can't chain her in the wine cellar, either, Rob. I tried locking her up. I can't keep her here against her will."

"You were of a mind to do just that. What changed your agenda?"

"We struck a bargain—to put up a front until after Evy's come-out ball. Hah! I wondered why she insisted upon having that blasted ball here instead of the town house. Now I understand. She wanted to have it close enough to give you a fighting chance."

"It won't matter, Simon."

"I'm going to have a little talk with Evy."

"If you do that, it will mean the end of our friendship. I swear it! I will never forgive you."

"Then you stand up and press your suit before some fopped-up Corinthian snatches her right out from under your nose at that bloody ball, ruins all of our lives and everything I've worked so hard to achieve for that girl all of these years. *That* would make an end to our friendship; you can bet your blunt upon it!"

Jenna had blown out the candles. She hadn't bothered to light the lamps when she came up to retire. Across the way, the hearth gaped empty, like a yawning creature of myth. It was far too warm for a fire.

The window was ajar. The fragrant garden smells laced with the tang of salt wafted in on a light breeze drifting landward from the sea. It stirred the dust motes to life on the shaft of light piercing the panes. She watched the tiny particles walk the moonbeam as if they had a purpose. She almost envied them. In that lonely moment, she could find none for herself.

Tears stung her eyes. She refused to indulge in them. She had made a bargain and she would keep it, but not for Evelyn's sake—for Simon's. She owed him that, after all. She'd nearly killed him, hadn't she? The worst of it was, the real culprit was still free.

Though Simon's dressing room door came open in a gentle hand, the windowpane rattled in its fretwork casing with the displaced air, and Jenna sucked in her breath as Simon's dark shape emerged from the blackness beyond. He was wearing his dressing gown. But he couldn't mean to . . .

She vaulted upright in the bed, clutching the counterpane to her trembling bosom as he drew near. "What do you think you're doing, my lord?" she demanded.

"I am beyond exhaustion, my lady," said Simon, "riding

down your highwayman all last night to no avail, not to mention what went before. Then, returning here to find my house under siege with come-out madness. I haven't slept in nearly three days, and I am going to bed."

"Not in this bed, you aren't, my lord!"

"This is my bed, madam, and I assure you I will sleep in it."

"There are scads of bedchambers in this mausoleum, my lord. If you will not play the gentleman, since I have already retired, then I shall find one. Kindly stand aside."

"And have you arouse the whole house with news of our . . . estrangement? I think not, my lady. Your mother and Evy are roaming about making 'lists' of what needs to be done to set this house to rights by Saturday, and will be doing so half the night if I am any judge and your mother has her way, which seems inevitable."

"You've a lounge in your dressing room, my lord."

"I do, and it's an arm's length too short for a comfortable lie-down with this deuced leg. This will do quite nicely, thank you," he said, throwing back the counterpane.

Uttering a stifled gasp, Jenna scrambled to the other side of the bed and made a bold attempt to escape, but Simon hopped around the foot of the four-poster, gingerly though swiftly on the lame leg, and blocked her exit, capturing her in strong arms she tried to dodge.

His hands were warm, holding her through the thin batiste nightgown. Why hadn't she stayed dressed? She should have expected something like this. Why had she trusted him to keep his word?

In the moonlight streaming in through the window, she stared up into blue-fire eyes hooded with passion; meanwhile, in stark contrast, stiff muscles ticked along his broad jawline, and his lips had lost definition. It was like facing a snarling dog with a wagging tail. She didn't know which symptom to believe, and she fought to free herself from the white-knuckled hands locking her in their embrace.

Simon was breathing hard as he drew her closer. Was it rage, or desire driving him? His heart beat wildly against her through the silk dressing gown between them, with the rapid motion of his broad chest bearing down upon her; and his strong arms wrenched her closer, molding her to the hard, lean length of him.

He smelled of latakia, and of the brandy he'd drunk with Robert Nast in the dining hall earlier. Was the man in his altitudes? No, hardly castaway. But she knew that what he had drunk had emboldened him far beyond what mere wine might have done.

All at once, the sound of her name caught in his throat, and she was undone by the raw, feral voice—scarcely recognizable as Simon's—that delivered it. His sudden, almost desperate kiss weakened her knees. He deepened it, and she sagged against him, all reason lost as he gathered her up in strong arms and set her down in the center of the four-poster.

He loosened her nightgown, and his mouth slid the length of her arched throat. It hovered over the pulse at the base of her neck, his silken tongue seeking, probing. Was he feeling for the rhythm of the blood coursing through her? Yes. Her pulse quickened beneath his skilled mouth as he located her life force. It began hammering in her ears, pounding beneath his lips, throbbing against his teeth and searching tongue, resonating with the primal sounds coming from him then. It was a strange, almost ritualistic intimacy where sensual delights spiraled quickly into pure animal lust. Frightening, this forbidden pleasure beyond imagining, and she wanted it to go on forever.

His hands roamed her breasts. When his lips followed, a rush of moist, pulsating heat surged through her loins and raced along her thighs. His erection leaned heavily against her belly, its bruising hardness excruciating ecstasy. This was not the restrained Simon of her wedding night. This Simon held nothing back. His anxious sex entered her. It was like mating with a riptide, and she was undone.

Husky and breathless, her own throaty voice sounded back in her ears as in total abandon, she murmured his name. He groaned aloud, a deep, guttural explosion of sound that echoed in her soul, and her body responded, arching against him. All resolution dissolved in the heat of his kisses—in the fire of his passion. Nothing mattered then but those lips—those arms— that long, corded body molded against hers, promising fulfillment she never imagined.

All at once, he rolled on his back, taking her with him, and he slipped her nightgown down to bare her breasts. He cupped those in his hands, his thumbs stroking her nipples erect, his sex plunging deeper as he moved inside her, rolling her on her back again, grinding his powerful body against her.

There was no pain this time, only delicious waves of scorching sensation riddling her belly and thighs. There was no need for wine. Foxed by his passion alone, her head reeled dizzily. There was almost a desperation in their joining—a sexual feeding frenzy, as though he'd been condemned to die and was partaking of his last meal. Though she didn't understand it, Jenna responded, calling his name again and again until his hungry lips made an end to the litany. His silken tongue plunged deeper inside, coaxing hers into his mouth. She tasted him deeply, as she never had before.

His passion was palpable, then; his need overwhelming. There was no restraint in his crushing embrace, in the bruising power of his kiss. Like his kisses in the garden at Moorhaven had bruised her lips, so would these kisses leave their mark—on her mouth, her throat, her swelling breasts, and on her very *soul*.

He didn't speak as he loved her. Only his pleasured moans and rapid breathing broke the strained silence. His hooded eyes staring into her own held some message she couldn't decipher, but she knew what hers said to him: *Simon, I don't want to end our marriage. I couldn't bear to lose you now, after . . .*

Her rapture disengaged the thoughts hammering at her brain. He must have felt it, for he seized her closer and dropped his head down to her shoulder, shuddering as he clenched, erupting inside her . . . filling her, making her whole.

His brow was running with sweat. Slowly, he took command of his rapid breathing, though his heart still hammered against her like that of a horse in full gallop. After a moment he withdrew himself and pulled her nightgown over her breasts with painstaking control, just as he had done with her riding habit the day he proposed in the conservatory. All that seemed like a lifetime ago to Jenna now. She could scarcely believe it was only a few short weeks since he'd held her there, promising her a happy future as his wife. Instead, he had lied to her. He had broken her heart.

Climbing out of the bed, he struggled into his dressing gown and cinched the sash around his waist ruthlessly, but not before Jenna glimpsed his lean, naked silhouette against the shaft of light the moon laid at his feet. He took a ragged breath and raked his hair back. It was a mechanical motion. For a long moment he stood staring down at her in the moonlight, the blank expression on his handsome face maddening. Was he just going to leave her, *just like that*? A breathless gasp escaped her at the thought.

"As God is my judge . . . I didn't mean for that to happen," he murmured, his voice hoarse, and strained. "Forgive me. I promise you, it shan't . . . ever again."

Then, without waiting for an answer, he spun on his heel and stalked off through his dressing room door, melting into the shadows beyond like a phantom in the night.

"Simon, *wait!*" Jenna cried. Surging to her feet, she started after him.

The echo of a key turning in the dressing room door lock replied to that, and stopped her in her tracks. There was a deathlike finality in the sound, and it riddled her with chills from head to toe. Shivering, alone in the darkness, she dissolved into tears. There was no way to prevent them this time.

CHAPTER TWENTY

The last person Simon wanted to face in that moment was Phelps, but the faithful valet was waiting as he always did until his master was settled for the night. Just how the man knew that Simon wouldn't settle when he'd entered the master bedchamber barefoot in his dressing gown earlier escaped him. Damn it all. It wasn't natural that anyone should know him so well, though deep down he loved the man for it.

"Don't give me that 'I told you so' look!" he responded to the valet's arched brow and pursed lips. "I'm in no humor for it, Phelps, I warn you."

"I haven't said a word, my lord," the valet replied.

"Mmm," Simon growled. "You don't have to. I know that look all too well. What made you so sure I'd be back?"

"It seemed likely, my lord."

"Well, you can gloat over it after you make up the lounge."

"It's done, my lord."

"The devil you say! You really were sure of yourself, weren't you?"

"I didn't imagine your invasion of the sanctum sanctorum would sit all that well, my lord, considering."

"No, it did not. I botched it, if you must know. Damn it all, man, you know how I get when I'm overtired. You know my . . . urges intensify with exhaustion."

"I take it she wasn't receptive."

"That's just the trouble—she *was*! I was well out of it . . . until my passions betrayed me. It's going to be difficult to walk away now."

"You're sure you want to do that, my lord?"

"I haven't a choice."

"There's always a choice, my lord."

"Not in this, old boy."

"Forgive me the observance, my lord, but you aren't exactly an expert when it comes to matters of the heart."

"And you are, I suppose?"

"Hardly, my lord. I'm well beyond all that, thank providence, but I do have more of a perspective on things than you do at the moment . . . due to the wisdom that age has bestowed upon me, my lord."

"And I shan't have peace until I hear that wisdom out, is that it, Phelps?"

"You might say so, my lord."

"All right, my wise and learned sage," said Simon, with a sweeping bow that he was well aware looked ridiculous executed in a gaping brocade dressing gown. "Since I do need some semblance of sleep tonight, by all means speak your piece."

"This isn't your usual . . . liaison, my lord, as I have pointed out on numerous occasions. You've never needed instruction regarding your affairs of the heart, because in the past, heart and loins have always been disjoined, as it were. Here now, they are conjoined, and in such cases one can only expect . . . difficulties, since the gauze of love clouds the mind and defeats reason. Simply put, aside from the physical attraction that feeds carnal lust, you and my lady are hopelessly in love with each other. To make an end to such a union would be a grave mistake, my lord. Few men ever find such a love in their lifetime."

"You seem to think I have a choice. It is my lady who seeks to make an end to this union, Phelps."

"You've lost me, my lord. How can that be? Didn't you just say that she was receptive? She said she wanted to end the marriage did she, then?"

"Not in so many words, no, but Phelps, there is no trust. She didn't trust me enough to turn to me; she went to Rob."

"Mr. Nast is a man of the cloth, my lord. That is his function."

"Yes, yes, I know, but she should have come to me. I am her *husband*."

"She is very young, my lord, and it's plain that she has no family example to follow or seek counsel from in such matters. I think you ought to take that into account."

"Hear, hear. On that fine point, I do agree. That mother of hers!"

"A harridan to be sure, my lord. If you would spend your energy, I should think you'd best invest it thanking God that my lady's fallen far enough from that tree not to be blighted by it, if you take my meaning, sir, rather than chastising her for making bad judgments heeding her own inexperienced counsel."

"I have my pride, damn you, man!"

"'Pride goeth before destruction.' So says the Bible, my lord."

"Then we're right on schedule, old friend, and it's too damn, bloody late!"

Jenna poured all her energy into the come-out ball preparations over the next few days. She kept to herself, avoiding Evelyn and Simon altogether. That, however, was no great feat. Except for meals, the two were seldom seen. Simon made no more attempts to visit the master bedchamber, as Jenna knew he would not, and there were no more lights in the tower. Though, on more than one occasion, she saw a sliver of candlelight seep under his dressing room door well into the wee hours, and heard the hollow echo of his ragged footsteps pacing to and fro over the creaking floorboards.

Adding to the tension that reigned supreme as Saturday drew nearer, Jenna and her mother did not share the same vision for the ball. The dowager's elaborate concept called for months of preparation to bring to fruition, not the few short days at their disposal, and it was no small matter for Jenna to convince her that realistically, a simpler plan was needed.

The staff was summoned, and each servant was given particular tasks to perform in preparation for the event, and specific duties for the ball itself. Since there wasn't time to engage a florist, the groundskeeper Tobias Heath and his wife were put in charge of the decorations for the Grand Ballroom. There were to be countless bouquets of fresh flowers from the Kevernwood gardens set about in tall porcelain jars. Graceful garlands and festoons would be draped about the vaulted ceiling and mantels, as well as the food tables in the dining hall, where an endless array of hot and cold viands would be set out for the guests. The dowager took charge of the food, and spent much of the time in the kitchen instructing Cook in its preparation. She insisted upon French cuisine. Exclusively. And more feathers than partridge and squab were ruffled in the larder over her strict attention to detail.

On Thursday, Evelyn's ball gown arrived from London. It was a lovely frock of white silk gauze over satin, with fetching puffed sleeves and a low décolleté edged with porcelain pink silk ribbon rosettes. But there were fitting problems. Evelyn had all but stopped eating since her last fitting in town. Olive Reynolds was summoned from Newquay village, and literally held hostage by the dowager, who assured her she would remain in residence until the alterations were completed to her satisfaction.

When Robert Nast arrived that afternoon to find Evelyn closeted with the dressmaker, and Simon gone to the village to arrange for the musicians, Jenna found herself alone with the vicar for the first time since her confession. She decided that a stroll in the garden would be the wisest choice for the interview. That way, if the conversation soured, she could easily excuse herself and retreat inside. Receiving him in the Hall would give him an advantage she wasn't about to tender. Besides, there were just too many ears that might overhear them indoors.

White and purple-red foxgloves, delphinium, and blue

speedwell genuflected in a salt-laced breeze that would soon turn to a gale force, driving mountains of diaphanous spindrift over the head of Kevernwood cliff. A telltale, jaundiced sky was bearing down upon the afternoon. Soon the servants would be skittering every which way, fastening shutters and battening down for the flaw. But now, the storm brewing between herself and Robert Nast was paramount, and it was the vicar who broke the awful silence that hovered like a storm cloud between them as they traveled the garden path.

"We dare not go far," he said, gesturing seaward. "That's an ugly flaw on the make."

"Believe me, we shan't," Jenna returned. Though if he were looking for an invitation to repair to the Hall, he could forget it.

"Jenna," the vicar said, stopping her beside the yellow vignette that featured sunny shades of cinquefoil, cowslips, and butter-and-egg plant under a bower of sculptured privet. "May we have a truce? Things cannot go on as they are between us."

"Truce, truce! All I hear is *truce*—first Simon, now you. Well, there it is! We're definitely at war here."

"Jenna—"

"Don't 'Jenna' me, Robert Nast. How cruel you are. How dare you pretend to be my friend all these weeks when all the while you were involved in Simon's madness? How did you expect me to react to that? You lied to me!"

"I didn't lie to you, Jenna. I kept a confidence for a friend."

"Aided and abetted a . . . a thief!" Jenna hurled at him.

"Simon is my friend, Jenna. I'd hoped you were my friend as well. I told you all along that you needed to speak with him. That was the only counsel I could give without betraying his confidence. You had no compunction about betraying mine, did you?"

"I didn't really betray it as a retaliation—not consciously, in the way you imply."

The vicar gave a bitter laugh, and continued along the lane.

"No, I didn't," Jenna defended, answering. "Simon and I were having a dustup, and he asked me why I insisted upon holding Evelyn's come-out ball here at Kevernwood Hall instead of in Town, where practically everything was already arranged, and I said because of you. I was angry, and it just came out. I didn't premeditate it, Robert. I'm not my mother."

"Heaven forefend," the vicar muttered in an undervoice, then said, "No harm's done. At least only Simon is aware, and he isn't going to betray me."

"N-no . . ." Jenna stammered.

A surge of adrenaline set prickly gooseflesh loose upon her, and made her miss her footing; she was scarcely aware that the vicar's quick hand steadied her. Guilt shot hot blood to her cheeks, and parched her lips. Not even the sting of the wind bending the hollyhocks' backs could cool the fire in her face. For a moment she toyed with the idea of making another confession, telling him that her betrayal went deeper than he knew. What made her hesitate was that knowing Evelyn was aware of his feelings might keep him away. Still, her hesitation was counter to her purpose; her silence condemned her.

"Jenna . . ." He stopped in his tracks, and turned her toward him. "You didn't."

"Robert, you may as well know that when Evelyn's come-out ball is over, Simon and I mean to . . . part," she said, her speech halting, "I haven't done anything maliciously; you have to believe that. Oh, I know you think I've vengefully betrayed your confidence, but the truth is . . . I wanted something positive to come out of all this. Believe what you will, but that was my only intent."

"Good God!" the vicar moaned. His hands fell away from her arms, and he seemed to sway in the wind like the hollyhocks.

"Do you still want that truce?" Jenna said dourly.

"*I* don't matter anymore," he murmured, "but not so you and Simon. Don't leave him, Jenna. It will destroy him if you do."

"He will never forgive me for seeking your counsel instead of his—of not trusting him enough to take him into my confidence concerning something so grave. A marriage can survive almost anything but lack of trust. Besides, it's a point of pride with him. It would always be there, like a wedge between us. It's too late for us, but not for you and Evelyn, Robert. Come

Saturday, that Hall behind us will be overflowing with potential suitors for that girl. You cannot just hand her over to some . . . toady, some pink-of-the-ton!"

"And if she laughs at me?"

"Bowl her over! Don't give her the chance."

"What was her reaction when you told her, Jenna? Tell me the truth."

"Surprise," she answered.

"She didn't laugh?"

"Actually, she cried," said Jenna.

The vicar took his neckcloth back from the wind, and raked his hair with a harsh hand. "I wish you hadn't done this, Jenna," he said.

"Oh, I don't know," she replied. "It could very well be the most singularly productive thing I've done since this farcical odyssey began—for all of us."

CHAPTER TWENTY-ONE

Rupert chose a table near the door of the taproom at the Heatherwood Arms to wait for the Bow Street Runner. Nursing the inn's dubious black ale, his face was a study of smug satisfaction. He hadn't been waiting long, but he fidgeted nervously, drumming his fingers on the scarred oak table and twirling his quizzing glass, his eyes darkened to smalt, hooded against the thick fog of smoke drifting in his direction from the patrons' clay pipes.

He knew the man the moment he entered. He was dressed in typical Runner attire: a plain black frock coat, stuff breeches with dark stockings, buckled shoes. The man knew him as well, though they'd never met other than through correspondence. They had arranged a signal. The Runner, one Matthew Biggins, was to wear a red flower boutonniere. When he entered, Rupert was to order two pints of ale and repair to one of the salons, which he had paid for in advance. After a discreet interval the Runner would join him there, where they could speak as privately as one could at the Heatherwood Arms.

"Your letter wasn't too clear, sir," Biggins said, working bulbous fingers around his tankard. "As murky as this ale here, it was, to be sure. We'd best get to it."

"Keep your voice down," Rupert cautioned. "These walls are sheer as gauze, and we can ill afford to be overheard."

"Aye, sir," the Runner whispered. "You say you know the identity of the Marsh Hawk. Just who might that be, then? There's many a Runner would like that feather in his cap."

"You'll see soon enough," Rupert returned. "I've a plan that will put an end to his escapades for good and all."

"So you've said, but I'm going to need a bit more before I commit to it, sir. You're going to have to tell me who you suspect, and why."

"I'd rather not say just yet," Rupert hedged.

"Then I'm afraid I can't help you, sir," the Runner said. Squeezing his paunch past the table, he lumbered to his feet.

"Wait!" Rupert barked, caught between a shout and a whisper. "Since you insist . . . Simon Rutherford, the Earl of Kevernwood, is the Marsh Hawk, and I don't just suspect the man, I *know*. He held up my coach and assaulted me not a sennight ago on my way to the Highlands."

"What?" the Runner cried. He erupted in boisterous laughter despite Rupert's pleas to keep his voice down. "Are you addled in the bean box? Kevernwood is a war hero. The ton idolizes the man. Why, he's built two hospitals for veterans since he left the service. You don't want to let any one of them hear you speak against his lordship, or they'll likely plant you a leveler, viscount or no. No wonder the land guards laughed you out of Headquarters."

"The guards hereabouts are fools, Biggins; they're protecting the man. Can't you see that? Kevernwood built those hospitals with money he robbed from the ton on the highway at gunpoint!"

"There's bad blood between you," the Runner observed, shaking his head. "Word's out in Town that he stole your intended, that he bested you in a duel, and that you didn't exactly take being bested in a gentlemanly way, if you take my meaning. Now, if I'd known about *that* I'd have hauled him in—and you along with him. Dueling is against the law. But accusing him of highway robbery . . . you'll never make it stick. Have you got any proof of what you're accusing? Because, if you don't you're going to be the ton's latest laughingstock."

"I have no tangible proof," Rupert said. "That's where you come in. I will soon have enough, with your help. I'm going to set a little trap for Kevernwood. We're going to catch him red-handed."

"You're going to have to," Biggins blurted. "He's got to have the goods on him when he's caught for me to make an arrest. He can go about all masked and gotten-up in highwayman gear, even hold up a coach at gunpoint, like he did to you—to settle a score, I have no doubt—if he's of a mind, but if he doesn't actually steal anything, we can't touch him."

"You just leave that to me."

"Mmm. I think you're a bedlamite is what I think, but since I've come all this way, let's hear this crack-brained plan of yours."

"Saturday next, Kevernwood is holding a come-out ball at his estate in Newquay for that little chippie he's been seen with all over town. Half the ton is scheduled to attend —"

"And you expect him to stage a robbery in the midst of *that*—right under the noses of the ton?" Biggins interrupted. "Hah! Why would he trouble himself to take to the highway when he's got half the wealth in England right in his own ballroom?"

"No, you nodcock! I'm planning to offer him another shot at me."

"Now, why would he take it, sir? You've just said he already accosted you once. What else has he got against you?"

"There are to be a number of young blades at that ball," Rupert said through his teeth, ignoring the question. "At least one of them is expected to make an offer for the little ladybird he's been diddling. Damaged goods, I daresay, but fine-looking damaged goods. At least one of those bucks is going to make an offer, I'll be bound, but not of marriage when I get through. I can guarantee it. I've seen to it that a certain young rake, whose reputation excludes him from such events, has received an invitation. 'Twas easy enough to forge. He'd do the job nicely with the little chippie. Oh, don't look so shocked. She might even enjoy it. That aside, I've passed the word that Simon Rutherford means to foist off his leavings upon society now that he's married. My plant might not be the only young buck standing in line."

"You mean to set him up? Oh, now—"

"Let me put it this way," Rupert cut in. "I've seen to it that he'll know I was the one who spread the rumor. He'll hear it from someone close to him—someone he trusts. And when his bride—the bride he stole from *me*—gets wind of her husband's lurid adventures with the little chit, I might just have her back. The Marsh Hawk killed her father, you know. Oh, yes! Once she finds out that she's *married* the thatchgallows, I'll have her back, you can bet your mother's last quid upon it. How grateful she will be when she learns that it was I who brought her father's murderer to justice!"

"I get the drift all well and good, but how is this going to prove Kevernwood is the Marsh Hawk? And you say he killed Baronet Hollingsworth? The Marsh Hawk has never harmed anyone, to my knowledge. Besides, I've never heard tell of him targeting military personnel, and old Hollingsworth served in the Colonies. You're going to need tangible proof to back up your accusations in that cause."

"I'm not going after him in that cause; only in mine. I'm putting it out that I'll be heading for Darby's gambling hell in St. Enoder, with a foreign houseguest—a high-in-the-instep, avid gamester, notorious for carrying more blunt than is prudent to squander in such places. St. Enoder is close enough to Kevernwood Hall for the Marsh Hawk to easily slip out and make an appearance with no one at his blasted ball the wiser. It would be too tempting to let pass by. What better alibi than a houseful of the ton's elite? I've heard even Lady Jersey herself will be there. He'll show all right. We will be waiting for him, and I'll yet see Kevernwood dance the Tyburn jig."

"*We*? What *we*?"

"Do you speak French?"

"After a fashion. Not fluently by any stretch. Why?"

"It will have to do. Hopefully, you won't have to do much talking. You shall be the Comte D'Arbonville, my very affluent houseguest, and I'll supply all the 'evidence' you need to tempt the Marsh Hawk. I'll get it all back, after all, once you collar the bounder."

"You'll never pass me off as a foreigner. I haven't a talent for playacting. You should be soliciting down 'round Drury Lane for a professional. Besides, I'm not plump enough in the pockets to make a show worth robbing."

"Drury Lane? There isn't time for that, you want-wit!"

"I don't know," the Runner hedged, rubbing his chin.

Rupert fidgeted during the moment it took for the information to impact the man, wondering if all Bow Street Runners were as dense. It was the perfect plan; why couldn't the gudgeon see it?

"Come, come, man, I haven't all night. Do you want to catch the Marsh Hawk or not? I can easily find another."

"I want to catch the Marsh Hawk, yes. Not lose my position for falsely accusing the earl of Kevernwood. I've got my reputation to consider, and I think you're daft!"

"You'll see how daft I am come Saturday, Biggins."

"That's another thing," said the Runner. "You haven't much time to put all this in place—three days, counting Saturday."

"Leave the fine points to me. You'll come to the Manor and stay on as if you were the comte. My parents needn't get wind of this. Then, Saturday at dusk, we'll ride the road to St. Enoder all night long if needs must until he holds up that coach. We'll have to get you up in something less provincial, for God's sake. That rig screams Bow Street. You need to look the part." He raised his tankard. "Well then, it's settled. To our mutual gains."

"Aye, sir, our . . . mutual gains," said the Runner, making a halfhearted salute. "But I still think you're bloody daft."

By Friday morning, Jenna was exhausted, but the house was nearly in readiness. The marble floors had been cleaned and polished to a mirror-bright shine, and neither a cobweb nor a speck of dust could be found. The faded, threadbare furniture had been replaced with fresher pieces from the closed-off upper regions. While they were for the most part painfully outdated, they made a far better appearance than the relics they replaced. At least they couldn't be held up to ridicule, and it wouldn't appear that the Rutherfords were putting on tick. All that remained was to prepare the food and deck the Grand Ballroom out in floral array, which would commence after the dinner hour.

But for the servants, Jenna found herself alone in the house, and she decided upon a walk in the garden before nuncheon. Her mother had taken Molly and set out for Bodmin right after breakfast in search of "last minute must-haves," as she called the decorative finishing touches. Simon had gone to the vicarage, where he'd spent most of the week, and Evelyn was closeted with Olive Reynolds, who was working feverishly on the final alterations of her ball gown.

Evelyn had kept her distance since their confrontation, and Jenna was glad of it. It was Simon, however, whose absence was painful; nothing had eased the ache in her heart, or the longing—the terrible longing—for his arms, for his kiss, for his love. She scarcely saw him except at meals. Then their eyes would meet, blue fire jousting with gray. She couldn't read their message. The line between the passions they exuded was too tenuous. No matter the message, he was unapproachable, and she tried to pretend that it didn't matter. Soon she would keep her bargain; after the ball, she would be free. But would she ever be free again of the invisible cord that joined their hearts? Was she the only one who felt its tug? The worst of it was that there was nothing she could do. She had lost him.

Having walked for some time through the lush Kevernwood gardens, she had become oblivious of time. The overwhelming scents surrounding her. Moss rose, tuberose, honeysuckle, and gillyflower dominated that sector. The clovelike top notes threaded through her nostrils, riding the wind that never ceased to blow along the coast. Like May wine, it made her giddy and light-headed. But that wasn't to last. Before she reached the foxglove and delphinium vignette, the Hollingsworth carriage came tooling into the drive. The dowager stepped down almost before the footman could set the steps, causing the brougham to tilt, and hurried toward Jenna over the lane while Molly and the footman struggled with their purchases.

"Good God, Mother, what's wrong?" Jenna breathed, steadying her. "What's put you in such a taking? You're as white as chalk!"

"*No!*" the dowager shrilled, digging her heels in as Jenna attempted to steer her toward the house. "I daren't speak it in that house! Just let me . . . catch my breath . . . !"

"What is it? What's happened?" Jenna demanded, shrinking from her mother's keening whine.

"I met Lady Warrenford at the linen draper's in Bodmin, and she shared a most disturbing on-dit," the dowager said. "Rupert's put it out that . . . ohhhh, I can't! I can't speak it! It's too dreadful!"

"Can't speak *what*, Mother?"

"Rupert's spread a tale about Simon and Evelyn . . . that they . . . you know!"

"That's absurd, Mother."

"I know, but, dear, he's slandered Simon all over the coast—even in Town! Do you hear? All London is buzzing with it. Our guests! What are we ever to do?"

"There's nothing to it, Mother. Rupert is jealous. No one will take him seriously. Pay no attention."

"Rupert is entertaining a French nobleman at Moorhaven Manor—the Comte D'Arbonville. I've never heard of the man, but Rupert is making a show of him at all the local clubs. Rumor has it that he and the comte are going to the gambling dens in St. Enoder tomorrow night. If he ever spreads that tale among the pinks-of-the-ton who frequent those places, Simon will be ruined! Simon should call him out over this, Jenna—if it's untrue, that is."

"What do you mean, 'if it's untrue,' Mother?" Jenna snapped. Three words would silence her, but they were words she dared not utter. She couldn't divulge that Simon was Evelyn's uncle. That was one confidence she would not break.

"Well, dear, men will be men, you know, and Simon is a man of the world, as it were. The gel is ravishing, after all, and I've noticed myself that they are rather . . . close for mere obligatory family friends."

"Evelyn and Crispin are practically extended family, Mother," Jenna said steadily; it was as far as she dared go. "Nothing more, I promise you. You are not to speak of this to Simon. Is that clear?"

"He needs to know, Jenna! He needs to be told before he learns of it from someone outside the family, dear. He has a right to know what's being bruited about behind his back."

"No!" Jenna shrilled a little too loudly, remembering her mother's colorful account of the Marsh Hawk's assault upon Rupert. If Simon heard, he would surely do worse. "You will say *nothing*," she charged. "You will leave it to me. Tomorrow is Evelyn's ball. Would you have it spoiled by a duel, or worse? Would you bring bloodshed upon us after all of our hard work?"

"And when he finds out that we knew and didn't tell him—then what?"

"Better his anger toward us than Rupert dead at his hands, and him dying on the gallows for it."

"Aren't you being just a little melodramatic, dear?"

"Mother, I must ask you to trust me. Stay out of this and keep your place."

"My *place*?" the dowager cried, bristling.

"Yes, your place," Jenna said, wondering what her mother would say if she knew that her place would be at Thistle Hollow once the ball was over.

"Have you gone addle witted?" her mother shrieked. "Your husband has been accused of fornication and adultery with a mere child! How you can be so calm escapes me."

"I am calm, Mother, because I know there is nothing to this; so should you be. I'm going inside. Don't you dare think to follow suit until you can do so without calamity written all over your face. You thrive upon chaos, Mother. I will not have you spoil the ball. I will not have you wreak havoc in that house with vicious slander! You will say nothing to Simon—*nothing*, Mother. I turned you out of this house not so long ago for less."

"Well!" the dowager exploded, indignant.

"You have been welcomed back by my husband's good graces—not mine," Jenna said, with a raised voice over her mother's bluster. "Behave, or face the consequences. I've reached the end of my tether here, I warn you."

Jenna went straight up to the master bedchamber. She was in no mood for nuncheon; she needed time to think. This new information had thrown her. All Cornwall knew that Evelyn's come-out ball was being held at Kevernwood Hall. According to her mother, all Cornwall now knew that Rupert and his wealthy friends would be gambling nearby at St. Enoder at the same time. It stood to reason that highwaymen would know as well. Enticed by such an amplitude of fortune, how could the thatchgallows resist? And her score still needed to be settled.

She knew the road to St. Enoder well. It wended its way from Newquay through St. Enoder proper where a juncture with the highway, heading north, led straight to Launceston. Barstow had taken it the night she tried to return home—the night the highwayman who'd killed her father held up her carriage. Her mind's eye conjured the very spot where the brigand must have lain in wait that night. There weren't many patches along that stretch that offered concealment.

She still had the key to the tower in her possession. What if she were to use that key and borrow Simon's costume and pistols? Simon would be occupied with the guests; he would have no need of the tower that night. Especially if no one told him of Rupert's spiteful comments. She could have one of the horses brought 'round early in the evening on the pretext that one of the guests had need of it, and hide the animal in the orchard. Then, later, she could excuse herself by feigning a headache. No one would miss her.

Her mind racing with the possibilities, with a workable plan half-formed, she went down to nuncheon almost cheerfully.

CHAPTER TWENTY-TWO

Much to everyone's relief, the unpredictable Cornish weather held for the ball. It promised to be such a glorious evening that the terrace doors in the Grand Ballroom were thrown open to the salt-kissed evening breeze, which was laced with the mingled scents of night-blooming orchids and roses from the arbor beyond. Decked in flowers and candles, the lit chandeliers casting dazzling rainbows of light over the marble floor, Kevernwood Hall had come to life in a way that no one expected.

Carriages began arriving before dusk. As Jenna had imagined, it was no great feat to borrow Treacle just after dark and conceal him in the orchard. Then, dressed in her most fetching gown of patterned silk, the color of peaches and cream, she joined the ball, making the rounds with Simon.

They greeted the Warrenfords, the Eccclestons, Lord and Lady Chester-White, and the Markhams, who joined with Simon's military guests and the aristocratic throngs come from London to welcome Lady Evelyn St. John into society. Only one thing dampened the occasion: the absence of Crispin, whose military duties prevented him from attending, but not from sending a huge bouquet of white old English roses for his sister's debut.

To Jenna's surprise, just when she thought to part from Simon with the imminent approach of several naval officers, he swept her into his arms and waltzed her out on the crowded ballroom floor. Her heart skipped. His warm hand pressed against the small of her back, drenching her skin in fire beneath the clinging peach silk, just as she had fantasized it would at the masked ball. But all that seemed as though it had happened to someone else; so much had happened since. She felt a tug deep inside, stirring her very essence to life in an involuntary reflex of spasms that coursed through her body and threatened her balance. Could it happen like this, on the dance floor, with no contact save the most casual of public intimacies? She disguised her quick intake of breath under the umbrella of a cough.

Her mother had once observed that dancing was nothing more than an excuse to make love in public to music. That dour comment had come about at a ball when no one had asked the dowager to dance. Oh, but if she only knew how true those words were.

"Thank you," Simon murmured, his voice throaty yet revealing nothing.

"For w-what?" Jenna stammered, hoping he wouldn't notice the blush on her cheeks, or the heat of her body through the cool rustling silk.

"For this," he replied, nodding toward the gathering. "You've done a capital job. I appreciate it."

"For Evy," she said tersely.

"Yes, for Evy," he parroted.

"I can hardly take all the credit, my lord," she said, matching his cool tone. "Mother and Evelyn herself did a great deal with the servants' help. I had very little to do with it."

"Yes," said Simon, his eyebrow inching up a notch. "But this pains you. Your heart isn't in it, and even so, you've kept the bargain."

"I always keep my word, my lord."

He smiled. Albeit cold, she wanted to melt. Every cord in her body was strung to its limit, wanted to snap, ached to give way and let her throw her arms around his neck and beg his forgiveness—beg him to take her up those stairs to that magnificent mahogany four-poster and make love to her again, and forever. That, however, her pride would not allow, though his closeness drove her mad. He smelled of tobacco and wine and raw maleness. Her head reeled with his scent, and she longed for the taste of him. It was torture being in his arms now that it was over, and she bitterly wished she'd never set eyes on the enigmatic Earl of Kevernwood, wished he'd never awakened her to unimaginable pleasures no other would ever be able to ignite.

She would *not* cry. Grinding her teeth and pursing stubborn lips, she blinked back the tears, refusing to be a watering pot for him again.

She hadn't been meeting his gaze, and when he continued speaking, she almost missed her step.

"Do you realize that this is the first time we've danced?" he said.

"And the last, my lord," she blurted, sorry the moment the words were out.

"Yes, the last," he mused. "That's what I was thinking. It's just as well. You put me to shame."

She would not sink to flattery. He was obviously fishing for compliments. She would not stroke his vanity. If this was his method of coercing her to prolong the bargain, he was in for a rude awakening.

Neither of them was aware that the music had stopped until the guests began to applaud.

Breaking his hold with flourish, Simon bowed from the waist and delivered Jenna to her mother's side with practiced military control and no emotion in his face. There he left her abruptly to join a uniformed rear admiral patiently awaiting nearby.

"Lady Jersey isn't here yet," the dowager fretted, craning her jewel-draped neck in search of the woman. "She's such a boor—notoriously late. She must always make a grand entrance. If she dares to show up in that dreadful chartreuse turban, I think I shall die!"

"It's early yet, Mother," said Jenna, still shaking from Simon's closeness, and dismayed in spite of herself that he'd dismissed her so casually. "Not everyone has arrived. There'll be latecomers till midnight. You know how these things go."

"Who is that young man hovering over Evelyn, dear—the tall fellow with the hair à la Brutus?"

"Why, that's young Sidney Hargrove," Jenna said with a start. "Lord Eccleston's grand-nephew. Don't you recognize him? Where is your pince-nez, Mother?"

"I can't wear that *here*, Jenna!" the dowager breathed. "It doesn't go."

"Why not?" Jenna snapped, rolling her eyes. "You needn't fear to be noticed. All eyes are on Evelyn tonight."

Jenna could scarcely see the girl for the press of young gentlemen crowding around her. She frowned, scanning the room with worried eyes, and finally focused upon Robert Nast, who was also monitoring the young bucks surrounding Evelyn. When one of them, tall and lean, wearing black pantaloons, a black tailcoat of superfine, and an elegantly embroidered waistcoat of plum-colored silk, led her out on the dance floor, Nast turned away and moved toward the punch bowl, where he poured himself a claret cup.

"Excuse me," Jenna murmured to her mother, and made her way to the vicar's side.

"I told you it wouldn't matter," he said emptily, gazing over the rim of his cup toward Evelyn gliding by in the arms of the dapper young dandy. Giving a start, he gestured toward the punch bowl. "May I pour you some?"

"No, thank you," Jenna declined, shaking her head. "Why haven't you asked her to dance?"

"I'm a dreadful dancer, Jenna," he confessed. "I'd maim her sure as check."

"I shall be the judge of that," Jenna challenged. Taking the punch cup from his hand, she led him out onto the dance floor in the midst of a gallop in progress. "You lie," she observed, as he easily swept her along without missing a beat. "A shamefully shocking foible for a vicar, I daresay."

"You mock me now."

"No, I'm not that cruel; I'm sorry that you think it. I'm simply trying to loosen you up a bit. You're strung as tight as a fiddle bow, I can feel it."

"Do we have a truce, then?" he murmured.

"For the moment," she replied. "I've put too much into this to risk failure. Did you come here simply to sit on the sidelines and moon over her all night? You make a poor wallflower. She isn't going to jump into your arms, you know, Robert. You're going to have to take some initiative here. I know you can do it. I've seen the other side of you—the bold and daring Robert Nast, who isn't afraid to come to the aid of his friends, pistols blazing if needs must. Remember?"

"Are things any better between you and Simon?" he asked, as Simon waltzed awkwardly by with her mother. "I was watching you two dancing before, and I thought perhaps . . . that is, I was hoping—"

"Don't change the subject," Jenna snapped. "You aren't at all adept at it, you know."

"I'm not trying to be. I'm worried about . . . about both of you."

"You'll have to take that up with Simon."

"That's just it. He won't say."

"Well, that's unfortunate, because you've had your last confession from me!" she snapped, well aware of the bitter tears in her voice. She couldn't disguise them, though she blinked them back bravely for the second time in less than half an hour.

"I thought as much," he said through a sigh. "Jenna—"

"I am not important tonight, Robert. Neither is Simon. You and Evelyn are. When the music stops, I want you to march out there and ask that girl for the next dance."

"I'm too embarrassed, especially now, since she . . . knows. Besides, her dance card is certainly filled, judging by that lot waiting in the wings."

"Embarrassed, is it? You're going to be a good deal more than that unless you swallow your ridiculous pride and fight for that girl!"

He didn't get much chance. The minute the musicians stopped playing, the other dancer swept Evelyn into the garden through the terrace doors. After a moment, acting on an instinct he couldn't explain, Robert followed, but discretely, at a distance close enough to observe unseen as the young buck led her through the rose arbor where the shadows hid them, forcing him to draw nearer still.

"I think we shall be missed, sir," Evelyn said, her voice unsteady and thin.

"James—call me James," the dashing young Corinthian replied.

"Yes, uh . . . James, I really think we ought to go back in now."

"But you said you were overheated from dancing. Let the sea breeze cool you a moment."

"It's very dark tonight," she hedged. "Th-there's no moon. W-why, I can hardly see you, sir."

"There's more than enough light for what I have in mind," the man replied. A guttural growl followed, then a rustling followed by Evelyn's muffled cries. The man seized her in rough arms and covered her mouth with his own. His familiar fingers plunged inside her bodice, groping the breast beneath. He had freed it from the low-cut décolleté, and was attempting to hoist her skirt when Robert's quick hand separated them and spun the dandy around, his white-knuckled fist splaying the man out flat at his feet.

The young man's outcries, more of surprise than pain, in concert with Evelyn's hysterical screams as she covered herself, ruptured the silence. The racket rose above the music filtering from the ballroom, bringing a flood of people pouring through the terrace doors into the garden.

"How dare you lay hands upon Lady Evelyn, sir?" Robert seethed, hauling the man to his feet.

"Look here! Do you know who I am, you gudgeon?" the Corinthian spluttered.

"I know that you are no gentleman, but a rake and a rattle!" the vicar said, shaking him. "That is all I need know."

"Oh, come now," the young man chortled. "It's not like I've offended the honor of a lady. Word all over town is she's been diddling her . . .'benefactor,' and that he's staged this whole vulgar show to trick some unsuspecting prospect such as myself to take her off his hands."

Simon had reached them. His arm shot past Robert's in an attempt to relieve him of the young buck, but the vicar would not relinquish his hold.

"Not this time, Simon," he said through his teeth. "Not— this—time!" Shoving Simon's hand away, he launched a rock-hard fist that splattered blood over the young buck's neckcloth and silk waistcoat, and sent him sprawling on the manicured lawn.

CHAPTER TWENTY-THREE

Jenna's firm hand on Simon's arm turned him around with a jerk. She didn't say a word, but her eyes and wagging head spoke an emphatic "no."

The crowd had increased, surrounding Simon and the vicar, who had knocked the young buck senseless, and Evelyn, who stood sobbing in the dowager's arms. Nobody noticed Jenna; she had fallen behind in the crowd. It was the perfect opportunity, and in the confusion of the moment, she slipped away.

The Grand Ballroom was deserted when she reached it. Even the musicians had fled, and she slipped the key to the tower from her beaded chatelaine purse, stole out through the Great Hall into the courtyard, and ran to the orchard.

She would not light the coach lantern inside the tower; it might be seen from the house. In minutes, she had rummaged through the chifforobe and exchanged her delicate silk frock for a pair of Simon's black pantaloons and shirt, and one of the light cloaks she found inside, along with his mask and dated tricorn hat—the perfect thing for covering her hair. The pantaloons were a poor fit to say the least, but that couldn't be helped, and the boots were a problem. Her feet swam in them.

Tugging them on over her morocco leather slippers took up some of the slack, however, and, hoping she wouldn't have to walk too far in them, she snatched a brace of pistols from the chifforobe drawer, loaded them, and picked her way gingerly through the woodbine groundcover to the burgeoning fruit trees beyond. Then, following the sound of Treacle's nervous snorts at her approach, she groped her way along in the darkness, as black as coal tar pitch without the moon to light her course.

The horse seemed to know his way through the orchard in the shortcut the vicar often took on his visits, and Jenna gave him his head until the path spilled out onto the road that stretched between Newquay and St. Enoder. There she took charge and moved more cautiously. The highway was deserted. She wasn't sure if that was a good sign, or bad. It was still early, and the stretch of road ahead was straight enough for her to see that there were no visible carriage lights One of the few wooded patches that might give a highwayman shelter caught her attention. Nothing seemed untoward, and she proceeded past the spot with caution, only to draw an easy breath once it was behind her, telling that her judgment was sound.

Revisiting this desolate stretch of road riddled her with gooseflesh. What madness was she embarked upon? What had possessed her to stage the same scene—re-create the same nightmare that had begun all her woes? That it was illogical had never occurred to her then, nothing had, except that she do what she'd set out to do what seemed a lifetime ago: avenge her father.

Was she really ready to gun down another brigand? No. She'd never meant to do that in the first place—which even Simon knew. *Simon.* Though her heart ached to put all to rights, she wouldn't even try. There wasn't any use. His pride was too obdurate.

How could she ever have thought that Simon was capable of murder? How could she ever have doubted him? What a ninnyhammer she had proven to be, knowing the measure of the man, his sterling devotion to those close to him and those under the yoke of oppression; his loyalty and tenacity to prosper their lives with a blatant disregard for his own. He had never shown her anything but kindness, and a heartfelt devotion the likes of which she had never known. How could she have thrown all that away? Her heart was rent in two over it . . . but it was too late.

She had nearly reached the bend in the road when she came upon another wooded patch. Instinct made her leave the path and take to the thicket beside. She saw no carriage lanterns, but there was . . . something ahead, some sort of foreign noise violating the quiet. Though she couldn't quite identify it yet, it spoke of danger, and she reached inside her cloak to reassure herself that the pistols were still tucked into her belt.

Edging closer, she commended Treacle for his silence with a fond stroking, but a pistol shot made an end to that. The horse pranced nervously, rearing back on hind legs, faced with the highwayman who had stopped a coach in the middle of the road. Jenna freed one of the pistols from her belt, cocked it, and rode out onto the highway. It wasn't until she came abreast of the carriage that she recognized the Marner device on the carriage door. It was too late to turn back now. She'd already been seen.

"Hold! Stand, sir, and deliver!" she demanded, her voice deep and disguised. Though apprehension nearly paralyzed her, she spoke forcefully, without a tremor.

The man had just stopped the brougham, and Rupert was climbing out. Her heart leapt for fear that he might recognize her, but she steeled herself as another man followed, a man she didn't recognize, dressed in silks and neck frills suggesting French nobility.

"And, just who might you be, Jack?" the highwayman inquired of Jenna, claiming her attention again.

"Drop the pistol," she replied.

"Come, come," said the man, addressing Rupert and his lace-bedecker companion. "Turn out your pockets, and hand over those baubles."

Jenna watched their eyes oscillate between her and the real

highwayman, as they emptied their pockets and removed their jewelry. Their confusion was evident, but what was more confusing was the highwayman's blatant disregard for her, and she fired a shot over his head to attract his attention.

"Give that here," she demanded, gesturing toward the sack he'd been cramming the spoils into. "And the pistol, sir."

The man ranged his mount alongside and, after a brief hesitation, tossed her the sack and relinquished his gun, though she had no doubt in her mind that he had another concealed somewhere on his person—just as Simon had that night on the old Lamorna Road.

Out of the corner of her eye, Jenna spied another carriage approaching around the bend from the east, where the road narrowed. Rupert's brougham was blocking it. The road wasn't wide enough to turn the vehicle, and the coachman snatched up his blunderbuss instead and took broad aim at the entire circumstance, jerking it this way and that, clearly at a loss to identify his target in the confusion of the moment. At sight of it, the first highwayman bolted, attempting to flee, and Rupert's companion's thunderous shouts rising over the ensuing racket ran Jenna through like a javelin.

"Hold where you are, the pair of you!" he demanded, drawing two concealed pistols. "I'm a Bow Street Runner, and you're caught dead to rights!"

The highwayman paid no attention, and Jenna watched wide-eyed as the Runner's pistol shot brought him to the ground in a cloud of road dust and acrid pistol smoke. A paralyzing rush of blood surged through every cell of Jenna's body. She was caught.

"Drop that pistol," the Runner barked at her, "and the sack." He waved one of his own guns, meanwhile backing toward the fallen first brigand.

" 'Tis all right, gov'nor, I've got 'im covered!" the driver of the other carriage called out, leveling his blunderbuss at her.

"Much obliged," the Runner replied. Rolling the fallen outlaw over, he felt his neck for a pulse then straightened, swaggering back in Jenna's direction. What a ridiculous figure he cut in his ostentatious French frills, barking commands in a Cheapside accent. "Come, come, hand it over," he charged. "He isn't going to help you, he's dead."

Shrill outcries were coming from inside the second coach—a woman's hysterical voice. Her turban was barely visible poking through the carriage window, with nothing but the coach lamps to pick it out in the moonless dark. Jenna's mind was racing. To obey meant imprisonment and hanging. She'd been caught with the spoils. Her only chance was to try and escape, and she took advantage of the darkness. Bending low in her saddle, she dug her heels into Treacle's sides and drove him straight toward the thicket.

Shots rang out: the thunder and boom of the coachman's blunderbuss, the sharp crack of the Runner's pistol. It was the pistol shot that brought her down, but all she felt was the impact that unseated her. She landed hard in a cloud of dust from the parched roadway, raised by Treacle's flying hoofs as the horse fled back along the highway the way they had come and disappeared.

Her hat was gone, and her hair had come down around her shoulders. She moaned as the Runner ripped her mask away, and shrank from his hot breath, fetid with stale onions and ale. The woman's screams seemed louder, ringing in her ears, but the Runner's face was fading.

"What do you make of this, Marner?" he barked, glancing back over his shoulder. He craned his neck. "Marner? Marner!"

But Rupert was gone, and the pain was coming now with the shock of impact subsiding. People were milling about, but Jenna couldn't see their faces in the dark, in the dim of evaporating consciousness that overwhelmed her. *Father is avenged* was her last conscious thought.

Rupert climbed out from behind the coach wheel where he'd crouched well out of the way of gunfire. Even now, he moved gingerly, and would have run but for his determination to make certain that the Earl of Kevernwood was dead.

Biggins had snatched one of the carriage lanterns. In its

light, Rupert was quick to catch the Runner scowling at him in disgust from where he stood over Jenna's inert body. The man beckoned Rupert nearer.

"What have we got here?" he inquired.

Rupert ventured closer, and nearly missed his step as he recognized the woman sprawled at the Runner's feet.

"Jenna?" he breathed. "G-good God! Was she in on it with him?"

"What the devil are you talking about, Marner?" Biggins brayed. "You *know* this woman?"

"Yes, I know her, you gudgeon," Rupert snarled. "I ought to know her. This is the woman I told you about. She was mine, before Kevernwood there—otherwise known as the Marsh Hawk—stole her from me. And he evidently enlisted her in his thieving exploits."

"What?" the Runner erupted.

"I-is she . . . dead?" Rupert stammered. "Damn and blast! I-I didn't mean for . . . I only wanted Kevernwood."

A scream interrupted them as the woman from the second coach shuffled close, and they both turned toward the sound.

"Rupert Marner, what have you done?" she shrieked, bending over Jenna.

It was Lady Jersey.

"My lady," Rupert gushed. "I . . . we . . . !" He spun toward the Runner. "Well, you nodcock, have you killed her, then?" he snapped.

"N-no, sir," he replied. "I barely grazed her shoulder. She's more stunned than harmed."

"You aren't going to climb out of this stew pot, Rupert Marner," Lady Jersey shrilled. "I heard you just now. I demand to know what you're about here!"

"I am 'about' putting an end to the Marsh Hawk's escapades along this coast, my lady," said Rupert.

"And what has this to do with Simon Rutherford?" she demanded.

"They are one and the same," Rupert pronounced, puffed up with pride.

"Are you mad?" she screeched.

"Go and see for yourself," he snapped.

Lady Jersey snatched the carriage lamp from the Runner, took his arm, and marched him toward the dead highwayman. Then, wagging her finger at the corpse, she stood while the Runner plucked the man's mask from his face. Thrusting the lantern close, she gave a start.

"Have you gone addle witted?" she said. "This isn't Kevernwood here. Where did you ever get such a ridiculous notion?"

"*What?*" Rupert breathed, striding over for a firsthand look. He stooped and cried, "Bloody hell! Who is this, then?"

"The Marsh Hawk is who he is, Marner," the Runner put in. "I said all along you were daft. What ever gave you the idea Simon Rutherford was the Marsh Hawk in the first place?"

"I told you, you clunch, he held me up. I recognized him— that damned queue of his gave him away, I tell you. I *saw* him. I *know.*"

"Silence, the both of you!" Lady Jersey bellowed. "Are we all going to stand here and let that poor woman bleed to death?"

"She'll keep," the Runner drawled. "Whatever she was up to, there's no question of her guilt." He gestured toward the prostrate highwayman. "She held *him* up; we all saw it. She's caught with the goods—trying to run with them, I'll be bound. I've never seen the like!"

"She needs to go to hospital," Lady Jersey cried.

"She's going to Newgate," said the Runner. "They'll doctor her there. The law doesn't play favorites, my lady. They'll fix her up proper so she'll give the folks a good show when she swings on the gibbet."

Rupert paled, and gulped the still air.

"Don't just stand there," Lady Jersey snapped, adjusting her turban, which had gone awry for her bristling. She pushed them aside and charged between them. "Get that coach out of my way! You haven't heard the last of this, Rupert Marner. I don't know what you're up to, but I'll see to it that Simon Rutherford sorts you out. I can promise you that. Stand aside!"

CHAPTER TWENTY-FOUR

Simon let Robert defend Evelyn's honor, in hopes that she would view him in a more romantic light, though he did have a hand in ejecting the offender privately, once Rob escorted him to the door. Afterward, he spent his time calming the rest of the guests, not the least among them Lady Hollingsworth, who had all but collapsed in a taking over the shambles the ball she'd labored so hard over had become. Finally, the merriment resumed, and Simon had almost succeeded in convincing the dowager that no harm had been done when Lady Jersey arrived—turban askew—and descended upon the Grand Ballroom with all the aplomb of a juggernaut.

He quickly committed the legendary hostess's simpering abigail to the custody of a footman, and led her to the study, trying to decipher her breathless babbling. The dowager and the vicar followed close on their heels. Only one thing came clear—Jenna's name, uttered in so shrill a manner that Lady Hollingsworth began screaming it again and again, her eyes darting every which way, as though she hoped to materialize her daughter from the very shadows that lived in the hallway.

A nod from Simon set Robert in motion, who quickly

poured a brandy at the gateleg table and brought it to Lady Jersey in the wing chair where Simon had settled her. He then poured another for the dowager, who took it, but she stood her ground, refusing the Chippendale chair he offered as well.

"What *is* it?" the dowager shrilled. "Will someone please tell me what's happened?"

Lady Jersey took a swallow from her snifter, and drew a ragged breath. "Simon Rutherford, what is going on here?" she demanded. "Why is Countess Kevernwood going about in costume in the company of the Marsh Hawk, holding up unsuspecting citizens on the King's highway?"

"What the devil are you talking about?" Simon erupted, giving a start.

"Not half an hour ago, the Marsh Hawk held up Rupert Marner's carriage on the road to St. Enoder. The countess was with him."

Lady Hollingsworth seized her breast and sank like a stone in the Chippendale chair, spilling brandy over her lavender silk voile gown.

"My wife is right here in this house, attending the ball," said Simon. "Where did you get such a ridiculous idea— from Marner?"

"No, I saw her myself. I was on my way here when I came upon the robbery. The viscount's brougham was blocking the road. Marner and a Bow Street Runner had evidently set a trap for the Marsh Hawk tonight, and the countess fell into it with him. Rupert actually believed that *you* were the Marsh Hawk. I have no idea what put such a notion into his head. He was livid when we unmasked the man and it wasn't you! What is going *on*?"

"What of my wife, Lady Jersey?" Simon urged, ignoring her question. He stood ramrod rigid, the hands at his sides balled into white-knuckled fists. "You saw her, you say?"

"With my own eyes," she replied. "She was shot by the Runner. Why, I nearly swooned when he unmasked her!"

Despite his already wooden posture, Simon's muscles clenched as though he'd been struck by cannon fire. For a moment he wasn't able to respond, and when Lady Hollingsworth jumped to her feet, Robert quickly voiced what Simon could not bring himself to put into words.

"Is she . . . w-was she . . ." he stammered.

"No, no," Lady Jersey hastened to say, shaking her head in a reassuring manner that set her green satin turban awry again at a comical angle. "Would I be this calm if such were the case? He just grazed her. I do think she ought to have been taken to hospital, though. She took a hard fall."

"Where is she now?" Simon said, his jaw muscle ticking.

"On her way to Newgate Prison via constabulary equipage out of St. Enoder," she told him. "I tried to intercede, but there was nothing I could do; she was caught with the spoils. The Marsh Hawk had relinquished them to her before the Runner shot him. Evidently she wanted it all for herself, because she was trying to rob *him*, if you can imagine such a thing. We shall never know for certain now, lest the countess speak it. The Marsh Hawk, thank the heavens above, is dead."

A moan interrupted her, and the floor shook underfoot as Lady Hollingsworth spiraled down to the Persian carpet at their feet with a shuddering thud, extracting an outcry from Lady Jersey.

"See to her!" Simon snapped through his teeth at his friend, and Robert yanked the bell pull to summon the servants, and knelt beside the dowager, rubbing her wrists.

"Now then, my lady," Simon pronounced, his words clipped and his voice strained. "You are absolutely certain of all this?"

"I was there. I *saw* it, Simon."

"Where is Marner now?"

"Gone back to Moorhaven Manor, I suppose. He left us to go 'round to the coaching station for fresh horses as soon as the Runner transferred the countess to the prison wagon. Why on earth did he think you were the Marsh Hawk? That's the part I can't fathom."

"We have issues," he said tersely. " 'Tisn't important. I'll see to Marner. I would appreciate it if —Lady Jersey, may I impose upon you to do me one more service tonight?"

"Of course, dear boy. I'm so dreadfully sorry to bring this news. Anything, you've only to ask."

"Keep all this from the guests. Take a moment to compose yourself, then go in as though nothing has occurred, and join the ball. I'm sure your distress was noticed when you arrived. Make something up. I know it's a lot to ask, but if anyone can accomplish it, it's you. I shall be forever in your debt. I shan't have all this spoil Evy's come-out."

"Certainly, dear. I daresay you're taking this far better than I expected. I'll tell them a half-truth—that the Marsh Hawk was shot dead by a Runner, and that delayed my arrival. I shall plead ignorance of the details. I shan't even mention the countess, or Marner. But you *are* going to give me an explanation, aren't you? Because, you may as well know, I shan't leave this house until you do."

"You have my word, dear lady, but there isn't time for that now. You may certainly stay as long as you like. Meanwhile, suffice it to say that things are not what they seem. All will be well. You have my word."

Two liveried footmen and three chambermaids were helping Lady Hollingsworth from the study. Simon instructed one of the maids to have an herbal tisane prepared at once to sedate the dowager, and to stay with her in her rooms for the rest of the evening. Then, ignoring the vicar's grip on his rock-hard arm, he stalked toward the Great Hall, literally dragging his friend alongside.

"Simon, what are you going to do?" the vicar pleaded.

"Go and find Phelps, and have him meet me at the tower," Simon ground out, breaking free with a vicious wrench that almost cost Robert his footing.

"Simon, you *can't*!" the vicar cried. Jerking him around, he shook him in place. "The Marsh Hawk is dead," he pronounced. "*Dead*, Simon! You're out of it. Now you've got to *stay* out of it. For God's sake, don't do this!"

"You know why she's done what she's done." He thumped his breast a scathing blow. "Because of *me*, that's why. Because I didn't avenge her father for her. I've been such a fool. I never should have come back here that night without that gallows dancer's head on a pike. But I didn't want to leave her locked in that room too long. I didn't know how things sat between us, Rob. I was so afraid she'd speak out—so afraid she'd turn me in, you along with me. You were, as well. Don't dare to deny it!"

The vicar's restraining hands fell away, and his posture slouched while he weighed his answer.

"All right, yes. I will admit there was a moment or two when I was worried she might bring you down," he conceded. "Her hatred of highwaymen was so acute, and you two were squared off for battle, but that passed when I saw the depth of her love for you—something *you* should have seen."

"You had nothing to lose. I stood to lose everything I've worked so hard for, to legitimize Crispin and Evy, to give them a future—a hope. For Edgar. *I* don't count, but I couldn't risk my alter ego ruining their lives, and it would have. They would never have survived the scandal of my exposure as the Marsh Hawk socially, and you know it. You should have warned me, Rob. You *knew*! All this might have been avoided if you'd only told me."

"Don't you dare presume to lay the blame for this upon me, Simon Rutherford! I couldn't do that. It had to come from her. Besides, you weren't even here to warn, blast you! And it wouldn't have done any good anyway; you were love-blinded, and I wanted this union for you. Dash it all, Simon, before any of this I told you to wait and get to know each other better. You didn't listen to me then, did you? You'd have pooh-poohed me, and told me to mind my own affairs, and you know it. I did what I could. I told her she was grossly mistaken, that the Marsh Hawk did not harm his victims; that he couldn't possibly have been the one responsible for her father's death, and I told her she should confide in you. She promised me she would—specifically asked that I let her broach the subject with you herself. Naturally, I assumed—"

"Well, there it is! You 'assumed.'"

"You are two grown adults, and she told me in confidence."

"Another confession, eh?"

"I take my calling seriously, Simon. There was nothing else I could do."

"Nothing but tell me."

"Tell you *what*?"Robert snapped, taking hold of his arm again. "I had no idea that she'd gunned you down during one of your forays! I learned that bit at the same instant you did, when she burst into the vicarage in hysterics and poured out her heart to me."

"Oh, and I suppose if I hadn't overheard, you'd have told me?"

"Simon, that isn't fair. You know there are strictures. You know I am under constraint to my calling. That I'm bound—"

"You wouldn't have, would you—not even then? Bloody Hell!"

"Do you hold *nothing* sacrosanct?"

"Not where my friends are concerned. You should know that. You've seen what I've been through because of the twins. Why I never married. Why, until now, I dared not afford myself that luxury, let myself hope for a normal life of my own."

"You are not a priest."

"Thank God for that!"

"Simon, please . . ."

"There's no time here now for this!" he replied. Wrenching free again, he strode through the Great Hall, and out into the sultry summer night to find Treacle grazing in the courtyard. Snatching the animal's reins, he charged toward the stables, his limp having become pronounced in his haste.

"What are you going to do?" Robert persisted, sprinting after him.

"I'm going to have a little chat with Marner."

"Not as the Marsh Hawk! I beg you not. The Marsh Hawk is dead. Let him stay so. Resurrect that brigand and you sign your death warrant, Simon!"

"Just go and get Phelps," Simon gritted out, raking fingers through his hair. "I know you mean well, Rob, but it's way too late for good intentions. My road is already paved."

He led Treacle into a stall, and motioned for the groom to tend the lathered animal while he saddled another, a chocolate stallion that answered to the name of Fury. He was about to mount when he noticed the vicar still standing there.

"The devil take it!" he roared, causing more than one animal to reply unattractively. "Will you go back in there and see to Evy? It doesn't take an Oxford scholar to deduce that Marner planted the seed of that disruption earlier. That young rake you just throttled in the garden was James Mortonson, Viscount Mortonson's son. He isn't received in polite society. He certainly wasn't invited here. Marner is behind it somewhere, and it could have been much uglier, if you hadn't had the presence of mind to monitor the situation, and I thank you for that. There's a score I have to settle with the viscount. Meanwhile, I need you to see to it that nothing else occurs while I'm gone."

"Simon . . ."

"Go to her," he commanded. "Let one positive thing come from this farce, but first get me Phelps! This ends tonight, by God, however it must!"

CHAPTER TWENTY-FIVE

Jenna leaned back against the cold leather squabs in the prison coach. The wound in her shoulder wasn't deep; the bullet had only grazed her, and the constable at St. Enoder had doctored and bandaged it, but the pain was dizzying. She couldn't help but wonder, if such a slight wound could pain her so, what Simon must have suffered when her pistol ball ripped through his shoulder. The irony of it all extracted a sorrowful moan from her, for she truly believed she'd gotten what she deserved. That was almost comforting in a ghoulish sort of way, she decided, and she accepted her penance gladly.

Most importantly, the highwayman responsible for all her woes was dead—and she had brought it about, though it was the Runner seated across from her in the austere conveyance whose pistol had felled him. It was over. There would be no more haunting the Cornish wilds in moon-dark, no more bloodlust for revenge, no more fear that she would be caught and bring disgrace upon her father's good name. That had already happened. Her worst fear had become reality.

Somehow, all this paled before the aching emptiness inside for the loss of Simon. How she longed for the comfort of his

arms, the consolation of his love—the love she had betrayed
and lost, if not then, surely now. Would he even know what had
happened to her? Well, of course he would. Eventually. She was
in no hurry for that. She had ruined Evelyn's come-out ball.
He would never forgive her for it.

Her eyes glazed over with unshed tears. She was still the watering pot, and he was still the cause. No. She would not cry.
But when she reached to brush the tears away, a hollow clanking called attention to the heavy iron manacles clamped around
her wrists, and the dratted tears fell anyway—a flood of them.
She dissolved in them.

The Runner seemed unmoved. He hadn't spoken a word
since they'd left St. Enoder. His contempt for female highwaymen was evident. His scathing looks were hard, and his resolve
unbending. She made no attempt to soften it by way of explanation: that she wasn't a highwayman, only dressed like one to
get close enough to do what the law would not, bring her father's murderer to justice. Her strategy was sound; it had
worked too well. The thatchgallows was dead. Her father was
avenged. But in the end, the strategy had damned her.

Her mind reeled back to the moments before she was shot.
Her memory was still fuzzy, but there was . . . something. A
woman's voice. Yes. She had heard a woman's voice from the
coach that came after. She'd only caught a glimpse of her in the
feeble light of the carriage lamp as she poked her turbaned head
through the coach window. There was something familiar
about her: that turban, that hideous chartreuse turban. How
well she remembered her mother's reference to it now. *Lady Jersey*. Could it be? She'd been late for the ball. Of course! Another moan escaped her. Jenna could only imagine her
mother's reaction to Lady Jersey's arrival in a taking over the
events of the evening. The picture wasn't a pretty one, and fresh
tears threatened.

Jenna had never felt so frightened and alone. But fear had always emboldened her, and her sobs were due more to anger
than despair. That, however, wasn't to last. From what she'd

gathered from the banter since her capture, despair would come when she reached the infamous Newgate Gaol.

The ball went on until the wee hours, much to Robert's chagrin. Rancor roiled in him at Simon's supposition that Rupert Marner was behind Evelyn's earlier unpleasant experience. It set his blood boiling, though one would never know it from the chivalrous way he conducted himself, taking the place as host in Simon's absence. Nonetheless, he was straining at the tether when the guests finally, mercifully, began to take their leave.

Lady Jersey was in her element, doing what she was famous for—playing the role of hostess in Lady Hollingsworth and Jenna's absence. The herbal tisane of skullcap, chamomile, and verbena prepared by Cook, whose skill with herbs was legendary, had rendered the dowager inert, and with Molly to administer subsequent doses, she slept soundly confined to her chamber in supine oblivion.

Soon everyone was gone. Evelyn smiled demurely as she passed Robert on her way upstairs to bed, or had he imagined it? No, the blush in her cheeks was genuine enough, though he dared not invest in it . . . yet. Instead, he offered her his warmest smile and most dutiful bow in return, and as soon as she was out of sight, steered Lady Jersey into the study, marveling that the woman's turban was still clinging tenaciously to her somewhat scraggly coiffure.

The woman sank wearily into the wing chair she'd occupied earlier, and waved him off with a hand gesture as he lifted the sherry decanter from the drop-leaf table.

"No! No more," she said. "Whatever this is, I would appreciate that you speak it quickly. I am quite done in, Vicar Nast, and I am definitely not at my most powerful at present. I long for my abigail to prepare me for a good night's sleep, so please be brief."

"I'm dreadfully sorry to detain you, but it's important. My lady, before you arrived, there was an unfortunate to-do here. A young rake made . . . improper advances toward Lady Evelyn, and had to be evicted from the ball."

"Oh, dear man!" she breathed. "How dreadful! Is there no end to the calamities this night?"

"Some ugly things were said," Robert continued. "The young scapegrace had the mistaken notion that there were improprieties between Simon and Lady Evelyn, and thought to take advantage—"

"Balderdash!" she erupted.

"Yes, I know, but—"

"I know who the St. John twins are, Vicar Nast," Lady Jersey interrupted.

Stunned, the vicar stared, and chose not to reply to that. How she could know and not the entire realm with such a juicy on-dit in her keeping, he couldn't fathom.

"Men make bargains with men, dear boy," she went on drolly, speaking to his silence, "ignoring the pure and simple fact that women overrule them. I know the Duke of York quite well, you see, and that mistress of his, Mary Anne Clarke, who never was known for her . . . discretion, and I am well able to make two and two come out to four, if you take my meaning. It's all quite straightforward, when one reasons it out."

"And, you've never . . . voiced your opinion in that cause?"

"You mean, have I never let on that I am aware? I only do to you here now because you are a man of the cloth, and I know how close you are to Simon."

Another confession. Would there be no end to them?

"Suffice it to say," she drawled, "that no one will ever hear that tale from me. I respect and admire Kevernwood for what he's done for those two poor children."

"I should like to get back to the point here," said the vicar, clearing his voice. He had gotten past one hurdle without having to commit himself or expand upon the issue; it was time to turn the tide before another confidence damned him. "The libertine that took advantage of Lady Evelyn was James Mortonson, Viscount Mortonson's son. He isn't received, and he certainly wasn't invited here. Simon believes Marner is behind this. Exactly what tales are circulating in Town?"

"You obviously know the answer to that already." She bristled, waving her be-ringed hand again. "*Balderdash*—all balderdash!"

"Yes, but who is spreading it?"

"Simon is right, Rupert Marner has had a good deal to do with what I've heard. I've no more respect for the maw-worm. It's all sour grapes over losing his betrothed to Simon, I daresay. Oh, yes, I heard all about the duel. The ton is buzzing over that. The viscount shan't be welcome at Almack's again—not while I'm hostess, and I plan to be till the place crumbles to dust. Have no fear of that. If it's any consolation, no one believes any of the gossip, you know. Everyone in Town adores Simon . . . and envies poor Jenna."

"It *is* true then. Marner is behind it. Simon thought as much, but I had to be certain."

"Why?"

"Where did you say you last saw the bounder?" he asked, ignoring her question.

"We parted company at St. Enoder. He was changing horses at the coaching station. Why?"

"Lady Jersey," he said, again ignoring her question, "I do so hate to impose, but since you are staying the night . . . may I presume upon you to look after things here until Simon returns?"

"Of course, dear man, but what of you? Aren't you staying on?"

"No, ma'am," he called, halfway through the study door. "I've stayed too long as it is."

Robert knew that Simon wouldn't approve of what he was about to do, of course, but he was well beyond caring. In his estimation, Simon hadn't shown the best of judgment in any regard since Jenna bewitched him. She would be his first concern now. Counting upon that, he borrowed a horse from the Kevernwood stables and set out for the coaching station at St. Enoder, since that was the last place Rupert had been seen.

It wasn't a rash decision. Certainly it wasn't something he hadn't thought through; and it wasn't entirely to do with Evelyn, either, though his blood still boiled at the thought of her abasement. What motivated him was that, by the time Simon got around to dealing with Rupert Marner, it could be too late. This was something he could do for his friend, something that would leave no taint upon Simon. There was no other sensible solution in his view, and that it was totally out of character for a vicar to run an aristocrat to ground in order to call him out mattered not a whit to him.

It was nearly dawn when he reached the coaching station—just in time. The stationmaster who had been on duty through the night was just about to give up his post to the day shift.

"I'm not no mind reader, ya know, gov'nor," the man groused.

"Surely not," Robert soothed, "but you must recall the direction the viscount took."

"Well . . ." the man said. Lifting his cap, he scratched his balding head and squinted off in space.

"Yes?" the vicar prompted.

"I'm thinkin', I'm thinkin'," the man grumbled. "You're a mite impatient for a man o' the cloth, 'ppears ta me."

"Yes, yes, I know. Just *think,* man! Which direction?"

"Do you know how many coaches tool through here of a night, sir?" asked the man, bristling.

"A good many, I imagine, but I'm only interested in one. Surely you remember? It had a device on the door picked out in gold—an Old English letter *M* in the center of a laurel wreath with a crown at the top."

"Ah!" the stationmaster cried, giving a lurch. "Well, why didn't ya say so? I remember '*im* all right, a regular cockscomb, he was, all got up in silks and frills—shirt points reachin' for the sky, belcher neckcloth, and all. 'Twas Plymouth he was headin' for."

"Plymouth? Are you certain?"

"Oh, aye. It was Plymouth right enough, with not even a bumbershoot strapped up top, much less a trunk or travelin' bags. He was askin' the whereabouts of coaching stations b'tween here and there. In a devil o' a hurry, he was."

"I need you to tell me where those stations are, sir," said the vicar.

"What's he done?"

"Never mind that," Robert returned. "The coaching stations; make a list. We're wasting precious time. It may already be too late to stop him!"

Rupert had dismissed his driver. He would have no more need of Wilby or the coach. He had booked passage on the *Clairmont*. She would set sail at dawn on the turn of the tide. He would be well on his way to Marner House in the Channel Islands for an extended stay, well out of the coil he'd set in motion and safe from Simon's wrath. He'd had a taste of that, and though he would never admit it to anyone but himself, he knew he was no match for it.

The stew he'd been served was hot and filling, if not palatable by his standards, at Plymouth's Albatross Inn, at the foot of Notte Street, beside the quay. He had begun to relax. No one would seek him in such a rustic dockside establishment, and he wasn't likely to run into any among the ton here, either. If not comfortable, he felt safe, despite the way the patrons eyed his Town togs and ornaments.

The inn was a respectable establishment, run by a husband and wife who catered to travelers like himself. The room he'd taken for the night was clean and adequate. He was smart enough not to have chosen one of the dubious havens for brigands and wharf rats that dotted the waterfront. Yes, all was well—or so he thought until Robert Nast's kid riding glove streaked across his face, knocking a spoonful of stew into his cream-colored, satin-clad lap.

"What the deuce?" Rupert cried. Vaulting to his feet, he scudded his chair out behind him. A rumble of dark mutters rose from the patrons, most of whom rose also, but kept their distance.

"You will give me satisfaction, sir," the vicar demanded.

"I don't even know you!" Rupert snapped, dabbing ruthlessly with his serviette at the greasy stain spread across his pantaloons. "I have never had the pleasure."

"Vicar Robert Nast, sir, and, yes, you have, one afternoon not long ago in the Earl of Kevernwood's orchard. I fired a warning shot over your head as you fled the place after accosting his be-trothed. Kevernwood is a friend of mine."

"Ahhhh!" Rupert exhaled. A tremor of recognition sparked in him. So, it was the vicar who had fired on him? He hadn't gotten a look at the man then; he had been too busy escaping. But it made sense. All the ton knew of the closeness between Simon Rutherford and the vicar of Holy Trinity at Newquay. A lopsided grin broke his scowl. "Ah, yes, the legendary Vicar Nast—of course," he mused. "And just what have I done to you, sir? I should think it would be Kevernwood calling me out. Has he gone soft, then, sending a vicar to fight his battles? Was that wise, I wonder, considering your bungling ineptitude when last we met?"

"I don't fight Kevernwood's battles, Marner," the vicar re-turned, "I fight my own. In your haste to bring Kevernwood low, you slandered an innocent young lady who is very dear to me. You shall answer for that on the dueling ground. Choose your weapons, and the field."

"The St. John chit he's been diddling?" Rupert blurted. "But I don't know why I'm surprised at that. It's what you do, after all, isn't it—redeem the fallen? I'm afraid I cannot accom-modate you, sir. There isn't time. I've booked passage on the *Clairmont*, you see, and, alas, you've caught me quite alone, without a second. Neither have you one, as it seems."

Before the vicar could reply, a group of seamen strolled alongside, doffing their caps collectively.

"Begging your pardon. Did I hear you say you were a friend of Simon Rutherford, sir?" said the tallest of the group to the vicar, though his steely-eyed squint never left Rupert. He was a weathered-looking man of middle age, whose swagger more closely resembled a limp. Rupert didn't know the man.

"I did, sir," Robert Nast replied, taking the man's measure.

"I'll stand for you, then," he offered.

"Impossible!" Rupert cried, incredulous. "You, sir, are no . . . no . . . gentleman. It won't do. You don't suit."

"Oh, aye, I can see how you might conclude that," the man returned levelly as he passed a glance over his attire. "But you can't always judge a man by the cut of his jib, so to speak. Why, at first look, I actually took *you* for a gentleman! Allow me to introduce myself, I am Lieutenant Nathaniel Ridgeway, Earl of Stenshire, at your service, lately mustered out of His Majesty's Royal Navy, where I had the pleasure of serving alongside Simon Rutherford at Copenhagen." He clicked his heels and swept his arm wide. Dismissing Rupert, he turned to the vicar. "Any one of us would gladly stand second for you, Vicar Nast," he said. "My shipmates here and I are just come from Ivybridge Retreat, on Dartmoor, one of the military hospitals Simon's built for us casualties of war. By your leave, I'll be pleased to make your arrangements."

"Thank you, sir," said the vicar with a nod and a handshake.

Rupert paled. There was no way around it now; the burden of supplying a second was put squarely upon him, and it was clear that no one in that establishment would rise to the occasion, much less protest the legality of a duel. He sized up the vicar. No threat there. What would *he* know of dueling? What weapon would he be accustomed to using from his pulpit? He smirked. A rapier perhaps, on an outside chance; the man certainly had the figure for it. But Rupert's gambling instinct told him pistols were the better choice, judging from the ineptitude Nast had exhibited on the occasion of their last meeting. Yes, pistols it would be.

"Since I'm sailing on the morning tide, we shall have to settle this locally," Rupert decreed, "On the Promenade, just before dawn. With pistols, sir?"

The vicar nodded.

"The innkeeper owns a fine brace of flintlocks," Ridgeway put in.

"My second will have to examine and approve them, of course," Rupert added.

"As will mine," replied the vicar.

"You'll need to *find* a second first," the lieutenant sneered, addressing Rupert. "And that might just be a mite difficult for you in these parts."

"I shall manage, have no fear," Rupert assured him haughtily.

"No fear whatever," the lieutenant chortled. "My friends here will accompany you on your search, just to be sure you don't happen to lose your way. They know the lay of the land hereabouts, and if there's a pink-of-the-ton to be found, they'll know where to locate him."

Rupert spread his frockcoat tails and started to resume his seat, but Ridgeway's hand on his arm arrested him in the ridiculous pose.

"You don't want that, 'tis cold" he said, gesturing toward the plate of stew. "And most of it's in your lap anyway." A nod to his companions snapped them to attention. "Best get on with the arrangements," he said, moving aside as the others led him away.

As the men ushered Rupert out of the inn, the lieutenant took his place at the table, and motioned for Robert to join him.

"A word, if you will allow," he said. "We, too, have arrangements to make."

Robert sank into the chair across the table. "Thank you, sir," he said. "I'm afraid I hadn't thought this out. You rescued the moment."

"Is he dead?" Ridgeway whispered.

"I beg your pardon?"

"Simon. Is he dead?"

The innkeeper's wife interrupted them before Robert could reply. He was grateful. He needed time to weigh his answer to that question. If the man was referring to Simon as the Marsh Hawk, he marveled that the news might have spread to Plymouth so swiftly.

"Thank ye for not startin' anythin' in 'ere, sir," the middle-aged woman said, with a nod in the lieutenant's direction as well. She was tall and slender, an intimidating presence standing arms akimbo between them.

"There will be no trouble," Robert promised. "Our . . . differences will be settled far afield of this establishment, and privately."

"Bring the vicar a plate of stew, May," the lieutenant charged, "and see that we aren't disturbed."

"In one of the salons, then?" she suggested, jerking her head in the direction of a hallway beyond the ale barrels. "It's goin' ta fill up in 'ere soon now."

"Aye, and bring a couple tankards," Ridgeway called after her as she turned away. He rose from the table and motioned for the vicar to follow. "Come," he said, "the air has ears."

The salon they chose was decently appointed for a wharf-side inn; the last in a row of five rooms, it was well out of earshot of any of the patrons. Robert was uncomfortable nonetheless. The conversation promised to be controversial at best, and Rupert was staying at this inn, after all.

"He's going to be occupied for a good while, sir," said the lieutenant, as if he had read Robert's thoughts. "That's been arranged. I asked you a question before we were interrupted: Is the Marsh Hawk dead? I need to know."

The vicar hesitated. He knew now exactly what Lieutenant Ridgeway was asking, and he knew how he had to answer. Simon was out of it. The whole circumstance was, at least as he saw it. Simon's golden opportunity to *stay* out of it, to give up his alter ego and claim a life of his own before his luck ran out at Tyburn, was within reach for the first time since the Marsh Hawk was born.

"The Marsh Hawk died on the road to St. Enoder, Lieutenant Ridgeway," he said steadily, on an audible breath.

"And how fares Simon?" the lieutenant replied without batting an eye.

"Simon is very much alive, sir, and at this very hour, I presume, at Newgate Gaol, trying to liberate his bride, who was inadvertently caught in a trap set by the viscount to ensnare him." That the lieutenant knew surprised Rob, and he hesitated. "Do the others know as well?" he asked.

Ridgeway shook his head. "No," he said. "I do, because when the Marsh Hawk first rode, I helped him out of a tight spot. But after everything Simon has done for them, there isn't a sailor in the Royal Navy who wouldn't crawl through fire for him."

The innkeeper's wife served them then, and after she left them to their fare, the vicar recounted the entire coil to the astonished lieutenant, making no connection between Simon and the Marsh Hawk, however. There was no need. The two men understood each other well.

"And so," the vicar concluded, "tomorrow will tell the tale."

"Are you skilled with the pistol, sir?" the lieutenant wondered. "Marner didn't seem to think so."

"Marner observed my holy side," he said with a wry smile. "I fired a shot across his bow, so to speak. I'm actually a better shot than Simon is; he'll vouch for that himself. My aim has saved his skin on more than one occasion over the years. It was expedient at the time I fired on Marner to let those present think otherwise."

"Well, if the blighter drops you on the Promenade tomorrow, he won't live to brag about it," the lieutenant assured him flatly. "You can bet your blunt on that."

CHAPTER TWENTY-SIX

Simon stormed out of Newgate Gaol and snatched his horse's reins from Phelps, who was waiting mounted outside. It had not gone well. For the first time in his life, his title hadn't benefited him. He may as well have been a dipped beggar in the Fleet, for all the clout his earldom carried in that infamous place.

"Don't say it!" he warned the valet, mounting his snorting stallion.

"I haven't said a word, my lord," Phelps defended. "But, by your leave to do so, permit me to say that you're going about this wrongly."

"Phelps, I am half mad with this," Simon returned. "They don't believe her, and she is denied representation by counsel. Under the law, she must speak for herself. Bloody hell! She's achieved her goal, by God, but she's going to die for it unless I can think of some way to prevent it."

"Was she seriously hurt, my lord?"

"I don't even know. They wouldn't let me see her." Though his hair was still tied back with a ribbon, it was mussed from the two-day journey on horseback, and he raked through it with both hands, as though he sought to keep his brain within the confines of his skull.

"Where do we go now?" the valet probed.

"Bow Street. I want to get these hands on this Matthew Biggins individual who put her in that hell there." Simon made a wild gesture toward the prison.

"Surely not like *that*, my lord?"

"Like what?"

"My lord, they'll lock you up for vagrancy. You haven't shaved. Your hair is . . . unkempt. You look as though you've slept in your togs. Don't you think you ought to freshen up a bit at the town house first? You haven't eaten or slept . . . Begging your pardon, my lord, but you look like a wild man."

"I'm going to lose her, Phelps," Simon moaned. He thumped his breast with a scathing fist. "*I* should have avenged her father for her. She wouldn't be in there if I had. I should have said 'the devil take the deuced ball' and addressed our differences. I should have swallowed my pride—my stupid, bloody pride! I *love* her, Phelps!"

"My heart goes out to you, my lord, but you aren't thinking clearly. This isn't like you, sir. You need to regroup and take stock. Nothing will be served by storming the bastions of Bow Street like a madman in the dead of night. How far did such tactics get you in that gaol just now?"

"I . . . love . . . her!"

"I know, my lord."

"I'm going to have to go after Marner for this, you know that. He's got to answer for Jenna—and the rest."

"I know, my lord."

"But not until I get her out of there!"

"Then come to the town house and let me tend you. I'll draw you a nice hot bath, and dress your queue. Why, Fury's tail there is more neatly groomed. Then, after a stiff brandy and a hot meal, you'll sort it all out, my lord."

"It's going to take more than a bath, a brandy, and a full belly to sort this out, old boy," said Simon ruefully. "It's going to take a bloody miracle."

* * *

In her wildest imaginings, Jenna never conjured the nightmare of Newgate Gaol. It never occurred to her that she wouldn't have a space to herself. Though she'd heard the shocking rumors, she wasn't prepared for the press of unwashed bodies milling about in the communal cell; mad and sane, old and young, women from all walks of life, petty thieves and cold-blooded murderers alike were thrust together in a pit of sewage.

She cowered in the shadows, scarcely believing her eyes. The stench permeating the air was a stifling mélange of filth, vermin, sweat, vomit, and human dung that promised to make her retch. The wound in her shoulder was scarcely more than a graze, but it had grown angry and sore, threatening infection for lack of tending. It hadn't been touched since the constable at St. Enoder bandaged it.

She hadn't slept. She was too afraid. One of the mad-women kept stalking her, fawning over her long hair. The woman dogged her, cooing and crooning, petting her hair as though it were an animal. Another, who had evidently bribed the guards for liquor, watched her constantly as well through bleary eyes. The woman was odious and coarse, not mad— worse, a governess who had kidnapped and murdered her charge, and had been sentenced to hang at Tyburn. Her issue seemed to be hatred of the aristocracy, and since Jenna was the only aristocrat among the motley crew, she was the woman's prime target.

Simon hadn't come. Of all the horrors cast upon her then, that was the worst. She hadn't really expected him to, but she had hoped. If only he would come—only that—she could face the trial, Tyburn—anything. She had done what she'd done for her father, but glancing around the stench-ridden squalor she'd been abandoned to, listening to the desperate outcries and mad, shrieking laughter of the inmates, she came to the conclusion that he never would have expected this of her. Strangely now, when her tears would have been appropriate, they would not come. Though she ached inside for the hopelessness of it all, and the loss of the man she loved until she thought her heart would break, she could not shed a one.

Crouching in her corner, as far from the madness in motion around her as she could manage, she desperately attempted to ready her defense. Her own words were all she would be afforded, and she prayed for the fog of confusion in her fever-clouded mind to lift long enough to allow her to prepare her case.

Matthew Biggins received Simon in his private office—a small, book-lined room, modestly appointed and cluttered with what the Runner defined as "loose ends"—as he gathered up the sheaf of rumpled papers before him and stacked them at the side of his desk blotter.

"I shan't belabor this," Simon told him. "I want a full account of the events that put Countess Kevernwood in Newgate Gaol, and—"

"It won't serve you, my lord," the Runner interrupted. "There's nothing to be done. Her trial is scheduled for tomorrow morning."

"—and a full account of your dealings with that jackanapes, Marner," Simon continued with a raised voice.

"That's privileged information, my lord—"

"Not any longer," Simon broke in. "He's dead."

"*Dead*, my lord?"

"Oh, yes—the minute I lay hands on him, sir! So you can consider that, from this moment forth, you are employed by me."

"Th-this is most irregular, sir."

"Indeed. Now are you going to answer me, or am I to extract the information in another manner? Make up your mind, Biggins. I am out of patience with Bow Street. Arresting Countess Kevernwood without a word to me—how did you dare, sir!"

"N-now, look here, my lord—"

"You have condemned her to death, you nodcock! Give account before I lose my patience altogether and take this place down stone by stone around you."

"A-are you threatening me, my lord?"

"You can bet your blunt upon it!"

"Sh-she was caught red-handed. She'd disarmed the man, and was running away with the spoils when I brought her down, my lord," the Runner said, clearing his voice.

"You shot her?"

"I-I was doing my duty. You seem to forget, the countess was engaged in highway robbery."

"She told you that, did she?"

"Well, no, but— "

"What *did* she tell you, then?"

"Well, she . . . didn't, that is to say . . . I mean . . . she was unconscious most of the way to St. Enoder."

Simon stiffened. Rage chased the blood through his veins to his scalp, and his hands balled into fists, drawing the tongue-tied Runner's eyes.

"You're sure she wasn't injured seriously?" Simon gritted through rigid lips.

"Y-yes, my lord," the Runner croaked, running his stubby finger along the inside of his collar. "I merely grazed her shoulder—her arm, really. 'Twas nothing—only a scratch, my lord."

"And that 'scratch' rendered her unconscious?"

"The fall rendered her unconscious, my lord. She was moving apace as she fled."

"She didn't try to explain when she regained consciousness?"

"Well, yes, she told a preposterous tale about avenging her father. Why, she tried to blame the whole deuced coil upon *me*. Well . . . not me personally, you understand. Upon the whole of law enforcement in general."

"You presume too much, imagining the likes of yourself as exemplary of the whole of law enforcement, you inept mawworm. Her story was *truth*. Did that possibility never occur to you, sir?"

"Well, no, as a matter of fact, 'twas too bizarre, my lord."

"Leave that," Simon seethed, looming over the Runner's desk, his nostrils flared, the veins in his neck straining uncomfortably against the modest shirt points Phelps had fixed in place with a triangular tied neckcloth. "What about Marner?"

"He thought that *you* were . . . were—"

"Yes, yes, I know," Simon cut in. "What made him think to accuse me of such a thing?"

"Y-your . . . eh . . ." The Runner stammered, pointing to Simon's queue with a trembling finger. "He claimed that you held him up at gunpoint and he recognized you."

"And you believed him," Simon replied, answering his own question. "It may come as a surprise, but I am not the only man in the realm sporting a queue, Biggins. Many of us old salts still cling to it as a reminder of our glory days. But enough about that. Where is he now?"

"I . . . I—"

"Don't dare hedge with me," Simon shouted, causing the man to give a violent lurch. "Can't you tell that you are speaking with a madman? You've been warned. My patience is at an end here, and there's no telling what I'll do. Where is the whoreson?"

"W-we parted company at St. Enoder," said the Runner. "He was still insisting that you—"

"Yes, yes, I'm sure. Where did he go?"

"He . . . he made mention of a manor house in the Channel Islands. Jersey . . . no, Guernsey."

"I hope you got your blunt from the bastard," Simon said, "because there's nowhere he can run to on the face of the earth to hide from me. And when I'm through with him, let's just say I'll have frozen his assets."

"My lord, my business with Marner is concluded. But let me warn you, if you carry out your threats, you'll answer to the law and follow right along in the countess's footsteps—earl or no. The Tyburn Tree makes no class distinctions, my lord."

"Is that a fact? Well, my good man, we shall just see about that. Enough! Since you ventured into my territory to serve Marner, ethical or no, you've set a precedent. You're on *my* payroll now, and I'd suggest that you start earning your keep. You can begin by telling me what the countess's options are."

"She has none," the Runner said. "She has broken the law; nothing changes that. She must stand trial like any other, and she must make her own defense to boot. She must represent herself. No counsel is permitted."

"There has to be . . . something?"

"Tell me your version of this, my lord."

"To what purpose, if she is denied counsel?" Simon gave a bitter laugh. "This is ludicrous!"

"Just tell it to me."

Simon raked his hair roughly and began to pace as he related Jenna's agenda, deftly omitting his own part in the coil and the circumstances of their first encounter on the old Lamorna Road. When he'd finished, he raked his hair again and leaned over the Runner's desk with his hands splayed on the blotter, waiting.

"So, you're saying she was holding *him* up?" Biggins said, rubbing his chin.

"She was—to see justice done. You just said she had disarmed the blighter."

"Yes, but how was I to know she was a woman, and on such a mission? I took them for rivals arguing over the spoils; so would you have. She was most convincing."

"She *knew* he was her father's murderer! The man held her up in my own coach not a sennight ago. She recognized the pistol he carried. It had belonged to her father, the very one the thatchgallows stole after he bludgeoned the man with it. There was no mistake, Biggins."

"H-how do you know it was the same highwayman?"

"It was only a fleeting glance, but I saw him myself the night he held up the carriage, and I viewed the body at St. Enoder. They are one and the same."

"And she took it upon herself, his apprehension?" He shook his head. "Madness!"

"I'm not condoning her actions, but the law forced that upon her. She went to the guards for help, and they put her off. You know the sort of law we have on the coast—volunteers, guards from the watch, half of them on the take."

"Still, it's a flimsy defense. Sh-she can never prove that pistol was her father's."

"Oh yes, she can. It was marked; his initials were on it. Where is it now?"

"H-here somewhere, I imagine."

"You *imagine*?"

"The constable at St. Enoder may still have it . . . I-I'm not certain."

"That pistol could make her case, man! You've got to find it! Could it clear her?"

"It isn't that simple, my lord. It could pose enough of a question to bring the case before the judge's peers, I suppose."

"How?" Simon urged, grasping at any shred of hope.

"Well, if—and I do say *if*—such were the case, the question posed might then be argued by counsel, not at court, mind, but rather at Serjeant's Inn. All the justices are members there. It's an outside chance, you understand, it's hardly a commonplace occurrence, but if it goes that far and they feel she has been convicted unjustly, she could be pardoned."

"You've convicted her already, haven't you?"

"It's almost a certainty, my lord. I don't want to raise your hopes. She's ill equipped to defend herself. She shan't be privy to the indictments beforehand. No copy is going to be provided her."

"Damn your eyes, man! Find that bloody gun!"

"I-I'll get right on it, my lord," said the Runner, righting the quill holder his fidgeting had knocked over. His hands were trembling, and his face had lost all color.

"Good! The sooner all this is behind us, the sooner I can settle my score with Marner," Simon replied. "The longer you sit there digging holes with that quill in your blotter, the closer my wife comes to the gallows, and the farther away that whoreson ranges himself from *my* brand of justice. Whatever Marner paid you I'll double it, but not unless you earn it. You put her in that gaol. Unless you fancy being without a feather to fly with—because I'll have your situation, sir, make no mistake, and see you raking seaweed out at Land's End if she dies on that damned Tree—you'll get your lazy arse up out of there, and *move!*"

CHAPTER TWENTY-SEVEN

Dawn broke over Plymouth heavy with cottony fog ghosting in off the quay. It drifted lazily inland past the headlands, and poured into the narrow lanes and byways that crosshatched the waterfront to spill over onto the Promenade where Lieutenant Ridgeway and Robert Nast waited for Rupert to make an appearance. The viscount was late—well past the fifteen-minute margin—and Robert was afraid that he might try and escape on the *Clairmont* according to plan.

"He isn't going to run," said the lieutenant. "My friends will see to that. He's probably having trouble finding someone who'll stand second for him. Marner isn't well liked in these parts, Vicar Nast—no one who means Simon harm is."

"The *Clairmont* will be sailing soon. It's almost light," Robert worried.

"The fog will hold her up for a spell, but that won't matter. Marner won't be sailing on her, you can bet your britches on that."

Robert was about to reply, when a group of men parted the fog. Rupert was at the fore, flanked by the lieutenant's com-

rades and a foppish, gangly individual tripping along on unsteady legs, outrageously outfitted in garish colors, not the least
of which were his purple brocade waistcoat and lime green
satin pantaloons. The man, who appeared to be in his early
twenties, was as white as the mist that issued him, his eyes darting among the men herding him unceremoniously to the center of the Promenade.

Robert gave him no more than passing notice. His scrutiny
was aimed instead at Rupert, and Rupert's complacent, lopsided smirk.

"There's no contest there," said the lieutenant, low-voiced.
He ground out a guttural chuckle. "They look like they're on
their way to a fete instead of a duel. That poor fellow's come
straight from one of the gambling hells, to be sure. Steady now.
Don't let them know you've got the cannon to back up your
fleet. Take them by surprise."

"I wish I didn't have to take them at all," Robert lamented.
"But if I don't, Simon surely will, and he doesn't need another
coil to unwind just now."

Before the lieutenant could comment on that, Rupert shoved
his reluctant young second forward.

"M-my lord," the man croaked, "Viscount Chester Hyde,
a-at your service. Present your w-weapons, sirs?"

The innkeeper's pistols had been laid alongside the Promenade on a low table borrowed from the inn as well. The morocco leather case that contained them was propped open with
the pistols on view, recessed in the burgundy baize lining. Several tense moments elapsed while the weapons were inspected,
and finally approved to everyone's satisfaction. There was a cursory display of nitpicking from the opposition, soon quelled by
Lieutenant Ridgeway and his closest associate, a man called
Lige, who had taken on the position of referee. By the time the
issue was resolved, the fog had been reduced to lazy ribbons of
mist hugging the ground.

"Do you want to offer to pardon the blighter if he tenders an
apology?" the lieutenant whispered in the vicar's ear.

"No," Robert replied. "It's too late for that. It ends right here right now, however it must. Not only over my grievance, but for Simon as well."

"Not exactly in character, are you now?" the lieutenant remarked.

"It isn't the first time I've strayed afield of character where Simon was concerned," said Robert. He ripped off his clerical collar and thrust it out. "Please God, it's the last."

"Look sharp," the lieutenant warned, tucking the collar inside his waistcoat. "Rumor has it that Marner's a backstabbing coward in a duel. Just because he's engaged in a gentlemanly tradition doesn't mean he's going to behave like one. Watch your back!"

"That's no rumor, 'tis fact," Robert admitted. "Don't worry, I'll be careful."

"Lige!" the lieutenant barked, nodding toward the referee. Set in motion, the man took two whittled stakes from the table. Stepping forward, he handed one to Lieutenant Ridgeway, and the other to Chester Hyde.

"Advance five paces, gentlemen, and drive in your stakes," the referee charged the seconds.

Both men paced off the distance, drove the stakes into the ground, and returned to the table where Rupert and the vicar waited.

"Choose your weapon," the referee said to Rupert, nodding to the pistol case.

Rupert examined each gun carefully again, hefting them in his hand, and finally made a choice. Robert took up the other. Then they both consigned their weapons to their seconds for loading.

The vicar watched Ridgeway ram the pistol ball into his gun with accomplished skill. Hyde, on the other hand, trembling hopelessly, dropped the ball twice, and had to search for it, groping the mist on his knees, whining all the while over the grass stains his pantaloons suffered on the wet Promenade lawn.

Rupert's impatience was painfully obvious; Robert monitored his nervous dance over Hyde's search for the pistol ball with not a little amusement. When their eyes met, Rupert's dark glower spoke volumes. But Robert met that scathing look coolly, and when at last Ridgeway put the loaded pistol in his hand, he held it steady with unprecedented calm.

"Backs to the stakes," the referee barked. "Pistols raised! The duel will begin at thirty paces. You will each take ten paces and turn. Then, when I give the signal, you will advance and fire at will any time before you reach the barrier stakes—"

"Yes, yes, let us get on with it! We know what we're about," Rupert cut in tersely.

"If you know what you're about, gov'nor, then you know it is my duty to present the rules, sir, so that there be no question afterward," the referee responded.

"Get on with it, then, you nodcock!"

"If there is a miss," the referee continued, "the opponent will not move, and the first shooter will allow the same distance for return fire. Pistols must be discharged in the direction of the opponent. If neither shooter hits, you will begin again. Is that clear, gentlemen?"

"Yes—yes—yes!" Rupert intoned.

"Then, gentlemen, take your places at the barrier stakes, and at my sign you will each advance ten paces, turn, and await my signal to cock your pistols and begin."

Rupert and the vicar responded, standing with their backs to the stakes, pistols upright, and waited.

Robert caught Ridgeway's narrow-eyed stare evaluating the entire circumstance, and when the lieutenant moved his coat aside, exposing a compact little pocket pistol concealed there, he swallowed dry. So, there was a backup. Ridgeway didn't trust Marner any more than he did. The pocket pistol was a comforting sight; as was the nod the lieutenant gave him. Robert wasn't in the least concerned over his shooting skills. Treachery was the only aspect of the duel that troubled him. After hearing Simon's account of Rupert, the last thing he wanted to do was turn his back on the man—even if it was only for the space of ten steps.

"Advance ten paces, turn, and wait for my signal to begin," the referee shouted, jarring him back to the present.

Footfalls crunching along the dew-drenched Promenade were the only sounds. The referee hadn't given the command to cock pistols, but Robert's thumb inched along the hammer in anticipation nonetheless. He had paced off, and was about to turn, when two shots rang out almost simultaneously, fracturing the stillness. In the same instant as he fell, from the corner of his eye he caught the blur of the lieutenant's arm drawing back his fired pistol. Just before his starred vision shut out light and consciousness, he watched at an angle through the wet grass spears against his face, the blurred image of Viscount Chester Hyde running away on spindly legs. With his coattails streaming behind him, the garish little fop disappeared into the crowd of spectators that the lieutenant's comrades could no longer keep at bay. Oddly, until that moment, Robert's focus had been such that he hadn't even noticed the gathering. But those people were the last he saw before the cold, wet, pain-ridden darkness swallowed him.

Robert opened his eyes to a wreath of pipe tobacco smoke, and Lieutenant Ridgeway stooping over his bed. Where was he? The room seemed familiar. It ought to be; it was his customary room at Kevernwood Hall, the one he'd often occupied on stay-over visits in the past. But . . . how could it be? Something tight girded his torso, like a second skin beneath his linen nightshirt. It pressed on grieved tissue with every movement, extracting from him a grimace and a deep throaty groan.

"Lucky for you," the lieutenant said, answering the sound as part of the conversation, "the pistol ball went clear through your side and made a clean exit. You're going to be just fine— he missed your vitals. How do you feel?"

"As well as can be expected for a man who's just been backshot," the vicar replied.

"Well, he won't be shooting anybody else in the back, that's for sure."

"Marner's *dead*?"

"I'm only sorry I wasn't faster," the lieutenant said, nodding. "He spun around on the ninth pace, and fired. He was quick enough, by God, but speed and my interference cost him accuracy. While I couldn't prevent what happened, I evidently distracted him enough to help spoil his aim. He saw death coming. I drilled him clean through the heart, and he dropped like a stone. You won by default, of course."

"B-but . . . how have I come here?"

"Hah!" the lieutenant erupted. He ground out a guttural chuckle. "You wouldn't pipe down till I brought you. You were off your head, but you kept insisting I bring you. Your duty was here, so you said, and you wouldn't have it any other way. You've no recollection of that?"

"I . . . I don't remember much except falling, and watching that weaselly second of Marner's run off through the crowd. I didn't feel anything at first, just the impact. Then, when the pain came . . . everything went black."

"There was a surgeon in that crowd, and we got you back to the inn so he could patch you up. You lost a good deal of blood, but he dosed you with laudanum and trussed you up good and proper so I could get you out here where one of your local surgeons could tend you." He cleared his voice and offered a wry smile. "I take it the lovely young lady that greeted us when we arrived is the reason for all this?"

A hot rush of blood sped to Robert's face, and he moistened fever-parched lips with a dry tongue. He owed the lieutenant an explanation.

"Lady Evelyn St. John and her twin brother Crispin are . . . orphans, and close friends of the Rutherford family," he explained haltingly. "Simon's just secured a naval commission for Crispin. It was here, at Evelyn's come-out ball, that she suffered insult because of Marner. He sullied Evelyn's name with an ugly rumor that had no basis in fact as an act of vengeance against Simon. I knew if I didn't call the bounder out over it, Simon would, and I thought to save him the bother. He has enough to worry about, what with the coil I explained. Lady Evelyn has no . . . feelings for me."

"Mmm," the lieutenant responded, clearly skeptical.

"C-can you stay until Simon returns?" Robert asked, attempting to divert the subject. "I know he will want to reward you."

"Oh, aye, I can stay, but I don't want any reward. It will do me good to see Simon again. It's been awhile, and I just might be of help—hopefully more help than I was to you."

"You have nothing to reproach yourself for," Robert assured him. "It all happened so quickly."

"The dueling ground is no place for a vicar—no matter how liberal. I knew the blighter would show his colors. I was ready for it."

"And if he hadn't?" Robert asked.

"Thank God we'll never know."

It took a moment for Robert to process that. He was still groggy from the opiate, and none of this seemed real. If it weren't for the pain in his side, he would have sworn he'd dreamed the entire episode, and when Evelyn burst through the door and ran to his bedside, her blue eyes swimming in tears, he was positive he'd lapsed into a very pleasant hallucination, indeed.

"You're awake—you *are*!" she sobbed, fussing over him.

"Stand back, girl, and let the poor man breathe," Lady Jersey chided, taking the situation in hand. "Is that tobacco smoke I smell? Put that filthy thing out at once, sir. This is no public house!"

The vicar's eyes were so filled with Evelyn, he hadn't seen the other woman enter, and had had no idea there was anyone else on earth until she spoke.

"Dr. Arborghast has come from Newquay," Evelyn announced. "He'll be up directly. He's instructing Mrs. Rees about a tisane for you." Then, in an aside to the others she said, "Mrs. Rees's tisanes are quite legendary. All the surgeons consult her. So, you see, you're going to be all right," she mewed, returning her gaze to him. "I just know you are."

"I-is there any word from Simon?" he wondered.

Evelyn shook her head no and lowered her eyes.

"Simon is well able to handle the situation, whatever it is," the lieutenant put in. "You needn't worry over that."

Evelyn fidgeted with Robert's pillow. "Whatever possessed you?" she sobbed in dismay. "You could have been killed!"

The doctor's entrance spared him making a reply, and he was grateful for it. If truth were told, trusting himself to make an intelligent statement in such close proximity to the inimitable Lady Evelyn St. John was a more painful thing than the hole in his side, and it was a great relief to him when Lady Jersey shooed the entire company into the hall and relinquished her command to the doctor.

CHAPTER TWENTY-EIGHT

"What do you mean, you don't have the gun?" Simon bellowed. He was pacing over the bare wood floor in the Runner's office in his ragged gait, made more pronounced for his lack of sleep. "It's nearly time for the trial to begin."

"It isn't here at Bow Street. I've made a thorough inquiry. I certainly d-didn't bring it, and it wasn't sent on with the bailiff's report."

"Where is that brigand's body now?"

"Why, I . . . I—"

"Come, come, man, you took the credit for his capture quickly enough—and claimed the reward, I have no doubt. Where's the bloody corpse?"

"B-back at St. Enoder, I imagine, that's where I left it—where you yourself saw it in the bailiff's keeping. It's probably been turned under the sod by now. It certainly isn't here."

"And the pistol as well, I suppose?"

"It would follow, my lord, that the pistol is still there somewhere. As I said, it hasn't been forwarded."

"Well, since the good Lord didn't see fit to endow me with

wings, how do you expect me to fetch it here in time for the trial?"

Biggins rubbed his chin and looked off into space, his bushy brows knit in a frown.

"Well?" Simon demanded.

"It was a fine piece, my lord. I doubt you'll find it now."

"Are you saying that someone at St. Enoder might have made off with it?"

"It's very possible, my lord. It was an exceptional piece. Or . . . or Marner himself might have taken it. Yes, that could well be . . . in all the confusion."

"By God, I will see this slipshod corruption you call 'law enforcement' reformed by the time all this is done. Before I go off on a wild goose chase, you are certain no such thievery has occurred *here*?"

"Absolutely, sir!" the Runner cried, indignant. "If it were brought here, it would *be* here."

"Yes, well, you should have done, shouldn't you? It has to be somewhere." He pushed his hair back from a moist brow, cleared his throat and pronounced, "I want you to think, Biggins. When did you last see that pistol?"

"Th the blighter . . . the Marsh Hawk—his name was William Hatch, by the way—eh, he . . . he didn't have it when I brought him down—"

"And? Come, come, there isn't time for this. The pistol, man—the pistol!"

"I'm trying to remember, my lord!" the Runner cried, waving trembling hands. "I don't think . . . *no*! You're confusing me. I didn't confiscate the pistol. Th-the countess took the pistol from the thatchgallows and made off with it—and the spoils—before he tried to escape."

"You recovered the spoils, though, didn't you?"

"Well, yes, my lord, but—"

"Bet your blunt, you did! Those things belonged to *you*, didn't they—you and Marner? Never mind. Can you get the trial postponed?"

"No, my lord. I have no say in court proceedings. Technically, my involvement in this brouhaha is over and done with."

"That's what you think," Simon seethed.

"Here! Where are you going, my lord?" the Runner called to Simon's back.

"To buy my wife some time," he replied, crashing through the doorway.

Jenna was grateful that she had no mirror. She could only imagine what she must look like. Her skin was hot and dry to the touch. It was fever; there was no mistaking it now. Her parched lips were cracked, and there was a buzzing noise echoing in her ears. As she awaited what promised to be an automatic conviction, nothing seemed to matter anymore. Simon hadn't come. He must surely know by now . . . and he hadn't come. Whatever made her think he might? It was over.

She dared not dwell upon any of that, not standing in the dock. The magistrate looked formidable at best, a hawk-faced prune of a man whose drooping jowls challenged his neckcloth.

It was early in the day, which was to her advantage. The man wasn't irritable yet from fatigue. That, however, didn't soften the look in his sharp, hooded eyes.

"Lady Kevernwood," he said, causing her to jump. "You are accused of armed robbery on the King's highway, a crime that carries the sentence of hanging at Tyburn if you are convicted by this court. Have you anything to say in your own defense?" She hadn't expected so thunderous a voice coming from such a wizened creature. It sent cold chills racing along her spine, and the rush of blood that accompanied them heightened her fever. Despite it all, she heaved a deep breath and spoke in her most eloquent voice.

"I am innocent of the charge leveled against me, Your Worship," she began steadily. "A year and a half ago, I went to the authorities for help in finding and bringing the Marsh Hawk to justice after he bludgeoned my father with his own pistol during a highway robbery, and subsequently caused his death. The law offered me no help, and so I took it upon myself to avenge my father by bringing the criminal to justice on my own. I dressed as a highwayman in order to get close enough to do so. That is what I was about on the night I was apprehended. I would have done it, too, but for the interference of the Bow Street Runner who interrupted us. The Marsh Hawk had already relinquished the spoils and the pistol—*my father's pistol*—to me at gunpoint, when the Runner—"

"But you ran with the spoils," the magistrate cut in.

"I *ran*, Your Worship. Period," she corrected. "I wasn't thinking of the spoils. I had accomplished my objective. The Marsh Hawk was dead and my father was avenged. I ran to spare my family . . . this. That the sack with the spoils in it was still attached to my saddle was not my primary concern, Your Worship. I certainly never meant to keep the contents of that sack. What need would I possibly have of spoils? Except for that pistol, my father's property, which was my proof of the brigand's guilt—the pistol that he had beaten my father to death with— the rest meant nothing to me."

"And, where is this legendary pistol, pray?" the magistrate barked.

"W-with the spoils, I imagine. I put it in the sack with the rest."

"Preposterous!" the magistrate bellowed. "No pistol was recovered, only the spoils planted by Matthew Biggins of Bow Street to trap your fellow robber."

"He was not my fellow, Your Worship! Haven't you heard me? I was apprehending him!"

"Lady Kevernwood, your social standing does not place you above the law. Do you suppose us all birdwits here? You ramble on about a mythical pistol that you cannot produce. Where is your proof? Are there any witnesses to speak for you, madam?"

"N-no, Your Worship," she despaired.

A hand gesture brought a bailiff with a black velvet pall, which the man placed on the magistrate's wigged head.

"Jenna Rutherford, née Hollingsworth, Countess of Kevern-wood, I hereby charge that you—"

"She is telling the truth," a voice boomed from the gallery stairwell. All heads snapped toward a tall, masked figure of a man emerging from the shadows.

Simon.

The gavel cracked furiously, as a surly rumble of voices crescendoed into an uproar. The spectators left their seats, craning their necks for a look at the masked, cloaked figure stalking to the center of what had become an arena, reminiscent of Jenna's imaginings of ancient Rome. She stood paralyzed, staring toward her husband who approached the bench like a Christian before the lions.

"You are out of order, sir!" the magistrate bellowed, vaulting from his chair. "What is the meaning of this charade? Unmask at once! Reveal yourself!"

Simon doffed his tricorn hat, removed his mask and bowed from the waist, triggering a collective gasp that rippled through the spectators, prompting another demand for order from the magistrate, punctuated by another furious assault upon the bench with the gavel.

"*L-l-lord Kevernwood?*" he spluttered, sinking back into his chair. "Have you gone addled, sir?"

"No, Your Worship," Simon replied. "The countess speaks truth."

"Of course you would say so," the magistrate scoffed. "How dare you interrupt these proceedings with your bizarre theatrics? Can you possibly think such a display will work in her favor? Leave this court at once, sir, or I will have you removed!"

"No, Your Worship, I can prove it!" Simon shouted, as the magistrate nodded to the bailiff.

"Simon, *no!*" Jenna shrilled.

"Silence!" the magistrate commanded, raising his hand.

"Your Worship," Simon continued, "I know that she speaks the truth firsthand, because she did the same to me."

"To *you*, sir?"

"To me, Your Worship," Simon parroted. "It is, in fact, the manner in which we met. The man that Biggins shot on the road to St. Enoder was not the Marsh Hawk. Oh, he possessed her father's pistol right enough, because he was the brigand who caused the baronet's death, but he wasn't the Marsh Hawk. He was only a ne'er-do-well by the name of William Hatch, who bears a physical resemblance to me and meant to capitalize on that. You see, *I* am the Marsh Hawk, my lord—at least I was—and the countess held me up last spring in the same manner as she did Hatch. I bear the wound to prove it."

Without further ado, Simon loosened his cape and shirt, exposing his shoulder wound before the flabbergasted magistrate's wide-flung eyes.

As a fresh uproar arose, a groan from the dock turned Simon's head, and he sprang to Jenna's side as she swayed and sank to the floor out of sight.

"Jenna, the pistol!" he whispered close in her ear as he crushed her close in his arms. "Where is that deuced pistol?"

His eyes, lit with feral lights, searched her face. His ragged heartbeat pounded against her, while his trembling hands roamed her body like a starving man groping a platter of food. The heady scent of his tobacco blended with the faintest trace of wine assailed her nostrils, just as it had on the night that seemed a lifetime ago on the old Lamorna Road, and she groaned again.

"Simon, what have you done?"

"Your arm—are you all right?" he pleaded. "You're burning with fever."

"Whatever possessed you?" she moaned, nodding against him.

"I'm trying to buy us some time," he gritted out through clenched teeth. "You've got to tell me—the pistol, Jenna! We need it if we are to get your case adjourned to Serjeant's Inn for deliberation."

"I–it was in that sack, Simon. I'm certain of it," she insisted.

"Take them down!" the magistrate thundered.

A swarm of bailiffs armed with truncheons descended upon

them then, and Jenna felt herself lifted. Others were dragging Simon away. The courtroom was in pandemonium. Milling figures swam before her. Spectators shouted in her face. The gavel banged incessantly. The magistrate had grown hoarse from shouting over the thunderous din. Above it all, the last thing she heard before she lost consciousness was Simon's thunderous voice demanding that a surgeon be summoned to tend her.

He hadn't abandoned her after all. Nothing else mattered, and she succumbed to the blessed release of oblivion.

"My lord, that display just now was foolhardy at best. Whatever possessed you?" Biggins railed. The Runner had spirited Simon away to his office once the bailiffs released him.

"It worked, didn't it?" Simon flashed. "Hah!" he erupted, as if to himself. "They didn't believe me—they laughed in my face—took me for a desperate husband trying to save his bride, the lack-wits!"

"I-it's true, isn't it?" the Runner breathed, as though a light had gone on in his brain. "It's all true, just as Marner said. You *are* the Marsh Hawk!"

Simon glanced at him. "The Marsh Hawk is dead, you nodcock. You shot him yourself on the road to St. Enoder, remember? It's best for all concerned that you let him stay as he lay—unless, of course, you fancy exposing yourself as the inept laughingstock you truly are."

"No! I'm right, aren't I? It's you! All along it was you."

"You and Marner gave me the name. I'm simply playing the game," Simon growled. "Now where is that bloody pistol? You had best come up with it posthaste. You heard them back there—I have less than a sennight to produce that gun, and even at that there are no guarantees. You were the last one with that bloody sack. Where is that deuced pistol?"

"A-actually, I wasn't, my lord," Biggins confessed.

"What do you mean, you weren't?" Simon demanded, crouching over the Runner's desk.

"M-Marner was."

"Explain! Be quick! I warn you, my patience ebbs low, Biggins."

"That dreadful woman, Lady Jersey, and her shrieking abigail, my lord, she was carping at us—interfering with official Bow Street business. I . . . I had Wilby, Marner's driver, give me a hand with the countess . . . she was unconscious, you see. He helped me put her in the carriage, and Marner collected the sack—at my direction, o-of course—then we took the countess on to St. Enoder, where we parted company. After I made my report, I hired a carriage, and brought the countess and the spoils here to Town."

"The gun, man—the *gun*!" Simon prompted, out of patience.

"Th-that's just it, my lord, there was no gun in the sack. Marner must have taken it."

"Marner, eh—or Biggins, perhaps? What was it you said, 'it was a fine piece'? You stressed that point as I recall. How fine, Biggins? Come, come, you must have examined it quite thoroughly to arrive at such an assessment. Is it fine enough to tempt a Bow Street Runner to let an innocent woman dance the Tyburn jig?"

"My lord!" Biggins cried, vaulting from the chair behind his desk. "Do you actually believe I'd sacrifice my career for a . . . a pistol, sir?"

"No, but you might be to save your career by covering up the theft of one. I strongly suggest that you make a clean breast of it, if such is the case—now, before I discover the truth. Because I *will* discover the truth, my man, and if my wife dies—"

"My lord! *I* conduct the interrogations here," the Runner interrupted hoarsely. "I think you'd best take your threats to Marner, sir. How dare you stand there and accuse me?"

"Your association with the jackanapes has earned that for you, and believe me I dare. I *have* to dare, sir; you give me no choice. Now then, didn't you say that Marner made mention of a manor house in the Channels—Guernsey, I believe you said?"

"He did, my lord."

"Well, it would do you well to pray that we can intercept him before he sails."

"*We*, my lord?"

"We," Simon enunciated. "You didn't imagine I'd let you out of my sight after this, did you? Besides, you're working for me now, remember?"

CHAPTER TWENTY-NINE

Before an hour was over, Simon had collected Phelps and hired a coach and four from the livery. With Biggins in tow, they were speeding along the highway on a course that would take them first to Kevernwood Hall.

Though he was not allowed to visit Jenna, he'd been assured that she would receive proper medical care. After seeing her in soiled and tattered highwayman's attire, he'd also managed to persuade the magistrate to allow her a change of clothing, which he would have Phelps collect at the manor and take back to Newgate Gaol.

The touch of her soft, supple body in his arms, yielding to his embrace, would not leave him, for she'd clung to him until his loins responded even in that dire circumstance. He was haunted, as ever a mortal could be by a ghost yet living; he had no peace. Would he lose her to the Tyburn Tree? He refused to accept it.

But for stopping at coaching stations to change horses along the way, the trio drove straight through. Simon never slept, and though Phelps pretended to, he didn't fool Simon for a moment. It was clear that the valet was keeping a close watch on the entire situation. By the time they'd put the second coaching station behind them, Biggins opted for a spell "up top," as he put it, to keep the coachman company. Simon was well aware that his own black looks had driven the Runner aloft. He didn't trust the man; it was that simple. Whether his suspicions were founded or not, remained to be seen. Guilty or no, the Runner certainly looked the part of a man with something to hide, and Simon was committed to making him sweat.

Biggins had scarcely scrambled up to the top of the coach when Phelps addressed the issue by posing the question Simon had seen in his eyes since they boarded.

"What do you hope to accomplish by bringing that . . . person along, my lord?" the valet queried.

"I don't trust the blighter enough to let him out of my sight," Simon replied. "He's safe enough up top. How far could he go that we couldn't run him to ground in open country? But that's as far as I'm prepared to go. Either Marner lifted that pistol, thinking to use it in some way as leverage to get to Jenna, or Biggins pinched the deuced thing and wants to cover it up to save his hide. If I cut him loose and he is guilty, he'll disappear. I can't take that chance, Phelps. He can go to blazes after I get my hands on that gun—not before."

"He will slow us down, my lord."

"Not 'us,' old boy; *me*. I'm not stopping at the Hall. I'm just dropping you off so you can have Molly pack a portmanteau for Jenna. You're to return to London at once with it, and if I don't get back there in three days, think of some way to stall for time."

"Me, my lord?" the valet cried, through a strangled gasp. "What can I possibly do?"

"You'll think of something, I have no doubt. You always come through, and we've been in tighter spots that this over the years, my friend. It's just that the stakes haven't ever been quite so high as they are this time. I'm counting on you, Phelps. Don't let me down."

"You know I'd sooner lose my limbs than fail you, my lord,

but that magistrate is a Neanderthal. If my lady couldn't charm him—"

"My lady charmed him well enough."

"Not without your . . . sacrificial performance. And that's another thing! What would you have done if they believed you? Hah! Are you even certain that they didn't?"

"I'm certain, or I wouldn't be sitting here right now. I've been such a colossal fool! I love her, Phelps. Without her, it doesn't matter what they believe."

The barouche wheels had scarcely stopped rolling in the circular drive at Kevernwood Hall when Evelyn came flying through the portico attached to the conservatory. Her sprigged muslin gown tinted peach in the rays of the setting sun, she raced across the drive, reached inside and flung her arms around Simon's neck, almost upsetting Phelps as he vacated the coach.

"Oh, Simon, thank God!" she sobbed. "The doctor said he was going to be fine . . . and now—oh, Simon! He was nearly killed! Lady Hollingsworth has taken a fit of apoplexy. She hardly knows us. Why, the doctor has practically taken up residence. We thought you would never return, and none dared leave to come after you."

"Who was nearly killed? Calm yourself and tell me, Evy. What's happened?"

"Robert . . . I mean, the vicar . . . he—"

"What's happened to Rob?" he demanded, gently shaking her.

"H-he's been shot, Simon!" she wailed.

"Shhh," he soothed. Catching a glimpse of Biggins's slack jaw and wide-eyed stare, taking it in with not a little interest, he said in a low-voiced aside to Phelps, "See that our Runner is made comfortable in the study. Instruct one of the footmen to dance attendance until I join him there once I've sorted this out. See that the coachman and groom are refreshed in the servants' quarters while Molly packs my lady's portmanteau, and then leave for London at once. I'll handle whatever this is here." Without waiting for a reply, he led Evelyn ahead, out of the Runner's range of hearing.

"Will you please tell me what the deuce you're talking about?" he snapped, hurrying her up the front steps.

"I . . . I saw your coach from the conservatory. I didn't mean to fly at you like that. Please don't scold me, Simon . . . it's been dreadful!"

"Where is Rob now?"

"In his old chamber. You know, the one he used to use when we had the hunts."

"How bad is he?" Simon asked, streaking toward the staircase.

Evelyn's stutters bloomed into a helpless spasm of blubbering, and Simon scaled the stairs two at a stride, leaving her behind. On the landing above, Lady Jersey appeared, and he raised his hands and jutted his broad chin out in a desperate plea for an explanation from the woman standing ramrod rigid in his path.

"The vicar was shot in a duel with Rupert Marner, Simon," she said levelly.

"In a—*Rob*?" he blurted, incredulous. "Was he foxed? Rob is a better shot on his worst day than Marner ever was on his best."

"He was back-shot, dear," she explained.

"Bloody hell!" Simon seethed, raking his hair with a rough hand. "What was he doing dueling with Marner in the first place?"

"Saving you the trouble."

"Damn and blast!" he said in an undervoice. "Where is Marner now?"

"Rupert Marner is dead," she informed him.

Simon searched the woman's eyes, which were dark in the shadows of twilight that had fallen over the stairwell, for the servants had not yet illuminated the landing. He nearly lost his footing. A low groan leaked from him, so charged with emotion it caused her to take a step back.

"What is it?" she murmured.

Evelyn's wails had grown louder, and she motioned the girl toward quiet with an impatient hand gesture that did little to quell the din.

"Rob killed him?" Simon said. His mind couldn't take it in.

It was like a nightmare. Evelyn's sobs, though shrill, were no more than an echo behind the desperate thoughts tearing around in his brain—thoughts that demanded action from all quarters at once.

"No," Lady Jersey replied, her voice edged with caution. "The lieutenant killed him."

"Lieutenant? What lieutenant?"

"A friend of yours, so it seems. Nathaniel Ridgeway, Earl of Stenshire. He's staying on. He and the doctor are with Vicar Nast now."

"Nate Ridgeway . . . here?" Evelyn's sobs had finally begun to invade his addled brain, and he gestured toward the girl behind. "My lady, please see to her," he said. "Perhaps one of Mrs. Rees's herbal teas will help. Once I've sorted all this out, I'll want a word with you before I leave. But now, you must excuse me."

Dr. Arborghast was standing over the vicar's sleigh bed, staring down, when Simon entered the bedchamber. At sight of him, Lieutenant Ridgeway came forward extending his hand. Simon gripped it hard, and clapped him on the shoulder.

"Nate," he greeted "What the bloody devil's going on?"

"Your friend here got himself back-shot in a duel with a coward on the Promenade at Plymouth," he replied. "We thought he was out of the woods, but then infection set in, and he can't seem to shake the fever."

"He's got to shake it." Simon decreed, uptilting his chin toward the doctor. "Arborghast?"

"I'm not liking this relapse," the doctor said. "He was getting on well at first. I'm not liking this at all."

"How long has he been delirious?" Simon asked.

"Since sunup, my lord. Mrs. Rees is preparing another herbal poultice, and a tisane to bring the fever down, but if it doesn't break soon—"

"Shouldn't he go to hospital?" Simon interrupted.

"No," said the doctor, with a quick shake of his head. "I don't want to take a chance on moving him again as he is. The trip from Plymouth has all but had its way with him. It isn't necessary. Mrs. Rees is as able a nurse as he'd find at hospital, I promise you."

Simon looked in dismay toward the vicar tossing in the bed alongside. Emotion choked him. He could never recall seeing his friend so helpless, nor could he recall himself in so helpless a state—so powerless to make things right for the two people that meant the most to him.

"I should be lying there in that bed," he said ruefully. "I should have known he'd do something foolish like this. Who's minding his church?"

"The deacons," the lieutenant said, laying a hand on his arm. "There's nothing you can do here." He nodded toward the doctor. "Come away and let the man work."

For a moment, Simon looked at him as though he were a stranger. Marner was dead, but where was the pistol? He had to find that pistol.

"Simon?" the lieutenant prompted.

"Come with me," Simon replied, shaking his head in a vain attempt to clear his hammering thoughts.

A sitting room adjoined the vicar's chamber, and Simon had a bottle of brandy and glasses brought there. They drank, while he and Ridgeway exchanged accounts of the events that had brought them together.

"So you see, I've got to find that pistol," Simon concluded. "We pushed four horses at a gallop, only allowing an hour at each coaching station to get here in less than two days. I'll need at least that much time to make the return trip, and that's not allowing for broken springs, sprung wheels, and lame horses—not to mention the weather. I was fortunate coming down, but I don't dare count upon providence to smile upon me so readily returning; not the way things seem to be stacking up against me. Time is running out. I've only got four days left, and one of those will be gone before I settle all this. What sort of weapon did Marner use in that duel?"

"They used a brace of dueling pistols that belonged to the

publican at the Albatross Inn, down on Notte Street by the quay."

"I know it. Go on."

"Your friend never got the chance to fire."

"Did Marner have a pistol on him any of the other times you saw him, Nate?"

"I never saw one. But that's not to say he didn't have one in his room at the inn."

"Where were his coach and driver? The Runner says . . ." He gave a start and slapped his forehead with the heel of his hand. "Good God! I'd forgotten all about Biggins! He's downstairs in the study waiting for me."

"Never saw a coach or driver," the lieutenant said. "Marner may have dismissed them. He had booked passage on a ship bound for Guernsey, you know. He wouldn't have needed a carriage."

"That deuced gun could be anywhere. Jenna insists that she put it in the sack with the spoils. Biggins says not. He's either lying, or Marner took it. The whoreson could either have left it in the coach, which I sincerely doubt, or he could have taken it with him. Could it still be at that inn, do you think?"

"You'd best pray not," Ridgeway ground out with a guttural laugh. "If it's still at the Albatross, someone's pinched it for sure. They'll never hand it over to you, Simon; not that lot. They're a wild bunch of pirates and brigands on that waterfront. You walk in there all got up in superfine and silk, and you'll be up against ten-to-one. They'll take your blunt, keep the gun, conk you on the head, and pitch you off the dock with nobody the wiser. Your friend in there—hah! and Marner, too, come to that—were fortunate that they ran into me and my crew, or they'd likely have met the fate I just described. It's a daily occurrence. It wouldn't have mattered in Marner's case, of course, but I think you get my drift."

"Phelps was right," Simon murmured. He'd begun to pace the Aubusson carpet. "Biggins is going to slow me down. But there's nothing for it. I don't trust the blighter."

"Look here," said Ridgeway, putting himself in Simon's path. "Do you want me to deal with this Runner chap?"

"For the moment, Nate, if you wouldn't mind," Simon decided. "Bloody hell, I haven't even thanked you for all your help, and here I am asking for more. Forgive my want of conduct. It's no excuse, but I'm half-mad with all this."

"Don't give it a thought. Whatever you need. That goes without saying, Simon."

"All right, then stay here, and keep Biggins till I return. That will free me for what I have to do. Also, I'm worried about Rob. Whatever he needs, see that he gets it. We've been friends since before we were breeched. I love him like a brother. And if he comes 'round while I'm gone . . . ask him if he knows anything about that gun. If by some miracle you manage to find it, don't come after me, deliver it to my valet at the town house— you know where it is, in Hanover Square—and tell him to take it to Serjeant's Inn. He'll know what to do."

"You really think the Runner might have that pistol?"

"I don't know what to think, but I can't afford the luxury of trust. He better *not* have it—not after I go off chasing my tail while the clock is ticking."

"Where are you going?" Ridgeway called, as Simon slapped his glass down on the table and bolted toward the door. "Don't you think I ought to know—just in case?"

"*I'm* not going anywhere," he hurled over his shoulder. "The Marsh Hawk is going to pay a little call at the Albatross Inn."

"Simon, the Marsh Hawk is *dead*! He needs to stay dead."

"Word travels fast, but not that fast," said Simon. "They won't know that yet in Plymouth, Nate. Just keep Biggins in your sites, and leave the Marsh Hawk to me."

CHAPTER THIRTY

Lady Jersey made it plain that she was only too glad to stay on and help with Evelyn and Lady Hollingsworth, when Simon broached the subject with her before he left. That he was taking advantage of her generosity worried him, but after speaking with her, he got the distinct impression that, short of being put out bodily, she had no intention of leaving Kevernwood Hall until his dilemma was resolved. It was obvious that her curiosity was piqued. Simon also knew she wasn't about to budge until she had all the particulars on what promised to be the juiciest on-dit since the Fordenbridge wreckers scandal, so that she could be the first to break the story—with his permission, of course.

Fury was the fastest horse in his stables, and Simon wasted no time having Barstow saddle the stallion. At the tower, he exchanged his bluecoat of superfine, embroidered brocade waistcoat, and faun-colored pantaloons for a black shirt and breeches. It was too warm for a greatcoat, so he chose a light black cloak instead, stuffed a tricorn hat and mask in a sack, loaded the brace of dueling pistols that lived in the chifforobe drawer, and set out for Plymouth under cover of darkness.

He didn't travel the main highways. He was well accustomed to less congested shortcuts from past experience. He stopped only once, to leave Fury at the coaching station in Liskead, where he hired another horse to take him the rest of the distance: a sleek bay with the long, muscular legs that hallmarked breeding for speed.

It was three in the morning when he reached the Albatross Inn. He had made good time. He couldn't have marched upon Plymouth in broad daylight; He needed the darkness to carry out his plan. But as he stopped outside to don his tricorn hat and mask, and cock his pistols, it occurred to him how futile a quest he'd undertaken. Not having slept, he was not at his most astute. All the separate pressures had melded into one gigantic mountain of complexity that seemed insurmountable. Still, there was nothing for it but to let the coil play out, and so he tethered the bay, squared his posture, and made his stealthy approach to the inn.

Such establishments along the waterfront at Plymouth harbor almost never closed their doors. The patrons were, however, usually cup-shot by this hour, and would, he hoped, cause little resistance if caught by surprise. Without further ado, he kicked the door open and burst inside, pistols raised.

A shriek from the innkeeper's wife roused a few fuddled patrons lazing about, and Simon quickly stepped away from the open door and put his back to the wall. He was out of his element, and he knew it. This was not his customary sort of banditry. He would have been much more comfortable in the open on horseback, targeting inept aristocrats, than the motley assortment of ne'er-do-wells and thatchgallows facing him now.

"Look sharp, and pay attention," he gritted out, as the lieutenant's warning ghosted across his memory. "I do not like repeating myself."

"T-take what ya will," the publican said hoarsely. "Just don't break up the place."

"I want only one thing," Simon returned. "You had a duel here two days ago, or thereabout. A man was killed. He had a pistol in his possession—a stolen pistol. I want it."

"Aye, a jumped-up popinjay back-shot a vicar out on the Promenade, all right, gov'nor, but 'twas my pistols they used, none o' his."

"Where are the dead man's belongings?" Simon demanded, a close eye upon the patrons watching from the shadows.

"B-belongins' gov'nor?" the publican stuttered. "He had nothin' on 'im but a wad o' blunt, which I figured he owed me for the business he cost me that mornin'."

"I care naught for the blunt. I want only the gun."

"There weren't no gun," the publican insisted, ducking as Simon fired a shot, into the bar.

"That should awaken your lodgers," Simon snapped, viewing all through a trailing plume of pistol smoke. He pointed toward what sufficed as a banquet table in the center of the floor with the barrel of his weapon. "Get them down here," he charged, "I want every gun in the place on that table there in five minutes." Then to the man's hesitation, he roared, "Are you deaf, man? Move!"

"Y-yes, sir," the innkeeper stammered. Jabbing his whimpering wife with his elbow, he sent her scurrying to comply.

Before the five-minute time limit had elapsed, all the guns had been assembled, and the lodgers stood groggy-eyed in their nightshirts, shifting their weight from one foot to another on the damp, ale-seasoned floor. There were a dozen men in the room, counting the patrons still seated, and Simon eyed them all with caution as he rummaged through the weapons heaped upon the table, examining every one.

"You're sure there are no others?" he pressed, not finding the service pistol among them.

"I told ya, *he had no gun*," the publican growled.

"Will it help any of you remember if I tell you that there's a reward of five hundred pounds for the return of that weapon? It was an army service pistol, engraved with initials, and marked on the stock—I'll not say how, so you can all run out and make counterfeits."

The publican swallowed audibly. *"F-five h-hundred pounds?"* he breathed.

Simon nodded. "In gold."

"Look here," the man braved. "What pistol's worth five hundred pounds I'd like ta' know?"

"One that could save a life," Simon replied. "Hear me—all of you—and pass the word. If the weapon I seek arrives at Serjeant's Inn in London, and the man delivers it there into the hands of the Magistrate, Sir Alexander Mallory, and leaves his name by Monday next, he will be rewarded with five hundred pounds, no questions asked."

"Aye, gov'nor, I'll pass the word, but if 'twas five thousand, 'twould be the same. There weren't no pistol," the innkeeper insisted.

"Very well," Simon conceded. He had no other choice. If gold wouldn't convince them, nor gunpoint, they had to be telling the truth. He'd come upon many such as these over the years. Men of their ilk would turn their mothers in to the Crown for a fraction of what he'd just offered. With no more said, he left as he'd come, muttering a string of expletives over the time that had been wasted, and he drove the bay at a gallop toward the coast. Biggins was his last hope.

It was just past nuncheon when Simon returned to Kevernwood Hall. He had stopped only to exchange the bay for Fury at the Liskead coaching station. He wanted neither food nor sleep. With scarcely two days left to find the pistol, every nerve in his body was like a short fuse.

Another summer storm was brewing off the headlands. Above-normal tides had unleashed heavy, white-capped swells along the strand by midmorning. The first fat, slanted raindrops had begun to lash down out of the southwest as he reached the Hall. Waterfowl were swarming inland riding the wind. All manner of gull, tern, cormorant, and curlew peppered the rolling lawn in the lee of the cliff, seeking shelter on the stable roof, filling the paddocks behind, and overflowing onto the drive. But those unfortunates soon lifted off again in a frenzied mass of squawking, flapping indignation at being so unceremoniously evicted by Fury's galloping hooves come so suddenly into their midst.

Stalking toward the house, Simon was aware of the cold splinters of rain stabbing down only as a vague annoyance. Passion had transformed his ragged stride from a limp to a long-legged stagger as he staved through the downstairs halls, crashing through doors in search of Biggins. He found him in the library with Lieutenant Ridgeway, who vaulted off the sofa as Simon's white knuckled fists—grabbing lapels and flesh along with them—lifted the Runner out of the wing chair he occupied, upsetting the table beside him, and scattering books and brandy over the Oriental carpet.

"Where's the bloody gun? I know you've got it, Biggins, I knew it from the start," he raged.

"Simon! Put him down!" Ridgeway shouted. "Let him go! You're choking him!"

Simon stared into the Runner's wide-flung eyes, and monitored the strangled sounds that were coming from his blue-tinged lips, but he made no attempt to comply.

"Put . . . him . . . down!" Ridgeway demanded, struggling with the rigid arms holding the Runner off the floor.

After a moment, Simon returned Biggins to earth, but he didn't release him.

"Give me that damned gun, you lying maw-worm," he snarled into the man's ashen face.

"No. *No*," the Runner pleaded, when Simon started to lift him again. "I . . . I don't have the deuced pistol. I never did—"

"Liar!"

"I . . . I don't. I swear it!"

"But you know where it is, don't you? You've known all along."

His bulging eyes glazed over with fear, Biggins shook his head frantically against the hands on his throat.

"You've got five seconds before I snap this scrawny neck of yours and gladly join the countess for the pleasure."

"All right, all right . . . j-just let me go," the Runner begged, clawing at Simon's fingers. "Just . . . just—"

"Not a chance. The gun, man. Where's the gun?"

"I've told you . . . Marner must have—"

"That gun was *evidence*," Simon railed, gripping him tighter.

"N-no, my lord—*no!*" Biggins defended. "The countess was armed. *Her* pistols were evidence. Hatch's pistol was in the sack with the spoils. The rest belonged to Marner . . . and me."

"When was the last time you saw that pistol? Think, man!"

"Let go! You're . . . choking . . . me . . ."

"Simon!" Ridgeway put in, gripping his arm.

"Stubble it, Nate!" Simon warned, shaking him off. Then, to the Runner; "Speak up, Biggins, this is your last chance. Don't think to put me to the test."

"It was in the sack with the rest of the spoils when I gave it to Marner out on the road," the Runner said one more time. "Look here, that was the least of our worries. I had a wounded woman, a dead gallows dancer, and Lady Jersey interfering in Headquarters business on my hands!"

"You took it, didn't you?" Simon seethed, shaking him again.

"I told you, Marner must have it. Why don't you go and knock him about over it?"

"Marner is *dead*," Simon spat through clenched teeth. "Killed in a duel in Plymouth. Now, I shall ask you again— where is that pistol?"

The Runner's beet-red face turned white before Simon's eyes, and when he spoke, his voice was thin and choked. "It's too late," he groaned. "Even if I did know for certain, it wouldn't help you now. Without Marner—"

"You knew Marner had it all along," Simon accused. "How is it that you are so certain? Did you give it to him? No! You wouldn't do that without personal gain. He paid you for it, didn't he? Good God, you sold him the damned thing, didn't you?"

"I . . . I . . ."

Simon buffeted him again. "Why?" he demanded. "Why did he want it?"

"How should I know? I'm guessing, just like you!"

"And, you coward, you let us waste precious time, knowing

all the while we wouldn't find it—knowing that the countess's very life depended upon it."

Simon didn't wait for an answer. Drawing back a rock-hard fist, he planted it squarely in the center of the Runner's face, sending him sprawling to the floor against the hearthstone, scattering andirons, shovels, and scuttles in all directions. Before Ridgeway could intervene, he'd jerked the Runner to his feet and pulled his fist back again.

"That's enough!" the lieutenant snapped, grabbing the fist in full swing. "He's no use to us dead. Let him go."

It was a long moment before Simon's rage-starred vision cleared. He was breathing through flared nostrils, his broad chest heaving. Slowly his fist relaxed in Ridgeway's grip, and he shoved the Runner down in the wing chair with force enough to nearly tip it over backward.

"I . . . I'll see you j-jailed for attacking an officer of the law!" Biggins stammered in falsetto. Vaulting to his feet, he straightened his lapels and wiped the blood running from his nose on a wrinkled handkerchief he'd snaked from his waistcoat pocket. When a mad laugh leaked from Simon's rigid lips, attesting to the absurdity of that prospect, the Runner quickly put the wing chair between them. "I . . . I will!" he reinforced feebly.

"Bring this gutless worm, who still thinks he's an officer of the law, and come with me," Simon charged. Prying Ridgeway's fingers from his shoulders, he raked his hair back from his brow and stalked toward the door. "What happens to him now depends upon what we turn up at St. Enoder."

Matthew Biggins wished he'd never set eyes on that deuced pistol—wished he'd never heard of Rupert Marner, much less let the man persuade him to give up that gun. But the offer had been too tempting. Who knew the pistol would play such a critical part in the investigation? If he had known . . . Well, it didn't matter now. What was done was done, and now if he wasn't very careful so would his career be. He'd worked too long and hard to reach his status at Headquarters to forfeit it all over one foolhardy mistake.

His brow was running with cold sweat—his neckcloth was wet with it—and his manacles were rattling. Somehow he had to keep his hands from shaking. He laced his stubby fingers together and clenched them until his knuckles turned white. He had to remain calm at all costs. They didn't know anything. How could they? It was his word against Simon's after all, and Simon was just guessing. The lieutenant didn't matter. Hadn't he come to the rescue more than once in the past few hours? The man was watching him rather closely now, though, that meddlesome lieutenant. There was something in the man's steely, hooded eyes that chilled Biggins to the marrow and set his teeth on edge. It was best to avoid both men, he decided, and embarked upon a strategy of muttered complaints. When that didn't work, he yawned and shut his eyes to feign sleep. Maybe if they thought he wasn't listening, they might say something he needed to hear. He never was one to favor surprises.

They were hoping to find the pistol at St. Enoder, and of course it wouldn't be there. They couldn't blame him for that. He'd never said it would be. Let them waste their time as they pleased. Not finding it there would only reinforce his explanation. He'd told them the truth, hadn't he? Marner did have the gun. That was truth enough for them. That he'd refused to give it up until the viscount paid him handsomely for it didn't enter into the equation. There was no way they would ever know, now that Marner was dead. Confident in that, he let the rocking of the coach lull him to sleep in earnest.

The road they took had never seemed so long to Simon. Less than three quarters of an hour traveling time by coach, the five-mile journey along that winding, desolate road seemed to pass at a snail's pace, though they kept up a reasonable speed. He thumped the brougham roof with his pistol barrel and called out to Barstow to push the horses to their limit.

Biggins was not permitted to ride up top on this excursion. Wearing his very own manacles, he sat beside the lieutenant, grousing and puling over the indignity of being pinioned like a common criminal, but his words fell upon deaf ears. What infuriated Simon most was that Biggins—run to ground, and caught out—still would not own up to his part in the coil; quite the contrary. And though Simon held his rage in check, it was all he could do to keep his hands from reaching out of their own volition and silencing the Runner's complaints for good and all.

The storm had worsened, and though it was only midafternoon, Barstow had to light the coach lanterns. Cold horizontal rain assailed the coach, sliding in sheets down the windows and drumming on the roof as though some frantic being begged admittance. Was it an omen? Simon wasn't given to superstition, but the eerie sound did call to mind the legends learned in childhood at his nursemaid's knee, of the gnomelike Knockers, as they were called. Their mysterious tapping on the walls deep in the tin mines was reputed to lead the miners to the richest veins of ore. Had he angered them? As he recalled, that was something one must never do, and, as luck would have it, he'd forgotten the rules. Was it food or gold one was supposed to ply them with? He couldn't remember. There was nothing for it; he was going mad. Nothing but utter and absolute insanity would have driven him back to those miserable, desolate nursery days made bearable only by escape into tales of Knockers and sirens and mermaids and trolls—anything but the reality of a bitter, loveless childhood.

The brougham bounced over a deep rut suddenly, jolting him back to the present. Impatient, he wiped the fogged window and strained his eyes toward the landscape. The rain was still sliding down in sheets that totally obscured the hedgerows and stacked-stone walls that lined the highway, where it narrowed at the approach to St. Enoder. Biggins had nodded off across the way, and Simon kicked the man's crossed feet smartly with the toe of his Hessian boot, jolting him awake. They had arrived.

"You had best pray that pistol has been left behind in honest error," Simon growled, remanding the Runner to Ridgeway's custody as they quit the coach. "Have you anything to say before we go inside?"

"Look here, I've told you all I know. Standing out here in this Cornish tempest isn't going to change anything. It isn't going to get the damned thing back. Get on with it, or turn me loose. You'd best think on that carefully before we go on in there, because I intend to have the pair of you up on charges the minute I get back to Bow Street—that I can promise you."

Simon and Ridgeway propelled the Runner up the constabulary steps, and all three burst inside on a howling gust of rain-lashed wind that had already soaked them to the skin. Simon recounted their mission to the slack-jawed officer, who spoke very little during the speech. When he'd finished, the gray-haired bailiff cleared his voice, and took an audible breath.

"Well, gentlemen," he said. " 'Twas myself on duty the night in question. I remember it well. I doctored the prisoner, and took charge of the dead thatchgallows and—"

"You doctored her?" Simon thundered. "No surgeon was called?" He was incredulous.

"Well, no, my lord. 'Twas in the dead of night, and the nearest surgeon is an hour away by coach. Mr. Biggins here was anxious to see the prisoner back to London. 'Twasn't all that serious, her injury. I cleaned and dressed it and sent them on their way."

"Was there an inventory taken of the contents of the sack of spoils Biggins brought in?" Simon asked the man.

"There was."

"Might I see it, if you please?"

The bailiff took a long, leatherbound ledger from the drawer of his desk and began leafing through it. "Here," he said, turning the book for Simon to view.

Simon read the entry, then read it again. Try as he would, he couldn't make the words *army service pistol* appear on the page.

"Just as I thought," he ground out through clenched teeth. "It wasn't in the sack. What have you got to say now, Biggins?" He was still seething over Jenna's care, and he stiffened at the touch of Ridgeway's hand gripping his arm. He'd almost forgotten the lieutenant was standing there.

"Belay it," Ridgeway said, low-voiced, leading Simon aside. "Remember where you are. You can't do the countess any good from the other side of those bars there. Fly up in the boughs at the blighter and that's just where you'll end up."

"We haven't got time to play his game, Nate."

"What do you want to do?"

"We know Marner didn't have the pistol on him," Simon reiterated. "He either discarded it, left it behind in the coach, or sent it back to Moorhaven Manor for safekeeping with Wilby, that dimwitted groom of his. I know it's a long shot, but I need you to go there and see if you can find it. If you do, bring it to the town house straightaway. If Marner hasn't tossed it, Wilby will know what's become of it. I want you to wring the truth out of him. I don't particularly care how. I've no doubt you'll be creative, as only you can be. It shouldn't take much. I've seen the blighter struck with terror, peeing in his britches—or rather the Marsh Hawk has—over far less than he's going to be up against at your hands. Just see if you can get that damned gun."

"And what are you going to do meanwhile?"

"Since I haven't got the deuced evidence, I'll have to settle for the next best thing—Biggins himself. I'll haul him back to Serjeant's in chains, if needs must, and choke the truth out of him before those magistrates. He knows he's caught now. I wouldn't even entertain the thought of removing his manacles. Look at him. I'd bet my last quid he's hatching a plan to make a run for it and disappear right about now."

Ridgeway was silent. His brow was pleated in a frown, and his mouth had formed a tight, lipless line.

"What?" Simon prompted.

"I don't know that it's safe to leave you alone with the gudgeon. I've seen that look before, and what it's led to. 'Tis battle madness, that—just like on the *Monarch*, when you practically took on the French singlehanded. I'll not forget that anytime soon. You cut them down like wheat sheaves."

"We won, didn't we? The stakes here now are higher, Nate. They're personal. I shan't do anything foolish . . . unless I have to."

Ridgeway said no more, and Simon was grateful for that. He wasn't in any humor for lectures. He strode back to the Runner. "All right, Biggins," he gritted out. "This is your last chance to tell me the truth. You'd best think carefully. You won't like the alternative."

"I've told you the truth. I've got nothing else to say."

"Very well, then, you leave me no choice but to have you back to Serjeant's Inn to tell the magistrates how you've just happened to have 'misplaced' a piece of critical evidence. Surely you must know Sir Alexander Mallory? It is he who is passing judgment upon the countess. He's about as stern an authority ever to sit on the bench. We'll just see what he does to you in the dock. He takes a dim view of renegade Runners, so I'm told."

"You don't frighten me, my lord. The countess was caught red-handed, don't forget. That pistol is a separate issue entirely."

"It was linked enough to get her sentencing stayed while I run it to ground."

"Do your worst, my lord. It's your word against mine after all, and my status as Runner gives me the edge, so to speak. I do believe you're quite mad—even said so yourself once. Now I believe it!"

"You're forgetting about me," Ridgeway drawled, swaggering close. "I'm as sane as the Honorable Alexander Mallory himself, and your odds just got a little slimmer. The word of two earls—two decorated war heroes, mind—against one Runner turned sour? You haven't got a prayer."

"I've got nothing to say," Biggins insisted.

"Come on, we're wasting time," said Simon. Fastening his fist in the Runner's shirtfront with little regard for the flesh beneath, he propelled him through the door, past the slack-jawed bailiff, and out into the horizontal rain to the waiting coach.

CHAPTER THIRTY-ONE

Time was bearing down on Simon like a dark rider in pursuit. It was gaining on him. He parted with Ridgeway at the coaching station in St. Enoder, and went on with Biggins alone—much to the lieutenant's chagrin, which was voiced at a waste of his breath. Simon was immovable. If his friend were to carry out his mission, Simon decided it would be accomplished faster on horseback than by coach, since Ridgeway's course to Moorhaven Manor would soon part them. Just how the lieutenant would accomplish his mission, he left to the lieutenant's judgment. His mind was too brimful of rage to bother with logistics. In that moment, he was ready to agree with Biggins that he was indeed on the brink of madness.

He had hoped to leave the storm behind with the coast, at least for Ridgeway's sake, but that was not the case. It seemed to have settled in over the whole land with relentless stubbornness, and what should have only taken two days, stopping only to change horses, stretched into three, bringing him to London on the brink of midnight, with time run out.

All the while they traveled, he hoped against hope to find Ridgeway waiting for him at the town house with the pistol that would give him back his wife—if she would have him after his stubborn pride had cast her this lot. But the lieutenant was not at Hanover Square when he reached it, nor had he ever been. Phelps was conspicuously absent as well. Could the valet have gone back to the coast? It didn't seem likely. There was nothing to be done until morning in any case, except to send a missive to the magistrate's address to the effect that he had arrived in London with proof of his wife's innocence, and would bring it to Serjeant's Inn first thing in the morning to present it. It was half-truth—not even—a ploy to buy some time. Meanwhile, he shackled the Runner to a mahogany four-poster in a locked chamber across the corridor from the master bedchamber. Then, after interrogating the staff without success in regard to Phelps's mysterious absence, he took himself off to soak his weary body in a steaming hot tub.

Matthew Biggins tugged at the manacles shackling him to the bedpost. It was no use. Even if he could manage to shinny up to its top, the bed curtains were in the way, and the finial was too large for him to slip the chain over. He glanced around the room. It was well appointed, though sparsely furnished. Aside from the bed, which dominated the space, there were several Chippendale chairs, a writing desk, a chifforobe, and a drop-leaf table before the window, where a branch of lit candles offered the only light.

The Runner licked his lips in anticipation. A plan to free himself was hatching. He stretched toward the table, but it was just beyond reach. There was nothing for it. He would have to move the bed. He was by no means an athletic figure, but desperation triggered a spurt of extraordinary strength and daring, and he slid off the bed, dug in his heels, and pulled hard on the chains. At first the bed didn't budge. Was the damned thing nailed to the floor? A quick glance told him that it wasn't, and his posture collapsed. Breath exploded from his lungs as he sagged against it in defeat, and he squatted there panting for a moment.

He had to get free. It was still his word against Simon's, but then there was Ridgeway, and he wasn't all that confident that he could persuade the magistrate that both earls were addled. The lieutenant's absence troubled him. He was certain Ridgeway would return to London with them to speak his piece at Serjeant's to back Simon up. He'd been sorely troubled since the lieutenant rode off hell-bent for leather in the teeming rain. Where could he have been going on horseback in a flaw? Judging from the direction he took, it could only be Moorhaven Manor. He was looking for the pistol. What if he were to find it?

Biggins drew a ragged breath of the stale, musty air in the room. It had obviously been long vacant. Dust motes dancing in the candlelight from the disturbed bedclothes choked him, and he loosed a string of blasphemies under his breath.

His mind was racing. He could always stick to his story, of course, and blame the theft upon Rupert. The blighter was dead after all; he could hardly contest it. If he stuck to his story, he might get off with just a censure for negligence, in that he let the deuced pistol slip through his fingers. The trouble was, he had always been a terrible liar, and with both Simon and the lieutenant hammering at him . . .

He'd been dogged by guilt since he took the bribe. Now that the countess's life was in the balance, it gave him no peace. And what if *Wilby* knew? Frantically, he wracked his brain trying to remember how private that transaction actually was. Dratted servants had an uncanny habit of getting wind of the most private affairs. Could Wilby have overheard Rupert begging for that pistol? Could he have seen the exchange? Could Rupert have even discussed it with him? He must have if he left it in his charge. Biggins couldn't be certain, and because he couldn't be, he dared not take the chance. He couldn't afford to wait around and hope for the best, either. No. There was only one solution. He had to escape and disappear. It would mean his career, everything he'd worked for, but that couldn't be helped. The way things were stacking up against him, he was about to lose it all anyway.

Right now, getting free of the manacles was the only thing

that mattered. There was only one way to accomplish that. Jumping to his feet, he tugged at the chains again and again, until his wrists were bruised and bleeding, until the old mahogany bed frame finally groaned and moved an inch—and then another. Sweat ran into his eyes from his brow, and drool dribbled from his open mouth. Like a man possessed, he put all his strength into the task until he'd finally breached the distance to the flaming candle branch denied him by the manacles. Then, praying that Simon had posted a guard outside who would hear him, he seized the candlestick in trembling hands, and touched the flames to the counterpane and bed curtains. They caught in a whoosh of fiery heat as the flames shot up the bedpost to the canopy above, slathering it like frosting in seconds. It happened so fast. *Too fast!* Burning bits of fabric began raining down, and he tried to back away, but the shackles prevented him.

"H-help! Fire! Help, I say!" he shouted, as tall tongues of writhing, crackling flame roared to life all around him.

Simon was exhausted, mentally and physically, and he'd nearly fallen asleep in the bath when frantic knocking at the dressing room door sent him scrambling to answer. Tugging on his pantaloons, he hopped to the door and flung it wide.

"Fire, my lord!" cried the breathless footman on his doorstep, waving his arms wildly toward the chamber where Biggin's had been incarcerated across the hall. Smoke was pluming out beneath the doorsill.

Barking a string of expletives, Simon snatched his key chatelaine from the drop-leaf table, and unlocked the smoldering chamber door. The Runner's shrill voice rushed at him as he flung it wide, releasing a billowing cloud of thick black smoke and a burst of flame-fed heat. He could scarcely see. Beating the smoky fog away with flailing arms, he staggered into the room coughing, his stinging eyes flooded with tears. Half-shuttered, they strained through the murky atmosphere for Biggins as he groped his way toward the bed where the man was chained.

The fire seemed confined to the immediate area of the bed. A quick assessment was all Simon needed to evaluate the situation. It appeared that, in an attempt to liberate himself, the Runner had knocked over the candle stand, igniting the bedclothes and draperies. The fire had come precariously close to the Runner's person, now. His hysterical shrieks rose above the cries of the servants who had come running with buckets of water and sand, dousing everything in sight with both, with little regard to the Runner in the midst of the spreading blaze.

Simon unlocked the manacles that pinioned Biggins to the bedpost—and for his pains took a blow to the head with the loosened chains and dangling bars that brought him to his knees, momentarily stunned. Groping his way up to his full height, he shook his head like a dog in a desperate attempt to clear his vision, blurred by smoke and the blow. Was that blood running down his face? He shook his head again and wiped it from his eyes, loosing another string of profanity as he staggered after the Runner, who was disappearing toward the door in the voluminous curtain of smoke.

Simon's head was throbbing. He reeled into the corridor, colliding with two footmen who doused him with the water they were carrying, spilling more over the parquetry underfoot. He was hard put to keep his balance, slipping on the puddles that had collected on the smooth waxed surface, but he crossed the corridor and burst through the master bedchamber door. There was a brace of loaded dueling pistols in the top drawer of his chifforobe. He snatched them up and followed after the Runner, who had reached the landing and was set to escape down the staircase in the confusion, still trailing clanking irons.

"Stand where you are!" Simon commanded.

But the Runner continued to flee.

"*Stop,* I say!" Simon shouted.

When the Runner still did not comply, Simon fired a warning shot over his head that hit a bronze wall sconce and ricocheted off the chandelier suspended above the landing, shattering prisms and candles over the steps below. Biggins froze where he stood, glancing back at the smoking pistol in Simon's hand.

"Not another step, or the next time I won't miss," Simon warned, moving nearer.

No one above was paying any attention. The servants that swarmed steadily up the back stairs from the servants' quarters, toting buckets and kettles of water, were far too occupied with the fire. Where the deuce was Phelps? It wasn't like him not to leave word of his whereabouts. Simon could certainly use him now, to back him up from below. But there was no sign of the valet, or any other to come to his aid.

The lame leg was a hindrance on the narrow staircase with wet feet, and he approached the Runner gingerly. Biggins stood motionless until Simon was almost upon him, and then swung the length of chain-trailing manacles at him again. Simon ducked, and it struck him in the shoulder this time, but the impact threw him off balance, between the dizziness, the blood in his eyes, and the stiff injured knee. The shackles glanced off Simon's hand on the downswing, and his other pistol discharged at close range. For a suspended moment, Biggins froze on the step before his hand gripped his chest and he fell backward, head over heels down the staircase in a cartwheel. He tumbled all the way to the bottom.

Simon staggered down the stairs and squatted over the Runner's inert, twisted body, his eyes flung wide to the shuddering chandelier above. Whether the pistol shot had killed him, or the fall, was irrelevant. The Runner was dead.

"*Bloody hell*!" Simon roared. He set the dueling pistols down on the step, and slumped beside the corpse. There went his hope of liberating Jenna; Biggins wasn't going to be of any use to him now. And he crouched there numb over the Runner's corpse with his bleeding head in his hands until a shadow fell across him through the drifting haze of smoke ghosting down the spiral stairwell from above.

Ridgeway.

"I knew I never should have left you alone with the blighter," he said. "Good God, Simon, what have you done?"

"Nothing that didn't want doing," Simon said with a dangerous tremor. "But, believe it or not, it wasn't deliberate. I gave him fair warning. The maw-worm set fire to the place, Nate— deliberately set off the bedclothes in the four-poster I'd chained him to upstairs. It was a setup, and I played right into his hands. I was turning him loose when he gave me *this*." He gestured to his gashed forehead, still oozing blood.

"That needs a surgeon, Simon."

"It'll mend without that. I needn't tell you I've had worse," he responded, waving the man off with a hand gesture. "To make short of it, he got away from me. I grabbed my pistols and went after him. At first he kept running despite my warning, then he stopped and let me get close enough to swing those damned chains again. In the process, the shackles hit my hand. The pistol went off, and the bounder toppled over backward and tumbled all the way to the bottom. His neck is broken. I don't know if the pistol ball killed him or the fall. I certainly wasn't aiming."

Ridgeway crouched down and went through the useless motions of feeling for a pulse in the Runner's throat.

"He's dead all right," he said, surging to his feet.

Simon eased himself onto the bottom step, and dropped his head in his hands.

"Did anyone see? Were there . . . witnesses, any of the staff?" the lieutenant probed. "Where's Phelps?"

"No," Simon replied. "The servants were all occupied putting out the damned fire. I assume they've succeeded, since the place hasn't gone up in flames around me. I haven't seen any of them since I took off after Biggins here, and God alone knows where Phelps has got to. Nobody's seen him."

"You're going to have to have the bailiffs. The man is dead, and he's a Runner, Simon. That isn't going to bode well."

"Doesn't matter anymore. I've . . . failed her."

"No, you haven't," Ridgeway said softly, tapping him on the shoulder with a pistol barrel. "Would this be the proof you're after?"

Simon's head snapped toward the gun, and he vaulted to his feet, snatching it in trembling hands.

"W-where did you find it?" he murmured, running his fingers along the barrel and stock. They paused over the notches and initials carved there, and he gasped.

"At Moorhaven Manor," said Ridgeway. "You were right on about old Wilby. Marner sent it back with him for safekeeping after he paid the Runner for it."

"H–how did you ever . . . ?"

"Let's just say I was creative, and leave it at that, shall we? I've brought Wilby along just in case there's any doubt. He'll not be much use to you yet awhile, though—not till he comes to."

"Nate, I don't know how I shall ever thank you," Simon groaned. "I'll take the pistol 'round to Serjeant's straightaway, and send for Wilby if he's needed."

"Hold there, ship oars!" Ridgeway called, arresting him with a quick hand. "What about him?" he said, nodding toward the corpse at their feet.

"I hate to ask, old boy, but can you have a surgeon and the bailiffs in and deal with this till I return? He isn't going anywhere, but Jenna is if I don't get to her with this in time." He brandished the pistol. "Straight to Tyburn."

An hour later, Simon was pacing in the courtyard at Newgate Gaol when a bailiff ushered Jenna through the great doors. The instant their eyes met, she called his name, and he streaked up the stone steps past the man and took her into his arms. Clasping her to him, he groaned, and her heart nearly burst with joy to be in those arms again.

"Simon . . . what's happened to you—to your head?"

"It's nothing. You're free. That's all that matters."

"Can you ever forgive me?" she moaned, clinging to him as he helped her down the roughly hewn stairs. "I've been such a fool."

"Shhh," he soothed, crushing her closer. "There is nothing to forgive, and I am the fool, not you. I don't care who you confide in." He pointed to a dusky figure perched on the roof. "Confess to that chimney sweep up there if the mood strikes you," he said, gesturing toward the man plying his trade aloft. "I nearly lost you!" He held her away and took her measure. She was still wearing the highwayman costume, and he frowned. "Where are the things I sent from the Hall—didn't Phelps deliver them?"

"What things?"

"I had him pack a portmanteau for you, and instructed him to deliver it to the gaol. He didn't?"

"No . . . no one came."

"No one at the town house has seen him, either. Something must have happened to him," he said, helping her into the waiting coach. "One more thing for Ridgeway to deal with."

"Ridgeway?" she said, nonplussed.

"I'm sorry, my love; so much has occurred since that deuced ball. I'll catch you up, but first you need tending." He ran his hand lightly along her shoulder to her wound, crudely doctored and bound. "Butchers," he snarled, pulling her close in the custody of his arm, meanwhile rapping on the carriage roof with his walking stick to signal the driver to move on. The coach sped off through the cobblestone streets toward Hanover Square.

"Simon, you're trembling," she murmured. He had such a tight hold on her that she could scarcely breathe, and his whole body was shaking.

"I passed the pardon through the aperture in that blasted door nearly an hour ago," he murmured. "When you didn't come out straightaway, I thought . . . Never mind what I thought."

Her lips silenced anything else he might have said. She melted against him, and they clung to each other in total abandon as the carriage tooled through the streets. His hands roamed her body through her black highwayman's garb like those of a starving man turned loose at a banquet, just as they had when he'd held her in the dock. Even now, his embrace shot waves of drenching fire through her loins. She hadn't slept in days—really slept; she hadn't dared, with so many mad and ruthless creatures cast about her. That terror hadn't left her yet; neither had the stench, nor the melancholy hopelessness that permeated the very walls of Newgate Gaol. And yet, Simon aroused her. Had she heard him correctly? Had he really forgiven her for . . . ? She couldn't even remember what had ever separated them.

During the short drive to the Square, in between the kisses he lavished upon her, taking her breath away—kisses full of longing and promise and passion—he told her about the duel, about Robert Nast's injury, about Ridgeway and his desperate attempt to find the pistol that finally set her free. Then, to her horror, he told her about the Runner lying dead at the town house.

When they reached Hanover Square, Simon lifted her down from the coach, swept her up in his arms, and carried her over the threshold, only to pull up short. Three bailiffs, a surgeon, a representative from Bow Street, and Ridgeway were engaged in a heated discussion. Simon put Jenna down and limped nearer the confrontation, only to be seized by two of the bailiffs, who disarmed him.

"What the deuce is going on here?" he thundered. "Take your hands off me! Don't you know who I am?"

"We know who you are, my lord," said the Runner. "Don't look to your title to save you."

"I'm sorry, Simon," Ridgeway put in. "There was nothing I could do."

"Are these your pistols, my lord?" the Runner barked, pointing to the dueling pistols Simon had left on the step earlier.

"They are," Simon snapped.

"And you gunned down Biggins here with this one, did you?" the Runner returned, exhibiting the weapon in question.

"Hardly," Simon retorted. "I gave him fair warning. He set my house afire, and was trying to escape before you found him out a renegade. I fired a warning shot over his head, and moved to restrain him when he struck me with the manacles, and my pistol discharged. He fell over backward. He was dead at the bottom of the stairs when I reached him. I think his bloody neck was broken."

"What say you, Dr. Smythe?" the Runner inquired of the surgeon.

"I'd be hard put to say for certain which injury did him in," the man observed. " 'Twas a mortal wound, but so was the fall fatal—but one is related to the other after all, so I expect which came first is a moot point, actually."

"Why is the deceased shackled, my lord?" the Runner inquired.

"Because he had knowledge that the pistol you took from me when I came in was the proof that would free the countess," Simon explained. "He and Rupert Marner were responsible for its disappearance from the scene of a crime that saw her ladyship wrongly accused. The Earl of Stenshire here just retrieved it from Marner's groom, who was privy to the transaction. He's brought the man along as witness—"

"Where is he, then?"

"Indisposed at the moment," Ridgeway said. "But he'll be fit enough in due course."

"I still don't see—"

"This has just come to light," Simon interrupted. "When Biggins refused to tell the truth about the evidence, I decided to have him before the bench as living proof instead—hence the manacles and this whole unfortunate situation."

"I see my lady has been freed," the Runner observed.

"Yes," said Simon, "thanks to Lieutenant Ridgeway, who brought the pistol on just in time. She was given a pardon. Nate, didn't you explain all this?"

"I did," Ridgeway replied, "but the blighters refused to see reason."

"The deceased was a *Runner*, my lords," the official clarioned. "I shall require more than the word of two earls who are obvious collaborators. I shall want—no, *demand*—proof, gentlemen, and in the meanwhile—"

"I–is that?" Jenna interrupted, gesturing toward a blanketed mound at the foot of the landing.

"Good God, Nate, how could you leave him there to greet her?" Simon railed.

"They wouldn't let me move him," Ridgeway defended.

Jenna couldn't take her eyes from the corpse. Her head was

spinning. Exhaustion and her badly healing wound sapped her strength without this new press. Simon was still tethered to the bailiffs. Why wouldn't they let him go? It was all perfectly plain. Why couldn't they see it?

"Meanwhile," the Runner was saying, "you're off to Newgate Gaol till we've sorted this muddle out." He cleared his voice. "Simon Rutherford, Earl of Kevernwood, I arrest you in the name of the Crown, for the murder of Matthew Elmore Biggins." He nodded to the bailiffs. "Take him away," he commanded.

Jenna found her voice and screamed. Rushing to Simon, she threw her arms around his neck and clung fast.

"No!" she shrilled. "Simon, no!"

"For God's sake, see to her, Nate," Simon thundered. They dragged him away, her hold on him notwithstanding.

Ridgeway took her in hand. She was too weak from the ordeal of Newgate, and this horrifying new development coming on the heels of their reconciliation, to prevent him. Though her fingers grasped with all their strength, Simon slipped away. And she screamed again as the bailiff's rough hands propelled him through the open doorway.

"You're in charge here in my absence, Nate," Simon called over his shoulder, as they hauled him down the steps. "Take care of her!"

Jenna strained against the lieutenant's grip. Was he speaking? Who were all these unfamiliar people—all these servants gaping at her, and at the shrouded corpse? She didn't know a one. What was she doing in this strange man's arms? Simon was gone. They were taking him to that awful place she'd just come from, and her last conscious thought was that she would never see him again.

CHAPTER THIRTY-TWO

The kindly housekeeper, who introduced herself as Mrs. Wells, took charge of Jenna in Simon's chamber once she regained consciousness. After the surgeon examined her and instructed the housekeeper in the makings of an ointment for her wounded arm and rat bites, the woman filled a French porcelain hipbath with lavender-scented water and helped her into it. But would she ever wash away the stench of Newgate Gaol, or purge it from her nostrils? Not even the reeking odor of scorched, water soaked wood and bedding seeping from the gutted chamber across the way could overpower it.

When she asked after Ridgeway, Jenna was informed by Mrs. Wells that the lieutenant had gone out straightaway once he'd delivered her to the master suite and the doctor's care, promising to call upon her as soon as he returned. But the surgeon dosed her with a sleeping sachet, and she drifted off the minute she crept between the sheets in Simon's enormous bed.

The sun was sliding low over the London skyline when she woke to a light tapping at her chamber door. A plump little maid in attendance who answered to the name of Nell hurried to answer, and admitted Lieutenant Ridgeway and Mrs. Wells, whose protests echoed along the corridor as they entered.

"I shan't disturb her long," the lieutenant insisted. "His lordship has asked me to act in his stead. That is all I am about here."

"Did you know she was bitten by rats in that place?" the housekeeper shrilled. "And now the master's shut up in it!" She burst into tears then, and he swept her into the adjoining sitting room and sat her down on the chaise.

"We don't want to upset her ladyship," he soothed. "It's unfortunate about her incarceration, but his lordship is well able to fend for himself, I assure you. In his present state, heaven help the rats." She almost smiled at that, and he gave her hand a reassuring pat. "Now then," he continued, "shall we go back in? I've come to put her ladyship's mind at ease, not to drive her farther into the dismals."

The woman nodded, and he handed her back over the threshold into the bedchamber.

"Is there news of Simon?" Jenna begged. They hadn't closed the door between when they spoke, and the bit about reassuring her had lifted her spirits somewhat.

"No, there is not," Ridgeway said. "Forgive the intrusion, my lady, but the surgeon has insisted that you remain abed, at least until tomorrow, and I agree. There is other news that I have come to tell."

"Please sit, Lieutenant," she offered, motioning toward the Duncan Phyfe lounge beside the hearth.

"Firstly, I have sent word to Kevernwood Hall that you have been released," he said, taking his seat. "It was Simon's wish that they be informed of that at once on the coast—particularly your mother."

"Thank you, Lieutenant Ridgeway. She must be beside herself with worry."

"Quite so," he replied. "There has been a communiqué from the Hall, meanwhile, that you need to be made privy to. It was sent by Lady Jersey—"

"Is she *still there*?" Jenna interrupted. She was incredulous.

"Yes. Simon left her in charge, and the missive was sent to inform him that Vicar Nast is much recovered. Since Simon left me in charge here, I took the liberty of opening it."

"Recovered? Recovered from what? I . . . I don't understand."

"Ah! Of course! You wouldn't. Forgive me, dear lady. So much has transpired since I came into this that I'm afraid I tend to loose perspective. That bit might be too distressing for you at the moment, however."

"No. Whatever has occurred, I should like to know. Please, Lieutenant, continue." She was almost sorry she'd suggested it by the look of him.

"Very well, since you insist. The vicar engaged in a duel with Rupert Marner, which is where I come into it. I acted as his second."

Jenna was wide-awake now, hanging on his every word, stunned, the aftereffects of the sleeping sachet notwithstanding.

"Marner and Biggins—the Runner Simon . . . shot—staged the little trap that got you flung into Newgate. Simon came here to London to try and free you at once. Meanwhile, the vicar tracked Marner to Plymouth—"

"Plymouth? Whatever was Rupert doing there?" she interrupted.

"He had booked passage on a ship bound for the Channel Islands. He knew Simon would run him to ground, and he was attempting to escape when the vicar arrived and challenged him on Simon's behalf. Well, that and to defend the honor of Lady Evelyn St. John."

"Robert was injured?" Jenna was afraid to hear and anxious to know all at once, and exceedingly glad that she had the four-poster underneath her.

"He was back-shot. Marner didn't conduct himself as a gentleman. Acting as the vicar's second, I brought Marner down. He's dead. I would have done so in any case. Couldn't have the vicar with that blighter's death on his conscience."

"And . . . the vicar?"

"It was touch and go for a time. He was in a coma when I left Kevernwood Hall. Evidently, he has rallied, and is much improved under the Lady Evelyn's care, my lady."

"Thank God!" Jenna breathed.

"Your mother suffered a mild collapse with the news of your arrest, but she, too, was showing signs of improvement when the letter was sent. I'm confident that my missive to the coast will set her on her feet again posthaste."

"Thank you, Lieutenant Ridgeway. It hardly seems enough. I don't know how I shall ever be able to properly thank you for your kindness . . . to all of us."

"Simon and I served together at Copenhagen. I was with him when our ship was hit and he went down saving others. I admire and respect what he did then, and what he has done since for the conscripted and commissioned men alike. I am on leave at the moment. I'd just come from one of the hospitals Simon built for us when I connected with Nast. We all owe Simon a great debt."

"What will they do to him?" she begged, though she feared the answer, and her heart had begun to hammer in her breast in anticipation.

"He goes before the magistrate in the morning."

"So soon?" she shrilled.

"Calm yourself, my lady, I've come to reassure you, remember?"

"Will they let him have counsel?" she begged.

"No, you know not."

"What then . . . Will they just . . . just . . ."

"He will be permitted witnesses."

"And . . . you will speak for him?"

"Ohhhh, yes," he replied through a guttural chuckle. "I believed Biggins was withholding information that would free you—we both did. Yes, my lady, I shall be there, have no fear. There is only one thing pressing that puzzles me."

"And that is?"

"Phelps's disappearance," he said. "I was at Kevernwood Hall when he left with a portmanteau filled with your things. Simon was given leave to supply you with a change of clothing. He was appalled at your state and condition, my lady, and Phelps left to carry that out straightaway. No one has seen or heard from him since, and Simon is concerned."

"I can't imagine Phelps just going off like this with a task undone, Lieutenant. He would have reported his failure at once. He and Simon are . . . very close."

"Yes, I know."

"Was he traveling in one of Simon's carriages?"

"No, my lady, it was a hired coach and four, and Phelps did reach the livery. But then he just . . . disappeared."

"I'm sure I don't know, Lieutenant," she said, puzzled. "That certainly isn't like the man."

"Well, no matter. Don't trouble yourself about it. We'll sort that coil out, one way or another. Now I shall leave you to your rest. Try not to worry, my lady. Know that there is a plan in place."

"But the man was a Runner. It doesn't bode well, does it?"

"He was a bad Runner, my lady, and he brought his death upon himself."

"This is all my fault," she despaired. "How Simon can even speak to me——"

"He loves you very much, my lady. That's all you need concern yourself with. Think on that, and leave everything else to me."

Simon hadn't been in Newgate Gaol half an hour when he made a startling discovery. From the midst of the madmen and desperate criminals roaming the filth-ridden communal cell, one bedraggled inmate staggered out of the shadows and touched his arm, spinning him around.

"M-my lord?" the barely recognizable voice murmured. "Is it really you? Don't you know me, my lord?"

It was Phelps.

"Good God, what are you doing here?" Simon cried. Having turned a few heads with the outburst, he quickly drew the valet back into the shadowy corner from which he'd come, displacing a few large, hunch-backed rats that had been feeding on moldy food in a discarded trencher.

"I tried to help, my lord, and botched it badly. What of my lady, is she . . ."

"Pardoned," Simon returned.

"Oh, thank God, my lord, thank God! They were set against her. That's why——"

"All right, old boy, from the beginning, how did you come here?"

"I brought the portmanteau to the magistrates, just as you instructed, my lord, but they told me it was too late, that her time had run out, and she was scheduled for sentencing on the morrow. I told them you were on your way with the pistol to prove her innocence, which was a bald-faced lie, of course, but I thought it would buy you some time. They were immovable, my lord. They laid hands upon me, and tried to throw me out, and I . . . I'm afraid I struck a bailiff, my lord."

"*You*, Phelps?" Simon blurted, suppressing a smile.

"Oh, yes, my lord. It was rather reckless of me in retrospect, but I mistakenly thought my bold behavior might convince the bounders of my lady's innocence. You did say that you knew I'd think of something. Well, it was the best I could do at the time. I'm so dreadfully sorry I failed you, my lord."

"Don't give it a second thought, old boy. I wonder why they didn't tell me, or release you with Jenna?"

"Oh, they couldn't do that, my lord—release me, that is. I've been sentenced to six months in this ghastly pesthole. They probably didn't even connect the two issues."

"Only six months," Simon chided, "for lobbing one at a bailiff? It's a wonder you didn't get life."

"I do believe they thought six months would be life for me in here . . . considering my age. I'm committed to proving them wrong, my lord."

"You won't have to if Nate Ridgeway has his way. We have a lot of catching up to do."

The valet gasped. "Oh, my lord, forgive me!" he cried.

"How have *you* come here? Is it because of—have they found you out, then?" Though he'd whispered the last, before the valet could bring the Marsh Hawk into it Simon covered his mouth with a quick hand.

"Shhhhh," he warned. "Nothing so simple as that, old boy. Biggins is dead, and I'm the one who killed him. Like I said, we've got some catching up to do. Now then, if we can find a spot that these damned rats have overlooked, I'll tell you all about it."

Two bailiffs hauled Simon before the magistrate the following morning. It was a different justice than he who'd tried Jenna, one whom Simon didn't know, though he looked much the same, leaving Simon to suspect that the office carried with it an infectious malaise. The man's tight-lipped scowl upon settling himself behind the bench was unnerving.

"Simon Rutherford, Earl of Kevernwood, you stand accused of the murder of Matthew Elmore Biggins, a servant of the Crown, and Runner of Bow Street, London. What have you to say for yourself?"

"I am innocent of the charge of murder, Your Worship," he responded. "Mr. Biggins suppressed knowledge of the where-abouts of a pistol belonging to my wife, a weapon that would have cleared her of a charge of highway robbery—which, I might add, has been recovered, and the Crown has awarded Lady Kevernwood a full pardon."

"Yes, yes, my lord, but what has that to do with the Runner's murder? I fail to see a connection."

"I had taken Mr. Biggins into custody, my intent being to bring him to make a confession before the magistrates at Ser-jeant's Inn, since he would not relinquish the pistol in question. He set fire to my town house in a mad attempt to escape. I un-locked his pinions, but one was still attached to his arm. When he made attempt to escape, I warned him to halt. He did, and when I approached him, he struck my hand with the chains. My pistol discharged at close range. He fell down the stairs."

"Is that all, Kevernwood?"

"I should think it enough, Your Worship."

"Cheeky upstart!" the magistrate blurted. "I shall decide what is 'enough' here, my lord. Have you any witnesses who will speak for you?"

"He does, your worship," came a thundering from the periphery. Ridgeway's voice rumbled through the chamber like cannon fire.

"Come, then," said the magistrate, beckoning with an impatient hand motion.

Simon stared through misted eyes. When the lieutenant approached, he wasn't alone. He had in tow Marner's coachman, Wilby, and the physician who'd examined the Runner. But even more impressive, they were flanked by two, four—no, there was no end to the line of men who followed, a virtual sea of faces, some familiar, some Simon had never seen before. There were so many men that the courtroom couldn't contain them. A roar of milling voices rose from the spectators to such a crescendo of ear-splitting noise as they continued to file past that it took the magistrate several minutes to dispel it with his shaky gavel.

"This is most irregular!" he intoned, bristling.

"Indeed," said Ridgeway. "Which of us would you like to hear first, Your Worship?"

Jenna had just finished nuncheon, which had been served on a tray to her abed, since Mrs. Wells would not hear of her leaving it, despite her insistence that she was perfectly able. She was just about to relinquish the tray to the chambermaid, when the door burst open and Simon streaked across the floor. He hadn't shaved, and dark stubble colored his jaw. His queue had come unbound. Were those tears in his eyes? And where had his limp gone?

All at once she was in his arms. The tray and dishes crashed to the floor, and lay somewhere out of her view on the carpet, which sent the plump maid scrambling to retrieve what was left of the china before she made a hasty exit.

Simon murmured Jenna's name. It was the most wonderful

sound she had ever heard, full of passion and love and longing, and she surrendered to it, to his kiss, deep and slow and intimate, a mating of souls. It was an endless time before their lips parted.

"It's over. You are free?" she begged, searching his face.

"Yes, my love," he murmured, pulling her to him again. "Nate rounded up a veritable army of men—naval officers, conscriptees, men whom I knew on my tours, and men whom the Marsh Hawk has helped since."

"Oh, Simon!"

"Nate backed me up, of course, and then there was Wilby, who testified to Biggins's guilt, and the doctor, who couldn't say for certain what killed the blighter . . . but I'm not sure any of that is what got me off. I believe there would have been a riot in that courtroom if things had swung the other way. I've never seen a look of fear quite like what I witnessed on that magistrate's face. He was positively gray with fright. There weren't nearly enough bailiffs to handle that crowd, nor space enough in that godforsaken pesthole at Newgate to contain them even if there had been. There, by God, is a cause worthy of attention, and don't you think I won't take it up once all this is behind us—even if I have to become an M.P. to do it, heaven forefend."

"You, in Parliament?" she blurted. "Isn't that a far cry from—"

"Masks and tricorn hats?" he concluded for her. "What do you think, my lady, should I give it a go?"

"I think I love you," she murmured, pulling him close in her arms.

He drew her to him so relentlessly then that she could scarcely draw breath. Easing her back against the propped pillows, he smothered her with anxious kisses. His hands roamed her body through the thin nightgown like a flock of starved birds descending upon crumbs. When they found her breasts she moaned, and he swallowed the sound with a hungry mouth that left her weak and trembling, totally aroused. Had he pressed her then, she would have surrendered to that one long, steamy, lingering kiss. But he did not press, and his lips had scarcely left hers when she gave a start, remembering.

"Phelps!" she cried. "Oh, Simon, no one knows what's become of him. He—"

"Shhhh," he soothed, burying his hands in her hair. "He's drawing my bath."

"You've found him? Where—what happened?"

"He was quite your champion you know. Trying to buy you some time, he got himself thrown into Newgate, too. The magistrate was only too glad to commute his sentence, considering Nate's show of force in that courtroom."

He kissed her again . . . and again. "Now, my love"—his mouth found the pulse at the base of her arched throat—"I shall have that bath"—he spread her gown open, and the skilled tongue glided lower—"make myself presentable"—his tongue teased her nipple then roamed back to her lips again, whispering against them—"and ravish you."

EPILOGUE

It was moon-dark as the barouche sped along just north of Newcastle on its way to the Scottish border. The night was soft, quick with mists that the rain would soon chase, and the coachman had just lit the carriage lanterns. Inside, Jenna sat cocooned in Simon's strong arms, scarcely daring to believe that they were finally embarked on their wedding trip.

"I feel dreadful making Phelps ride up top in all this damp," she said. "He's going to catch his death."

"That was his idea, my love," said Simon. "He wanted to give us some privacy. I do believe the old boy's an incurable romantic. Who would have thought it?"

"I feel a little guilty leaving Robert and Evelyn to fend for themselves while we traipse off to the Highlands," she said, clouding. "He is still on the mend, after all."

"Don't you think they deserve a little privacy of their own?" he chided. "After all your hard work bending Cupid's arrow in that direction, I should think you'd be gloating."

"As much privacy as Mother will give them," she returned. "I shudder to think. But then, if they can survive Mother, I expect it's a match made in heaven that can withstand anything."

Simon laughed outright, and pulled her closer in his arms as their carriage tooled along the highway in the still darkness.

"I wouldn't be at all surprised if when we return next month we'll be decking Kevernwood Hall out for another wedding breakfast," he observed.

"I told him to take the initiative with that girl," said Jenna, "but I never expected that he'd go to the lengths of a duel, for pity's sake. How bizarre."

"I've known Rob nearly all my life, and the man never ceases to amaze me. I could tell you stories passing bizarre that would raise the hair on your head. But we'll leave all that for another time. Suffice it to say that I've always looked upon Rob as family, and now that it's about to become official, I couldn't be happier."

Jenna was about to agree when all at once a shot rang out, and Phelps, scrambling down from the driver's seat, came crashing through the barouche door, pistol drawn, with an agile lunge that dropped her jaw.

"A highwayman approaches, my lord," he announced, out of breath, "a young one, too, by the look of him. Green as grass."

The coach pulled to a shuddering halt. The masked man, dressed in black, mounted on a dark horse, had ranged himself on Jenna's side of the barouche, and Simon quickly moved to the seat facing her, motioning her back.

"Put that away, Phelps," he charged, nodding toward the pistol in the valet's hand. "Keep it down out of sight. Unless I miss my guess, what we have here is a novice in need of a lesson. Novices have a tendency to be rather . . . trigger-happy. I can personally vouch for that, by God."

Jenna caught his raised eyebrow and half smirk, and frowned. Would he never let her live it down? Her breath caught when, to her surprise, he reached into the pocket of his greatcoat and removed a black silk half-mask.

"This will have to do, since I don't have the hat with me at the moment," he said. He offered it to her. "Well, my dear—shall I, or would you rather deal with the brigand?"

"Stand and d-deliver!" the highwayman's shaky voice intoned, interrupting him.

Jenna stared at the mask. Surely he couldn't mean to . . .

"Don't worry, my love, I was just offering you a professional courtesy," Simon assured her drolly, tying the mask in place. "Allow me," he said, and burst from the coach, both pistols blazing.

The young man's hat went flying, having taken one of Simon's pistol balls, and his weapon spun off into the scrub having taken the other. Simon had managed both without inflicting so much as a scratch upon the horseman, whom he promptly yanked out of the saddle and pulled close for observation.

Phelps had climbed down and stood at the ready, his own pistol aimed at the quaking youngster in Simon's white-knuckled grip. Jenna remained where she was, staring through the coach window, streaked now with rain, watching Simon rip off the man's mask and throw it down, revealing a terrified youth of scarcely twenty.

"And who might you be, laddie?" Simon growled, close in the man's face.

"Lemmee go!" the youth shrilled, struggling.

"Answer me first," Simon demanded. "Your name—and be quick. You've wasted enough of my time tonight as it is."

"J-Jeremy . . . Jeremy Higgins," the youth replied. "Ow! Ease off! I told ya, didn't I?"

"And why have you taken to the highway, Jeremy Higgins?" Simon demanded, ignoring his plea.

"Why have *you*?" the youth flashed.

"Plucky little whelp, isn't he?" Simon observed to no one in particular. "I've just given up the trade, actually," he went on, "and so shall you, if you want to stay out of the place I've just come from." The youth struggled to free himself, and Simon jerked him to a standstill. "No?" he observed. "You mean to defy me, do you? Maybe I should find a bailiff and see you there straightaway; you can take my place. Have you ever been inside Newgate Gaol?"

"N-no, sir . . . lemmee go! I'm sorry I come inta your territory."

"You're going to be a whole lot sorrier if you ever put that there on again," Simon snarled, grinding the mask into the mud of the road with the toe of his polished Hessian. He reached into his coin purse and pulled out a crown. "Here," he said. "It's not quite what you had in mind, of course, but it'll get you where you're going. Do you know Stenshire Manor, on the moors south of York?"

"Aye," said the youth, "I know of it. Never been there."

"Well, you're going there now. When you arrive, tell the Earl of Stenshire that you met with the Marsh Hawk's ghost on the old road to Newcastle, and that it was none other than he who has recommended you. He will see that you are gainfully employed."

"The M-m-m—" the youth stuttered.

"Don't think to disobey me, laddie," Simon warned, shaking him in punctuation. "I'll know. And you won't like my haunting."

Simon let him go then, and the youth leapt up on his mount and rode off in a southerly direction without even trying to locate his pistol. Simon laughed, plucking it out of the mud. Staring after the boy, arms akimbo, he stood with Phelps until the sound of hoofbeats grew distant, and the horse and rider were long out of sight. Then, as though nothing untoward had occurred, the valet resumed his seat beside the coachman, and Simon climbed back into the brougham.

"Oh!" Jenna cried, exasperated. "Do you really think Lieutenant Ridgeway is going to appreciate this, Simon—foisting off a thief on him after all he's done for us?"

"You don't know Nate," he replied through a chuckle. "He'll straighten that little would-be thatchgallows right out. Don't worry, I'll write him from Roxburghshire." He chuckled again. "That poor young ne'er-do-well doesn't know yet if he's just had an encounter with flesh or spirit, he was so struck with terror."

"You can't save every brigand in the realm, you know."

"No, surely not, but there's hope for that one. Poor bungling lack-wit would be dead in a week but for the Marsh Hawk's ghost."

"Is that why you put the mask on? I don't understand."

"That lesson needed to be taught anonymously, my love," he replied. "Believe me, the Marsh Hawk was far better suited to the task than the Earl of Kevernwood." Pulling her closer, he attempted a kiss.

"Ohhhh, no, not until you give me that mask," she demanded, turning her head aside. If he thought he was going to fox her with his kisses, he had another think coming. She extended her hand, working impatient fingers. "Give it here," she said with resolution.

He reached into his pocket and withdrew the mask. Serving her one of his irresistible lopsided smiles, he placed it in her open palm, closed her fingers around it, and kissed them gently. When she promptly tossed it through the barouche window, he burst into deep throaty laughter.

"I fail to see the humor in this," she said frostily.

"The humor in it, my wonderful, beautiful Jenna, is that you presume it to be the only mask I own."

"Oh!" she cried, pounding his chest with playful fists. "Simon Rutherford, if you ever, even for a moment, entertain the thought of—"

His warm mouth swallowed the rest as he pulled her closer still. It was no use. His kisses held sway over her heart, mind, and soul. And she surrendered to the promise of his passion, melting against the lean, turgid length of him as the coach rumbled on through the misty green darkness toward what promised to be a very provocative future.

Blood Moon

✠ ✠ ✠

Dawn Thompson

Jon Hyde-White is changed. Soon he will cease to be an earl's second son and become a ravening monster. Already lust grows, begging him to drink blood—and the blood of his fiancée Cassandra Thorpe will be sweetest of all. Is that not why the blasphemous creature Sebastian bursts upon them from the London shadows? But Sebastian's evil task remains incomplete, and neither Jon nor Cassandra is beyond hope? One chance remains—in faraway Moldavia, in a secret brotherhood, in an ancient ritual and in the power of love.

Don't miss Victoria Morrow's sweeping
saga of passion and revenge, set amid
the blood, sweat and tears of linking
East and West with the transcontinental
railway.

Coming in September,

THE EAGLE
AND THE DOVE

CHAPTER ONE

Sangre de Cristo Mountain Range,
May 1851

He had been born in the dark of a November night twenty-four years before near the Canadian border. He was a Celt. The stark Highlands of his ancestry were apparent in his pale skin, which contrasted sharply with his dark eyes and hair. He towered over most men and spoke Gaelic fluently, the language his father spoke to him, as well as a curious mixture of French, English and Pigeon Blackfoot. He was a white man raised in a red world and comfortable in his skin.

He came from the high country where Old Man Winter still had a stranglehold on the land and the world was blinding white and his traps were full. He had ridden hard for nearly a week, pushing his big, dun-colored stallion until its powerful body was bathed in lather and its once nimble legs shook from exhaustion.

He slept little and ate less. Pulling a piece of deer jerky from his pack every now and then, he would suck on it until it softened and the smoky juices ran down his parched throat. He was going toward the dunes at the base of the ridge, a mountain man covered in buck-skins and fur with a shock of wild, midnight hair blowing in the wind and piercing, black eyes locked onto the horizon. He wasn't alone.

Above him in the zinc-colored sky, an elegant falcon-hawk circled lazily, easily keeping pace with his relentless speed; traveling beside him loped a lean slant-eyed wolf. The three were companions, a trinity of primitive power; beating wings, talons, fangs, sinew and cunning, bound together by the knowledge that they were of the same clan: predators. Yet, though all were formidable, the mountain man was, by far, the most dangerous of the three. Cresting a bald ridge of rock, he pulled back on the soaking reins, stopping abruptly in a shower of powder-red dust and fragments of nail-thin shale.

"Ease up, horse," he growled as he absently wiped the sweat from his upper lip. "'Tis the blighted camp of the Philistines."

His voice, though companionably soft, was filled with such unmistakable menace that his horse's ears came to attention and began to dance as nervously as its feet. Narrowing his eyes, the man studied the scene below.

Hatred, there was hatred in every breath he took, in every shuddering beat of his heart. And he didn't turn away from it—instead he touched it, breathed it in, owned it until he became it.

Other men might have walked away, trusting God or a badge to fight their battles for them. But not him. His blessing and his curse was the nobility of his soul. He knew right from wrong and took responsibility for every thought, action or deed his mouth uttered or hand performed, expecting others to do the same.

God might show mercy, but Jesse McCallum wouldn't.

Beneath him, nestled as contentedly near the root of the Sangre de Cristo Mountains as an infant to its mother's teat, was a small, crudely built cabin. Massive dunes of rolling sand surrounded it on three sides while on the fourth, a vertical wall of granite effectively sealed the basin from the rest of the range. No one could approach from across the dunes without being seen for miles.

Jesse knew the odds and weighed his options carefully. He knew it was certain suicide for anyone to attempt to approach the cabin on foot or by horse, especially in daylight. Yet he knew that even if he had to go through the front door with his guns blazing, he would do whatever it took to bring his father's killers to justice.

Calmly he noted that behind the house stood a makeshift pen fashioned with posts of thorny mesquite and rails of frayed hemp, spliced now and then with bits of knotted rags that still hinted at some nearly forgotten color. Every few feet, empty cans that were once filled with succulent peaches, tangy stewed tomatoes and other such citified delicacies, were tied to the uppermost rope, clanking noisily like a poor-man's chimes with each passing gust of wind. The "gate"— and it was charity to call it that—was nothing more than the mummified remains of a buckboard, bleached nearly white and laid on its side. Decorating its sagging top were stiff gray blankets, mile-worn saddles, tangled leather traces and rusty bits, one for each of the dozen horses and the odd assortment of New Mexico mules, mingling without prejudice, in the little pen. Just outside the corral and within mere spitting distance from the front door of the house was a pyramid of packs filled to overflowing with stolen booty.

All of this Jesse noted without a hint of surprise, as though he had beheld the scene many times before in the misty landscape of his mind. Yet he knew the picture wasn't complete, so he continued to search, scanning the grounds until he found the missing pieces to the puzzle he had come so far to solve.

"There you are!" he said.

His voice sounded strange. His words were whispered, barely more than a phantom of sound, spoken so gently they seemed less than a sigh. But what a frightful expression colored his eyes! They gleamed like black opals filled with infernal fire, hellish in intensity and intent.

Cursed.

It was as if the tortured soul imprisoned within the massive tower of flesh was slowly dying. A once proud soul ravaged so savagely by the cold hand of guilt that it believed itself lost forever. Beyond hope. Beyond forgiveness. Dead to everything except pain.

He suffered in silence, and he suffered alone.

"And here I am," he said at last.

He announced his arrival in a voice so heartbreakingly soft, so filled with sorrow and regret that the fickle wind seemed to moan in sympathy as it passed.

His journey was over; the circle was about to close....